THE RUTHL

Spiteful

R.A. SMYTH

Pretty Spiteful

ASIN: B09QXYYLC9

Cover by Vicious Desires Design

Editing by Lunar Rose Editing.

Created with Vellum

She wants our protection, but her safety comes with a price.

Emilia Harrison. The girl I attended Pacific Prep with. My sister's best friend. The greatest sex I've ever had.

I never expected to see her again after graduation, so when she shows up in my kitchen in the middle of the night, I don't know what to think.

Apparently there's some psycho after her and she needs my help. My family owns a private security firm, but I can't protect her from Wilder.

And maybe I don't want to. Her presence brings up old feelings I don't want to confront. It's easier to blame her for the past than face the truth.

With all of us living under one roof, it's only a matter of time until tensions reach a crescendo, and this time, none of us will escape.

Welcome to Ridgeway, Em, where you will have to survive more than just your stalker.

TRBOR PLAYLIST

Numb Little Bug – Em Beihold
3days – Nightcore
Hyponotize – Flights Over Phoenix
Damaged People – Connell Cruise
Tonight, I Love You – Latency
Louder Than Love – Emphatic
Reckless – Lowborn
sTraNgeRs – Bring Me The Horizon
Pray – Ryan Vasquez
She Ain't You – New Hollow
Work Off My Hurt – Havelin
Reflections – We Are The In Crowd
Shapeshifting – Taylor Acorn
Blinding Lights – All Time Low

Play Now

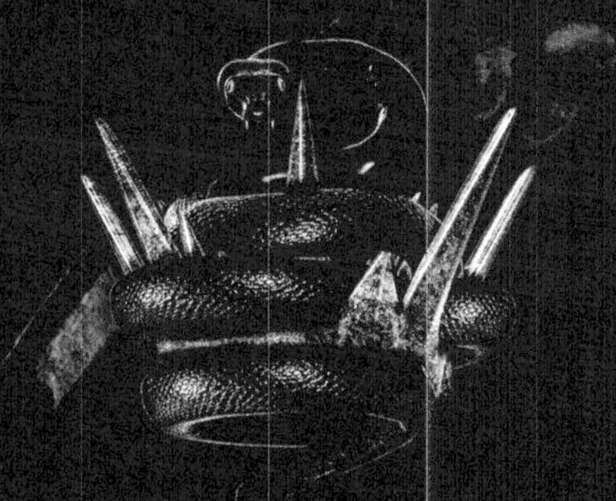

THE RUTHLESS BOYS OF RIDGEWAY

Anonymous

PROLOGUE

I twirl the bloody penknife in my hand as I stare down at the man with disgust.

Weak.

That's exactly how he looks, lying at my feet with his sightless eyes staring at nothing, his mouth parted on a silent scream. The pathetic wimp barely even put up a fight. It was *so* fucking easy to kill him.

It just proves that I was right. He *isn't* good enough for her. No one is.

Only me.

I'm the only one who truly cares for her. The only one who sees who she really is. Everyone else thinks they know her, but they only see what she wants them to. *I'm* the only one who can see past the lies. See through the deception.

He thought she was happy with him? Wrong!

She's been slowly dying inside, and he couldn't even fucking see it!

Yet he had the audacity to think he was worthy of spending the rest of his life with her?

Ha!
Well, I proved him wrong.
I'm the only one worthy of Emilia's love.
... And she's the only one worthy of mine.

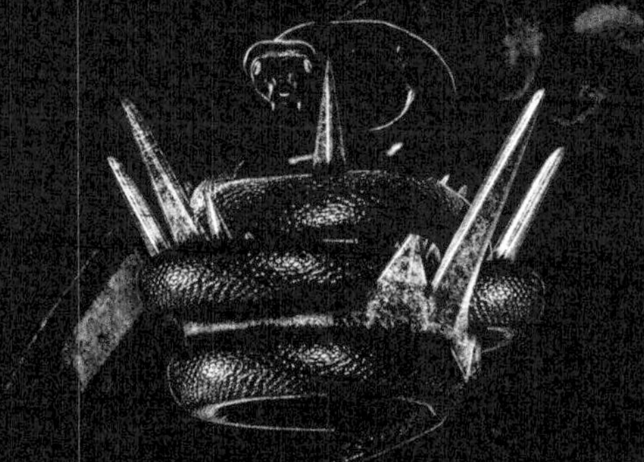

THE RUTHLESS BOYS OF RIDGEWAY

Emilia

CHAPTER 1

Pinot Grigio or Merlot. White or red. I glance back and forth between the bottle of wine I'm holding in each hand, indecision warring within me while one of my best friends talks away in my ear.

"Cathy is such a bitch. I swear she makes a point of passing my desk at least four times a day just so she can scowl at me."

Ah, fuck it. Both it is.

"So just scowl back at her," I respond as I set both bottles beside my groceries for the week and push the cart down the aisle.

"She's my boss, Em." She sighs in exasperation. "I have to play nice."

I laugh because playing nice is not something Mel is good at. We met on our first day at Halston University four years ago. Both of us were there on a scholarship—me as an English major and her to study finance. We hit it off immediately, and when we graduated last summer, we both moved to the same city.

She got a job in a bank, and from the stories I've heard, she has the boss from hell. However, her pain is my endless amusement. Every day there's a new story.

I hear rustling on the other end of the line, followed by heavy pants. "What are you doing? You sound out of breath."

"Oh, I'm just taking out the trash."

"Oh."

"Anyway, are we still on for a girls' night tomorrow?"

"You know it. Just don't let me drink too much," I respond, eyeing up the two bottles of wine in my cart. "Richard's taking me away for the weekend."

"Ooh, fancy. Special occasion?"

I pause mid-aisle, oblivious to anyone around me. "Uhh..." I wrack my brain, trying to remember if it's our anniversary, but no, that's sometime in April or May. His birthday? Nope, that's not for a few months yet. And it's definitely not my birthday. "No, I don't think so."

She snorts. "I'm pretty sure you're supposed to know these things without having to think about it."

"Shut up," I grumble, not wanting to get into this conversation... again.

"I don't understand why you stay with him when you're clearly unhappy."

"I'm happy," I argue, reaching the register and loading my groceries onto the conveyor belt while tossing the checkout woman a warm smile.

"Happy people don't have to convince themselves—or their friends—that they're happy. You should be with someone who is right for you."

"He's a good man," I sigh. "Safe. Reliable—"

"Boring."

I frown. "He's not boring. He's taking me away on a surprise weekend trip. Boring people don't do that." A non-committal grunt is all the response I get from her. "Look, I'm at the checkout, I gotta go, but I'll see you tomorrow."

"Yeah, yeah, whatever. I'll see you tomorrow."

Hanging up, I pay for my groceries and begin the short walk to my apartment block. I barely notice the people passing me by on the street, already accustomed to city living. I moved to Springview as soon as I graduated from Halston University. With a major in English and a minor in journalism, I was offered a job at a world-renown publishing house straight out of college. Of course, having only started the job a couple of months ago, I'm at the bottom of the food chain, doing the grunt work to prove myself before I can work my way up the corporate ladder. But I'm no stranger to hard work. My entire life has been about hard work. It's all I know, and I *like* it. I'd much rather be busy than twiddling my thumbs.

Dodging a woman walking seven dogs, my thoughts drift back to what Mel said. Now that she's raised the question, she's got my mind spinning off in crazy directions trying to work out Richard's reasoning for the surprise weekend getaway. I just assumed he was trying to be more spontaneous. We have been together for over a year. It's natural that the initial excitement of a new relationship would wear off, although I'm not sure if we ever had that hot and heavy, *I can't keep my hands off of you,* beginning. Richard and I had a critical writing class together our junior year, and we became fast friends. As time passed, it became apparent that he wanted more, but I was hesitant to cross that friendship line with him. I'd been there, done that before, and I still hadn't recovered from the fallout.

He eventually won me over with his compelling arguments —I am a sucker for a well-thought-out argument. Besides, on paper, he's everything I've ever wanted. Stable, dependable, trustworthy. He listens when I talk, he always texts to say good-night, and he *always* walks me to my door after a date. He's the perfect gentleman—husband material. And yet, everything about our relationship feels... flat. We still have that close friendship, only there's no spark. My body doesn't melt beneath his stare, and I don't lose all common sense when I'm around him. I don't want to pounce on him and lick him all over the second he walks into a room... not like I wanted to do with *them.*

God, even now, my face heats at the thought of that night. I've always been *the good girl.* I always got good grades, went to a prestigious high school, then to one of the top universities in the country, and now I work at one of the best publishing houses in the world. I've had my moments of fun, especially when I was at Pacific Prep. When you lock a bunch of teenagers on campus together, you have to expect at least some debauchery... but I never fully allowed myself to be wild and carefree until that night.

Except, instead of the one night of dirty, sinful deeds with my best friend's brother and her *kind of* fiancé, things snowballed. Feelings got involved. Mistakes were made—mostly on my end. I didn't handle the situation well, and everyone ended up hurt. Well, probably not Hawk. That man has the emotional bandwidth of a peanut. But Wilder was definitely hurt, and I... honestly, I've never been the same since, even though I know I made the right decision at the time. It was the end of school, and I was heading off to college, so it just made sense to sever any and all ties and start fresh.

Besides, I was a scholarship student at a prestigious school for the rich and arrogant—two things Hawk and Wilder had in spades. I didn't fit into their world. All that glitz and glamor. The fake smiles and over-the-top parties. I'm more of a *glass of wine in my sweats on the couch on a Friday night* kinda girl.

I'm more than happy to leave all that angst and drama to the dirty books I read. At least then, when it all becomes too much, I can just set it aside and return to the safe existence I've carved out for myself. Although Richard is the kind of man I have always pictured myself ending up with, he doesn't make my heart thump or my throat dry up like the Sahara. He's the type of guy I'm *supposed* to want. The kind who will one day be a caring husband and doting father. He's not all hostile aggression and crazy mood swings like two other assholes I used to know... and occasionally still get off to with my vibrator.

By the time I make it to my apartment building, I'm pissed off and feeling like crap, and the smile I give the concierge as I pass by is tight and forced. I feel awful that I'm thinking about two other men when I'm in a happy, steady relationship, and I feel even worse that no matter how hard I try, I can't seem to make myself feel for Richard what I felt for those two assholes. It has resulted in me stringing him along, not wanting to let him go but never being able to fully commit, either.

God, I'm a fucking mess.

Getting out of the elevator on my floor, I notice a small cardboard box sitting on the mat outside my door. *Huh, that's weird.* Looking around, there doesn't seem to be anyone about. Any outside packages get left with the concierge, so it must be something one of the neighbors left at my door by accident. Maybe they meant to give it to the guy next door. He moved in shortly after I did, but unlike me, he's friendly and sociable and has actually made an effort to get to know the other people on our floor. Whereas I mumble a *hello* and walk on past like the anti-social bitch I am. I'm too drained after a day's work to engage in small talk.

I'm not exactly sure what happened to the girl from high school who was always up for a good party and enjoyed hanging out with her friends. Somewhere along the way, I lost a fundamental part of myself. Which is ironic, considering the whole point of working hard and obtaining my scholarships was so that I'd end up here—with an excellent job, a financial security net, and a life that I chose for myself.

Sliding the key into the lock, I open the door, which leads straight into a large, spacious living room, furnished simply with a white, modern, leather sofa that faces the floor-to-ceiling windows. They provide an expansive view of the city. There are also two cozy armchairs that sit in front of overstuffed bookcases and dark wood furniture interspersed throughout the room.

Off to the left is a small yet modern kitchen, and I set my grocery bags down on the counter before heading back out to grab the package on my doorstep. Lifting it, I turn it over in my hands, frowning when I don't find a name or address.

I'm already peeling back the tape to open it as I head back inside and close the door behind me. Another two steps, and I have the cardboard flaps pulled back, before I freeze halfway across the room.

I blink, then blink again, before my brain finally computes what my eyes are seeing. Hysteria descends like a mist as I double over, my trembling hands dropping the box as some strange, strangled noise escapes my lips. The sound only escalates as a bloody, detached finger rolls out of the box onto my cream carpet.

I can't do anything but stare at it as the wailing sound bounces off the walls. I can't even get my brain to think straight, to do *anything*. It's just completely shut down as I stare wide-eyed at the severed digit in horror.

I'm faintly aware of a loud bang somewhere in the apartment, but it's not enough to force my gaze from the floor. A second later, large hands are on my shoulders, turning me away from the grotesque sight, and a face obstructs my vision. I distantly note the handsome features of David, my next-door neighbor—his broad jaw with a dimple right in the center of his chin, a dark dusting of stubble over his cheeks and atop his upper lip, a broad nose, and intense green eyes lined by thick eyebrows, and dark wavy hair that's fallen across his forehead.

He gives me a shake, and I focus back on his plump, pink

lips... lips which seem to be moving, but no words are coming out. Blinking rapidly, I try to focus on the attractive man standing before me.

"Emilia. Em! Are you okay?"

Am I okay? I mean, yes, I'm absolutely fine, except, you know, for the bloody finger lying on my clean, cream carpet. How does one even get blood out of a carpet, anyway? I feel like white vinegar and elbow grease aren't going to cut it. Isn't the key to getting red wine out of fabrics to put something on the stain as soon as possible to soak it up? Maybe the same logic applies to blood; it's similar in color, after all. But then, is my carpet technically a crime scene now? I mean, a crime was committed... somewhere, on someone... and now my carpet's going to be cut up and taken away as evidence.

"Okay, let's get you sitting down before you pass out, yeah?" David says as he directs me to a seat out of view of the finger.

"Do you know how to get blood out of carpet?" I ask him, vaguely aware that I'm fixating on entirely the wrong issue as he crouches down in front of me.

He frowns, looking even more concerned than he did a minute ago. "I don't think you need to worry about that right now."

Right, of course. Yes. I nod absently in agreement. *We need to call the cops. And oh my god, whose finger is that?! Are they alive? Oh god, what if the person is dead?* I groan as I wrap my arms around my waist. Why the hell would some psycho send me someone's finger?!

"Are you okay with sitting here for a sec?" David asks.

I nod again, pretty sure I'm not capable of forming words yet. He hesitates for a moment longer, running his gaze over my face—which has probably turned ashen—before standing and moving over to where the box is lying on its side from when I dropped it.

Closing my eyes, I hang my head as I suck in deep lungfuls of air, trying to calm the hysteria threatening to consume me. I need to think rationally. Panicking doesn't help anyone, least of all the guy walking around out there with a missing finger.

I bury my face in my hands. Deep breath in. Long exhale out. Deep breath in, long exhale out. I repeat that until my arms and legs stop trembling, then for another minute until I'm confident I won't spiral when I turn to face David and the destruction that is now my apartment floor.

David is an ex-Marine, and it's obvious by the way his eyes run over the scene, cataloging every detail yet careful not to disturb anything. Unlike me, the sight of a bloody finger doesn't seem to churn his stomach. I guess he's probably used to seeing stuff like this... well, not *this* exactly, but you know, blood and guts and gore.

"Do you have any idea who'd do this?" he asks when he notices me watching.

I shake my head. "No. I've only been here for a few months. I don't know anyone well enough to have pissed them off yet."

Moving to the kitchen, he grabs a drying cloth before moving back to the box and carefully lifting it to peer inside. His brows furrow. "There's something in here."

"If it's another finger, I'd really rather not see it," I grumble, a fresh wave of nausea causing sweat to bead along my forehead.

Frowning, he carefully reaches in, using the cloth to avoid contaminating any evidence. "There's a note."

Although I'd prefer not to get closer to the finger, curiosity has me rising to my feet and moving to stand beside him as he lifts out the piece of white notecard. Ignoring the bloodstains, I lean in to read what it says.

Sorry to spoil the surprise, but I don't think Richard will mind.

The only ring you'll be wearing is mine.

The words swim before my eyes as a coldness like nothing I've ever felt before seeps into my bones and takes me hostage. "W-what do th-they mean?" I stutter, still staring at the piece of paper that threatens to destroy everything I know. Until this moment, I'd just assumed it was all one big mistake. The finger was a fake. It was a prank. It wasn't meant for me. But Richard... that can't be a coincidence.

I must lose myself to the downward spiral of my thoughts until David's nudge against my shoulder jolts me back to the cold, harsh reality of my current predicament. "Look." He points toward the discarded, bloody finger, and unwillingly I look at where he's pointing, gasping when I notice what I missed before. Shoved onto a too-large, masculine-looking finger is a ring. No, not just any ring. An *engagement* ring.

"Oh fuck," I gasp, unsure if I'm going to pass out or vomit.

Nope, vomit. Definitely vomit.

I rush to the bathroom, just about managing to get my head over the bowl before the contents of my stomach hit the porcelain. "Richard," I sob, flushing the toilet and sagging against the cool bathroom tiles as the last of my energy drains out of me. Looking up through wet lashes, I notice David standing in the doorway. His shoulder is pressed up against the doorframe as he watches me, pity shining in his dark green depths. "M-my boyfriend. We were supposed to go away this weekend." Bringing my knees up to my chest, I grind the heel of my palms into my eye sockets. "Oh god," I groan. "He was going to propose. He wouldn't tell me where we were going. It was supposed to be a surprise."

I feel wrung out and a fucking wreck as I push to my feet, standing on unsteady legs. "We have to find him. Help him. He could be bleeding out o-or have an infection. He needs medical attention!"

Moving until he's standing in front of me, I see the truth in

David's eyes, but I refuse to believe it. "Emilia, someone who clearly thinks they have a claim on you just delivered your boyfriend's finger to your doorstep." He says each word slowly, emphasizing the gravity of this situation since my poor little broken mind can't seem to grasp it. "You need to think about yourself. You can't stay here. You're not safe."

"Right. You're right," I agree, nodding while I try to work out what to do. "We need to contact the cops. They'll know what to do. They can find Richard and catch this guy." I continue to nod my head in agreement with my own plan, determined to believe the police are the solution. I mean, they're who you turn to when you're in danger or feel unsafe and need help, right? This is totally within their wheelhouse.

Except David doesn't seem to agree based on the hard frown lines around his mouth and the scrunch of his brows. "The police can't do jackshit." His sharp tone catches me by surprise, making me jump.

"B-but they can run DNA tests and dust the box for fingerprints," I stammer. I watch crime shows. I see the brushes and the DNA lab reports. They do that stuff.

"They can't do jackshit to protect *you*," he growls. "While they're running their tests and canvasing the street and pussyfooting around, who is looking after *you?*"

My mouth opens and closes while I scramble for some sort of response before coming up empty and snapping my mouth closed.

"Exactly." Standing to his full height, he barks out, "Pack a bag. You have five minutes." Before I can ask a single question, he strides out of the room, his phone in his hand as he types away on the screen.

Too much has happened today, and I'm reeling from all of it, unable to get my head on straight and think for myself. Which is the only reason why I actually do as the man—who is practically a stranger!—says. I guess it won't matter if I stay at his place for a few days until I figure out what to do next.

Moving on autopilot while my brain spins at a hundred miles an hour, I pull open my drawers and start throwing stuff into a bag. I don't even know what I'm putting in there. For all I know, it's nothing but underwear, yet I can't bring myself to care. I'm just numb. So. Freaking. Numb.

"Ready?" David asks, stepping into my room. I'm not sure how long has passed. Minutes? Hours? In a daze, I nod my head, and he grabs the bag from my bed before placing a palm against the center of my back and ushering me forward. "Do you have your phone on you?"

"Ehh. It's in my purse, in the kitchen." Beside the grocery bags I never put away and the wine I'll never get to drink. Wine I could seriously fucking do with right about now.

"Okay. Good." He doesn't elaborate more than that as we cross the living room. As we pass the *crime scene*, I notice the finger and box are conveniently missing, and a rug that I had placed in front of the sofa has been moved to hide the bloodstains. *Well, I guess that's easier than trying to scrub them out.*

David only leaves my side to quickly grab something from the kitchen, but I'm in too much of a daze to take in whatever he's doing.

Stepping into the hall, I expect him to direct me toward his apartment next door to mine, but instead, he applies pressure to my back, pushing me toward the emergency stairwell. Digging my heels in, I lift my head to look at him. "Uh, where are we going?"

"Somewhere where you'll be safe."

"Ehhh..." Going anywhere alone with a stranger is a big no-no. One of those things my mom ingrained into me from a young age. Don't talk to strangers. Don't go anywhere with strangers. Don't accept food from strangers. And yet, as he gives me a little nudge, I find my feet moving toward the stairwell. I mean, there are strangers and then there are handsome, helpful in a crisis, friendly neighbor strangers. David has never set alarm bells ringing in my head, and given the fact my options are currently either staying here and probably getting stabbed to death by some crazy psycho or leaving with David... I think I'd rather take option number two, please.

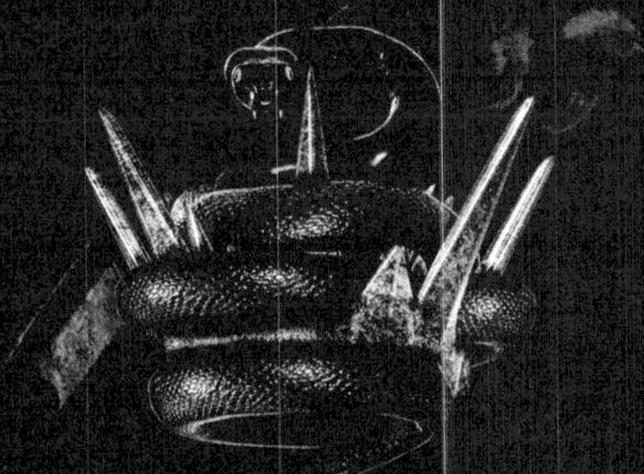

THE RUTHLESS BOYS OF RIDGEWAY

Emilia

CHAPTER 2

"So... where are we going?" I repeat, once I'm sitting inside the confines of a luxury sedan.

David pulls out onto the street before he responds. "If you don't mind, I'd rather wait a bit longer before telling you that."

Okay, so now those alarm bells are starting to go off... a little too fucking late!

I slowly edge toward the side of the car, wanting to put as much distance between us as I can within the small space. "Why?" I question warily, working hard to keep the panic out of my voice.

My eyes are glued to his face, reading his expression, so I don't miss when he grimaces. "You're just... It's better if we wait."

What the hell does that even mean?!

My brain scrambles to figure out what the hell is going on and how the fuck I got myself into this situation. "Oh my god," I gasp as a thought strikes. "Y-you're the one who left the box on my doorstep. Aren't you?" My shoulders rise and fall as I begin to hyperventilate, quickly spiraling into the throes of a panic attack. "Oh, my god, you killed Richard. And now you're going to kill me." The world outside the window fills with black splotches as tunnel vision sets in, and a whooshing sound in my ears distorts any other noise around me.

"What?!" David balks, taking his eyes off the road to gape at me. "No! God, no! That is not... Fucking hell, Emilia." He swipes a hand down his face, and even in the midst of my meltdown, I'm still with it enough to note the look of absolute horror on his face. "No, you've got it all wrong. I'm just trying to look out for you. I've *been* looking out for you."

His cryptic words do nothing to shine a light on the situation, and I get momentarily distracted as he pulls off the road onto a private airstrip. We approach a hangar where people are busy working on refueling a plane and getting it ready to fly, by the looks of things.

My confusion only heightens as we pull to a stop and David gets out, coming around the front of the car to open my door. I'm seriously regretting not taking my chances with the crazy psycho as I hesitantly step out, wondering what the hell I've gotten myself into. Seriously, I always obeyed my mom's rules, and *now* I choose to break what has got to be one of the most important ones?!

Stupid. Stupid. Stupid.

He places his hand in the middle of my back again, and even though I'm freaking out, the heat from his palm is strangely reassuring as he ushers me forward. Turning to take in the luxury jet before me, I stumble over my feet when I notice the large owl painted on the tail.

"Um, why is Hadley's plane here?"

Hadley Davenport. My best friend. The one whose fiancé and brother I slept with.

"Just keep walking. I'll explain it all on board."

Feeling a little more reassured that he's in some way

connected to Hadley and maybe not my crazy finger-leaving psycho, I don't argue as I climb the steps onto the plane.

"Wow." I whistle as I take in the plush interior. The comfy leather chairs look like they belong in a fancy hotel or nightclub rather than on a plane. Giving the flight attendant a weak, exhausted smile, I move to claim one of the cozy-looking seats by the window.

David moves to sit beside me, but I ignore him as I stare out the window, watching as the men finish fueling the plane and they pack up their equipment before the doors are closed as we're waved out of the hangar. I remain quiet, deep in thought, as we accelerate down the runway and lift into the air until the flight attendant approaches.

"Can I get either of you a drink?" she asks in that polite, professional tone all good customer service people have perfected.

"No, thanks. We're—"

"Yes, actually," I bite out, cutting David off. "A *large* glass of white wine would really be appreciated."

"Of course, I'll get that right away."

"Hadley sent you here, didn't she?" I question when the woman has gone to get my drink, finally giving David my attention.

"She did."

"You work for her?"

"Hawk, actually." I wince. Even hearing his name hurts my chest. Hadley quickly learned not to bring him or Wilder up in conversation, and on the odd occasion when I visited her, she always ensured they weren't around. Or perhaps they have been avoiding me as much as I've been avoiding them. Either way, hearing Hawk's name after so long is... jarring. It's both unwanted and savored all at once. "But I'm here under Hadley's orders."

I nod, my thoughts churning as the flight attendant returns with my glass of wine. I wait until we're alone again before taking a sip and voicing them aloud. "She told you about the stuff at college."

"She was worried about you."

Sighing, I return my attention to the blue sky and the blanket of white clouds outside my window. I should have known Hadley would overreact.

Except, given today... maybe it wasn't an overreaction. Maybe she was right to be concerned. Maybe I was *under-reacting*—making light of a hazardous situation and waving it off as if it was nothing.

"Is your name even David?" I hiss, angry at all the secrets and deception.

He winces, an apology in his eyes, giving me an answer before he even so much as opens his mouth. "It's Kai."

I roam my eyes over his handsome, boy-next-door features. Kai. It suits him, much more than David. Not that there was anything wrong with David, he just never seemed like a David to me.

I shake my head, too tired to care that he lied about his name. "I thought, now that I'd graduated, it would stop," I explain. The feeling of being watched. The flowers. The gifts.

"Has there been anything else since you finished college?"

"You mean other than a severed finger and my boyfriend's possible limb removal or death?" I sigh. "No." I haven't received anything since I moved into my new apartment. Not until today.

"Em, Richard's dead. You may as well get that into your head now."

I practically give myself whiplash with how quickly I turn on him, nearly spilling my drink in the process. "You don't know that! How can you possibly know that?! He could be chained up in a basement somewhere! Or maybe they just took his finger, and he's in the hospital right now, unconscious and unable to contact me." Hysteria raises its ugly head as tears overflow and run down my cheeks. "We just left him there. I didn't even try to help him." I duck my head, wiping at the tears, annoyed that I'm completely falling apart in front of this hot stranger.

"Do you remember that guy you slept with freshman year?"

"Fucking hell, you just know everything about me, don't you?" I gripe, buying time as I struggle to compose myself. I remember him, in any case. Ben. He was the first guy I slept with after Hawk and Wilder. One of those *just rip-the-Band-Aid-off* situations. I figured if I just got the first one over with, it would get easier. Spoiler alert, it didn't. I tried again with a couple of other guys before finally giving up... until Richard. "What about him?"

"Did you know he transferred schools?"

"So? What does that have to do with me?"

"He transferred because someone threatened to sabotage his scholarship."

"What?" I ask, incredulous. "How do you even know that?"

"I asked him. And guess what?"

"What?" This time the question comes out with an edge of wariness.

"The other two guys you dated also transferred shortly after meeting you."

"That doesn't..." I trail off, shaking my head. "That's not possible." But even I can't deny it doesn't look good. "And what does that have to do with Richard being d-dead?"

"The second guy you dated, his family was threatened and a fire was started in the family home. Thankfully, no one was inside at the time." My brows furrow, but he continues. "The third guy was beaten with a baseball bat, bad enough to require hospital admission. There's a clear pattern of escalation."

"A pattern of escalation?" I squeak, unable to wrap my head around what he's saying. "Why do I not know about any of this?"

He shrugs. "You were done with the guys, and Hadley didn't want to freak you out."

"So she sent you," I finish, my mind reeling. "Why did this psycho not go for Richard earlier? Why wait until now?"

He shrugs, not seeming to have an answer to that one. "I'm guessing the ring was the trigger. Perhaps before then they didn't think he was a threat."

"And you think he's dead?"

He grimaces. "I'll look into it, but I doubt he's just walking around with a missing finger." He hesitates before stating, "The fact that whoever this is also sent you his finger is concerning. It shows not only an escalation of violence, but that they want you to see how far they are willing to go for you."

My mouth suddenly feels like sandpaper, and I gulp down the rest of my wine, desperate for the alcohol to numb me from the terror currently rocking me to my core. My gaze once again drifts to the window as I lean my head against the wall and just stare at the clouds, not really seeing them.

This morning I woke up and went to work like it was any other day. Where the hell did it all go wrong? How did what was supposed to be an ordinary Wednesday end up with a severed finger, a possibly dead boyfriend, and a creepy ass stalker? And that doesn't even touch on the fact that Richard was going to propose. *Propose.*

As if he could read my thoughts, or maybe I was muttering to myself, Kai asks, "Would you have said yes?"

Sighing, I turn my head to look at him, frowning as I try to navigate through my feelings. "Maybe." I wince, because that is not the indecisive answer Richard deserved. He deserved way better from me than the half-assed effort I put in. It wasn't for lack of trying, but no matter how much I wished I could be madly in love with him, I just... wasn't. It's a head-over-heart matter, and I'm honestly not sure who would have won out. My head says he ticks all the boxes and I'd be a fool not to marry him, but my heart screams for passion, heat, and excitement.

And more concerningly, for the only two men who have ever made me feel that way.

"I think the fact your answer isn't an immediate yes is an answer in itself," Kai says softly.

Not long later, the pilot speaks over the intercom, letting us know we are beginning our descent. Fifteen minutes later, we are hitting the ground and rolling to a stop. Kai grabs my bag, along with a bag of his own things he must have packed when I was in my frenzied state earlier, and we exit the jet to a waiting car.

Ah, I'd forgotten how the other half lived—no commercial flights and waiting for the bus when you have money.

A driver meets us at the car and takes the bags from Kai, putting them in the trunk while Kai ushers me into the back seat.

"So," I begin as the driver climbs in behind the wheel, and we start moving. "Was everything else you told me a lie?"

"I didn't want to lie to you," he insists, his voice soft and sincere, tinged with regret that's mirrored in the deep contours of his brow. "It was necessary for my cover. We didn't want anyone tracing me back to Nocturnal Enterprises or Hadley if anything like this was to happen."

"So you were expecting... *this*?"

He gives an easy shrug of his shoulder. "You hope for the best and plan for the worst. I genuinely hoped, for your sake, that it would be all over when you graduated. However, I made sure to have an exit plan in place just in case." I simply nod, unsure how to respond to that. "But I told you the truth when I could."

"So you were in the Marines?"

"I was. I enlisted the day I turned eighteen and served for six years. When my tour finished last year, I got a private security gig at Nocturnal Enterprises. It was only meant to be a short-term thing until I worked out my next move, but they've been an excellent company to work for, and I've gotten to know Hawk, Hadley, and her guys pretty well."

"And you really do hate peanut butter and jelly sandwiches?" My lips quirk as I remember our first conversation. The first time I met him, I was stuffing a peanut butter and jelly sandwich into my mouth while I ran out the door, late to meet Mel for a shopping trip. I'd somehow managed to smear jelly on my face and had no idea until he kindly pointed it out. Talk about making an excellent first impression. Not that it seemed to bother him, finding humor in the situation while I wished for the ground to swallow me whole.

He smiles with a glint in his eye as if he recalls that first meeting too. "I really do."

The car slows to a stop, and I frown as I look out the window, squinting through the darkness to see where we are. "Ehh, where are we?" I ask when I realize we are in some back alley. I'd just assumed we were going to Hadley's.

Before Kai can answer, headlights flash through the front window, momentarily blinding me until they are switched off.

Kai steps out of the car, and a second later, a grinning blonde pops her head in.

"Hadley," I gasp, more relieved to see her than I'd ever been before.

"Hey, girl, how are you holding up?"

She slides into the backseat beside me, and I throw my arms

around her. That's when the tears start, like her presence is the wrecking ball that smashes through the dam holding my emotions at bay.

Wrapping her arms around me, she lets me fall apart as I sob into her shoulders, today's events finally hitting me.

"I'm sorry about Richard," she says softly when my sobs have trailed off to sniffles.

Pulling back, I swipe under my eyes. "He was going to propose."

"I know."

"I didn't think we were at that point."

She grimaces. "Well, you were together for over a year. He probably assumed marriage, kids, and the whole shebang was where it was heading."

I sigh, not wanting to dwell on thoughts of all of that. Not only because it makes me feel guilty but because, in all honesty, every time I tried to picture a future like that with Richard, I just couldn't. It had nothing to do with him. I couldn't imagine a future with *anyone*. The future with the pretty house in the suburbs and neat lawn, with two kids and a golden retriever running around that I'd always pictured as my future never comes to mind anymore. It hasn't for quite some time. Instead of having that goal to work toward, I've had nothing but an unfocused image of my future for years now. I'm just not sure what that means. That I no longer want that? That it's no longer in the cards for me? Perhaps I'm destined to end up alone as a crazy cat lady.

Shaking that unwanted thought from my mind, I focus on the significance of today's events, my thoughts sticking to what Kai told me on the plane. "How could you not tell me about the threats?" I argue. "I feel so stupid."

"You'd just graduated when you told me about the phone calls and gifts. I know you tried to play it off, but I could tell you were a little freaked out by it all. I didn't want to frighten you, especially if whoever it was stopped."

"But you didn't think they would."

"No. In my experience, people like that don't just give up because of a change in circumstance or geography."

Hadley would know. She had her own obsessed psycho when we were at Pacific Prep, although her situation was entirely different.

"I sent Kai to watch over you. He's one of the best men we have, and I trust him," she says earnestly. Hadley doesn't hand out trust easily, so if he's earned hers, he must be okay.

"What's his story?" I ask, flicking my gaze out the window to where the man himself is standing guard, his back to us while we're granted this moment of privacy.

Something flashes across Hadley's face, but it's gone before I can pinpoint it. "That's his story to tell, but he'll do everything he can to keep you safe."

Sighing, I return my gaze to her. "So what happens now? Am I staying with you for a while?"

An apology flashes in her eyes and her lips press into a flat line.

"You can't stay with me," she states apologetically. "Whoever this is, most likely knows about me. My house will be one of the first places they look..." Her expression changes, and my eyes narrow as I try to place what she's feeling. Then it hits me. Guilt. What the fuck does Hadley have to feel guilty about?

Unless...

"Hadley," I growl, putting two and two together, even as my mind rebukes the idea. "No." I shake my head adamantly. "No!"

"It's the safest place for you without sending you away somewhere," she pleads. "I don't want you to be miles away if something goes wrong. Besides, I doubt anyone from Halston, or Springview even knows about them." She quirks a brow in challenge, and I sigh.

"No. No one knows, but you're delusional if you think Wilder isn't going to rip my head off when he sets eyes on me."

She snorts, and I glower at her, not appreciating her amusement at the complete disaster that is my life. Reaching out, she takes my hand in hers. "Look, I know things are complicated between you, Hawk, and Wilder, but don't you think enough time has passed? It's been years. You all need to talk and sort it out, because you're all such huge parts of my life. None of you are going anywhere, and I *need* you all to get along."

"Fine," I relent, knowing it's not fair of us to put her in the middle.

She beams, rewarding me with one of her rare genuine smiles as she gives me a quick hug. "I promise it will be okay. And Kai will be staying there too, so you won't be alone with them."

I paint on a fake smile as she reaches for something in her bag.

"Here's a new phone. It has all our numbers in it. Don't use it to call anyone else." She hands over the phone while she continues, "We also sent an email from your account to your work, explaining that a family emergency had occurred and you needed some time off."

I'd ask how she managed to do that, but West, one of her boyfriends, is a tech genius, so it was probably disturbingly easy for him to hack into my emails. Instead, I ask the more pressing question. "Am I even going to be able to go back to work? What is the plan here? Do I just hide out and hope this psycho gives up when they realize I've disappeared?"

"I don't have all the answers for you yet, Em. It would be best if you stayed hidden while we work out who this guy is. I've sent a couple of people out to keep an eye on your apartment, see who shows up and snoops around, but I don't know how long it will take."

I sigh, rubbing at my temple as a headache begins to form. "I need to tell Mel. She will freak out when I just disappear off the face of the earth."

"Okay, I'll get West to message her and make it seem like it came from your number. Is there anything in particular you want us to say?"

I bite my bottom lip while I try to think of what will appease Mel for now. "Just tell her something has come up with my mom and I've gone home, and I'll reach out to her when I can."

Nodding, she gives me a final hug. "Alright, I'll be in touch soon." Opening the door, she slides out. Except at the last second, she turns around. "By the way, Hawk and Wilder have no idea you're coming."

"Wha—" The car door slams shut. "Hadley!"

The bitch ignores me, sharing a few words with Kai before disappearing into the other car.

Pulling open the car door, Kai ducks his head in. "Come on." He gestures for me to get out while he grabs our bags. Frowning, I slide across the backseat and follow him. I step into the narrow alley, trying to figure out what the hell we are doing now. Walking down the alley until we reach a garage door, Kai inputs a code into a keypad, and it automatically opens.

I follow him over to a dark blue sedan and climb into the front passenger seat as he throws our bags in the back and gets in behind the wheel. We make our way across town to wherever Hawk and Wilder live in silence, as I try—and fail—to prepare myself for seeing them for the first time in over four years. While Hadley has been careful never to bring them up in conversation, I have seen photos of them when they've all been away on holiday together or simply out for a night. Every time I look at those photos, a pang of regret hits me steadily in the chest. I always end up wondering what would have happened if I'd stayed. If I'd taken a gap year with them, then if all of us had gone to Ridgeway College together. At the time, Wilder had wanted more. He'd even planned a whole summer vacation for us together—one that was perfectly tailored to me and gave away just how much he'd been paying attention when I hadn't realized he was even looking.

Nevertheless, everyone knows long distance doesn't work, and I was terrified of ruining our friendship. Of course, I should have seen that it was already ruined. The second we slept together, it went up in flames.

Although, if I'm really being honest with myself, I was scared. It wasn't really about preserving my friendships with them. I caught feelings I hadn't been expecting, and the sheer intensity of them scared me. It threatened to destroy everything I'd worked for; everything I had planned for myself. Pacific Prep and then Halston had been the plan ever since I was old enough to understand the sacrifices my mom made for me. She was a single parent. A nurse who worked herself to the bone to provide for me. Even at that, she still had to scrimp and save to make a living for us. She raised me to want more for myself. From a young age, she ingrained a strong work ethic in me, fostered my love of reading and learning, and encouraged me to be independent.

I never knew my dad, and I don't care to know him. When my mom was twenty-one, she was getting her nursing degree and she fell in love with one of the doctors she was working with. From what I gather, it was a whirlwind affair. One that resulted in her getting knocked up. When my father found out, he held his hands up and claimed no responsibility. He broke her heart, dumped her, and shunned her until she was forced to move to a different hospital.

The fear of something similar happening to me has followed

me my entire life, influencing my decisions and becoming deeply rooted in my psyche. My mom never really put the pieces of her broken heart back together. It was like she gave up after everything that happened with my dad. She's been an excellent mom and provider, but she definitely closed herself off. She never dates or puts herself out there. Literally, she lives for work and me.

Maybe it's because I grew up in that environment, where work comes first, that I have put so much emphasis on putting my own career above all else. My career is the culmination of years of hard work, and it scared me that two men could possibly interfere with that. I could easily have lost myself in Hawk and Wilder. I could already feel it happening, and I didn't trust myself to not develop blinders and fall head over heels for them until they became all I saw, all I cared about. *That's* why I ran.

I'm jolted out of my thoughts as we pull up to the curb, and I stare up at the wide stone steps leading to a three-story brownstone. I can't see any lights on inside, making it appear dark and intimidating, and I swallow nervously as I rub my palms, slick with sweat, against my jeans.

"You're here to protect me?" I question, unable to tear my gaze away from the foreboding townhouse.

Kai shifts to face me, even though I still don't look at him. "I'll do everything within my power to keep you safe."

I finally find it within me to tear my gaze from the looming building and turn to stare at him, my expression flat as I say, "Even against Hawk? He's your boss."

His lips pull down in a frown, confusion causing lines to form along his forehead. "*You* are my number one priority. Although, I don't believe Hawk will do anything to hurt you."

Unsure if he knows about my tumultuous past with Hawk and Wilder, I simply murmur, "I guess we'll find out," and push the door open before I can chicken out and beg him to take me somewhere else.

Following me out of the car, we head up the steps, and I wait while Kai unlocks the front door. Ushering me into a small lobby, he reaches around me to open the inner door, calling out Hawk's name as we step inside. The place is decorated in dark wood and soft lighting, making it appear warm and cozy. It's at complete odds to the racing of my heart, which accelerates to dangerous levels when I hear Hawk's gravelly voice call out in response. "Kitchen." *God, did he always sound that sexy?* Every nerve in my body responds to that one word, firing to life and making me feel more alive than I have in years.

Anxiously, I follow Kai across the hall and into a kitchen that's situated at the back of the house. Given the late hour, most of the lights are off, with just the under-cabinet lighting providing a low glow. I'm sure the rest of the kitchen is gorgeously furnished with top-of-the-line finishes, yet the shirtless man in the kitchen is all I can see.

Hawk has his back to us, wearing only a pair of sweatpants that hang low on his hips. I get an eyeful of the finely sculpted muscles of his back as they flex and tighten with his movements. *I never knew someone's back could be so erotic.*

"Hadley mentioned you'd be stopping by," he says before turning to face us. "Is everything..." He tapers off as his cold gray eyes clash with mine. His entire body tenses as he stares at me standing in his kitchen, probably looking like a haggard mess. I really should have taken a second to look in a mirror before getting out of the car, and I have to fight against the instinctual reaction to lift my hand and flatten my hair.

"Em?"

My mouth dries as my eyes fall to his exposed chest. God, if I thought his back looked good, it's nothing compared to the six-pack abs and hard pecs I'm struggling not to drool over. My gaze lingers on a tattoo on his left pec that he didn't have the last time I saw him. It's an image of a phoenix rising from the ashes, similar to the one Hadley has, and despite the fact that I'm on the verge of a heart attack at being this close to him after so many years, my heart swells at the love for his sister.

Once upon a time, the two of them were at each other's throats, ready to kill the other. The tattoo is a symbol of how far they've come. I'm honestly a little envious of their close relationship. What would it be like to know you have someone who will always have your back? Not that Hadley doesn't deserve everything she's got. She had to go to hell and back to achieve it all, and there's no one who deserves happiness more than her.

Hawk's gaze snaps to Kai, the initial smile on his face now replaced with an angry scowl that I'm more than familiar with and definitely haven't missed seeing in the last four years. "What is she doing here?" he bites out. It takes everything in me not to flinch at his arctic tone. There was once a time when I was practically immune to his brusque attitude, but it seems, with time and distance, that immunity has worn off.

"Maybe you should put on a pot of coffee," Kai suggests with a sigh. "We need to talk."

THE RUTHLESS BOYS OF RIDGEWAY

Hawk
CHAPTER 3

I can't stop staring at her. Even while she's hugging her mug of coffee like it's a lifeline, with her shoulders hunched as her eyes dart around the kitchen, landing anywhere and everywhere but on me.

She doesn't look dissimilar to the last time I saw her, and at the same time, she seems completely different. Her raven hair is longer, styled differently than it was in high school, and her curves have filled in more. The surge of want that I used to experience in her presence flares to life, and the image of grabbing onto those hips while I rail her from behind flashes across my mind, making my sweats tent, and I'm thankful the kitchen island blocks me from view.

"Hawk!"

"Huh?" My gaze snaps to Kai, realizing I missed whatever he was saying.

"I asked if Wilder is here?"

"Oh, no. He's at the frat house tonight."

Kai purses his lips. "Fine. We can fill him in tomorrow, then."

As if her body is a magnet drawing my attention back her

way, I once again find my gaze resting on her. I note the exhaustion tugging her shoulders down and her unnaturally pale face with dark purple rings under her eyes. It's probably fucked up that a thrill runs down my spine at seeing her haggard appearance. I guess life hasn't worked out too well for Emilia Harrison since she left us all behind to move to her fancy college.

Not that I give a shit. Sure, she was hot as fuck and a fun lay. And maybe I went back for seconds and could have gone for thirds, but it was just sex and convenience. She was the only girl in school who wasn't looking for something other than a good time from me, and *that's* the only reason why I slept with her more than once.

Unlike Wilder, who lost his goddamn mind over her. She practically chewed him up and spat him out, leaving him to put the pieces of his psychotic little heart back together all by himself with duct tape and super glue. *That's* why I feel pacified in knowing she's suffered too, even if whatever the reason for her hollow eyes and the fact that she's currently sitting in my kitchen has nothing to do with Wilder. She's still suffered, and there's some satisfaction in that.

I once again have to rip my gaze away from Emilia to focus on Kai, and I realize I missed what he was saying—again.

"Sorry, what?"

He frowns, spearing me with a look that says whatever he's trying to tell me is important and I need to pay attention. I've known Kai for just over a year now, and even though he's technically my subordinate, we have an easygoing rapport.

After working to turn Nocturnal Enterprises into an entirely legit operation, offering private security to the rich and famous, I started an outreach program offering security and protection for those attempting to run from dangerous situations. It's primarily battered women looking to escape their abusive partners, but we get other cases too. It was when I was recruiting men who could help get these vulnerable people to safety that I crossed paths with Kai. It's difficult to find men who are competent and will take their job seriously, who won't take advantage of such a situation, but I instantly warmed to Kai.

His years of service and the pride in his eyes at having served his country reassured me that he would put the lives of these men and women above his own, but it was his backstory that confirmed he was the perfect candidate for the job. After hearing that, I *knew* he would never let the same fate befall whatever charge he was protecting. He'd do whatever it took to ensure they were safe.

Over the following months, we fell into an easy companionship, and his knowledge and insight have been invaluable in ensuring the project has thrived. It's thanks to him that we have successfully helped over fifty men and women escape life-threatening situations.

Several months ago, he'd come to me, asking for some time off. He didn't give a reason and I hadn't wanted to pry, but now that he's here, in my kitchen with Emilia, I have to wonder what the hell he's been up to and how she's involved.

"Emilia has a stalker."

Well, those words get my attention, and I finally listen to what Kai has to say as he fills me in on Emilia's past with this so-called stalker, the events of today, and Hadley's hastily thrown-together plan. Of course, my sister went to Kai asking for help. With his bleeding heart and history, there was no way he wasn't going to jump to Emilia's rescue. However, the fact that Hadley sent them here, knowing damn well that she was delivering Emilia like a sacrificial lamb to the slaughter... What was she thinking?

Hadley is more than aware of the safe houses we have dotted across the country. She could easily have sent Kai and Emilia to one of them. Hell, it would probably have been safer, and yet, it's my kitchen Emilia is currently sitting in. My infuriating sister is playing with fire, and she damn well knows it.

The entire time, I watch Emilia, noting the fact that she never removes her gaze from the countertop while Kai talks. The only reaction she gives is the tightening of her hand around the mug when Kai mentions her dead boyfriend and the threats her previous ones received. Seeing as she's not a blubbering mess on my floor, she couldn't have been too attached to this boyfriend.

"So, Hadley thinks you'll be safer here?" Kai's already said as much, but I want Emilia to know that she may be safe here from her stalker, but that does not mean she is safe. I hitch a brow. "Under the same roof as me and Wilder?"

Emilia attempts to suppress her flinch at hearing his name, but I catch it, smirking at the knowledge of how uncomfortable this situation is for her. Given the fact that we hadn't heard from or seen her since high school, I bet she never thought she'd see us again.

I can feel Kai's gaze as it flicks between us, and I wonder if she's told him anything about our past. Regardless, I ignore his questioning stare as I drill my gaze into Emilia until she squirms in her chair. I watch as her shoulders tense and her spine turns rigid as she gathers the courage she needs to lift her head, meeting my steely gaze with a resolute one of her own.

I can see the fire burning deep in her eyes, and I smirk at the challenge. Bring it on, Little Sparrow. This time, you're playing by our rules, and you won't escape unscathed.

Dismissing her, I flick my gaze to Kai. "Fine, you can stay." As if I had any choice. "You can take the two bedrooms on the third floor."

With an appreciative nod, Kai downs the last of his coffee before placing his and Emilia's mugs in the sink. He grabs the two duffel bags they arrived with, and Emilia moves to follow him as he heads out of the room, but I quickly round the island and wrap my arm around her waist, pulling her back against me before she can run away.

I ignore the heat of her body radiating along mine, and the way she fits snuggly against me, her soft curves pressed flush against my hard edges. Lowering my face to her neck, my breaths fan over the sensitive skin beneath her earlobe, and I smirk as she reacts to my touch, her tense body trembling as goosebumps pebble along her skin.

"Don't think your safety won't come at a price, Little Sparrow."

Dropping my arm, she scurries from the room without a backward glance, and I watch her go, both apprehensive and curious about this new development. For the first time in a long time, I find myself excited for tomorrow. Wilder's going to obliterate every remnant of the safe world Emilia has built for herself, and I can't wait to watch him.

Leaning against the headboard of my bed, I get comfy before dialing her number. It's late. I had to wait until I was sure Emilia was locked away in her room for the remainder of the night, but I knew she'd still be awake, expecting this call.

The call only rings once before it connects, and I smirk as I'm met with silence. Hadley has never been intimidated by me, though that doesn't mean we don't like to one-up each other every chance we get, even if it is as petty as who will break the silence first.

Eventually, her frustrated sigh is followed by, "Aren't you calling to yell at me?"

"That would imply you've done something wrong, dear sister."

I swear I can hear her eye roll before she says, "No, but I knew you'd be against the idea, which is why I didn't tell you."

"Mmm, you'd have been right." My tone turns serious as I question, "What are you thinking by bringing her here?"

"I'm thinking that my best friend is in some serious trouble, and the only people I trust to keep her safe from this psycho are currently living under your roof."

I sigh, pressing the pads of my fingers into my eyes in an attempt to relieve some of the pressure. "You know what this is going to do to Wilder."

"I know. You'll keep him in line, though?"

With a scoff, I retort, "Do you seriously think Wilder will listen to me? When it comes to her, he won't listen to what any of us have to say."

She's silent for a moment, and when she speaks again, her voice is softer. "What about you?"

"Don't worry about me, sis. I wasn't the one who had their heart stomped over."

"Right." Her tone is unreadable, grating on my nerves.

"Don't start that shit again, Hadley," I growl angrily. For fucking ages after we graduated high school, she was insistent that my funk was because of Emilia. But it wasn't. After the year I'd had—discovering my parents' company was responsible for kidnapping and training children to become ruthless mercenaries, finding out I had a sister only for her to be kidnapped, working to dismantle said mercenary ring and bring down everyone responsible, and watching my mother die right in front of me after witnessing her torture one of my best friends—it's only to be expected that I would struggle to bounce back to my normal self. Just because Emilia happened to be the final factor in that entire fiasco of a year, doesn't mean she had anything to do with it.

"Okay, I won't. I will tell you the same thing I told her,

however. The three of you need to get past this. You're all important to the guys and me, and I'm sick of being put in the middle, unable to mention her when I'm around you and Wilder, and then forbidden to talk about either of you with her. It has to stop. The three of you *have* to work it out."

Forbidden, huh? That piques my curiosity. Is that because Emilia didn't want to be reminded of us? Or because she didn't want the reminder of her past mistakes?

"Wilder's the one you need to have this conversation with, not me."

"Well, you're the one I'm talking to right now, and since you're so unaffected by Emilia's presence, you can be the one to start fixing things." Her tone makes it clear that she doesn't believe for one second that I'm *unaffected*, and I just grunt in acknowledgment, not wanting to go around in circles with her.

"Fine," I hiss reluctantly. My goddamn motherfucking sister knows I can never say no to her. She's the one person I'd do anything for. The one person who can get me to do the exact opposite of what I want to do. "But I'm not making any promises. You know Wilder won't take this well."

Hadley sighs, but she knows I'm right. "Just don't hurt her too much."

When we hang up, I pull up my chat with Wilder and fire off a text, telling him to come home before classes in the morning. Better to rip the Band-Aid off before he accidentally stumbles across her on his own. God only knows how he would react to that.

Knowing how manic it can be when there's a party at the frat house, I'm not expecting a response, so I drop my phone onto my covers and allow my eyes to trail skyward to where Emilia rests in the room above mine, as I wonder what she's doing at this moment. I wonder how it feels to know she's trespassing on our playground once again. Is she scared? 'Cause she should be. Of more than just her stalker.

Wilder is more than just a little unhinged, and while most of the time his brand of crazy comes out in the weird shit he says and does, in the lack of fucks he gives and the quirky way he dresses, I've seen the flip side of that switch when someone gets on his bad side. The crazy glint in his eye is not something you should take lightly, and I have a feeling Emilia is going to get a rude awakening to his instability.

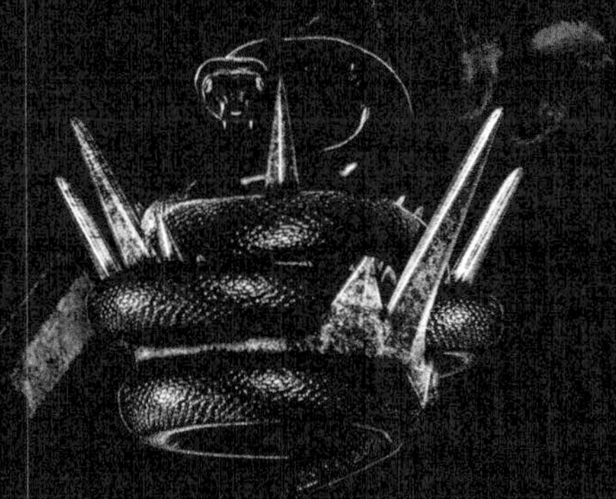

THE RUTHLESS BOYS OF RIDGEWAY

Emilia
CHAPTER 4

I toss and turn all night, my mind unable to shut off after the events of the last twelve hours, not to mention the fact that one of the guys I've actively been *not* thinking about for the last four years is sleeping on the floor below me. And I'm inside his fucking house. How the hell did my whole life get turned upside down in less than a day?

And, *holy hell*, did Hawk look good. So good. *Too* good. I can't figure out if he's gotten even better looking since I last saw him or if I downplayed his hotness in my mind. He was always one of those guys who was abstractly attractive, but until our senior year, I'd never really *looked* at him. He was an arrogant asshole, and no matter how hot he was, it wasn't enough to make me overlook that. Not that it would have mattered if I had. Until Hadley showed up, Hawk had never looked at me twice. He probably didn't even know my name.

I only ended up on his radar because Hadley incurred his wrath. Later, when he discovered Hadley was his sister, and their relationship went from hate to one of reluctant siblings united in their cause to destroy their parents, we were forced to be around each other. It was only then that I really started noticing just how stupidly attractive he was. I'd catch myself staring at him, and even though I still hated him and didn't trust him one bit around Hadley, I couldn't deny how his close proximity set my body on fire in a way I'd never experienced before.

Still, I never let myself act on it. It was he who made the first move one night when Hadley and the guys were away, and he invited me to watch a movie with him. I thought he was just bored, and outside of his circle of friends, there was no one else he could hang out with. But after falling asleep and waking up to him getting me off... *damn.* I thought for sure I was still dreaming.

Hawk's eyes simmer as they rake over me. "You're such a tease, Emilia. You think I don't notice the extra sway of your hips when I'm looking or your fuck me eyes, but I do."

Stepping into me until my breasts brush against his chest, my nipples harden into peaks as he stares down at me with nothing but undisguised heat burning in his gaze. His hands move to rest on my hips, the heat burning my skin, before he slides them around to palm my ass. With a tight squeeze, he uses his hold to grind against me.

"You have no idea how long I've wanted this for," he purrs, dipping to nibble on my earlobe before trailing a path of searing hot kisses along my neck. In the space of one blink, Hawk's clothes evaporate, leaving him in just his boxers, the thick length of his erection straining against the cotton.

Glancing down at myself, I realize my own clothes have disappeared, and when Hawk makes a pleasurable noise in the back of his throat and moves to cup the heavy weight of my breast in his hand, I moan in delight.

His other hand reaches between my thighs, his fingers trailing through the moisture gathering before he starts playing with my clit. I gasp at the delicious tingles that emanate outward from my core.

"Hawk." His name is nothing more than a soft exhale, a pleasure-induced moan as he does incredible things to my body.

"Damn right, baby. I'm the one making you feel this good."

His thumb rubs tight circles around my over-sensitized bundle of nerves, and I bite down on my lip to trap another wanton moan. My body quakes in his arms, hungry for more, and when he moves lower, sliding two thick fingers inside of me, I arch my back, clinging to his shoulders as he sends me catapulting toward oblivion.

I'm right on the edge, dancing precariously along the precipice of what promises to be a one-of-a-kind orgasm, when the image in front of me distorts, and I'm pulled away, sucked into darkness. The only thing that remains is the lingering exhilaration of his touch.

As I'm tugged back into the land of the living, I expect the residual effects of my near orgasm to fade, but instead, they heighten, wave after wave of pleasure coursing through my body until I want to scream.

Clearing the sleep from my eyes, I gaze groggily up at the mass of blond hair hovering over me. As if sensing I'm awake, Hawk lifts his head, his dark, stormy gray eyes clashing with mine. His pupils are dilated with lust, making it look like I'm staring at a cross-section of a tornado; his pupil the eye of the storm, and his iris the swirling chaotic energy that destroys anything in its path.

I lose myself in the turbulence for a moment, until another thrust of his finger makes me realize that my dream wasn't just a dream. My entire body goes rigid, my arms snapping up so I can grasp his shoulders, attempting to push him back.

Instead of getting off me, Hawk uses his superior strength to maneuver us until I'm sprawled across the sofa, pinned beneath him.

My lips part with some sort of protest, but before I can gather the words, he speaks over me.

"I know you want this. Need it." Another thrust of his fingers.

"Don't fight it." His pace quickens, and any objections I had, fall away as my back arches and my breath hitches.

With skilled movements, it doesn't take long until the ball of energy in my core explodes outwards. Hawk drinks in every second, his eyes never once leaving mine as I fall apart beneath his touch, and for a split second all the animosity and distrust that usually bounces between us falls by the wayside. For a moment, he hasn't always despised what I am, and I haven't always hated his righteous arrogance. We're just two people who find each other attractive.

That bliss only lasts a moment before the reality of our situation penetrates my mind, like a sharp pin bursting a bubble. Our past rushes in, along with the reminder that this is Hadley's brother, and I shove him backward.

"What the hell was that?" I snap, jack-knifing off the couch in my desperate need to put some distance between us before I can convince myself to take this any further.

The emotion on his face from a moment ago is wiped clean, his usual mask of indifference firmly back in place as he shrugs. "Just giving you what you wanted."

What I wanted? What does that even mean?!

My mouth opens and closes as I try to find the right words, but every time I go to say something, I can feel my mind twisting it into something different, something dirty, something that my body craves but I know I can't indulge in.

Giving up, I throw my hands in the air in exasperation, and needing to get the hell away from him before I cave and climb aboard his dick. I storm out of the apartment, not stopping until I'm locked behind my own closed door, wanton and needy, and completely confused.

As the memory of the night that things turned a corner between Hawk and me fades away, the faint rays of daylight start to break through the darkness outside my window. Rubbing at my gritty eyes, I check the time, finding that it's shortly after five a.m. *There's no hope of me getting any more sleep.*

Giving up on even trying, I throw back the covers and climb out of bed. Wearing my thin pajama top and matching shorts that are covered in pictures of different breeds of dogs, with the words, written in large letters across my ass, *bite me*, followed by *and I'll bite you back* in much smaller writing, I poke my head out of my room, checking if the coast is clear before daring to venture any further.

On silent feet, I pad down the stairs and into the kitchen, turning on the under-counter lighting. I open and close cabinet doors until I find everything I need to put on a pot of coffee, and while I wait for it to brew, I lose myself to my tired and groggy thoughts.

It's the same thing that's been keeping me awake all night. Hawk. Or, more precisely, the hard glint in his eyes and his stone-like expression. All of it is something I should be more than used to. It was his standard expression when we were at Pacific Prep. The only one he ever used on me, until he didn't. Somewhere along the way, in our final year, that look changed. It wasn't even something I realized at the time. Outwardly, his face was still set in the same veneer, but it was different from how it had been before. His eyes were no longer hard and cold but burned with an intensity that scorched my skin and made me self-combust.

It was only when I mustered the courage to meet his harsh gaze last night that it resonated with me. The realization practically knocked the air from my lungs. Even now, my shoulders deflate, knowing I'm back to square one with him, and this time Hadley and the guys aren't around to soften his edges.

I'm so caught up thinking about Hawk that I fail to realize a more dangerous threat has snuck up behind me, and I practically jump out of my skin, a high-pitched yelp escaping when a large hand grabs a handful of my ass. "Don't mind if I do," Wilder growls low in my ear in a voice that both soothes, excites, and terrifies me.

He chuckles, the sound a seductive purr that resonates with every atom in my body, flushing my skin and heating my core. Before I can brace myself, he spins me to face him, and the playful, hungry smile on his lips drops away, his eyes widening almost imperceptibly as he roams his gaze over my face.

In the blink of an eye, his umber eyes grow hard, his body stiffening as he shuts down right in front of me. I'm helpless to do anything but watch, my insides feeling like they're being shredded to pieces as I watch the Wilder I once knew being methodically tucked away, a colder version of him rising to the surface to take his place.

A sharp tug on the back of my head makes me gasp as it's forced back, until I'm openly staring up at him, unable to hide from the anger, hate, and malicious intent staring me directly in the eye. One side of his lip lifts in a snarl, his eyes boring into mine, and I have no doubt he wishes his ire alone could incinerate me.

With the way he's holding the back of my head, my neck is bared to him, and he wraps his other hand around it, squeezing. I can feel the intent in his fingers as they press firmly against my skin, his hand shaking with the desire to crush my windpipe until nothing but the faintest wisp of air makes it past his tight hold.

"What the fuck are you doing here?"

His face is so close that spittle lands on my cheek, and I part my lips, although to do what exactly, I'm not sure. I can hardly breathe, never mind speak. And even if I could, I'm sure he doesn't want to hear anything I have to say.

He crowds me against the counter, the edge digging

painfully into the lower part of my spine as he uses his tight hold on my hair to force me to arch my back. The move only presses me against him more fully, my pelvis and thighs flush with his.

By now, I can hardly think straight. Blood rushes in my ears, deafening me as black spots appear in my vision. I'm distantly aware of the hardening of his cock against my lower stomach, but it's little more than a passing thought before my lack of oxygen sends it scurrying off into the recesses of my mind.

Just when I think I'm going to pass out, he abruptly lets go, stepping back as my weak knees give out and I sink to the floor, gasping for air as I cough and splutter. When I no longer have tunnel vision, I lift my head, watching as Wilder stalks toward Hawk, who is leaning against the doorframe, apparently having observed our interaction and clearly didn't feel the need to intervene.

I glower at him, although given the tears in my eyes and the trembling in my hands as I lift them to touch the tender skin along my neck, I doubt it looks all that impressive. He barely looks at me anyway, before returning his focus to Wilder.

"She shouldn't fucking be here," Wilder snarls venomously before storming past Hawk and disappearing through the door. Hawk remains where he is, still leaning casually against the doorframe like this is any other morning, watching me with those stormy gray eyes of his that always leave me feeling unsettled.

"I told you your safety came with a price. You better get ready to pay up, 'cause that was only the beginning."

On that disturbing note, he pushes off the doorframe and follows after Wilder. Their footsteps have long since faded by the time I pull myself off the kitchen floor. Forgetting about my coffee, I sneak back through the house, taking the stairs as quickly and quietly as I physically can until I reach the relative safety of the third floor. Rushing past my bedroom door, I head straight for the bathroom, slamming the door shut behind me and pressing my forehead against the wood as I suck in a steadying breath of air.

"Are you okay?"

What the hell?! It can't even be six a.m. yet. Why is the entire house awake?!

With another fortifying breath, I turn to face Kai, but holy mother of Mary, my mouth instantly runs dry as I drink in every exposed inch of his torso. It's only as my eyes trail the water droplets as they drip from his wet hair onto his shoulder, then over the hard planes of his torso until they soak into the towel wrapped around his narrow hips, that I notice the bathroom is steamed up from his shower.

A moment passes when I can't seem to look away. Everything from the kitchen is forgotten as I commit every hill and valley of his prominent six-pack, his lightly bronzed skin, and the short dusting of dark chest hair to memory. It's only when my eyes trail further south, following a neatly trimmed happy trail, that my cheeks pinken and I snap my eyes up to his face.

When I do, I find his gaze zeroed in on my neck. Self-consciously, I lift my hand to cover the no-doubt red marks on my skin, but before I can, he steps toward me, batting my hand away. With gentle fingers that are at complete odds with Wilder's rough touch, he grasps my chin, tilting it up while he inspects my neck.

"Which one of them did this to you?"

His voice sounds like gravel, ominous and seductive all at once, and when I don't immediately respond, he lifts his gaze, meeting mine. His jaw is clenched tightly, and something I can't place simmers in his emerald, green eyes, turning them a darker shade than I've seen before.

"Wilder." His name is barely more than a whisper on my tongue, but Kai hears it.

"Why?"

I push against his chest until he takes a step back, and refusing to answer him, I move over to the sink, craning my neck to get a better look at the fingerprint marks that will definitely bruise and stand out against my otherwise pale skin.

Sighing, I turn on the tap and run my hands underneath the cold stream before splashing my face. The cool water soothes my heated skin and helps steady my nerves. Even so, I can feel the heat of Kai's intense stare drilling into my back.

"Why?" he repeats, his voice sounding more strained than it did before, and when I flick my gaze to his in the mirror, I catch him staring at me, his fists clenched at his sides like he's debating going out there and punching Wilder on my behalf. I don't know why he's so worked up over this. Surely he knows Wilder's crazy ways, and even if he doesn't, he barely knows *me*.

His words from last night come to mind, his promise to protect me. I'm honestly not sure if this falls under his purview, nor do I know if I want to clue him in on all the details of mine, Hawk, and Wilder's complicated and sordid past.

Instead, I wave away his question. "It doesn't matter." Looking away, I say quietly, "I deserve it, anyway."

It's the truth. I do. Every time I close my eyes, I see the pain on Wilder's face the day I basically told him to go shove his summer plans for us. The second I told him what I was actually going to spend my summer doing, it broke the thin thread of inexplicable feelings that had been blooming between us.

I CAN'T DO anything but gape at Wilder while he literally ticks off what sounds like the vacation of my dreams. A vacation he planned... for us.

I don't...

I can't...

"Wilder," I trail off, lost for words. "That's... insane. Like, completely crazy. Why would you even organize all of that without asking me first?" I dart my eyes around the busy dining hall. We're in the middle of our last school dance at Pacific Prep, yet none of it really matters as I stare into Wilder's enigmatic eyes that shine with excitement. So much excitement. He can hardly stand still; he's so ready to burst with it. Like this trip means as much to him as it would to me.

Except, I can't.

"Why would you even assume I want to spend the whole summer with you? How do you know I don't have plans already? Hell, you haven't even given me any say in what we're doing."

"Well, tell me what you want to do, and I'll add it to the plan."

I hesitate, still gaping at him like an idiot.

Could it be that simple? Could I just...?

No. I've already made my plans.

God, I feel like I'm being torn in two, my heart and head yanking me in opposite directions while I just flail around in the middle, unsure of which way to go.

It feels like the internal debate goes on for a lifetime before I whisper the words past numb lips, "I can't... I just can't with you right now."

Before he can gather any sort of argument to entice me further, I run off into the crowd, desperate to put some distance between us. Tears blur my vision as I push blindly past the milling students. I just need to get away from him, because if one more word passed his soft, pillowy lips, I'd have been a goner. I'm not even sure how I managed to get those final words out, because I'm pretty sure every bone in my body was urging me to go. To go on the trip with him. To give him a chance. Give us a chance.

By the time he drags me off the dance floor later that night, I've got my mental walls firmly back in place and fortified with steel. I've spent all evening ignoring his allure and reminding myself of the bigger goals. College. A stable job. Looking after my mom.

I can't afford to lose myself in Wilder Clearwater. He'd take everything from me and leave me with nothing. It's not that he'd do it deliberately. Hell, he probably wouldn't even notice he was doing it at all. I'd happily hand over every part of who I am to him, but then when the heat of our lust burnt out, I'd be left with nothing. I'd be an empty husk. A hollowed-out version of the girl I am now.

Because it would eventually come to an end. A blazing, self-destructive, take-the-world-down-with-us kind of end. We're only eighteen, and Wilder is, well, Wilder. He's wild and carefree, and he lives in a world where he can so beautifully be those things and not have to worry about the real-world stresses that the rest of us have to deal with.

My mom never picked herself back up. Who's to say I would? And despite how much I want to—and I really fucking want to—I can't risk my future for the inevitable heartbreak. So, tucking the quickly growing feelings I have for him into a lock box that I know I'll stroke often but make myself promise I'll never open again, I turn to face a fuming Wilder.

"I don't get it. I thought you'd love to spend the summer traveling, seeing new places."

"I would love that, but what made you think I wanted you to dictate the next two months of my life? I don't need or want you making decisions for me. Did it ever cross your mind to ask me if I had any plans or if I wanted to spend the summer with you?"

The words hurt even as I say them, but I will myself to stay strong. This is what has to happen. Wilder and I, we were never meant to be. We're two stars passing in the night. For a while, our lights burnt bright together, but now we're drifting away, moving in opposite directions to one another, and there's no changing course. No going back.

"Alright, I'm sorry. I should have involved you. I thought it

would be a nice surprise. That doesn't mean you have to say no just because you're annoyed, though."

Fuck. He's not making this easy, and with every passing second, my resolve weakens, my heart hammering against my chest in its desperation to break free. My voice is strained when I next speak, knowing exactly what hammer to use to drive the final nail into the coffin of our relationship.

"Wilder, I can't."

Before I can continue, he plows over the top of me. "You can. It's my treat. You won't have to pay for anything."

"It's got nothing to do with money. I already have plans."

"What are they? I'd need to review my itinerary, but I'm sure we can squeeze it in."

Gathering the last of my strength, I deliver the final blow. "No, Wilder. I'm spending the summer touring with Death on a Matchstick. They asked me a couple of weeks ago and... I agreed."

"When? Cancel." The sharp command snaps off his tongue. A direct order that I don't obey.

"I emailed them back to confirm last week."

"After our night together?"

There's the hurt I was looking for, although I take no pleasure in causing it as I murmur a pathetic and useless, "I'm sorry," before he storms off.

Death on a Matchstick had played a concert for Hawk's birthday party our senior year of high school, and well, I had an exclusive after-show with two of the band members that night. We'd kept in touch via text and emails over the following months, and when they asked me if I'd be interested in spending the summer on tour with them, I thought long and hard about it before I agreed.

It wasn't an easy decision, but at the time, it felt like the right one. I was falling in love with Wilder, and that scared the shit out of me. I hadn't been prepared for such intense feelings, and I couldn't work out how they factored into the life plans I'd spent the last four years putting together for myself and my mom.

So, I ran... right into the arms of three tortured musicians.

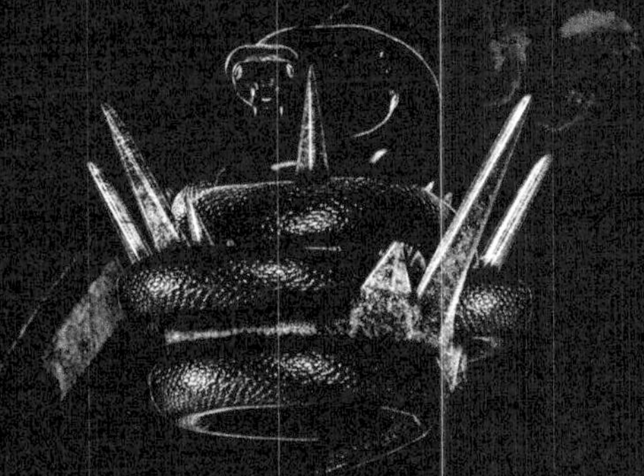

THE RUTHLESS BOYS OF RIDGEWAY

Wilder

CHAPTER 5

I'm still fucking fuming mad when I step onto the campus grounds an hour later, Hawk at my side.

"Forget about her for now, man. She's not here, and we're staying at the frat tonight. Kai can babysit while we let off some well-deserved steam."

"Thank fuck. I'd have lost my shit if I had to be around her for one more second."

The asshole snorts. "You mean, that wasn't you losing your shit this morning?"

The death glare I throw him would have anyone else screaming like a baby as they ran away like the hounds of hell were on their ass, but the jerkweed simply rolls his eyes, knowing damn well that when it comes to him, I'm all bark and no bite.

Well, maybe a little bite.

Still, that's why we're brothers. Brothers in every fucking way. Ride or die, brothers. Frat brothers. Nearly actual, real-life bros-in-law—back when I was his sister's fiancé. Well, fake fiancé if you wanna get specific about it. Pussy brothers, although I no longer like to think about that one. We've only ever been pussy brothers when it comes to *'she who shall not be named'*. So, I guess we're no longer pussy brothers, but still, brothers in every other way that counts.

"Thanks for the heads up, by the way."

"How the fuck was I supposed to know that she'd be in the kitchen at the ass-crack of dawn?"

"She's lucky she didn't get a throatful of my cock," I snark, making Hawk smirk.

"Damn, I hope I'm there to see it when she does."

I scoff. "Not. Fucking. Happening. Been there, done that, got a stupid fucking t-shirt somewhere to prove it." I really do, assuming I kept it after all these years. I bought one each for Hawk and I, only he just scowled at the time and most likely threw it away. We weren't on great terms back then. He was still adjusting to having me as his ride-or-die, but I wore him down eventually, and now I'm his bestie. The Bonnie to his Clyde. The peanut butter to his jelly. The condom to his jizz. Eww, well, maybe not that last one, but you get the gist.

Hawk makes a noise in the back of his throat that sounds a hell of a lot like he doesn't believe me, but before I can reinforce what I'm saying, some doe-eyed freshman catches his attention, and with a mumbled goodbye, he takes off after her. At least one of us hasn't been completely thrown off kilter by Emilia's sudden and unexpected presence back in our lives.

Dammit, there I go thinking about her again. Despite myself, I smirk at the memory of blocking her in against the kitchen cabinets. The flash of fear in her eyes. The erratic flutter of her pulse beneath my hand. She seemed so fragile, so breakable.

Good. I want her to break, to make her feel what I felt when she shredded my insides with her caustic words and abrupt departure from my life. She made me fucking care about her. Then she just left me behind, like I meant nothing. Which is fine because now, *she* means nothing to *me*. She's at *my* mercy. Relying on *me* to keep her hidden from some deranged psycho. If I ever meet this crazy stalker, I'll be sure to let them know the selfish bitch really isn't worth their time or energy, but in the meantime, I can have some fun. Exact some revenge and level the playing field. She wanted to treat what we had like it was just sex and a fun time, then fine, that's exactly how I'll treat her.

Except, I'm not fucking sleeping with her. That's where it all went wrong last time. The fucking sex. It was too good. Even now, my dick stirs in my pants at the memory. *Not. Fucking. Happening,* I remind it as I stride into my first lecture of the day and take a seat near the back of the hall.

Pulling my textbook and laptop out of my bag, I flip open the book to what we are studying today but pause when I find a cream envelope tucked inside the pages. Hesitating to touch it, I glance around at the other seniors slowly filing into the room, but no one is paying me any attention.

Flicking my gaze back down to my textbook, I tentatively lift the envelope, feeling the smooth texture of expensive cardstock between my fingers as I turn it over and carefully remove the rectangular card from within.

I run my thumb over the embossed emblem along the top—a snake coiled around a crown, before lowering my gaze to read the rest of it. There's nothing except a time and place.

Midnight. Kappa Epsilon Library.

Frowning, I flip the card over, but there's nothing on the back. Focusing on the front of it again, my gaze snags on the snake and crown. Something niggles at the back of my mind, but I can't see the thought clearly. I can't remember ever seeing that symbol before, but it seems somewhat familiar. Perhaps I've seen it around the frat house. Whatever this is about must be related to it since they've requested that we meet in their library. Only frat members are allowed in there. The room is locked on nights when we throw campus parties, and non-Kappa Epsilon members have never set foot inside the library. It's not anything special, although I'll admit that libraries aren't really my thing. It's a lot smaller than the main college library, but apparently, it holds rare one-of-a-kind texts or some such shit that I couldn't really care about. Essentially, it's a room with old, dusty books that only select people—such as myself—are allowed to peruse.

The professor momentarily catches my attention as he strides into the room and begins today's lecture, but it's not long before I zone him out, my focus once again returning to the card in my hand and what it could mean. I dig my phone out of my bag and text Robbie, hoping he might have some answers, but I hesitate before I hit send on the message.

Robbie is my cousin. I'd never even met him until I started college, yet somehow he recognized me from an old family photo and sought me out. It was weird as fuck, and I was definitely skeptical at first, but I couldn't exactly argue the truth when it was staring me in the face in the form of old family photographs.

Besides, given the fact that my father had no contact with the rest of his family, and I'd never met any of them, it wasn't beyond the realm of possibility. I'd often wondered if I had other family out there, even though, honestly, I just assumed they were all as messed up as my father and was probably better off not knowing them.

Except, according to Robbie, they *aren't* anything like my father. The family apparently disowned my father after some scandal that would have dragged the family's reputation through the dirt if not for my grandfather's influence—i.e., money.

Although, they have been hesitant to have any communication with me—besides Robbie. Robbie claims they simply need time to assure themselves I'm not my father. I guess the mistakes in my past don't help with that. At one point, I definitely wasn't what a family who cares primarily about their reputation would want to be associated with. Honestly, I'm probably still not. I truly only care about the opinions of a very limited number of people, and the Clearwaters definitely aren't one of them.

Nonetheless, Robbie and I have become good friends over the last three years. When I first started at Ridgeway, he was a senior. Within a year of graduating, he became the Dean of the Political Science Department, thanks to his name and the clout of Kappa Epsilon, so I still see him around campus, which is cool.

It was Robbie who first told me of the Clearwater tradition of rushing for Kappa Epsilon. Every single Clearwater before me was a member of the frat. In fact, every single Clearwater has attended Ridgeway College. Such a small world that I'd unknowingly ended up here too.

It's almost like fate was pushing me to bridge those familial ties. Here, was a family legacy that I had no knowledge of, and while I've never been one for tradition or legacy or any of that hocus pocus, I am a fan of wild, drunken parties and having a good time. Especially back in freshman year when my pain was still fresh, when that was the only way I could temporarily forget about *her*.

However, sometime over the last few years, I guess my attitude has changed somewhat. I've watched Hawk and his father turn the Davenport name around, and the plans Hawk has for

Nocturnal Enterprises only ensures further that everyone will know it—and his—name. He's proud to be a Davenport, and I've come to realize I want that too. I want something I can be proud of. All my life, I've flitted from one thing to the next—friends, hobbies, cars, drugs. You name it. Hadley, Hawk, and the guys are the only constants that have stuck with me. They saved me when I was in a really dark, fucked up place, and while I've come to view them as my family, it's no longer enough. I want something that's solely mine.

I once thought Emilia could fill that empty void in my chest. It certainly felt like she could, but I was wrong, and now I understand that I can't rely on others to give me what I want. I can't allow my wants, needs, and desires to be contingent on another person. I have to reach out and grasp them for myself.

My focus returns to the card still clutched tightly in my hand. Kappa Epsilon is my family's legacy, and perhaps whatever this card represents is mine.

The rest of my morning classes go by in a blur, and when lunch rolls around, I'm sitting in my usual chair, surrounded by Hawk, Hadley, and her guys at our regular table in the on-campus food court. I'm present, but I'm not really here. The card burning a hole in my back pocket has all of my attention. I can hardly sit still in my chair, my leg bouncing underneath the table in anticipation of tonight.

"Wilder? Wilder!" Hadley's elbow drives into my side, and I turn to glower at her.

"What the fuck, Sunshine? That's not cool."

"Are you even listening?" she asks, ignoring me. "West was asking how you're getting on with your classes this semester?"

My gaze darts up to West, sitting opposite me, with a quizzical look on his face. "Oh, yeah, they're fine. Same old. You know I'm only here for the parties, girls, and to hang out with you guys. I couldn't care less about my classes."

I hear Hadley sigh, but I'm already back to my theories about tonight. Everything from the mundane to the intriguing to the downright ludicrous. You name it, I've thought of it. Someone playing a prank. A two-month belated surprise birthday party for yours truly. A private audience with Beyonce. The possibilities are endless.

"Is this about *you know who*?" Hadley whispers, leaning in so our conversation can't be overheard.

"Of course not," I scoff. "I'd actually completely forgotten she existed."

Lie. While the invite and meeting tonight are a welcome distraction from *she who shall not be named*, it would be impossible for me to ever forget her—especially now that she's taking up residence in *my* house.

"Rightttt," Hadley drags the word out, clearly not believing me.

Whatever.

"The two of you need to work out your shit. You're both my best friends, so you can't avoid one another forever."

"I beg to differ. Haven't the last four years proven exactly that?"

She huffs out a frustrated sigh. "The opposite, actually. I'm sick of being stuck in the middle. I just want all of us to get along."

At her uncharacteristically deflated tone, I glance her way out of the corner of my eye, finding her staring at me with big puppy dog eyes as she flutters her eyelashes like an idiot. "You suck at pulling off the innocent pleading look," I deadpan.

"Yeah, I know," she says with a shrug and a small smirk. "But figured it was worth a go."

"Because you couldn't use violence in front of a room full of people."

"Who says I won't resort to violence just because other people are around?"

With a blur of motion, so quick I don't even see it, she has my hand twisted in such a way that it feels like something important is about to snap. I bite down so hard on my tongue to keep from crying out that the coppery tang of blood fills my mouth.

Just as quickly as she incapacitated me, she lets go, and I growl furiously at her while massaging my aching wrist and ignoring the curious stares we're receiving from the others around the table.

As if nothing happened, she continues talking. "Please, just find a way to co-exist. For me."

Still snarling at her, I spit out, "Fine, I'll try," earning a rare Sunshine smile from her before she resumes eating her pasta salad.

Damn, that almost makes me feel bad for lying to her.

THE REST of the day felt like it crawled by at a snail's pace until, finally, classes were done. Hawk and I agreed to stay at the frat house for the rest of this week—something I foresee myself doing every week until a certain black-haired ghost vacates *my* house. I'm already thinking up ways to break my promise to Hadley, and that's not a good sign. I can't be around that girl without losing my self-control—and let's face it, I barely had any to begin with.

I can still feel the thudding of her pulse beneath my skin and recall the surprise in her eyes when I wrapped my hand around her throat this morning, and against my wishes, my cock begins to twitch in my pants, straining to get to her.

Calm the fuck down, I demand of it, subtly readjusting myself so Hawk and the other frat guys we're hanging out with tonight don't notice. *She's off-limits.* Not listening to reason, my dick continues to harden. *Remember how that worked out for us last time? You got wet, and I got kicked to the side.* Yeah, no, he's not fucking listening to me. Unwilling to continue attempting to reason with him, I instead focus on the two guys playing a game of darts. Except, within a matter of seconds, I'm bored out of my skull and back to thinking about *her.*

Getting pissed off now, I instead direct my thoughts toward tonight. I only have to kill a little more time until midnight, then I can find out what that note was all about. Finally, the need to fuck Emilia until she can't fucking think straight ebbs away and excitement takes its place.

"What's up with you tonight?" Hawk asks, nudging me with his knee. We're sitting in two armchairs, slightly off to the side, away from the others so they can't overhear our hushed conversation. "You're disturbingly quiet." Before I can wave away his concern, he brings up the one topic I without a doubt do not want to discuss. "Is this about Emilia being back?"

God fucking dammit, I only just stopped thinking about her.

"She's not back," I hiss furiously. "She's being forced to hide out at our house, but as soon as this stalker is taken care of, she'll go running right back to her idyllic little life in wherever the fuck city she came from."

"So, her unexpected appearance doesn't bother you?"

I glower at his cocked brow. "No."

A round of cheers goes up from the other side of the room as someone lands a bullseye, and Hawk glances in that direction before refocusing on me and asking in a quieter tone, "What do you think of this whole stalker business?"

I shrug. He explained to me this morning everything Kai and Hadley had told him last night, but Emilia hasn't been a part of my life for four years. I don't know anything about her now;

who she hangs out with or what guy she might have performed her witchy voodoo on and lured under her spell until he was so fucking obsessed with her he had to threaten and kill every man she got close to.

"I think if you don't wanna end up like her last boyfriend, you better keep your distance."

He scoffs. "I have no intention of getting close. It's you I'm worried about."

"Well, don't be. She's nothing but an annoying house guest. Hopefully, Kai will find her stalker soon, and she can fuck off back to wherever she came from."

"Right," Hawk snarks with a snort. "An annoying house guest who you nearly choked to death this morning."

"I was just... taken by surprise. She's the last person I expected to find in our kitchen. Next time I'll be prepared."

Hawk quirks a brow, a devilish smirk playing along his lips. "I'm not sure if I should be reassured or concerned, but either way, I hope I'm there to see it."

"Whatever." Wholly fucking done with this conversation, I knock back the last of my beer and check the time on my phone. I'm a few minutes early, but I can't fucking sit here any longer. "I'm calling it a night." Getting to my feet, I don't wait for Hawk to try and talk me into one more beer before heading for the door.

I saunter casually through the long corridors toward the library. The frat house is a large colonial-style mansion, complete with a copious chapter room and dining hall, library, private study areas, four lounge areas, a state-of-the-art gym, forty bedrooms, and, of course, a swimming pool.

After Robbie told me about the Clearwaters' history with Kappa Epsilon, I convinced Hawk to rush with me. Okay, so maybe Hadley twisted his arm—have I mentioned that he wasn't such a big fan of mine back then? It was hardly my fault, in any case. He was pissed because his parents and my father had made an agreement for me to marry Hadley. And maybe I didn't totally hate the idea. I mean, Hadley's hot, and she had a look in her eye I recognized. One only someone who's been through similar shit to you could identify. It made me curious, but the four guys marking their territory like lions prowling around their lioness, and the big brother who made it clear with one look he'd tear me limb from limb if I made one wrong move toward his sister, was a little off-putting. I'm all for a challenge, but attempting to go after Hadley would have been as dangerous for my health as begging the gods to smite me with a bolt of lightning—guaranteed death.

Instead, Hadley and I became friends. More than that, even. She's more like a sister to me. She gets me in a way no one ever has, and even now, she recognizes when I'm close to the edge. I'm a lot better than I used to be, but some days the memories of my past are closer to the surface than others. And on those days, you better not fucking cross me.

As I walk, my fingers brush lightly along my side, where my skin is toughened and uneven as images of my past—scorching heat, flames, blood—flicker unwantedly across my mind. As always, when I think about that night, sweat gathers along my hairline and down my spine, and my breathing turns ragged.

It's only when I notice a student walking toward me that I manage to pull myself out of my downward spiral. Snatching my hand away, I drag my thoughts back to the present and stare down the guy heading my way until he picks up the pace, scarpering past me like he thinks I'm about to slam him against the wall. Given my current head space, that's not a complete impossibility.

Reaching the library, I falter outside the door and glance around before cautiously opening it and peering in. Not seeing anyone, I open the door wider and step into the room, looking around the deserted space. The walls are lined with floor-to-ceiling bookshelves, with more breaking the room up into various aisles. Reading nooks and study desks spread out around them, and the dimly lit wall sconces cast shadows in the corners of the room. Combined with the musty smell of old books, it might appear comforting if the knowledge of the ominous note wasn't burning a hole in my pocket.

The floorboards creak beneath my shoes as I walk further into the room, peering down aisles. "Hello?"

My brows scrunch, and I pull the note out of the back pocket of my pants, re-reading it once again.

Midnight. Kappa Epsilon Library.

Right time. Right place.

Wrong date?

I rake my eyes over the piece of card, as if expecting more words to magically appear. Unsurprisingly, they don't, and I'm left frowning at it as I try to figure out what I'm missing.

I'm still staring at the card when the sharp click of a door locking resonates around the room, and I snap my head up to look at the door I just entered. I traverse the room with quick strides and begin yanking on the door handle, but it doesn't give.

Before I can put more force behind my attempts, a hissing sound from behind me has me spinning around, and I find mist pouring in from a vent high up in the wall. *What the fuckity fuck?*

The effects of the gas hit me immediately, making me feel lightheaded and woozy. My brain goes fuzzy as I take an unstable step away from the door and the vent. Another couple of steps, and I collapse to my knees, fighting desperately to stay conscious as whatever the fuck I'm poisoned with seeps into my system.

I crawl across the room on my hands and knees, but I already know it's pointless. There's no other exit, and as darkness creeps across the edges of my vision and my limbs turn heavy, I know I only have seconds left until I succumb.

My arms and legs give out beneath me, yet I don't even feel the pain as I faceplant the wooden floor. Right before unconsciousness claims me, the last thing I see is the toe of brown suede loafers, and with the last of my energy, I manage to drag my eyes upward to a black rubbery face making a weird, heavy breathing sound. *Great, I've been lured into a trap by demon monsters, and now I'm going to die.*

It's the stinging pain of a cold stone floor digging into my knees that rouses me, followed by the stiff ache of my neck, as if I've been sitting in the same position for hours. Opening my eyes, I blink several times, but still, all I see is pitch-black darkness.

Wariness begins to grow inside me, a low groan escaping my lips as I stretch out the kinks in my neck and strain to see through the darkness. A noise on my right has me looking in that direction, squinting. Before I can call out, a hiss echoes around the room, quickly followed by a flicker as flames ignite all along the walls.

I blink. Then blink again. *Huh.* Either I've been given some seriously high-quality hallucinogenic, or I really am surrounded by mysterious cloaked figures. I slowly turn my head, noticing that I'm positioned in the center of a ring of black cloaks. Two other guys I recognize as seniors in the frat are on their knees beside me, taking in the weird-ass scene with similar wide eyes and wary expressions.

Focusing straight ahead again, there are three cloaks standing front and center. I'm guessing they're the ones running this show. My eyes rake over their robes, hoping to find some identifying feature, but the only difference I can spot is the gold stitching in the middle guy's robes and the corresponding silver in the two cloaks standing on either side of him.

"Welcome to the King's conclave." The middle robe's voice booms out around the chamber, reverberating off the stone walls and drawing my eyes skyward to the pitched roof disappearing into the darkness high above me. "Your bloodlines have marked you as our new initiates, and should you succeed, you will be welcomed into the ranks of the King's Elite."

I haven't the faintest fucking clue what he is going on about. Hell, I'm still not entirely sure if this is real, a drug-induced hallucination, or maybe I hit my head when I passed out in the library.

My eyes again dart around the room, and I try to peer under people's hoods, hoping to identify Robbie amongst the statuesque figures. When I have no luck with that, I return my attention to the man in front of me as he steps forward.

"Over the coming weeks, each of you will be given tasks you must complete. A point of contact will be individually assigned to you. For now, it is imperative that you do not speak of this to anyone. I cannot emphasize enough that the consequences will be dire."

The man must give some sort of signal that I don't notice as, in the next instant, a hood is thrown over my head, blocking my vision. I immediately begin to fight against whoever is holding it in place until a voice I recognize hisses in my ear, "Calm down, asshole."

"Robbie?" I whisper-hiss.

"Shh." Yanking me to my feet, he directs me to god knows where. I can hear the other initiates being wrangled, but considering the number of people that were in that room, I don't hear any other footsteps or noises.

We move in silence, Robbie only murmuring a word here or there when we turn or begin climbing a set of stairs that feels as though it goes on for-fucking-ever. It's not until we're standing back in the library that he whips off the hood, and I turn to glower at him, noting that we're alone.

"What the ever-loving fuck was all that? Did you drug me?" I snarl angrily.

He just rolls his eyes like I'm being fucking dramatic. "Of course not."

"So that weird-ass robe shit was real?" I point toward the door, but honestly, I have no idea why. I have no fucking clue how we got back to the library or where the fuck that chamber is in relation to here. "What the fuck even is the King's Elite? Sounds like some fucking power trip shit for egotistical assholes."

That snarky comment earns me another eye roll. "*That,*" he emphasizes, "was your legacy."

I just look at him in confusion. "I thought Kappa Epsilon was my *legacy.*" Using my fingers, I put air quotes around the word legacy.

"I mean, yeah, it is. Kappa Epsilon is the first stepping-stone to the King's Elite."

Still confused, I ask, "And what's the second?"

"Coming from the right family. Clearwaters have been Kings since the beginning of time."

I scrunch my nose. "Honestly, it just sounds like a bunch of elitist bullshit to me, and that's not really my thing. I couldn't give a crap about ensuring the rich stay rich, all so they can lord their money over everyone else."

Robbie is already shaking his head. "It's not like that." Seeing my skeptical expression, he tacks on, "Okay, so I'm sure there's an element of that, but don't you want to be a part of something our forefathers helped build?"

"Not really," I state, scrunching my nose. If the Clearwaters aren't interested in treating me like a member of their family, then why should I care about being a part of something *they* built?

"This could be your opportunity to prove yourself to the family," Robbie continues.

"How is joining some creepy as fuck club proving myself?" I argue skeptically.

"The Kings matter to us. They're our bloodline. Our birthright. We are as much a part of them as they are of us."

Oookay. My brows scrunch in confusion.

"If you can prove to the family that you are taking your initiation tasks seriously, then Grandfather has already agreed to accept you back into the family. I already know you're nothing like your father, so prove that to them and come home where you belong."

Where I belong.

I never felt like I belonged anywhere until I met Hadley and the rest of the gang. Then, I finally felt like I'd found a place where I fit in, but now with Emilia back, it's thrown a wrench in everything and made me realize I'll never truly be rid of her. As Hadley's best friend, Emilia will always be around in some way or another.

Perhaps friends aren't meant to become your family.

Perhaps my place is with my family.

I mean, surely, if I'm going to belong anywhere, it will be with my own flesh and blood, right? Just because that place wasn't with my father, doesn't mean I don't belong with the rest of my family.

I'm still frowning as I say, "Alright, and what exactly are these tasks?"

Grinning, Robbie fishes a white envelope out of the inner pocket of his blazer and hands it over. It's made from the same expensive cardstock as the one I found in my textbook earlier.

I glance up at him before flicking my gaze down to the envelope in my hand and slowly opening it, pulling out the card inside.

Ridgeway's President is a long-time stylophile with an impressive collection. Steal one.

"What the fuck is a stylophile?" I ask, still frowning at the page.

"Someone who collects fountain pens."

I dart my gaze up to Robbie, cocking a brow in an *are you fucking serious?* expression.

"So you want me to steal a fountain pen? What the fuck does the King's Elite want with a fountain pen?"

"It's not about the pen. It's about whether you have the gall to do it." Robbie's tone is pure challenge. One I readily accept as I lift my chin and stare him down.

He smirks, stating, "You have one week," before turning and leaving me alone in the library.

One week to steal some stupid pen? Easy!

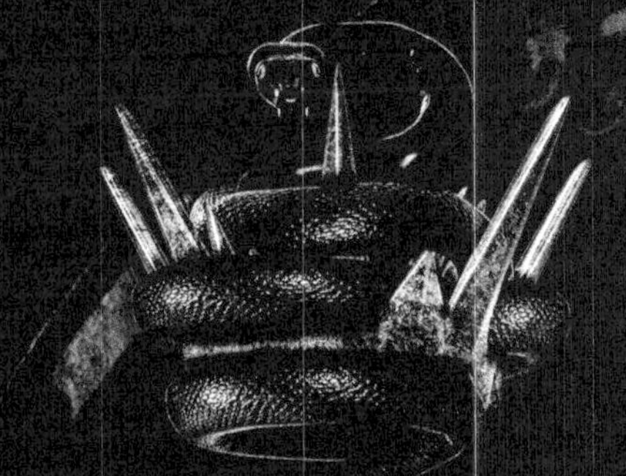

THE RUTHLESS BOYS OF RIDGEWAY

Emilia

CHAPTER 6

Embarrassingly, I hide in my room until I'm certain Hawk and Wilder have left for class. Only then do I sneak down the stairs and take a second attempt at making my morning coffee before curling up on the sofa in the living room. Grabbing the remote, I channel surf before landing on the morning's news report, although I struggle to focus on what the reporter is saying as my thoughts jump back and forth between my confrontation this morning with Wilder and the fresh round of terror at knowing there's a stalker somewhere out there looking for me. I honestly think I was in shock yesterday and I didn't fully comprehend the significance of that revelation, but after having all night to fret over it, the reality of it all is hitting me and zapping any remaining energy I had.

Looking at my watch, I note that I'd usually be sitting at my desk by now, with a steaming cup of coffee, going through emails and hoping Martha, my boss and mentor, will send a manuscript my way. Instead, I'm stuck in the last place on earth I want to be, with housemates who have made it crystal clear they don't want me here, unable to go outside or get away from them for fear that whoever this psycho is will be lying in wait.

My thoughts run over everything Hadley and Kai told me yesterday, about what happened to the previous guys I dated or slept with and the escalation in this stalker's actions. I can't believe how fucking blind I was to all of that. How fucking naive it was of me to shrug off every surprise gift and strange note.

"Ooh, someone's got a secret admirer," Mel jokes, nudging me in the shoulder when we spot the large bouquet of peonies—my favorite flower—at our dorm room door.

Bending down, I notice a card tucked amongst the petals with my name scrawled across it. "Shut up," I grumble, my cheeks heating as Mel coos behind me.

"Well, who are they from?" she asks far too excitedly as I lift them off the ground, tilting my head to breathe them in.

Choosing not to answer, I cock my brow in a silent gesture for her to hurry up and open the door. When she finally does, I step inside and set the bouquet on the table, extracting the card before she can snatch it up and deliberately turning my back on her so I can have some privacy to read it.

You looked beautiful today.

I have to read it twice, not sure how I feel about the blunt statement.

"Oh, how sweet," Mel fawns, having obviously read the card over my shoulder.

"You don't think it's creepy?"

"What? No! It's probably someone who has seen you around campus and is just too shy to approach you."

I think it over for a second before deciding she's probably right. "Yeah, probably."

. . .

That was the first of many gifts, but there was never anything that stood out as an obvious red flag. I hadn't felt wholly comfortable about any of it, especially the strange complimentary notes bordering on weird or socially inept, but they were only gifts. I assumed they were from some socially awkward guy who wasn't great at flirting. I never suspected anything more sinister.

Despite the fact that I'd left Pacific Prep telling myself that I'd forget all about Hawk and Wilder, I spent most of my freshman year in a fog, especially when it came to boys and dating. Instead of seeing what was right in front of me, I'd placed my uncomfortableness over the gifts down to the fact that I wasn't ready to move on. Maybe if I'd actually done what I'd told myself I would do—leave them in my past—then I'd have seen the threat staring me in the face before anyone got hurt. Before poor Richard had to die.

I don't even realize I'm crying until I feel the wetness on my cheeks. Sniffing, I wipe hastily at the tear tracks and redirect my thoughts to this morning. To the surprised look in Wilder's eyes, mixed with something darker and slightly unhinged. It's a look I've seen before, just never directed at me.

I remember seeing that maniacal glint in his eye a time or two. Sensed the change in his aura when he or someone he cared about was threatened. You see, Wilder is the type of guy who, when he decides you are worth his time, will give one hundred and ten percent. He'd go to the ends of the earth for you, even if his methods are a little unorthodox and outside the box.

Once upon a time, I was one of those people. One of the few in this world he allowed into his inner circle. At the time, his attention terrified me, but honestly, the coldness in his eyes today was far more alarming. Back then, I was a kid scared of the overwhelming feelings that were beginning to overshadow everything else in my life. I was afraid I'd get hurt or be let down. Worried Wilder would break my heart. He was the first one—the only one, really—who has ever had the power to do just that, and after watching my mom go through life like a zombie, I would have done anything to avoid that life for myself. Except, in my attempts to avoid making the same mistakes as her, I ended up living a life that was just as detached and void of emotion.

I hadn't even realized how numb I'd become until I saw him this morning, and all those feelings I thought were long buried came rushing to the surface. Even seeing Hawk yesterday elicited more emotion than I've felt in a long time. I couldn't tell you the last time I found a guy attractive, yet I couldn't stop looking at Hawk from beneath my eyelashes last night. And despite the hostility in Wilder's gaze this morning, heat still coiled in my core at his close proximity.

"Uh, sorry, am I interrupting?"

I startle out of my thoughts when I hear Kai's voice. Thankfully, he's found a shirt and pants since this morning, although he still looks drool-worthy in his form-fitting workout top and black cargo pants. Just another guy in this house who manages to make me feel things I haven't felt in years.

"No, you're fine. I was just thinking." I chew on my bottom lip before plucking up the courage to ask, "Has there been any update on Richard?"

Kai's eyes soften, taking on a pitying look that I *hate*.

"I know you said he was..." *Dead.* I can't say the word aloud, however. "But I just can't give up hope until I know for sure."

"I get that. And, Emilia, I really do hope I'm wrong."

But he doesn't think he will be. That's what he doesn't say.

"To answer your question, no, there's been no sign of him."

Moving to stand in front of me, he reaches out and gives my shoulder a squeeze. "I promise to let you know as soon as I have anything."

"Thank you," I croak, swallowing around the lump in my throat.

He smiles sadly. "I can only imagine how difficult the last twenty-four hours have been on you."

I sigh, the combination of fear and feeling overwhelmed and completely out of my depth threatening to drown me.

"So, what is the plan?" I ask, changing the subject and needing to do something more productive than wallowing in self-pity. "How are we going to catch this guy? How are we even going to figure out who it is?"

Straightening, any sympathy is wiped from his face as Kai goes into work mode, explaining, "Since Hadley has had me on the job, I've been looking into the people in your life. I started with those closest to you—Mel, Richard, anyone in your building, and your colleagues at work—and one by one, I've ruled them out."

My shoulders drop. Kai's been living next to me for months, presumably working that whole time, and yet he has zero leads. "So basically, you have nothing?" I ask dejectedly, a fresh wave of panic slamming into me. What if it takes us weeks or months, or—holy crap—*years* to identify this asshole? "Kai, I'm going to go out of my mind cooped up in this house. What about my job? I can't hide out here indefinitely."

Most likely seeing my escalating panic, Kai moves to perch on the sofa beside me. "It might sound like no progress, but I promise you it is. Every person I rule out is one less person I need to look deeper into. I started with the people least likely to be the culprit—your friends and people you only crossed paths with since graduating. Now, we can focus on everyone associated with Halston, which is most likely where we will find this guy. It's a slow process, but eventually, we will have ruled out everyone, with the exception of a small handful of suspects. Besides, now that I no longer have to dig into your life without you knowing, I'm hoping that with your help, we can dwindle down the pool of suspects much faster."

"If you think this person is someone I met at Halston, then why did you start with people I only met a few months ago?"

"Ruling people out is just as important as ruling them in. Now that I know for sure that no one present in your life since you graduated is involved, I can put all my focus into investigating anyone who was associated with Halston while you were there."

"Okay. So, what can I do to help?"

In answer to my question, he passes over the stack of books he's holding, and I glance down, reading the cover of the top one. *Halston University: Scientia ac Labore.*

Through knowledge and hard work.

"I didn't know Halston made physical yearbooks anymore. Aren't they all digital now?"

"They are, but I got them to send me physical copies. This way, we can highlight and make notes beside anyone we need to look at more closely."

Cracking open the top yearbook, I flick through the pages, hardly recognizing anyone.

"I want you to go through each of these yearbooks and see if anyone stands out."

"Stands out?" I question, still thumbing through the first book.

"Anyone you remember paying you any extra attention or making you feel uncomfortable. Anyone you noticed hanging around your dorm or whose presence struck you as odd."

"But these people were seniors when I was a freshman."

"Doesn't matter. Anyone who was at Halston when you

began getting gifts is a suspect. It was during your freshman year, right?"

"Yeah, just before winter break."

He taps on the pile of yearbooks in my lap. "Better get cracking then."

Holding out his other hand, he hands over a pen, a highlighter, and a stack of sticky tabs; his level of organization reminding me of my high school and college days and making my neat-freak heart sing.

"Shouldn't I start with my yearbook?" I question, taking the proffered items. "Isn't it more likely that whoever this is, was a freshman at the same time I was?"

"It is, but I figure you'll be able to get through these years faster. There will be a bigger suspect list in your year group. It's easier to rule out people in other years first, and then we can focus on those in your year."

"Makes sense." Agreeing with his logic, I return to the front of the yearbook in my lap. Before I can start looking at the first page of faces, Kai snags my attention as he settles more comfortably beside me on the sofa and cracks open the lid of his laptop. "What is it that you are doing?"

"Now that I've ruled out the few people closest to you and anyone you've had contact with since moving to Springview, I'm running background checks on all Halston staff members."

Hearing him talk about all of this in such a clinical manner sends a shiver down my spine. "Have you dealt with many stalking cases?"

"A few," he answers in a brisk tone, his concentration mainly focused on the laptop on his knee.

"And how do they usually end?"

His fingers pause on the keyboard, and he seems to think over his response before answering. "It varies. Sometimes the guy is caught in time, and sometimes the pieces don't all come together until it's too late."

I want to ask him what exactly he means by that, but I'm terrified of the answer. It's clear by the way his entire body has tensed that it's not something he wants to discuss, so instead, I start scanning the multitude of faces in front of me.

"UGH," I groan, hours later, slamming the yearbook shut. Even when I close my eyes, unfamiliar faces swim in front of me. "This is pointless. I don't remember any of these people." I'm seriously beginning to think I walked through college with blinders on. I don't recognize a single person.

Kai looks up from his laptop, glancing at the yearbook I just shut before meeting my gaze. "The next one is your year group. Hopefully, you'll have more luck there."

I shake my head, defeated. "What if this guy wasn't someone at my college? He could literally be anyone. Someone I crossed paths with in a coffee shop, a checkout person in the supermarket, a cab driver. *Anyone.*" I can hear the panic in my voice as the endless list of possibilities run through my mind. It's like looking for a needle in a haystack—impossible to find.

"Emilia." Kai waits until I lift my head to meet his steady gaze. "You can't think like that. Whoever this person is, they will have attempted to insert themselves into your life. Even if your initial contact was brief and unassuming, they would have pursued you. Maybe started up a conversation with you or showed up in other places you frequented. They won't have been happy sitting on the sidelines. They'll have wanted to integrate themselves into your life in some way."

I shiver, feeling more and more bothered about all of this with every passing second.

"You told Hadley there were phone calls?"

I nod slowly. "Yeah. Only when I was out of town, here or visiting my mom."

"Tell me about them."

I blow out a breath, shaking my head. "There's nothing to tell. No one ever spoke to me. I'd answer and hear silence on the other end for a second before they'd hang up." I shrug. "I assumed it was a wrong number, except it happened every time I left campus."

"Probably because whoever this is couldn't keep an eye on you then," Kai says thoughtfully, unaware of how concerning his words are. Does that mean someone was watching my every move when I was on campus?

"Sometimes it felt like someone was watching me," I murmur quietly, chewing on my bottom lip as I think back. "I'd feel eyes on me when I walked between classes or when I was in the dining hall." I shake my head. "I thought I was just being paranoid, being in a new environment and all that. I figured I'd gotten more comfortable than I'd realized having Hadley, Wilder, and the guys around, and now that I was on my own, I was being hypervigilant."

"There was probably an element of that, too," Kai says reassuringly.

"Except, I still felt eyes on me four years later, long after I'd gotten used to being alone."

"Was it just on campus?"

"No." I shake my head. "I worked summer jobs off campus, and did an internship in the city one summer, and I felt it then too. Not all the time, but some nights when I worked late, I'd feel the hairs on the back of my neck standing on end as I walked home."

"What happened that made you tell Hadley?"

Memories of that last day in my dorm come to mind. "I'd

just graduated, and I was packing up the last of my belongings. Hadley called me on my way back from grabbing a coffee."

"You should come visit before you start that fancy-pants job of yours," Hadley says, her crisp voice coming through the earbuds.

"You should come here," I counter, jiggling my key in the lock while holding my coffee in the other hand.

She sighs down the line. "Em, you hardly ever come here. It's been four years. You need to fish out those big girl panties."

"Sorry, they're already packed, and I have no idea which box they are in."

"Har. Har."

"What are your summer plans before senior year?" I ask instead, changing the topic as I set my coffee cup down on the kitchen counter before moving to my bedroom to grab the last box of my belongings.

Stepping into the room, Hadley's words fade into the background as I spot a black envelope sitting in the center of my bed. My sheets and covers have all been stripped off the bed, leaving the bare, white mattress. The contrasting color only serves to emphasize the obsidian envelope, making it stand out in an ominous way that sends an eerie chill through my body.

It definitely wasn't there when I went out for coffee, and I locked the door behind me.

Ignoring Hadley, I call out, "Mel?" wondering if she's here and left it there. When she doesn't respond, I cross the kitchen-living space to her closed bedroom door and push it open, but her room is empty. She's already moved into her new apartment, so unless she forgot something, there's no reason for her to be here.

"Em? Everything okay?"

"Yeah," I respond absently, walking back to my room and once again staring at the envelope. "There's an envelope on my bed."

"Okay..."

I realize the insanity of that statement and tack on, "I don't know how it got here."

"Your roommate didn't leave it?"

"She's not here."

"Maybe she came back while you were out."

"Maybe."

"What does it say?"

To answer her question, I move over to sit on the edge of the bed and carefully lift the envelope. There's nothing written on the front of it, and I turn it over, cautiously sliding out a folded piece of paper. Opening it, I begin to read.

THERE WILL COME a time when you believe everything is finished. That will be our beginning.

"WHAT THE HELL DOES THAT MEAN?" Hadley asks when I read the note aloud.

"I have no idea."

"Where did you say you found it?"

"It was just sitting on my bed when I walked in."

"And your roommate isn't in?"

"No, she left already."

"Em, what the fuck?! That's not normal."

I swallow roughly, my palms sweaty as I scan my eyes over the card again and cast my mind back over all the weird things from the last four years. "There have been other... things."

"What do you mean other things?" Hadley's tone is dead serious.

"Gifts. Notes. Phone calls."

"What?! Why have you never told me about this?"

"I didn't think it was a big deal. I'm still not sure that it is."

"Since when? When did all this start?"

"I don't know, freshman year."

"Freshman year?! What the fuck, Emilia?"

I sigh, already regretting saying anything to her. "Calm down, Hadley. I'm sure it's nothing. Probably just some crush who never found the balls to actually speak to me. What does any of it matter now, anyway? I'm done with college. Whoever this weirdo is will be moving on too."

A noncommittal grunt is all I get in response, although I still cling tight to the knowledge that this will be the end of it all. When I'm no longer on campus with this guy, where he can most likely see me all the time, he'll move on. Out of sight, out of mind, right?

Convincing myself of that, I tear the card into pieces and dump them in the trash. Grabbing the last of my belongings, I don't even look in the direction of my trash can before exiting the room, determined that I won't let the creepy envelope or weird quote be the last memories I have of Halston.

"There will come a time when you believe everything is finished. That will be our beginning," Kai repeats thoughtfully. "Sounds like whoever this is thought things would change between you and him after graduation."

"But how?" I question, my voice coming out a pitch higher than usual. "I was dating Richard, and we were both moving to the same city."

There's an empathetic understanding in Kai's gaze when he looks at me. "I don't know, but college wasn't the end for him. If anything, he planned to take things up a notch."

"But until yesterday, there hasn't been anything. No gifts, no notes, no phone calls. Nothing."

Kai shrugs, clearly not having an answer. "He was maybe planning or lying in wait. My guess is, Richard's plan to propose forced this guy to act."

I swallow around the lump of panic in my throat. "So what happens now?"

"Your sudden disappearance will most likely cause this guy to spiral. Hopefully, he'll make a mistake, and we'll be able to find out who he is."

"And if he doesn't? Make a mistake, that is?"

"He will. The level of his obsession with you... not knowing where you are, not being able to contact you or see you. He'll be driven to do anything and everything to find you."

"Well, that's not absolutely terrifying," I mumble, my eyes darting toward the window, half expecting some creep to be peering in at me.

I practically jump out of my skin when Kai reaches out to place a hand on my knee, giving it a reassuring squeeze. "You're as safe here as you can be. I won't let anything happen to you."

I force a small smile to my lips. "How do you know about all of this?" I wave my hand toward the textbook and laptop. "The inner workings of stalkers?"

He smirks, but it doesn't reach his eyes. "It's my job to know." Ending the conversation before I can ask him anything else, he pushes to his feet. "I'm starving. How about some lunch?"

More than ready to forget all about this psycho for a while, I let the conversation drop. "God, yes, I thought you were never going to feed me."

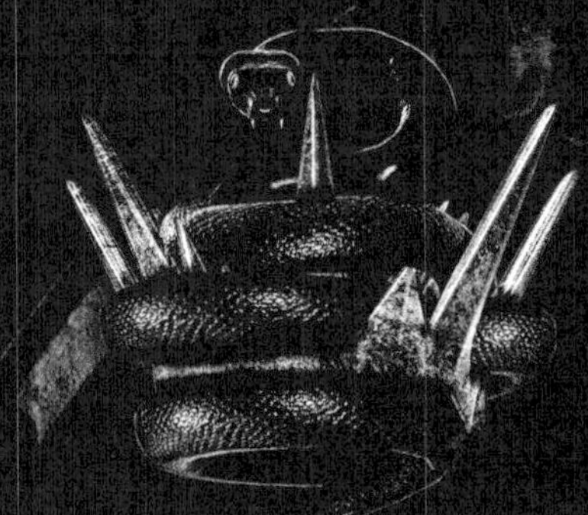

THE RUTHLESS BOYS OF RIDGEWAY

Hawk

CHAPTER 7

"Don't forget, essays are due next Friday," my macroeconomics professor calls out at the end of class, making me sigh. We're only a month into the semester, and senior year is proving to be the toughest year yet. I'm already bogged down with assignments. As much as I've surprisingly come to enjoy college, I'll be glad to be done with it. Juggling studying and working at Nocturnal Enterprises can be challenging on the best of days. Now, throw in Emilia's untimely reappearance, and I can already tell this year is going to be a headache of epic proportions.

My phone vibrates in my pocket and I pull it out, finding a text from Wilder. *Meeting Robbie so can't make lunch. Catch up later at the frat.*

What the hell? That's the second day in a row he's skipped lunch with us to hang out with his cousin. It's fine, except he *never* misses a chance to hang out with Hadley and the guys. Lunch and our once-a-month Sunday dinners are the only opportunities the seven of us get to catch up.

I've met Robbie briefly a few times. He's never shown much interest in hanging out with all of us. Personally, I think he's a bit standoffish. I've never warmed to him, but he's Wilder's cousin, so I've kept my mouth shut. Wilder's never talked much about his family. I know from personal experience that his father is a piece of shit, but the rest of his family is a mystery to me. The fact that Wilder had no idea that his cousin was enrolled at Ridgeway would imply to me that they're also a mystery to him.

As someone who initially hated his sister when he found out she existed, I'm not one to judge, and I'm sure as hell not going to stand in Wilder's way if he wants to get to know his family. I understand better than most just how important family is—and how fucked in the head they can be.

Pocketing my phone as I stride into the campus dining hall, I grab food before dumping my ass into a chair beside Hadley at our regular lunch table.

"Are anyone else's classes kicking their asses already?" I grumble, already back to thinking about the mountain of work waiting for me in my room.

Hadley shrugs. "My zombie apocalypse class isn't too bad."

All I can do is roll my eyes and bite my tongue. Hadley seems to have made it her life's mission to find the weirdest courses Ridgeway offers.

Sometimes I envy her, but then I just feel like a dickhead because, after a childhood spent in captivity, she's only now getting the opportunity to find herself. Something I've had the luxury of my entire life, and yet I took it for granted. I've had an entire lifetime of being an irresponsible kid, doing dumb shit with my friends, and basically being angry at the world for the shit hand I thought I'd been dealt—if only I'd known then just how good I actually had it.

Now, I'm trying to make better choices. Trying to be the brother I never had the opportunity to be when we were growing up. Trying to appreciate everything I've been given in life and forge my own path.

"What the hell does one even learn in a zombie apocalypse class?" Cam—one of Hadley's boyfriends—asks, dropping his tray on the table as he takes a seat opposite her. "It's gotta be the easiest A ever. I'm still pissed you didn't tell me about the class before I submitted my choices for this year. I could really do with an easy A."

"I *tried* to tell you," Hadley grouses.

"You need to stop trying to tell me this shit during sex. You know I'm not listening!"

"Eww." Grabbing a chip from my tray, I chuck it at Cam. "Fucking gross! Do you *not* see me sitting right here?!"

Cam smirks. "Cover your ears then, you big baby."

"How's Emilia coping?" Mason asks when he joins us, taking the seat beside me.

Taking a bite of my burger, I just shrug my shoulder, not having any other response. To answer that, I'd actually have to spend more than five minutes with her. Except, Mason stares at me until I'm finished chewing, his eyebrow quirked with impatience.

"What?" I bite out. "How would I know? I've been here all week."

"You haven't checked in on her once?" Mason's lips purse in obvious disappointment, making me scowl.

"Kai's with her. She's fine."

His expression clearly says *sure, whatever you say*, and I feel the need to tack on, "*Someone* had to stay on campus and keep an eye on Wilder."

"Oh, yeah?" Mason makes a point of looking around. "Where is he then?"

My frown only deepens. "Not coming."

"Again?" Hadley questions with a frown. "That's not like him."

Yeah, no shit.

I get that Emilia's presence at the house has thrown him, but that doesn't explain why he would skip out on our lunches.

Unless he's avoiding fielding the same Emilia questions I'm left to face from Hadley and the guys.

Yeah, that's probably what it is. Even mentioning her name is likely to send him into a fit of rage that will devastate the dining hall.

"How bad has he been?" Hadley asks, worrying her bottom lip.

"How do you think, Hads?" I turn my head to look at her, my voice softening when I see her pained expression. "He was alone with her for five minutes, and he had her pinned against the kitchen counter, his hand around her throat while her lips turned blue. More than that, he's refused to talk about her all week. Won't even acknowledge her existence. So, yeah, I think it's safe to say he didn't react well to finding her in his house."

Not that I can blame him, exactly. Hell, I was convinced my eyes were playing tricks on me when I saw her standing in my kitchen that first night. She was the very last person I would have expected to walk through that door. I was so shocked that I didn't even know what to feel at first.

But then this low simmering anger started brewing. Nothing like Wilder's raging inferno that had him catapulting across the room, but a bubbling heat that was both reminiscent of the way I used to feel around her—that grating anger where she both annoyed and intrigued me—and felt entirely new.

I was angry on Wilder's behalf. Angry that she just left him without so much as a goodbye. Angry that she left me to pick up the fractured pieces of his heart. A heartbroken Wilder is no fucking joke. He's barely tolerable on a good day, let alone when he's pissed at the world and searching for an outlet for all his anger and hurt.

But perhaps I was also a little bit angry for myself, too. Angry that she just waltzed into my life after all this time, and all I could fucking think about was how good she looked. How fucking *right* it felt to have her in my space.

Like, what the fuck even is that?!

"He'll get over it."

At Hadley's words, I'm pulled out of my thoughts and dragged back into the dining hall.

A sharp pain in my palm draws my eyes downward to where my fist is clenched so tight that my nails are digging into my skin.

Slowly, I unfurl my fingers, stretching my hand out to ease the tight muscles.

See? Even thinking about Emilia inflicts pain.

Returning my gaze to Hadley, I take in her pinched expression.

"That, or whatever thin thread is tethering him to his sanity, will snap and he will actually kill her," I grumble in response, earning a deathly glower from my sister.

"Alpha Sigma Phi is having a party tonight," Wilder informs me later that evening when he bounces into my room at the frat house. "We're going."

Great. Another party where I get to watch Wilder get shitfaced and hit on hot girls. Exactly what I wanted to do with my Thursday night.

"Oh, goodie," I deadpan, not even bothering to lift my head from the textbook I'm buried in while I try to make a dent in the never-ending list of assignments I have due.

"It's senior year," Wilder unhelpfully reminds me. "Pretty soon college will be over, and you'll regret not taking a more active role."

I somehow seriously doubt that. I used to think parties were my thing. I loved a good Pac Prep party, but I quickly realized when we started Ridgeway that it was hanging out with my friends and listening to music or laughing at the drunk idiots that I enjoyed more than the actual partying.

Once I discovered that, parties got boring pretty quickly. Besides, once you've been to one college party, you've essentially been to them all: same shit, different theme.

"We were at a party last night," I remind him. "And the night before that."

Basically, every night other than our first night here after Emilia's reappearance has been spent at some party or other.

"It's excessive, even for you."

"So?" Wilder bites out defensively.

"So, maybe you should stop distracting yourself from the problem and go face it."

"No."

I inwardly sigh. "I take it you're staying here this weekend, then?"

"You can assume I'll be staying here for the foreseeable future."

All I can do is pin him with a *really?* expression. If he thinks avoiding Emilia until she leaves is the solution to the problem, then he's deluded. Not that I know what the solution truly is. Hell, I've been avoiding her too. But unlike Wilder, I haven't been pretending she doesn't exist. I just don't know what the fuck to do with her. My response to her presence here threw me for a loop.

Perhaps it would be best if we just avoided her until she left. I mean, Kai is great at his job. He'll probably find this guy within a week, then Emilia will be back to her regular life, and Wilder's and mine can continue as normal.

Except...

"You have to be at the house on Sunday for dinner."

Wilder scowls, and I can see the excuse forming on his lips.

"You can't fucking wimp out of this one! You've skipped lunch twice this week, and Hadley is worried about you. So you'll damn well show your face."

Wilder's lips pinch as he throws an angry glare my way, but then hisses out, "Fine, but we're going out tonight."

"Fine," I sigh. God knows, someone needs to keep an eye on him.

"SHE'S A MANEATER..."

A very drunk, off-key Wilder sings later that night as I practically drag his ass back to the frat house.

"Make you fall real hard in love. Make you wish you never met her at all."

I'm pretty sure he's missing a few lyrics somewhere in there, but whatever. I'm too busy stopping his face from meeting the asphalt to bother correcting him—not that I have any fucking idea what the right lyrics are. I don't even know what song he's singing—well, trying to sing.

I do my best to block out his horrific singing skills as I haul him into the frat house and up the stairs to his bedroom next to mine. Finally managing to hold him upright and simultaneously open his bedroom door, I practically shove him onto the bed. He falls onto his back, his eyes already closed as he continues sing-mumbling under his breath, thankfully now too low for me to hear.

As I stare down at his pathetic, wasted ass, a fresh wave of anger crests. *This* is why I was pissed to see Emilia in my kitchen. I haven't had to deal with *this* Wilder in a long time. Four years, actually.

If spending *five minutes* with her has him resorting to *this,* then what the hell will happen if they actually spend time together?

"Why did she have to come back?" he mumbles. His eyes are still closed and given how much he had to drink, he's probably mostly asleep.

"I dunno, man," I answer anyway, feeling bad for him.

"I was over her."

Yeah, I don't think he was, but he'd definitely fooled himself—all of us—into thinking he was.

"Need to get her out of my system." His words are barely more than a whisper as sleep claims him.

"So do that," I tell him, even though I'm pretty sure he's not listening now, and even if he was, he's too drunk to remember any of this in the morning. "Do whatever you have to do to move on. Ignore her. Fuck her. Punish her. Whatever you need to do."

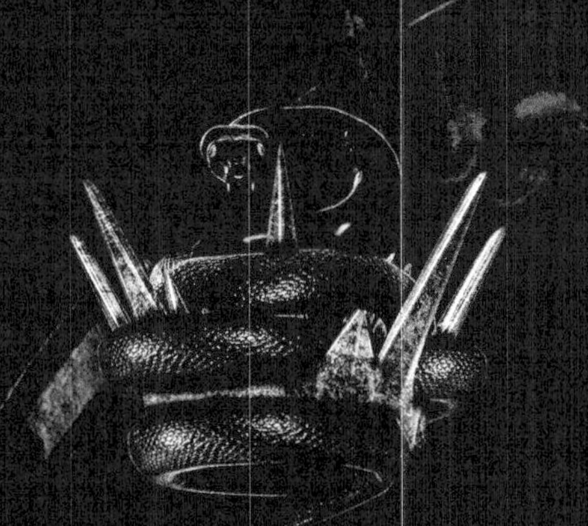

THE RUTHLESS BOYS OF RIDGEWAY

Emilia

CHAPTER 8

Without the routine of work, each day blurs into the next until I lose all track of what day it is. I haven't seen Hawk or Wilder all week. I'm pretty sure they're both avoiding me, and I feel equally grateful and guilty for that. I don't think I can emotionally handle another run-in with either of them—especially Wilder—but I feel bad that they both feel like they can't come back to their own house.

It's just been Kai and me alone in the house together all week. There's still no sign of Richard, and with every passing day, I fear that Kai is right. Apparently, he quit his job the same day I received the unlabeled package, which raises red flags. Richard loved his accounting job. There's no way he would have just upped and quit. According to Kai, his social media has been dead, too, with no posts or updates.

Richard doesn't have any family. His parents died in a car accident during his freshman year at Halston, and he was an only child, but I suggested reaching out to some of his friends to see if they had heard anything from him. However, Kai said it was best not to. For now, all we can do is wait and see if he shows up anywhere.

To prevent myself from constantly worrying over Richard, I've been spending my days going through the stack of yearbooks or looking at photos of staff members from Halston or any other photos Kai deems relevant while he does whatever it is he does on his laptop, only pausing to make phone call inquiries and give orders to others working for Nocturnal Enterprises. That constant has formed the basis of a familiar, comfortable routine which has helped me not completely lose my shit.

I've been able to give him a few names of possible suspects, though I'm not holding my breath that any of them are the right guy. They're just people from my classes who talked to me at parties or who I noticed around campus. Not exactly anything strange about that.

Honestly, I'm going a little stir-crazy cooped up and staring at faces all day. I'm frustrated that I don't feel like I'm helping in any way, and I'm sick of being stuck indoors hiding. I'm stressed out over being in the same house as Hawk and Wilder and the tension that I can feel in the air, even though they aren't around.

"You aren't even looking at the pictures," Kai chastises from across the kitchen table when he catches me flicking blindly through the pages in the yearbook.

Sighing, I close the book, knowing he's right. There's no point in continuing to search if I'm not actually paying attention.

Reaching across the table, Kai grabs the piece of paper where I've been keeping a list of potential stalkers. There are only a handful of names on it, and none are newly added today. He runs his eyes over the list before grabbing a pen and crossing a couple of them out. Ones he must have researched and ruled out.

He's still staring at the list when he asks, "Is there anyone else you can think of? Anyone from outside of college?"

"I thought you said this guy was someone on campus during the same time I was?"

"That's most likely the case, but anyone could walk around a college campus unquestioned if they make an effort to blend in. Same with college parties."

Swallowing around the uncomfortable lump that has formed in my throat at the thought of any weirdo strolling around campus, pretending to be a student, I shake my head. "No, not that I can think of." I've been wracking my brain all week trying to think of possibilities. If this person has made an effort to integrate themselves into my life like Kai believes, regardless of how abstractly or distantly, then I must know them. However, no matter how hard I try to rack my brain, I come up blank every time. It's gotten to the point where faceless shadows haunt my dreams at night, nothing but white eyes staring at me from the darkness.

"What about the summer before you started freshman year? You went touring with Death on a Matchstick, right?" It should probably bother me how much he knows about my life, but I've kind of gotten used to the fact that he knows everything about me while I know next to nothing about him. It's not for lack of trying, but whenever I ask him about his past, he changes the topic or shuts it down altogether. "Was there anyone you came across there that made you feel uncomfortable or who gave you an odd vibe?"

I pause. I hadn't even considered the possibility that this person could be someone I met *before* I started at Halston. "You think it's someone I knew from before college?"

He shrugs a shoulder. "It's possible. Just because you were in college when you started receiving gifts, doesn't mean that's when whoever this is first noticed you."

Jesus, that's not at all terrifying. The thought of this creep following me around before he made himself known is somehow even more bothersome. Instead of dwelling on how fucked up it all is, I think back to that summer.

"I was only there for a month, and most of the time, no one paid me any attention. Everyone was there for the band, and when I wasn't hanging out with the guys, I faded into the background."

"Most of the time?" Kai queries.

I chew on my bottom lip, because there was someone who I didn't like being around. He always gave me the creeps with the way he'd leer at me and how he always managed to corner me when I was alone. He never actually did anything to me, but when the band was on stage and I was standing on the sidelines watching, he'd always saunter over to me and stand too close. I'd feel his eyes on me when we were all hanging out after a show too. It used to bother me, but I was a guest along for the tour, so I never felt like I could say anything, and when I said goodbye to the guys that summer and went off to college, I never gave him a second thought.

"Steven Carmichael." I watch as Kai adds his name to the list. "He was the band's manager."

"Okay, I'll look into him. I'd looked briefly into the band, but nothing in depth."

He gets back to work, and I try to focus on the yearbook in front of me, but after a few minutes, I end up pushing it away and instead I watch while he works. It's a habit I've formed over the past week. There's something reassuring about the furrow that forms between his brows when he's concentrating and the astute look in his eye as he scrutinizes data that means nothing to me.

"So, what's it like working with Hawk?" I ask after a few moments of silence.

The question seems to catch him by surprise, and he quirks a brow as he leans back in his chair to study me. "Not what I thought it would be."

"What do you mean by that?"

"I thought this job would involve me wearing some ridiculous suit and protecting actresses from crazed fans or standing guard backstage while some popular band did their thing."

"And that's not what you do?" I question. Other than knowing Nocturnal Enterprises offers personal security, I don't know much else about it.

One side of his lips lifts in a smirk. "Not quite. Hawk specifically recruited me for a special outreach program he was starting that was created to help people in abusive relationships or in helpless situations—"

"People like Hadley," I murmur, unable to believe Hawk would do something like that.

"Yeah, exactly." My eyes widen at his words, not realizing he knew Hadley's history, but I guess if she trusted him enough to look out for me, then she trusted him enough to know her story. "I'd just finished up with the Marines and was looking for work. Hawk and I hit it off from the first meeting and became friendly from there. He introduced me to Hadley and her guys, and when they found out I had no family in the area, they started inviting me to their family dinners every month." He smiles as if remembering fond times, and I can totally picture Hadley taking him in like a stray cat.

The moment passes, and his gaze turns curious as he focuses his attention back on me. "I think the better question is, what is your history with Hawk and Wilder?"

I snort. How the fuck do I put the complex nature of my history with Hawk and Wilder into words? "That is not a conversation I want to have sober."

A roguish grin plays along Kai's lips. "There's no way there isn't a bottle of overpriced scotch around here somewhere."

I scrunch up my nose. "I'm not really a scotch person."

"There's probably wine and beer in the fridge." Getting to his feet, he goes to check. "Bingo," he calls out when he opens the fridge door and pulls out a bottle of chilled white wine. Grabbing two wine glasses, he walks back over to me and pours us both a large glass each.

I hum as the cool, crisp wine slides down my throat, and he lets me drink half the glass before topping it up and saying, "Well?"

Sighing, I rehash my whole sordid past with Hawk and Wilder. I explain how Hawk and I were at Pac together. How Hawk and I basically hated each other, until we didn't, and the surprising friendship that budded between Wilder and me. How he looked out for me when Hadley went missing. I have to fight back the blush that threatens to burn my cheeks when I tell him about my threesome with the two of them, but he gives no visible response other than a slight raise of his eyebrows.

I finish by telling him how it all went to shit, and I confess the truth aloud for the first time. "I was scared. Scared of the intensity of these new feelings, scared of giving my heart to Wilder, and scared of getting hurt. I ran away, and in the process, I destroyed any hope of there ever being a me and Wilder."

"I won't deny, you definitely did some damage to Wilder if those marks he left on your neck the other day are anything to go by, but I wouldn't be so hard on yourself. You were young, and from the sounds of it, you hadn't known Wilder all that long. As someone who thought he was destined to marry his high school sweetheart, let me tell you, life has a seriously fucked up way of messing with you, and if you cling to the ifs and buts, you'll never move forward. Hindsight and regret are bitches. What happened, happened. What's important is what you are going to do now that you're back in each other's lives."

Slotting away that little tidbit of information to mull over at a later date, I shake my head, disagreeing with him. "He hates me, and I can't say I blame him. Besides, I'm only here for as long as there's some psycho out there searching for me. Once you've caught him, I go back to my life."

"Is that what you genuinely want?" he questions, staring at me with a far too knowing look for my liking.

"I have an apartment, a job, a *life* waiting for me."

"Jobs and apartments come and go. You need to ask yourself if you were truly happy with the life you had, 'cause it sounds to me like you have a lot of regrets." He holds up his hands in a defensive gesture when he sees the protest written all over my face. "All I'm saying is, this could be your one chance to correct old wrongs. Your opportunity to mend bridges with Wilder and maybe even Hawk."

I laugh humorlessly. "I don't have anything to worry about when it comes to Hawk. He's pissed because of Wilder, not because of anything I did to him. At least with him, we were on the same page. Unlike Wilder, he knew there was a time limit on *us*. There were no feelings there, just sex."

There's a sharp pinch in my chest at the lie that flows seamlessly from my lips. Well, half-lie. Hawk may not have developed feelings, but I can admit to myself that I was definitely starting to fall for him. Standing on the sidelines and watching him step up to become the brother Hadley needed, how could I not develop feelings? It made it more painful to walk away, but I was equally aware that what we had was transitory.

Nothing and no one was going to stop me from going to Halston, and Hawk had his newfound family. Besides, I'm not convinced there's even a future between us. Hawk and I are like chalk and cheese—total opposites. He'd piss me off, or I'd irritate him into leaving.

No, despite the chemistry between us and those old feelings I had for him that makes it painful to look him in the eye now, there's nothing concrete between us. Nothing that could withstand the test of time.

"Regardless, this blip in your life plan could be a blessing in disguise. It sounds to me like you haven't been able to fully accept the decision you made four years ago. I just don't want to see you repeat that. If I were you, I'd make sure I'm absolutely certain before I walk away this time, because you might not get another chance to come back."

We lapse into silence while we each sip on our wine and his words play on repeat in my mind. There's much wisdom in what he's saying, however, considering that neither man can even bear to be under the same roof as me, never mind in the same room, I'm not sure how feasible an idea that is.

"Well, now that you know all about my sordid past, what are your dark, dirty secrets, Kai?"

He chuckles, emptying his glass before giving me an evasive answer. "I think we'll leave my past for a different day."

My curiosity is piqued, but it's obvious he doesn't want to discuss whatever happened in his past. Before either of us can change the topic, there's the sound of the front door opening before it slams shut, and a moment later, Hawk enters the kitchen.

He pauses in the doorway, cocking a brow. "How cozy," he drawls, before continuing into the room. "By all means, make yourself at home."

"Figured someone should, since you two have been playing frat boys all week," Kai retorts. "Or were you too busy avoiding confronting your past?"

I kick Kai under the table as Hawk glowers at him before

leveling me with an ice-cold glare that makes me feel like I'm two feet tall and completely insignificant. Except, he *has* been avoiding the house all week, and if it's not his usual M.O. to spend the week at the frat house, then what other reason could he have for staying away other than me?

"What is there to confront?" Hawk questions, his eyes never once leaving mine. "An old fuck buddy who was so unmemorable that I can't recall a single detail?"

Ouch. There's no denying how much that stings, but I refuse to give him the satisfaction of knowing his barb hit the mark. Instead, I shove the hurt down and hold his steely gaze. "Not so unmemorable that it stopped you from coming back for seconds."

"Only because there was no one else. A guy has needs, you know."

The burn sears my skin, but I don't let the pain show. I glower at him while he scowls at me with narrowed eyes until he spins on his heels and storms out of the kitchen. When we're alone, Kai snorts. "What were you saying about you two not having any unfinished business?"

I'M HAVING a lazy morning in bed on Sunday—or more like avoiding Hawk and Wilder, who I heard banging around downstairs late last night—when my bedroom door bursts open, making me jump. A boxer-clad Kai rushes in, his face set into a hard mask that immediately has me tensing.

"What's wrong?"

"A private number has been calling your phone non-stop the last few days. After what you said about the phone calls when you were out of town, I think it might be your stalker." He shows me the phone screen, which is lit up with an incoming call.

"How did you get my phone? I thought I left it behind in my apartment."

"I grabbed it before we left," he rushes out, pushing the phone into my hand. "Answer it."

I reach out to take it without the meaning of his words actually penetrating. "Wait. What?!"

"Answer it," he urges, more insistent this time.

Swallowing nervously, I hold his gaze while I press the answer button and put the phone on speaker. I don't say anything, instead waiting for the usual silence that would dominate these calls.

My heart hammers against my chest and my stomach churns dangerously before a frantic-sounding, "Em?!" comes over the line.

I swear my entire body collapses in on itself, the tension from a moment ago bleeding out. "Mel?" I question. "Why are you calling me on a private number?"

"Oh, I was a total klutz and dropped my phone down the toilet. I'm using my work phone in the mean—hold on, *I'm* the one asking the questions here! Where the hell have you been, bitch?!"

My brows draw together. "Didn't you get my message? Something's come up with my mom, and I had to go home."

She scoffs disbelievingly. "Yeah, I got that weird text, and I called your mom. She said she hasn't seen you since the summer."

"Uhhh..." Unsure how to answer, I flick my gaze back to Kai for some direction, but he just shakes his head, his order crystal clear.

"You scared the shit out of me. I thought you'd been

kidnapped or something. I was on the verge of calling the cops. Where the hell are you?"

"I'm sorry, Mel. I didn't mean to scare you. Something's happened, but I can't tell you about it yet, I'm sorry." I continue rambling, not giving her a second to argue with me, "It will hopefully be all cleared up soon, and then I'll be back and can tell you all about it. But don't worry, I'm safe. I'll call you soon. Okay, bye." I hurriedly hang up the phone, still feeling the adrenaline pumping through my body from the possibility of that being my stalker. I should have known it would be Mel blowing up my phone. She obviously didn't believe whatever message Hadley sent, and she's probably been freaking the fuck out over my sudden disappearance.

"She might be able to help, you know," I tell Kai when I've managed to calm my heart rate down a bit.

"No." That one word is an unarguable order. "The fewer people who know, the better."

"Yeah, but she was my roommate in college. We went everywhere together. She may have seen something I didn't or remember something I don't." He seems to think about it for a second, and I push my advantage. "You ruled her out, right?"

"Yeah, she's clean, but by telling her, you could be putting her in danger, Emilia." That gives me pause. I hadn't thought about that. "Let's just see how these few leads pan out. If they are dead ends, then we can discuss bringing Mel into the fold, okay?"

"Yeah, okay."

"Good, now you better get up. It's the last Sunday of the month."

Confused, I question, "Yeah, so?"

"So, Hadley and the guys are coming over for our monthly dinner."

My mood suddenly brightens at the prospect of seeing Hadley and the others. Not that Kai isn't good company, but it's just been him and me and a tension-riddled house all week. Having Hadley and the guys here as a buffer might make it easier to be in the same room as Hawk and Wilder. Besides, it will be great to catch up with them all. In my attempts to avoid Hawk and Wilder, I've actually missed hanging out with everyone.

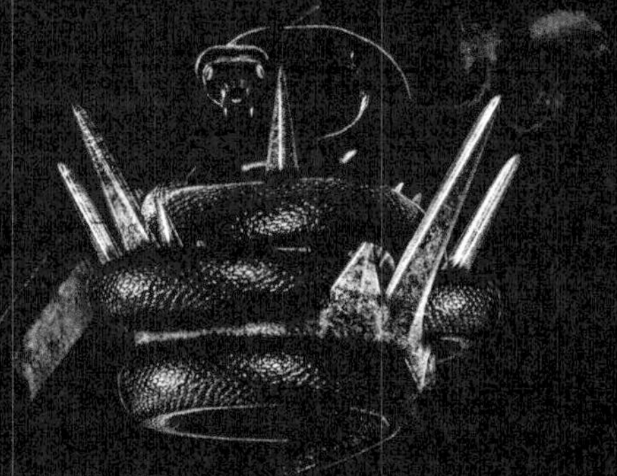

THE RUTHLESS BOYS OF RIDGEWAY

Emilia

CHAPTER 9

After spending an hour on the phone with my mom and reassuring her that everything was fine while trying to convince her that it had all been a misunderstanding —that I'd lost my phone and Mel had panicked when she couldn't reach me—all of us are sitting around the table, having stuffed our faces with a delicious roast that Cam and Kai made. It's been great seeing Mason, Cam, West, and Beck and having some time with Hadley. We've remained close over the last four years, but we haven't had this—hanging out all together the way we did at Pac.

I hadn't realized how much I needed today, how much the stress of everything and being thrown into Hawk and Wilder's sphere of existence has been getting to me, but today I've laughed harder and smiled more than I have in a long time. It's almost like the last four years never happened. Except, Hawk and Wilder are noticeably sitting on the opposite side of the table from me. Wilder is more subdued than his usual brash self that I remember from school, only really talking when someone speaks to him.

"It's great to have you back again, Em," Cam says. Hadley

elbows him in the ribs, and he tacks on, "Oh, uh, other than the whole stalker business. That must suck. I just mean it's good to see you. How, eh, are you doing with all of that?"

I shrug a shoulder, not really sure how to answer that. Thankfully, it's Kai who speaks up. "She's doing as well as can be expected."

"Do you have any solid leads?" Hadley enquires.

Kai shakes his head. "Nothing definitive. We've been working on putting together a list of suspects all week, but I've managed to eliminate pretty much everyone."

"Who's left?"

"Steven Carmichael. He's the manager for Death on a Matchstick, and, so far, I haven't been able to find out where he was the day, uh, Richard's finger was delivered to Emilia's apartment." He throws me an apologetic look, and I swallow back the rush of emotion at the reminder of Richard. It's not that I miss or even grieve him—which probably makes me a bitch. This suffocation I'm feeling, is guilt. Guilt that he might have died because of me. If I'd known dating him was putting him in danger, I would never have strung him along the way I did. *God, I really am a bitch.*

"I also found a restraining order that an ex-girlfriend of his filed a couple of years ago. Apparently, he kept showing up at her house and workplace, even after she had made it clear that they were over."

"That's not suspicious at all," Mason states sardonically as Wilder snorts, muttering something under his breath that I can't hear from the opposite side of the room.

"What was that?" I snipe at him, sick of the mumbled jibes and furious glowers he's been tossing in my direction all day.

Undeterred by my angry tone or pissed-off expression, he meets my gaze with a blank one of his own. "I was just saying that maybe if you hadn't gone running off with some pathetic boy band like a goddamn groupie, none of this would be happening to you."

"So it's my fault that some crazy-ass psycho is out there stalking my every move and threatening any guy who so much as looks at me?"

He just shrugs, but it's more than evident that that's precisely what he thinks.

"It's no one's fault," Beck interjects. "We don't even know if this has anything to do with the band."

"What does any of it have to do with us anyway?" Wilder continues, clearly not done. He waves in my direction. "She left. Now, we're all supposed to jump into action and save her ass just because she's in trouble?"

"I haven't *asked* anything of you," I snap angrily at him.

"Wilder." Hadley's low tone is a warning that draws his ire her way. "I'm the one that brought her here."

"Well, I don't want her here. I've got enough shit going on, never mind worrying about her bringing some fucked-in-the-head crazy person to our door. Not to mention, I'm fucking sick of having her in my house."

"Wilder!" This time, his name comes out as a harsh snap from Hadley's mouth, but Wilder's done listening as he shoves to his feet, sending his chair scraping across the wooden floor before he storms from the room.

Everyone falls into an awkward silence in the wake of his departure, the lighthearted afternoon turning sour. I can feel Kai's watchful gaze on me. It's a weight that I'm becoming familiar with, as I've felt it on me numerous times this last week. He's always watching, assessing, trying to get a feel for my emotions. It's not intrusive, though. It feels more like he's checking to ensure I am okay. That I'm not about to break.

Perhaps he's just waiting for me to implode, but whatever

the reason, it feels nice. Especially when I'm surrounded by Wilder's hate and Hawk's indifference.

"Do you feel the same way?" Hadley snaps at Hawk.

God, I've never felt so unwanted, and I can feel the embarrassment in my cheeks as I duck my head, choosing to commit the knots in the wooden table to memory rather than meeting anyone's gaze.

There's a pregnant pause before Hawk responds, and while I'm glad his response isn't an outright agreement, his apathetic tone and callous words sting just as much. "I don't give a shit, Hadley. She can stay, or she can go. It's all the same to me."

Despite knowing I brought all of this on myself, I can feel the pinprick of tears in my eyes as I get to my feet, and still without looking at anyone, I mumble an excuse to leave and scurry from the room.

Locking myself in the bathroom, I lean back against the door and close my eyes against the onslaught of tears. This is why I've been avoiding coming back here all these years. I didn't want to face the damage I left behind. When I left Pac, I was certain Wilder would easily move on. Hell, I'd convinced myself of the same thing. Clearly, I was wrong on both counts.

And Hawk… before I left, we'd come to an unspoken amicable agreement. The hateful glowers and distrust had morphed into heated stares and mutual respect. While we may not be back to where we started, the cold shoulder he's giving me is just as brutal. I can't handle all of this past resentment on top of everything else that's going on. I need to do something to try and mend the bridges between them both. We may not be able to go back to what we once were, but perhaps we can all live peacefully under one roof for the duration of my stay.

Bolstered, I peel myself off the bathroom door and yank it open to go in search of Wilder. I hear the dull thud of his music through the wall when I reach the top of the stairs, and nerves somersault in my stomach as I hesitate with my hand raised in front of the door before rapping on it.

"Fuck off, Hadley," Wilder shouts.

I debate for a second before turning the handle and pushing open the door. Wilder looks up, and when he spots me in the doorway, his face hardens into a sharp mask. "What the fuck do you want?"

Digging deep to find the confidence I felt in the bathroom, I lift my chin and straighten my spine. "I want to apologize—"

"Apologize?" he scoffs. "I don't want your lame-ass apology. I want you to leave me the fuck alone."

Chewing nervously on my bottom lip, I try again. "I was hoping we could maybe start fresh—"

Before I can continue, the weight of a warm body crashes into me, and I stumble back against the wall. Wilder follows until his hands are planted against the wall on either side of my face and he's towering over me, effectively caging me in as he stares down at me with derision and fury. "What the fuck do you not understand by *I don't want you here?*"

I grit my teeth as anger rises to the surface. "Do you think I want to be here?" I argue. "That I wanted my life completely turned upside down? That I wanted to be stuck under the same roof as you, facing what is possibly the biggest mistake of my life?"

His nostrils flare, and I'm readying myself for another cutting remark when he spits out, "Were you going to marry him?"

His left-field question gives me whiplash, and it takes me a second to comprehend what he's asking. "I—" I pause with my brows furrowed, unsure how to answer that. Before I can gather my thoughts into something coherent, Wilder cuts across me as he pushes back, putting space between us.

"Nevermind. I don't care what you do anymore." Moving over to the door, he pulls it open wider and snaps, "Get out."

I hold my ground for a beat, searching his face for something, *anything*, but when all I see is an uncaring blank slate, I sigh and silently pad out of his room. Unable to let me go without getting in one last dig, Wilder practically snarls, "Stay out of my way, and I'll stay out of yours, and before you know it, you can go back to your cushy little life and forget all about us again," before slamming the door shut in my face.

Defeat makes my shoulders drop. *Well, that was a disaster of epic proportions.*

I guess I shouldn't have expected anything different.

"How have you been holding up?" Hadley asks later that evening when we've snuck off for a moment alone. She quirks a knowing eyebrow, already hazarding a guess at how the last week has gone.

"Oh, great. Just like old times," I reply sarcastically with a half-smile. "Really, what were you thinking when you had Kai bring me here?"

Hadley gives me an innocent doe-eyed look that doesn't suit her one bit. She can only hold it for a second before the two of us are bursting out in laughter. "I don't know. You've all just seemed... lost these last few years."

"All of us?"

She rolls her eyes like I'm being dense. "You, Wilder, and Hawk."

"My leaving meant nothing to Hawk."

With a shake of her head, she explains, "He's buried himself in his studies and the company since we graduated high school."

"Isn't that a good thing?"

"It is. Don't get me wrong, he's helped our dad get Nocturnal Enterprises back on its feet, and with his plans for the future, I'm certain he'll take the company to new heights. It's just... It's like he's forgotten there's more to life than work. I don't even think he's dated anyone in years."

"Please," I scoff, not buying that for a second.

"I'm not saying he hasn't slept with anyone." Hadley shrugs her shoulders, seeming unsure. "I don't want or need to know that shit. He just hasn't seemed interested in anyone."

I wave away her concern, even as my mind races with possibilities. "I'm sure when the right girl comes along, he'll be all over her, and you'll be thoroughly sickened by it and wish he'd go back to being a workaholic."

Hadley laughs lightly before quirking a brow. There's a serious underlay in her tone when she says, "Maybe the right girl already came along, just neither of them knew it at the time."

"Hadley," I gripe, shaking my head. "Abandon that train of thought right now."

"Why?"

"Because... No. Just no. Hawk and I are polar opposites. Besides, didn't you see the way he was at dinner?"

"That?" she waves her hand in the direction of the door. "So he's harboring a little anger. That's nothing. He'll get over it."

"Anger? No, Hadley. That was so much worse than anger, or hate, or any other negative emotion. That back there was the *absence* of emotion. That was someone who couldn't care less."

"Em," Hadley begins in a reasoning tone. "I know my brother pretty well, and he can try to convince you, and himself, that he doesn't care, but he does."

"Oh? And how do you know that, oh wise one?"

She smirks. "Because I've been there, shoving my feelings

down and pretending they don't exist. I know what that looks like, and it looks a lot like the way you and Hawk look at each other."

"I think you need your eyesight checked," I grumble, not sure what to make of this conversation.

Laughing, she thankfully changes the topic. "Well, how are you getting on with Kai? He doesn't hate you, too, does he?"

"Not yet. Give it time. I'm sure I'll do something to hurt or piss him off." There's an edge to my voice that detracts from the jesting tone I was going for, and Hadley leans in, resting her arm against mine.

"Don't be so hard on yourself, Em. You did what was right for you. You're not responsible for their feelings. Don't carry that burden."

"But did I? Do what was right for me?"

"Em, you have a top-rate education and an amazing job in a killer career. Isn't that everything you wanted? Everything you worked so hard for at Pac?"

"It is, don't get me wrong. It's everything I wanted, and I love it. Or, at least, I thought I did." I shake my head as I struggle to put my mishmash of feelings into words. After a moment, I sigh, unable to really explain it. "I don't know. I thought I'd be happier, but I don't think I am."

Hadley gives me a soft, empathetic smile and squeezes my shoulder. "Then you should probably work out what will make you happy. Life's too short not to love every second of it. Trust me. You've got the education and the career path, now focus on you. You deserve to be happy, Em. I don't know if that happiness lies with Wilder or Hawk, but I think it's worth exploring. You need to know for sure before you can put the past to bed."

HADLEY'S WORDS still play on my mind when I'm curled up in bed later that night. There's a ring of truth in what she said. I'm too busy wondering how life might have played out if I'd gone on that summer vacation with Wilder; if I'd given up my dream of going to Halston and attended Ridgeway with all of them. I can't move forward when I still have one foot stuck in the past. I thought I'd dealt with my feelings for Wilder and Hawk, but being around them has emphasized just how much I was fooling myself. Distance had enabled me to bury those feelings deep, except they never went away, and now, like a can of worms, the lid has popped open, and the contents are spilling everywhere.

I toss and turn for a while longer before pushing back the covers and getting up. Perhaps a hot chocolate will help calm these turbulent thoughts. Wearing my *bite me* pajamas and my Disney 3D Stitch slippers, I trudge down the stairs and into the darkened kitchen.

Flicking on the under-cabinet lighting, I move on autopilot, boiling the water and adding the chocolate powder while I figure out how to do what Hadley suggested and find my own happiness. She's right, it all comes back to Wilder and even Hawk. Are they my happiness? God, I hope not, but they're definitely occupying every spare space in my mind at the minute, so it makes sense to rule them out as definite no's before moving on.

I'm so lost in my turbulent thoughts that I fail to realize I'm no longer alone until I feel the hair rise on the nape of my neck. In a fluid movement, I spin, pressing my back to the counter as I turn to face the darkened figure hovering in the doorway, just outside of the pool of light from the kitchen.

Images of the faceless shadow man with the white eyes from my dreams flash across my mind as terror freezes me in place with my heart lodged in my throat and my hands clasping the edge of the counter.

"Thought I told you to stay out of my way," Wilder grunts, still not moving from his position. Even so, the sound of his voice somewhat settles the paralyzing fear, and I let out the breath I hadn't realized I was holding.

"Jesus Christ, you nearly gave me a heart attack," I chastise with my hand resting over my racing heart.

"Did you think I was your scary stalker?" he scoffs. "Trust me, *Angel*, you should be much more fearful of me." He pushes off the doorway and stalks toward me. "Your stalker wants to wrap you in bubble wrap and keep you all to himself, but me?" He waits until he's standing directly in front of me and I can see the unhinged look in his eye. The shadows reflecting back at me are like nothing I've ever seen. They speak of trauma and pain, of hurt and desolation, and have me wanting to reach out and comfort the man in front of me. "I want to tear you down until you're nothing but a broken doll at my feet."

"Why?" I croak in a hoarse whisper, warring with myself on closing the gap between us or ducking and running. I'm shocked by the extent of the vitriol dripping from his words. I know I hurt him, but I hadn't expected *this.* Yet, the damage is clear to see in the crevices lining his eyes.

"Because I can." Lifting his hand, he reaches for me until the pad of his thumb brushes along my lower lip. It's a strangely gentle touch that is so at odds with the callous way he's talking that it causes goosebumps to rise along the exposed skin of my forearms. "Because I want you to feel a fraction of what I felt." His thumb presses harder against my lower lip as he drags it down until my lip slips free and his hand drops to rest over my collarbone. "Because you just had to come back here and bring everything up again when I'd finally gotten you out of my mind." His fingers twitch, and I can feel his desire to tighten them around my throat like he did the last time we were alone in here together. "Because I'm not a forgiving man, and you, Emilia Harrison, are not deserving of my forgiveness."

"Do you think I haven't suffered these last four years, Wilder? That I haven't questioned if I made the right decision and wondered how different things might have been if I'd—" He cuts me off with the press of his finger against my lips.

"I don't think you've suffered enough." He once again runs his thumb along my lower lip before pushing it into my mouth. Instinctively, I wrap my tongue around it and suck it deeper into my mouth. All the while, my eyes remain glued to his, watching as he remains hyper-focused on where his thumb has disappeared between my lips.

Despite his cruel words, electricity charges the air around us, leaving it thick with desire and hate. Creating a potent blend that both rattles me and has me quickly melting into a puddle on the floor.

When he pulls his thumb from my mouth with a wet pop, I try again to reason with him. "Wilder—"

"There's only one thing that mouth of yours is good for, and it sure as fuck isn't talking. Now, get on your knees, or you can get the fuck out of my house."

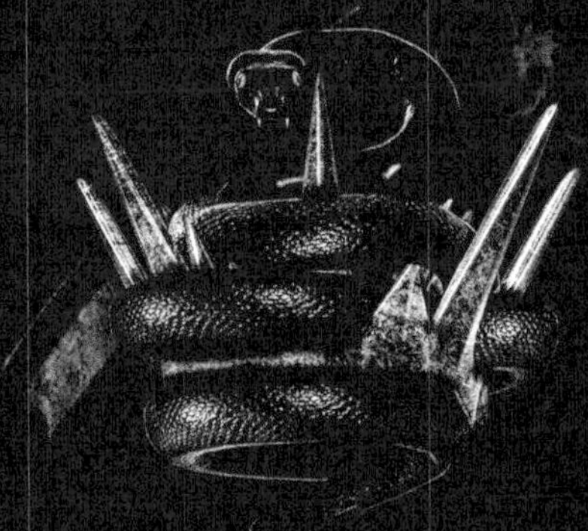

THE RUTHLESS BOYS OF RIDGEWAY

Wilder

CHAPTER 10

I watch with a cold detachment as Emilia sinks to her knees. She peers up at me, the jade green of her irises visible beneath the thick line of her eyelashes. God, my memory has not done her justice. I'd forgotten just how beautiful she is, and she's especially captivating when she's kneeling at my feet, staring up at me with a mixture of fear and lust, waiting to see what I'll do next.

Once upon a time, my instincts were to protect her. Sure, I wanted to push her boundaries in the bedroom and explore unfounded territory with her, but I would have ripped apart any asshole who wronged her. I'd have stood between her and a moving bullet. Helped her cover up a murder and take the fall for whatever crimes she committed. Now? Now, I want to be that asshole who shreds her world into pieces and leaves her as adrift as I felt after she walked away.

Punish her.

I don't know if that was an alcohol-fueled dream or a real conversation, but Hawk's words have been circling around my head since Thursday night, and every time I think of punishing her exactly as I plan on doing right now, an excited hum shoots through my body. It's certainly a far better response than pretending she doesn't exist. When I stormed out of here after the first time I saw her, I'd decided I'd stay at the frat until she fucked off again, but why the fuck should *I* be the one inconvenienced? This is *my* house, and if she wants to stay here, she can damn well live by *my* rules.

Well, I guess it's only really one rule: If I see her spiteful little face, then she's going to get punished.

Holding her captive with my gaze, I slowly move to unbuckle my belt and pop the button on my jeans before lowering the zip. "Open that mouth of yours," I order, pulling my hard cock out of my boxers and fisting myself as I watch her hesitantly part those luscious lips of hers. Precum leaks from the tip as I watch her quietly obey me. Now, this is a version of Emilia I could get on board with. Compliant. Submissive. Acquiescent.

When her mouth is open wide enough, I push the tip of my cock past her lips. I feel the slight graze of her teeth along my shaft, and even though it makes my dick twitch, I growl, "Unlike what's written on your shorts, I will do a hell of a lot worse than bite you back."

I pause, waiting for her to relax her jaw before placing my hand on the back of her head and pushing forward until her throat constricts around my length. I groan. *Fuck, that feels good.* Gritting my teeth as I hold myself deep in her throat, I can feel her muscles spasming as she struggles to accommodate my size and adjust to breathing through her nose.

Just when she starts to relax, I push deeper, my balls hitting off her chin as I completely block her airway. Satisfaction courses through me as her eyes widen in fear and tears gather at the corners before spilling over.

Reaching out, I brush my thumb through the trail, bringing it to my lips and sucking the salty tear into my mouth. The taste dances across my tongue as I remain buried in her throat until her fingernails dig into my thighs and panic shines in her glassy eyes. Only then do I pull back, waiting until she sucks in a hasty breath before pressing forward.

Setting a punishing rhythm, I lose myself as I arch my back and drop my head so I'm staring at the ceiling. For a moment, everything between us falls away—all of the hurt, my animosity, her fear. There's nothing but the feel of her lips wrapped around me, the perfect combination of suction and saliva driving me closer to the edge.

That is until my balls draw up and I glance down at her, shattering the moment of peace I'd found. All those feelings I once felt slam into me, mixed with the pain when she told me she was spending the summer with some fucking boy band, and the earth-shattering realization that I wasn't enough when I found out she'd left campus without so much as a goodbye.

My hands fist tightly in her hair, no doubt hurting her. She stiffens, attempting to pull away. I hold her steady for a moment before letting her pull back until my still rock-hard erection bobs in front of her face. With one hand clasping the back of her head, holding her still, I fist my cock with the other until strings of cum erupt from the tip, hitting her cheek and swollen lips before dripping onto her chest.

I smirk down at her as I tuck myself away, and she stares up at me with wide, shocked eyes as though she can't believe she just let me do that. Not that I gave her much choice. Emilia is my doll to use and abuse, to play with and discard. We'll see how she likes being tossed aside like unwanted trash.

Her lips are slightly parted, and I take advantage of the opportunity, smearing my cum along them. I smirk cruelly at her the entire time, happy to have finally replaced the doe-eyed image of a freshly-fucked Emilia lying on Hawk's bed that night.

Holding her gaze, I call out, "Enjoy the show?"

Her brows pull together in confusion before footsteps cause her gaze to snap behind me. I heard him enter the kitchen before I'd even gotten my dick out, but based on the embarrassment currently coloring Emilia's cheeks, she didn't know he was there.

She tenses as Hawk approaches, her eyes darting back and forth between us. Stepping up beside me, Hawk drinks in the sight of her coated in my cum. Now that the heat of the moment has passed, wariness has entered her eyes, and she makes a move to get up. Except Hawk pushes her back to her knees with a firm hand on her shoulder.

"Hawk?" she questions, her voice small and hesitant. My new favorite sound.

"Shhh, Little Sparrow," Hawk coos, stroking his hand down her hair as he moves to crouch behind her. "It's just like old times." His knees press into the floor on either side of her hips as he slips his hand beneath the waistband of her sleep shorts. We all know this is nothing like old times. It's more nightmarish, filled with friction and the air thick with bad blood and unsavory intentions.

Despite that, Emilia melts like butter beneath Hawk's touch. Just as she did with mine. I might not have been good enough for her—and perhaps I shouldn't blame her for that, who would want a damaged fuck up like me anyway?—but she can't deny the way her body reacts to mine. To us.

Emilia's breathing turns ragged as Hawk's hand slides lower, and despite myself, my cock twitches in my boxers when I drop my gaze and find the hard peaks of her nipples straining against the cotton of her pajama top. My voice is deep and gravelly when I ask, "Is she wet?"

A sound of approval rumbles up the back of Hawk's throat. "Drenched. You enjoyed Wilder using you, didn't you, dirty girl?" I can see Hawk's hand moving beneath her shorts, and Emilia's eyes drift shut in response to his touch.

"Answer him," I bark, the sharp tone of my voice causing her to snap her eyes open again.

Whatever Hawk does elicits a pleasure-filled moan and she arches her back as she grinds down on his hand. "Yes," she says breathlessly as Hawk works her over.

The sound of her rapid pants and seductive moans fills the room as Hawk and I watch while he effortlessly drives her toward the edge. Pleasure softens her features as she loses herself in Hawk's touch until her head is resting against his shoulder, her hips moving rhythmically in time to each thrust of his fingers. For a moment, I wish I could see as her wet cunt sucks him in, before remembering that I no longer give a shit about this girl. I used her for my own gratification and nothing more.

On the precipice of exploding, her whole body trembles with her impending release, until I bark out, "Stop."

Hawk immediately obeys, pulling his hand from her shorts as she whimpers with frustrated need. Her cheeks are flushed with desire, her chest heaving as her angry, lust-darkened green eyes bore into mine. Only when Hawk groans does she break eye contact with me, turning to look at him as he releases his fingers from his mouth with a pop.

It hits me how easy it would be. How effortlessly we could fall back into what used to be. I can see the fire burning in Hawk's eyes that he tries to hide, can feel it in the hardness of my cock. We could so easily fuck her like we did that night, claim her as ours, and mark her with our cum. Except she's not ours. Truthfully, she never was.

And we were never hers.

Suddenly furious, I can't be around her for another second without completely losing it and either fucking her or killing her. With my jeans still undone, I turn my back on the two of them and storm from the room. Emilia would be fucking wise to heed my warning and stay the fuck out of my way. There are only so many times I can cross paths with her and keep myself in check. She got off easy tonight. If she'd caught me in a mood, she would have been left with a lot worse than a denied release and cum on her face.

"Done," I state, slamming the pen down on Robbie's desk. "Like taking candy from a baby."

Although, I could have done without running into fucking Emilia when I got back last night. What the fuck does that woman not understand about *staying out of my way?!* It's almost as though she *wants* to be punished. Wants *me* to punish her.

My dick twitches in my pants and I quickly shut down that line of thought.

"Good," Robbie says, leaning back in his chair with steepled fingers. He watches me for a moment before reaching into his top desk drawer. "Perhaps you'll find this next task more challenging."

Lifting out the envelope containing my next task, he hands it over, and without any fanfare, I rip it open.

Senatorial candidate Compton is a client of Nocturnal Enterprises. Obtain a copy of his file.

"What the fuck is this?!" I snarl, snapping my gaze up to glower at Robbie. "I'm not doing that." I toss the card down on the desk, refusing to jeopardize my friendship with Hawk.

Unfazed by my anger, he shrugs casually. "Then you won't get to join the King's Elite. And you won't get to meet the rest of your family." There's a pregnant pause, long enough for me to question whether all of this is worth it.

I still don't have an answer when he lifts the discarded card and holds it out to me. "Think about it. You have one week."

Holding his gaze for a long second as a war wages within me, I reach out and snatch the card from his outstretched hand before turning tail and storming out of his office.

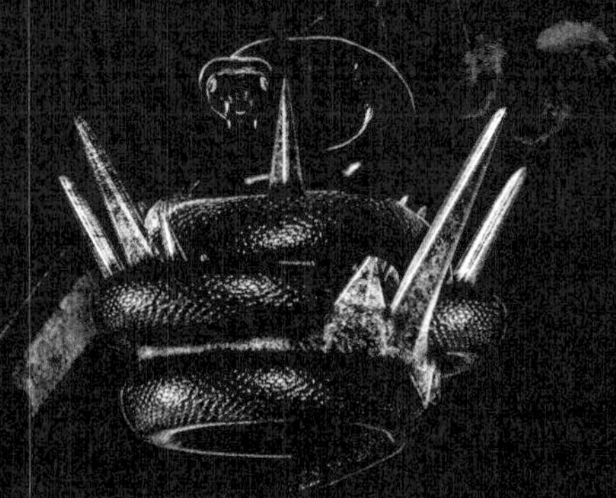

THE RUTHLESS BOYS OF RIDGEWAY

Hawk
CHAPTER 11

The stench of sex-drenched pheromones quickly dissipates from the air as Wilder's receding footsteps taper off, and I get to my feet, ignoring the lingering sweetness of Emilia's excitement on my tongue.

Stepping past her, I move to follow Wilder, concerned about the look I saw before he stormed off. He's been acting weird recently—weirder than usual—and I'm pretty sure the cause for that is currently covered in his cum and on her knees behind me. I thought he'd gotten over her, but she's getting to him more than I'd anticipated.

Perhaps I should have insisted Hadley get rid of her. Although, tonight has been one of the most entertaining nights I've had all year. Not that I have the most active social life. Wilder is the one who has really embraced the whole college experience, while I've dedicated my time to my studies and helping Dad get Nocturnal Enterprises back on its feet. It maybe hasn't been as exciting as Wilder's experience, but it's come with its own perks. I'm in the top fifteen percent of students in my major and Nocturnal Enterprises is thriving.

Over the last four years, Dad has taught me the ropes and

given me more and more responsibility within the company, preparing me for when I graduate and I can step up beside him as a director.

There's a seat at the table for Hadley too, but she's not interested in running the company. Not that I can blame her, given her past. She's content to know the company is doing well—and, most importantly, is operating within the legal confines of the law. Now that she has made a life for herself and has opportunities she never thought possible, she would rather spend her freedom discovering what she enjoys and pursuing that than getting sucked into the corporate world of board meetings and accounting spreadsheets.

I, on the other hand, have been surprised to find that I genuinely enjoy it. Nocturnal Enterprises has always been my future, but when I was younger, the thought of being forced into working there was like watching the bars of a prison cell slam into place. It was suffocating, and I'd never felt more trapped. However, after we *removed* the corrupt members of the board—which basically consisted of my own mother, West and Beck's Father, Cam's Dad, and Mason's—it's like we were able to form an entirely new company. My father and I worked together to change the organization's outlook and purpose. Together, we developed something financially sustainable that we could be proud of, and somewhere along the way, it became a labor of love for me. Something worthwhile to invest my time and energy in.

Not to mention, having that first-hand insight and experience has gone a long way in helping me with my college classes and ultimately convinced me to pursue a business degree.

All of that to say, I've been a little too preoccupied to have much time for parties and dating. Not that anyone has really caught my attention. Girls have always just been a way to pass the time for me. Back at Pac, having every girl at school drooling over you was a huge ego boost. They were easy and willing to do whatever I wanted, but it didn't take long for that to become boring. Easy? Who the fuck wants easy?

That was when Emilia first came onto my radar. She wasn't like the other girls at school. She didn't want to suck up to me—or suck me off. Where my money and last name were a turn-on for other girls, they did the exact opposite for Emilia. Initially, I liked that about her. That, and the fact she was the only girl I could sleep with who didn't expect her orgasm to come with a wedding ring attached.

Her quiet, studious, holier-than-thou attitude had always been off-putting, but watching her face her fears and stand up to me, all in the name of being a true friend to Hadley, was intriguing. I enjoyed pushing her and seeing how she responded. The battle that ensued as she worked up the courage to go toe-to-toe with me. I fucking loved it when the fighter in her won. The way she'd straighten her spine and jut out her chin. The fire that would burn in her eyes promising destruction. I'd never been so fucking turned on in my life.

"Hawk?" The fragility in Emilia's voice gives me pause, and I turn to face her. Slowly, my eyes rake over her slumped position on the floor before landing on the confused and somewhat despondent look in her eye. *God, as much as I loved her moxie, I don't think she's ever looked more beautiful, all broken and defeated.* There's only one other night she's looked this breathtaking...

Memories of *that* night flicker through my mind when all three of us chucked our inhibitions—well, Emilia and I did. Wilder's never given a shit about inhibitions. He does whatever the hell he wants. That night he wanted Emilia, except it was more than that. He wanted Emilia to give in to *her* desires. To set aside her fear and concerns over what others might think or say and act on her impulses.

I don't think I've ever been more shocked than when she

launched herself at me and kissed me like she'd die if she didn't taste me right that second. After that night when she'd fallen asleep on my couch, moaning my name in her sleep, and then I'd gotten her off with my fingers before she stormed out of my apartment, pissed as all hell, I'd constantly find my mind drifting to her. Remembering how her face relaxed right before she came, the way her eyes darkened to a forest green when she was turned-on.

The night everything changed, I'd been watching her dance with Wilder. It was obvious to anyone watching that he was obsessed with her, even then. The way she melted against him when he wrapped his arms around her... she was into him, too. That night, he was pulling out all the stops, and I knew the only way it was ending was with both of them in bed together.

When I realized that, I stormed away from the party like a toddler who wasn't allowed to play with his favorite toy. Until that moment, I hadn't even realized I wanted her. I found her attractive, sure, but I thought the only reason I was even remotely interested in her was that she was the only girl—other than Hadley— at Pac who saw me for me, not my money or my last name.

So, when she catapulted herself into my arms and said she wanted both me *and* Wilder, there was no stopping me. I slammed my lips down on hers and spent the rest of the night intimately acquainting myself with her body.

She was like a drug after that. Every time I was around her, I needed another fix, but it was still just sex. Admittedly, inexplicably mind-blowing sex, but I didn't catch feelings like Wilder did. I didn't fall in fucking love with her. I knew she was leaving, knew that she was meant for a life far better than anything she'd find with me—with us. Emilia wanted a life she'd built for herself, one she'd worked hard for. Not one that had been handed to her. Wilder would have given her the world, but that's not Emilia's style. She wants to earn her place in this life, and I can respect that, even if I can begrudgingly admit that I did actually miss her after she left.

It had caught me by surprise. I hadn't expected to, and it took me a while to identify why I was feeling a little adrift. But once I figured it out, I threw myself into rebuilding Nocturnal Enterprises—along with establishing a family dynamic with both my father and Hadley—and by the time we started at Ridgeway the following autumn, Emilia was nothing but a distant, fun memory... until she crash-landed in my life again.

Now, I'm just fucking confused about how I feel. What I *should* feel. *If* I should be feeling *anything* toward her.

"Do you really think leaving was a mistake?"

Surprised by my question, she takes a second to think—or maybe she's still reeling from her near orgasm—before answering me. "I'm not sure. Not necessarily a mistake, but more that I wish things had turned out differently."

"With Wilder."

She shrugs a shoulder, the movement seeming delicate and poised, even with the cum drying on her face.

"Not just him." She chews on her bottom lip. "Hawk, I—"

"You don't owe me any sort of apology, Em. You and I are okay. We always have been. We both knew where we stood back then, and for what it's worth, I think you did the right thing by leaving. You might be wondering *what if*, but I don't think you could have lived with yourself if you'd stayed. Your regrets would have been far bigger than they are now, and they would have come between you and Wilder."

"Maybe it didn't have to be an either-or option."

I shrug, not having a sure answer. "Maybe, but I still think you had to achieve your success on your own. You wouldn't have accepted Wilder handing you anything, which is exactly what he would have done. You would have questioned whether his name or influence was the reason for your achievement instead of your hard work. And, honestly, Wilder wasn't ready either." With another shrug, I finish off, "Now, if Wilder can get over his bruised ego and hurt heart, the two of you could have something real."

Silence follows my speech, an uncomfortable tightness forming in my chest. Pushing past the feeling, I ignore the strain of my cock against my pants and walk out of the kitchen, choosing to go in search of Wilder instead of what I actually want to do—paint Emilia in my cum too.

On Tuesday, I'm sitting in my office in Nocturnal Enterprises, reading over the report one of my men compiled on a recent job they completed for a high-profile client of ours.

I work at Nocturnal Enterprises on Tuesdays and Wednesdays, with the rest of my week spent on campus. The balance works well for me. On days when I have classes, I stay at the frat house and usually let Wilder drag me along to whatever party is happening. Except, on Tuesday and Wednesday nights, I sleep at the brownstone to give myself a break from the constant buzz of fraternity life.

There's a knock on my door as I sign off on the report and put it in the tray to be filed away, and my father pops his head in.

"Morning, son. New client meeting in five."

"Sure thing." Getting to my feet, I button my suit jacket as I step around the desk and move toward the door.

"Tell me about the client."

"Briana Larson, AKA Ember, is a twenty-five-year-old singer," I begin, knowing the client's file off the top of my head. I've sat in and ran several of these meetings now, but as the

CEO, my dad likes to come along to make the client feel special. "Her newest release jumped to number one in the charts, making her an overnight sensation and unsurprisingly bringing with it a lot of unwanted attention. The client is looking for home security plus protection when she's out and about."

"What about at concerts?"

I nod, already knowing the answer. "She has a tour organized for later this year and wants us to provide bodyguards to travel with her, coordinate with venue security, and to provide an extra layer of protection."

"Have you thought about how to organize that?"

"I have. I've assigned the job to Jasper's team. They will be sitting in on the meeting this morning as well. Once he has a list of venues and has spoken with the head of security at each of them, we can get a plan in place."

There's a proud smile on my father's face as we reach the meeting room, and he turns to face me. "Sounds like you've got it all worked out." He claps me on the shoulder. "I'm proud of you, Hawk. I wouldn't have been able to revive this company without you."

A warmth floods through me at his praise. My father and I have come a long way in the last four years. He's made many mistakes in his time, but he's worked hard to make up for them and build a relationship with both Hadley and me. For the first time, I feel like I have stability. Friends I trust, a sister I've learned to embrace and care for, and a father who I can look up to and respect.

The meeting with the new client goes smoothly, and an hour later, I'm back in my office when Hadley comes storming in, disrupting my otherwise quiet day.

"Didn't you ever learn it's rude to enter without knocking," I snark with a glower.

"No," she bites out, dropping into one of the chairs opposite my desk.

"You realize I could have been indisposed."

Her nose scrunches up. "Eww, Hawk. Gross. I don't need that fucking imagery."

I cock a brow. "Why, what a dirty mind you have, little sister. I meant I could have been on the phone or in a meeting."

"Sure you did," she drawls with a roll of her eyes.

"What are you doing here anyway?" I question. "Other than annoying me. Shouldn't you be at school?"

She sighs, her shoulders dropping as she spears me with a serious look. "I wanted to check in and see if things were any better with Emilia after Sunday's dinner."

I shrug. "Things are fine. Wilder's been staying on campus." Images of Sunday night rise to the forefront of my mind, and I have to suppress my grin at the memory as I subtly shift to ease the sudden tightness in my pants.

"Him hiding out on campus does not mean everything is fine," Hadley snaps irritably, and I throw my hands up in the air.

"And what do you expect me to do about it? He's a grown-ass adult. If he wants to hide at school and pretend she doesn't exist, that's his prerogative."

"No. He needs to deal with the problem head-on. The two of them need to talk."

My mind flashes back to Wilder telling Emilia there was a better use for her mouth than talking. "Yeah, I think talking is about the last thing Wilder wants to do when it comes to Emilia."

Hadley huffs out a breath, shaking her head in exasperation. "Then fuck it out. Whatever will help him move forward. He needs to get past this."

At Hadley's insistent tone, my eyebrows pull down, and I analyze her more closely. "Why are you so determined that the three of us learn to get along?"

She doesn't quite meet my eyes when she responds. "Because it's been over four years now. It's past the point of ridiculous. You're my brother and Emilia is my best friend, and Wilder is... Wilder. No matter what, you will all be a part of each other's lives, so you need to goddamn learn to get along. Besides, don't tell me you aren't enjoying having her around. I see the difference in you already, and it's only been two weeks."

I scoff. "What difference? I'm no different than I always am."

She rolls her eyes like I'm being dense. "Sure. You tell yourself that, but I saw how you tracked her from across the room with your eyes on Sunday. And you've been less uptight—"

"I am *not* uptight! And don't change the subject. This is about more than you suddenly wanting us to be all buddy-buddy. We've been successfully ignoring one another for four years now, so why the sudden urge to upheave all our lives and force us to confront the past? What are you not telling me?"

Completely exasperated now, she pushes to her feet, looking furious as all hell as she stands in front of my desk, peering down at me.

"Because I'm getting married." The words are a harsh snap, delivered with zero finesse, that leaves me staring open-mouthed at her. It takes a long moment for the meaning of her words to sink in.

"You're what?"

Her shoulders drop, and her tone is softer when she repeats, "I'm getting married."

"What... When... How...?" My gaze drops to her left hand, not seeing an engagement ring, and my confused frown deepens.

Sighing, she rubs at her temples. "The guys proposed right before Kai called to tell us about Emilia," she explains. "We were going to tell you on Sunday, but after Wilder stormed off, it didn't seem like the right time." My forever fierce and headstrong sister shows me a rare moment of vulnerability as she ducks her head.

"You're getting married." Shock colors my words. A small but excited grin pulls up the corner of my lips, and she flicks her gaze up, scrutinizing me through her eyelashes.

"Not until after graduation, at the earliest, but... yeah."

Her eyes jump all over my face before a matching grin lifts her lips.

Jumping out of my chair, I round the table. "You're getting married!" I pull her in for a hug, and she wraps her arms around my waist. I rest my chin on her head. "I'm so happy for you, Hads. You deserve every moment of happiness."

She returns my hug for a moment longer before pulling back, and when she looks up at me, happiness shines in her stormy gray depths, though there's a seriousness in her tone when she says, "You deserve happiness too, Hawk. I wish you'd let yourself have it."

I squeeze her arms before dropping my hold. "Don't worry about me, Hadley. I'm happy so long as you are happy."

A soft smile tilts her lips even as she shakes her head and pokes me in the chest. "You need to find your own happiness. What you're building here is great, and you should be incredibly proud of everything you've achieved, but you're only fooling yourself if you think all of this is enough."

Hadley leaves my office not long after, and her words are still churning over in my mind at the end of the day as I log out of my computer and lock my office door. I'm not sure about finding my own happiness, but one thing is for sure, I'm more excited than I reasonably should be at the fact that I'm going back to the brownstone tonight... where a certain raven-haired hellcat awaits.

THE RUTHLESS BOYS OF RIDGEWAY

Emilia

CHAPTER 12

Dropping a slab of butter into the heated pan, it hisses as it starts to melt, and I move to chop up the vegetables for the salad. Since it seems that Hawk and Wilder are back to avoiding me and staying at the frat house, I thought I'd make Kai dinner as a 'thank you' for all the time and effort he's put into tracking my stalker down. He's been chasing down leads all week, not that he's had any success. However, as he keeps reminding me, every person we rule out is one less person we need to spend time researching. I can see the sense in his logic, even if it is disheartening.

Once the vegetables are chopped, I grab the bottle of red wine I found in the cupboard and pop the cork, pouring myself a glass while I wait for Kai. He usually makes an appearance around six o'clock to sort out dinner before returning to his laptop and spending the rest of the night staring at it.

At the sound of the front door opening and closing, I stiffen in my chair, staring at the entrance into the kitchen with trepidation. *So much for hoping for a quiet night.* My features are set into an expressionless mask by the time Hawk appears in the doorway, wearing a suit, the top button undone and his tie hanging loosely around his neck.

His eyes bounce from me to the bottle of wine to the stove before once again settling on me, studying my guarded expression before holding up his hands. "I come in peace."

I scoff, not buying his bullshit for a second, and my gaze darts behind him, half expecting Wilder to make an appearance and completely ruin my plans for tonight.

"Don't worry, I'm alone." At his words, my gaze snaps back to him, tracking his every move as he walks slowly into the room, almost as if approaching a wounded animal. "Wilder's staying at the frat tonight."

"Why aren't you?"

"I work at Nocturnal Enterprises Tuesdays and Wednesdays. I usually stay here on those nights."

"Oh." My shoulders slump with disappointment. I just wanted an easy night without any hostility or angry glowers. Is that too much to ask for? Apparently so.

"Sorry to disappoint," Hawk snipes angrily, his nostrils flaring as he surveys the kitchen again. "I guess I'll go and leave you to your *date*." He spits out the last word, the vitriol in his tone causing my brow to furrow in confusion as I glance around at the dinner prep. It's only when my eyes land on the bottle of wine that it clicks. Does he think I'm preparing some sort of dinner date for Kai? *Oh my god.* But also, why does that seem to infuriate him so much?

He turns on his heel and stomps toward the door, but I rush around the island, calling out his name. "Hawk! Wait!" Not listening to me, he continues walking away. "It's not a date!" He stops in his tracks, spinning to face me, suspicion and doubt written in his eyes. "I was just making dinner for Kai as a thank you for all he's doing to help me. You, uh... You can stay. There's enough for three." I chew on my bottom lip, noticing how his eyes dart down to track the movement, and with a fortifying breath, I steel my spine. "On one condition."

At my no-nonsense tone, his stormy gray eyes snap up to meet mine, his tone guarded as he asks, "What condition?"

"We leave our past at the door. I just want an easy night. No snide remarks or angry glares. Just three people having dinner together."

He thinks it over, taking his time, and with every passing second, my heart beats nervously inside my chest. Eventually, he steps toward me. "Okay," he agrees slowly. "No snide remarks and no angry glares, but if you think I can just forget about our past"—his eyes drop down to my feet before slowly rising, raking over every inch of me with lust burning in their depths—"then it must not have left as lasting an impression with you as it did with me."

Gobsmacked, all I can do is gape at him. His words are completely at odds with the angry barbs he threw at me last week, but the heat simmering in his eyes affirms that this time he's telling the truth.

The asshole smirks, leaning in until his uniquely rich, mellow, smoky scent, mixed with pine that reminds me of sitting around an open campfire as a kid, envelopes me. With his lips against my ear, he murmurs, "Better close that mouth, Little Sparrow, unless you want a repeat of the other night."

My eyes widen, and I snap my mouth shut, making Hawk chuckle, this deeply masculine rumble that vibrates straight down to my bones. "I wonder what Kai would think if he walked in and found you eating my cock for dinner?"

Speechless, I swallow around the lump in my throat, fighting and failing to dispel the flush that rises to the surface of my skin at the imagery he's painting. It's not at all normal that the thought of it has me clenching my thighs. I'm seriously beginning to think I'm a closet exhibitionist, with how much it turns me on, thinking about being watched. Discovering that Hawk had been watching Wilder and me in this exact room turned me on like nothing else, and now picturing Kai watching Hawk and me is heating me up just as much.

Taking mercy on me, Hawk releases me and steps away to pour himself a glass of wine, and I conveniently ignore him as I go back to preparing dinner. By the time Kai makes an appearance, Hawk is sitting at the table, engrossed in his phone and pretending not to glance my way out of the corner of his eye while I act as though he's not here, the two of us co-existing in relative peace.

"Mmm, something smells delicious."

I beam, moving to pour a glass of wine and handing it over to him. "Thank you. Grab a seat. I'm making steaks and salad. They'll be ready in a minute."

Moving back to the stove, I turn over the steaks and pile salad onto three plates, all the while listening to Kai and Hawk's conversation.

"I'm surprised to see you here," Kai says in a teasing tone as he takes a seat opposite Hawk.

"Well, this *is* my house."

"How are things at Nocturnal?"

"Good. We've had a few new high-profile clients recently, and I've put the expansion plans for the outreach program into motion. So far, I've got three new safe houses outfitted."

"We'll need more manpower to cover the new areas."

"We will. I have a few potentials. I was hoping you could look over them for me?"

I flick my gaze up in time to see Kai nod. "Send me through their files, and I'll have a look."

Watching the two of them talk business, it's more like they are partners. Hawk clearly respects Kai's opinion and experience, and I find it fascinating to watch. I'm so busy watching them that I almost forget about the steaks, and I whirl around just in time, yanking the pan off the heat before they end up as lumps of charcoal.

Plating up, I bring everything over to the table and sit beside Kai. Hawk notices, his gaze darting back and forth between us before focusing on his meal.

"God, this is delicious, Emilia," Kai groans around a mouthful of food. I duck my head, mumbling a thank you before trying a bite for myself. I wouldn't say I'm a great cook, but I do enjoy the monotony of it. It allows me to forget about whatever my current stress and problems are and just focus on the task in front of me.

"He's right," Hawk speaks up. "This is really good."

Sincerity bleeds through his words, and I smile softly, glad to see our agreement is holding up.

We eat in silence for a while before Kai breaks it, turning to face me. "I have some good news for you."

"Oh?" I question with a raise of my eyebrows, taking a sip from my wine glass.

"Steven Carmichael. A credit card bill confirms he was booked on a flight to New York when Richard's finger was delivered to your door."

"Oh." My shoulders deflate. I know that's good news—ruling out another suspect—but I was hoping for something more concrete.

"And do you remember Jack Horner?" Kai continues, apparently not done with his *good news.*

"Uhhh." I wrack my brain for a second before his face floats to the surface and recognition dawns. "Yeah, the guy that was in my Literature and Ethics class who kept asking me out for coffee even when I told him I wasn't interested?"

Kai nods. "Well, guess where he moved to after graduation."

"Uhh, the same city as me?"

He smiles. "Try the same apartment building."

My eyes round as I stare at him in shock. "Are you shitting me?!"

He chuckles. "I am not. He's renting an apartment four floors below yours."

"What are the chances of that?"

"Exactly!"

Excitement has me practically bouncing up and down in my seat as I grin broadly. "So what do we do now?" I ask hopefully, picturing us hunting this sicko down and making him regret ever taking the same class as me.

"Well, I need to do my due diligence first," Kai says, holding his hands up in a clear gesture for me to chill. "I have I's to dot and T's to cross."

I frown. "What does that mean?"

"It means we can't jump the gun and accuse the wrong person of stalking you," Hawk interjects. "Not only could it be detrimental for this guy if he's actually innocent, but it will alert the real stalker to the fact that we're looking for them and could draw their attention here, meaning you would no longer be safe."

"Okay," I begin slowly, drawing out the word as I direct my attention back to Kai. "How long will it take you to do your *due diligence?*"

"No more than a day or two," he assures. "Just sit tight for another couple of days, then we can hopefully make a move."

"Two days," I say aloud, mostly to myself. "I can do that."

The rest of dinner goes by in easy conversation and even a few laughs. Kai and Hawk banter back and forth, their effortless friendship clear to see. I mainly sit and watch them, listening to stories of the people they've helped through Hawk's outreach program, and for a few hours, I actually manage to forget all about the worry plaguing me.

By the next morning, the light banter from the night before has disappeared, and I wake up early after a restless night of sleep. The thought that we could be so close to catching this guy has me all worked up and on edge, and yet, it wasn't thoughts of him that kept me awake last night. It was the thought of leaving here. Of leaving Hawk, and Wilder, and even Kai. Of going back to my life far removed from Hadley and the guys.

The last two weeks haven't been easy. In fact, I think it's safe to say they've been the worst two weeks of my life. Despite that, I've felt more alive than I have in years. Even my run-ins with Wilder, while terrifying, have also been exhilarating in a way I can't explain. But every time I'm around him—and Hawk, and admittedly even Kai—this humming sensation starts up beneath my skin. It's like I'm a live wire just waiting for the current of electricity only they can provide to make me feel animated.

I'm sure I look like shit, with my bedhead and haggard appearance, still in my pajamas with zero fucks to give when I step into the kitchen. I momentarily pause when I find Kai already at the kitchen table, an empty cup of coffee beside him and wholly engrossed in whatever is on his laptop.

He glances up at me, and I see the dark rings under his eyes that most likely resemble mine. *God, did he go to sleep at all last night?* Something both soothing and guilt-ridden blooms in my chest, seeing how hard he is working to help me. *It's his job,* I remind myself, but the illogical part of my brain isn't listening. She's too busy fawning over the fact that no one has ever gone to such lengths to ensure my safety the way he has these last few weeks. And I know it's more than just tracking down leads on his laptop. I've heard him on the phone, barking orders to people. He's doing everything within his power to keep me out of my stalker's hands. There's something incredibly sexy about that. About watching a man take charge and do what's necessary to protect those in his care.

"How long have you been up?" I ask, moving to grab his empty coffee cup so I can refill it.

"Never went to sleep," he mumbles, not taking his attention away from the screen in front of him.

"Kai," I chastise. "You need sleep."

"You need answers more."

I shake my head. "You shouldn't put me above your health."

Something in my tone has him shifting his gaze to me, and he smiles softly. "One night of no sleep won't kill me, Em."

Not seeing the point in arguing with him, I instead ask, "Have you had any luck?"

His shoulders drop, an apology in his eyes. "Not yet, but I will. Just be patient a little longer, okay?"

I chew on my bottom lip anxiously but nod anyway and move to refill his cup and grab one for myself.

Returning to the table, I set his mug down beside him and take a seat opposite, watching while he works. Creases line his forehead, his brows dipped in concentration, and I find myself tracing the lines of his face while my leg bounces restlessly under the table. He's handsome. I've always thought so, but the early morning light makes him appear softer, younger. Although, he can't be more than a couple of years older than me. Mid-to-late twenties, I'd guess.

"Emilia," he sighs eventually. "I can't focus with you staring at me like that."

"Oh." I duck my head, embarrassed to have been caught openly staring at him. I can only hope I wasn't drooling too. "Sorry."

Staring into my coffee, I don't last long until the anxiety becomes too much and I cannot sit still, so I get up and start opening and closing cupboard doors until I find some cleaning supplies. I can feel Kai's eyes on me as I don a pair of bright yellow rubber gloves that go all the way to my elbows and begin scrubbing at the kitchen sink like it's personally offended me.

We work in silence as the early morning sun climbs higher in the sky, the birds tweeting outside the window, oblivious to the tension inside the house. At eight a.m. Hawk strides into the kitchen, wearing a suit similar to the one he wore yesterday, and just like yesterday, I find myself thinking, *this man has never looked more devastating.* My panties disintegrate at the mere sight of him.

His gaze lingers on me, taking in my bed head that probably looks even worse than it did when I woke up, now that I've had several hours to run my fingers repeatedly through it, before slowly dropping over my pajamas. I've worked up a sweat cleaning the kitchen, and my top sticks to me like a second skin. Something he seems to enjoy as his eyes linger on the strip of skin showing above the waistband of my shorts. One side of his lips quirks up in a quick, barely there smirk before he glances over at Kai.

"You two look like you got plenty of rest last night." Moving toward the fridge, he pulls open the door, lifting out a carton of orange juice and bringing it to his lips. My eyes widen in horror as he drinks directly from the carton, and I hurriedly grab a glass and thrust it into his chest.

He looks down at me questioningly, and with a roll of my eyes, I explain, "It's unhygienic. Other people don't want to drink your backwash."

His lips quirk again, drawing my attention to them, and his voice drops an octave as he says in a quiet voice meant only for me, "You didn't use to mind my saliva in your mouth."

Oh, fuck me. Any remnants of my panties have just self-combusted.

I can feel the heat in my cheeks, and as though he can't help himself, Hawk reaches out to brush a thumb over the flushed skin. "I love the way you blush for me." His eyes drop to my chest, which rises and falls rapidly beneath his gaze, my nipples having no issue with letting him know just how badly he's affecting me.

I have absolutely no idea what is happening between us. Where is his apathy from Sunday night? I'm getting whiplash from how quickly he goes from hating me to being interested to being indifferent. Which version is the truth, and which are the lies he's telling himself?

Appearing completely unaffected, he pours the juice into the glass and drinks it down in several large gulps while I watch the bob of his Adam's apple with a thirst that can't be quenched by anything we have in the fridge. When he's finished, he presses the glass back into my hand, his fingers brushing along mine. That buzzing I felt before starts up, and it's as if his touch has triggered a chain reaction, heat flaring out from my hand until it encompasses my entire body and I feel like I'm being incinerated from the inside out.

The only outward appearance that indicates he's as affected by this as I am is the heat that simmers in his stormy gaze as he steps away. Clearing his throat, he stores the carton back in the fridge. "I've gotta get to work." He makes a point of not looking at me, instead turning to focus on Kai. "Keep me updated, yeah?"

Lifting his gaze from the screen, Kai nods. "Will do, man."

Satisfied, Hawk straightens his suit and strides from the room, once again leaving me with the after-effects of his whiplash.

THE RUTHLESS BOYS OF RIDGEWAY

Wilder

CHAPTER 13

I lie with my back against the headboard, turning the card containing my next task over in my fingers as I replay the scene I walked in on last night. The three of them laughing over the dinner table, drinking wine, and acting like it's not completely fucked up that she's here.

How the fuck can Hawk just park his feelings and act so casually around her? Why doesn't he fly face-first into a fit of rage the way I do? I can't even look at her without wanting to wrap my hand around her neck and shove my cock down her throat until her eyes stream and her lips turn blue. It's the only time I can stand to fucking look at her, when she's choking on my cock.

My hand crumples around the card, crushing it, and I have to close my eyes and suck down a deep lungful of air, forcing myself to calm down.

Focusing my thoughts back on the perfect family dinner I stumbled in on last night—not that any of them noticed—I open my eyes and uncrumple the card, reading over my task once more.

. . .

Senatorial candidate Compton is a client of Nocturnal Enterprises. Obtain a copy of his file.

I don't want to betray Hawk, but the more that image from last night assaults my brain, the more I feel like maybe I no longer fit in here. Perhaps my time with Hawk has been nothing more than a stepping-stone, and now I'm ready to move on to better things. Move on to my *real* family.

To do that, I need to get the file of some pretentious asshole running for senator.

Robbie's words from my first task come to mind: *It's not about the pen. It's about whether you have the gall to do it.*

This is exactly the same, except instead of a pen, it's information. It's not like the King's Elite are even going to use it. They just want me to prove... what exactly, I'm not sure. That I'll do it? That I'll risk getting thrown in jail? That I'm willing to piss off Hawk? I don't know exactly, but if it will get me one step closer to meeting my real family, is it worth it?

When I was first given the task, I thought no. Nothing was worth affecting my friendship with Hawk. But wouldn't Hawk do the same for his family? He'd do anything for Hadley, even stab me in the heart if he had to. I'm not saying he'd like it—although there are definitely days when I swear he looks at me like that's precisely what he'd like to do—but he'd do it because that's what you do for family.

Now, I don't know if my family is worth killing my best bro friend/frat brother/roomie over, but the Kings aren't asking me to kill him. They just want some pointless information about some old dude who thinks he can cut it as a senator. He probably won't even get elected.

If it means that I might finally find a place I belong, with people like myself, where no heartless bitches can come storming into my life out of the blue and fucking it all up, then it's gotta be worth it, right?

Yes. Abso-fucking-lutely, yes.

Before I can second guess myself, I jump off the bed and throw on some clothes. It's Wednesday, so Hawk will be at the office. Great, that provides me with an excuse to be there. Now, I just need to figure out how to get him out of his office for five minutes so I can gain access to his computer.

I mull it over the entire taxi ride to Nocturnal Enterprises, and I still don't have a plan in place by the time I step into Hawk's office.

"Hey," I greet, forcing my face into a casual smile.

I didn't expect for this to feel so... wrong. I'm not one for giving a shit about morality.

It's just because this is Hawk, I assure myself. What I'm doing might not be *right* per se, but if it reunites me with my family, then Hawk can't be mad. He knows exactly what that feels like.

Glancing my way, his eyebrows raise in surprise. "Don't you have class today?"

"Not 'til later," I answer, dropping into a chair opposite his desk.

Leaning back in his chair, he watches me. "What's up?"

I shrug a shoulder. "Just thought I'd stop by and catch up."

"Everything okay?"

"Why wouldn't it be?"

He cocks a brow, not buying my bullshit for a second.

"About the other night—"

"I don't wanna talk about that," I growl. The memory of Emilia's lips wrapped around my dick is still too fresh. I swear I can still feel the perfect amount of suction she applied.

"Well, she might not be around for much longer, anyway. Looks like Kai's got a lead. He should have it confirmed in a day or two."

I'm not sure what I feel at hearing that news, but I grunt out, "Good. About fucking time she left us alone."

Hawk's astute gaze watches me far too closely before he gives a vague, "Uh huh."

Frowning, I move the conversation on to safer territory before we can come to blows—again—over this girl. For someone who claims she wants to move on from the past, she's sure creating quite the wedge between Hawk and me. "Will you be back at the frat on Thursday night?"

He hesitates before answering, my eyes narrowing in a glower at the fact that his answer isn't an automatic yes.

He's saved from responding by a knock on the door, and some guy pops his head in. "Mr. Davenport, sir, can I have a word?"

"Mr. Davenport?" I mouth, using my hand to hide my smirk from the guy.

Hawk scowls at me before shifting his attention to the guy at the door and donning a polite smile. "Sure." Pushing out of his chair, he says to me, "I'll be back in a sec," before stepping toward the door.

I watch as he closes the door behind him, listening as their voices disappear down the corridor before hastily shoving out of my seat and rounding the desk.

Giving the mouse a shake, I thank my lucky stars that the computer hasn't logged him out yet, and hurriedly search through his hard drive until I find a file labeled *Clients*.

Seems like a good place to start.

Clients are arranged alphabetically by surname, so I quickly make it to the C's. There's a moment of panic when I realize there might be more than one Compton, and I have no idea what this guy's first name is. It's not like I keep up to date with the latest political drama. A donkey would have to become President for me to actually take notice.

Whooshing out a breath of relief when I find a file for only one Compton, I stick the USB drive I brought into the computer and quickly copy over the file. My leg bounces as the bar takes its sweet fucking time filling up, notifying me of its progress. It takes forever before it jumps forward a smidge, and the entire time all I can do is glance back and forth between the computer screen and the door, straining for the sound of Hawk's returning footsteps.

Hurry up! I silently demand. *Come on! Hurry the fuck up!*

The second a box pops up on the screen telling me the transfer is complete, I yank the device out and scurry around the table.

By the time Hawk returns, I look as casual as a sloth on a Sunday as I give him a broad grin.

He frowns.

Oh, right, we were in awkward territory when he stepped out.

Jumping to my feet, I clap him on the shoulder. "Well, it's been real, but I've gotta get to class."

Not hanging around, I hurry out of his office, not taking a full breath until I dive into the back of a taxi, blurting out where I want to go and barking at him to put the foot down.

My foot taps against the floor of the cab with a nervous energy the entire way to Ridgeway. The USB drive feels like it's burning a hole in my pocket, and I keep staring at my phone, expecting it to light up with Hawk's name, him calling to demand why the hell I defiled our friendship.

When I finally step out of the car on campus and my phone still hasn't rung, I suck in a deep breath. *Maybe I actually got away with it.*

"Wilder! Hey!"

My head snaps up, my gaze widening as Hadley strides toward me.

Oh, fuck! I did not get away with it. Hawk decided to sic Hadley on me instead. Abort mission! I repeat, abort mission!

She glances at the taxi as it pulls away, her brows furrowing. "Where were you?"

"Went to see Hawk before class."

She smiles, and fuck does it not make me feel sick to my fucking stomach because, now, I haven't only betrayed Hawk. I've betrayed her, too. Betraying Sunshine is the very last thing I'd ever want to do. I'd rather cut off my own arm with a rusty saw.

"Good. He says you've been spending a lot of time on campus recently. I think he misses you at the house." She smirks, and I force out a strangled laugh.

"Just making the most of my senior year, Sunshine." I sling an arm over her shoulder, directing her away from the parking lot.

She spears me with a *don't try that bullshit with me* expression, and I paste a wide grin on my face.

Her eyes narrow, her gaze searching me for a moment before she says, "You're acting weird."

I snort. "What's new?"

"Weirder than normal."

"I'm fine," I grouse.

Her lips purse as she continues to stare up at me, and I begin to sweat beneath her scrutiny. *She knows. She fucking knows!*

"Is Emilia's presence really that bothersome?"

My shoulders practically hit the asphalt as relief sweeps over me. *She thinks I'm acting weird because of Emilia. Phew.*

"Yes, actually, it is."

"You could just accept her apology, and the two of you could move forward with your lives."

I'm fairly certain my deadpan expression tells her precisely how likely that is to happen.

"I'm just saying," she says, holding up her hands.

"Well, don't. I'll deal with Emilia how I see fit." I pull her to a stop outside one of the campus buildings without even bothering to check if it's the right one. "Anyway, I've got class"—I gesture toward the building beside us—"I'll catch you later, Sunshine."

With a quick kiss to her cheek, I hurry off before she can grill me any more about Emilia or my 'weird mood'.

THE RUTHLESS BOYS OF RIDGEWAY

Emilia

CHAPTER 14

The next thirty-six hours go by in an entirely stressed-out, cleaning-frenzied daze. I try my best to leave Kai alone to work, yet I constantly find myself peering over his shoulder until he gets frustrated and tells me to go away. That's when I pick out a room and decide it's my mission in life to make it sparkle like it's never sparkled before. By now, the entire house is probably cleaner than it's ever been. Even the goddamn cutlery shines so damn brightly you could use the back of a spoon as a mirror.

I don't think either of us has slept more than an hour or two, and the tension is at an all-time high. The only thing I have to be thankful for is the fact that Wilder hasn't come home. I couldn't possibly deal with him on top of everything else right now. Hawk came back after work again last night, but none of us were in the mood to banter over wine and good food.

"Food's ordered. Now come on," Hawk says, looping his arm through mine and tugging me away from Kai. "I'm sure having you breathing down his neck isn't helping him find answers any faster."

"But..."

"He's right," Kai sighs, sounding exhausted. He looks it too, with his bloodshot eyes drooped with tiredness and encased in dark rings. "There's nothing you can do to help. Go with Hawk and try to take your mind off everything. Trust me to find the answers we're looking for."

I hold his gaze. "I do trust you."

He smiles, and even though it's not one of his gorgeous, boy-next-door ones, it's filled with gratitude.

"There you go," Hawk states, tugging on my arm. "Leave the man to it."

I let him drag me into the living room, and I sit and watch with a strange kind of detachment—like I'm here, but I'm not really here*—as he flits around the room, grabbing a big fluffy blanket and the TV remote before sitting on the opposite end of the sofa.*

He browses through the various movies before selecting one. I'm thankful that he doesn't ask for my opinion because, honestly, I don't care. It's not like I'm going to pay attention anyway. All of this is an exercise in futility. Nothing short of the apocalypse could distract me from wondering if this Jack guy is the one.

I remember he was annoying, but I wouldn't have labeled him as mentally unstable. But then, if whoever this is, acted crazy, I'd probably have a better idea of who he is. Whoever is stalking me is fantastic at acting normal. At blending in. Which is what makes them so damn dangerous.

The movie is background noise to my chaotic thoughts as the minutes tick by. Occasionally, I feel Hawk's eyes on me, searching, probing, but I keep my gaze glued to the television. The last thing I want is to start up a conversation, least of all with him. I don't even understand what the hell is going on between us. It's starting to feel like our truce last night was more than a temporary ceasefire.

Either that or he feels sorry for me, and this is all some type of pity affection.

God, please don't let it be pity affection.

I don't think I could handle that right now. I'd much rather he be his usual grumpy, apathetic self than only be kind out of pity. Although, if it's not pity and this is an amnesty, then what the hell does that mean? Are we friends now? Are Hawk and I even capable of being friends?

No.

Hawk and I have never been friends. During high school, there was always animosity between us. It was only when we both acknowledged the underlying sexual tension that we set aside our barbs and cutting words in favor of tearing one another's clothes off.

But if that's the case, where does that leave us now?

When the food arrives, Hawk hands me mine, and I mutter a thank you before we return to our mutual silence. Something about his presence is reassuring in an odd, foreboding kind of way that I can't quite explain. I just know that it steadies me. It doesn't distract from the churning anxiety in my gut, but it prevents me from diving head-first into the deep end.

Eventually, I tell him I'm going to bed. His lips part as though he's going to say something, but I don't want to talk about it—or anything—right now. I just want to be left alone with my thoughts, so I scurry out of the room before he can say anything.

In the hall, I notice the kitchen lights are still on, and I debate going to check on Kai's progress. He will come and tell you if there are any updates, *I reassure myself, forcing my body in the direction of my bedroom.*

I spend the rest of the night staring at my bedroom ceiling. Kai never knocks on my door, and I never hear him enter his room.

I'm currently rearranging the books on the shelf in the living room that I'm pretty sure no one actually reads when the creak of a floorboard behind me announces Kai's presence. On cue, my body begins to tremble, apprehension pouring off me in waves as I turn to face him.

The second my eyes land on Kai's face, my exhausted, wrung-out body drains of the last of its energy. My hand flies out to grab the back of a chair as my knees crumple beneath me. "No," I cry.

"I'm sorry, Em." Sympathy, frustration, and something that seems a lot like shame is written into the haggard lines of his face, but I'm too close to falling apart to truly take it in.

"But he was supposed to be the one." My vision blurs, tears stinging my eyes before they overflow and race down my cheeks, and a sob rips from my throat. I've been trying so hard to keep it together, but I'm slowly losing my mind with stress and worry.

"I know. I'm sorry. I genuinely thought it was him."

My arms shake violently, and when I try to take a step forward—not that I have any idea where I'm going, I can't leave this goddamn house—my legs give out, and I go crashing to the ground. I don't even register the pain in my knees as I hit the solid wood floor. My body is numb, my mind shutting down as I spiral into the hole I've been circling precariously for weeks now.

A deep-seated coldness seeps into my bones, nothing but emptiness blanketing my thoughts, muting them and my senses until nothing exists. Not the world around me. Not even the sound of my own breathing or the thud of my pulse. Time loses all meaning, becoming nothing but an abstract concept as I sink deeper into this well of helplessness.

Eventually, something penetrates through the cold numbness—a dull heat that intensifies with every passing second, slowly pulling me out of the fog that's cloaking my mind. The comforting weight of something wrapped around me like a therapy blanket brings me back to the room, back to the situation, and I blink several times as I register the source.

Kai.

Kai is the source. He's on the floor with me, his muscular arms wrapped around my middle as he holds me against him, using his broad frame and firm grip to radiate warmth and comfort.

As I slowly begin to relax, he shifts, getting us both more comfortable as I perch in his lap, my face buried against his chest while he strokes my hair. It's so soothing, and I can't recall being held like this since I was a young child. I should probably be embarrassed, and I should definitely be removing myself from his embrace. Kai has done far too much for me already. He doesn't need to comfort me as well. However, instead of pulling back, I press my nose more firmly against his t-shirt. He smells like sage, only softer and sweeter, and it chases away the final remnants of my panic attack.

I'm not sure how long we sit like that, but it's a while. The entire time he just holds me, stroking my hair while I breathe him in, as I feel my heart rate slow down with every sage-infused inhale.

By the time I lift my head, I still don't feel ready to leave his arms, but I know we've been sitting on the floor for quite some time, and I'm sure it can't be comfortable for him.

We lock eyes, worry shining in his as he checks to see if I'm okay. With one arm still banded around me, he lifts his other hand to cup my face. "I promise you, Emilia. I *will* get this guy. I won't stop until he can no longer hurt you."

Unable to muster a smile, I simply nod, but his words dig into my soul and stay there. I know he means them. Not only can I see the truth of his promise burning in his bright green eyes, but I know Kai isn't the type of man to just give up on someone. He's in this with me until the very end, no matter what happens, and there's something incredibly consoling about that.

"Come on." He urges me to get up. "You need a distraction, and I need a night off. Pick a movie and I'll make us some popcorn."

I quirk a brow, surprised. The whole time we've been cooped up in this house together, we've never sat down and watched a movie together. Occasionally, I'll flick through the channels while he's on his laptop, but we've never sat down to watch anything *together*. Yet, now that he's suggested it, it sounds like exactly what I need.

"Okay."

He watches me until I plonk myself on the sofa and grab the remote before he leaves the room to grab the popcorn, and I search out a movie for us. I have one cued to play by the time he returns and takes a seat next to me on the sofa. He sits so close that his thigh brushes mine, and I startle, taken aback at his close proximity. The other night when I watched a movie with Hawk, he sat on the other side of the room, and although Kai and I have often sat on this sofa together, we've never been this close before. As the heat of his body warms mine, I relax against him and press play to start the action movie.

We watch in companionable silence, munching on popcorn. Only the entire time, I'm fully aware of his thigh pressing against mine and the way he radiates heat like a goddamn furnace. I don't know if it's because he comforted me in a moment of weakness, but I can't stop darting my gaze his way. Especially when he snorts out a laugh or scoffs at something ridiculous on the screen.

I'm so busy focusing all my attention on him that I don't even realize the movie has ended until he grabs the remote. As he does so, he turns to look at me, his eyes roaming over my face as if checking that I'm okay. Although I still feel like crap, the last two hours have been a pleasant distraction—and, no, I do not mean the movie. I barely paid it any attention. The second Kai sat down beside me and his heat infused my skin, I was sidetracked. It feels like something has shifted between us—at least on my end—but I can't quite put my finger on what or why.

"Feeling any better?" he asks, still watching me closely.

"Yeah, a little. The movie helped."

He quirks a brow, as if he somehow knows I wasn't paying any attention to it, but thankfully he doesn't call me on it. "Good. Do you want to watch another?"

"Sure," I find myself saying before I've even really thought about it. Whatever keeps both of us planted on the sofa with his comfort and heat oozing into me and keeping me calm.

With a twitch of his lips, he surfs through the channels until he finds some late-night horror movie. It's not really my style, but again, it's not like I have any intention of watching it. I just want to continue living in this moment of peace, where I have Kai's silent strength bolstering me and holding my demons at bay.

In an effort not to appear like a total creep leering at him, I focus back on the television. I flinch when the psycho killer starts chasing the dumb blonde, my thoughts once again beginning to spiral. The movie had already been on TV for nearly an hour before Kai switched to this channel, so I have no idea what the storyline is, but I can't help wondering if one day I'll be that dumb blonde. Or maybe I already am, except instead of being chased by a psycho killer, I have my very own psycho stalker.

My palms sweat as my breathing becomes shallow, that downward spiral building up all over again until I'm no longer paying attention to the TV, which is why I don't notice Kai has paused it until I feel his hand on my face, coaxing me to look at him.

Rather than seeing the look of terror on the female character's face, I focus on the brilliant green of Kai's eyes. They look like two emeralds, warm and soothing, and I let them do exactly that as I all but fall into them.

"I'm sorry. A scary movie was a pretty stupid idea, huh?" He gives a small, self-deprecating smile, making me chuckle.

"No, it's fine. I didn't think it would..." I trail off, unable to put words to exactly what it did. Trigger me? God, am I one of those people now who have traumatic triggers they have to avoid? It's not that I think less of those people—because I definitely don't. I've seen how very real and debilitating they can be. I just feel like I haven't been through anything traumatic or particularly distressing—other than having Richard's finger delivered to my door and finding out I have a crazy stalker. But it's not like this stalker has done anything *to me.* He hasn't hurt me or abused me. Hell, if it weren't for Hadley and Kai, I wouldn't even know he existed. Compared to what Hadley has suffered, I've lived in a sheltered bubble. I have absolutely nothing to be *triggered* over.

As if he can see where my thoughts have gone, Kai, whose hand is still cupping my cheek, strokes the skin with the pad of his thumb. "It's a normal reaction," he assures.

"How?" I argue. "I haven't been victimized or harmed."

"Haven't you?" Kai lifts a brow in question. "You're the victim of a stalker, Emilia. Just because he hasn't *physically* hurt you doesn't mean he hasn't hurt you. Because of him, your entire life has been uprooted. He's the reason you're currently hiding in this house, on edge and stressed out. The reason you can't go to work and do the job you've worked so hard to achieve. The reason your boyfriend isn't the one here comforting you."

At the mention of Richard, I chew on my bottom lip and glance up at Kai through my lashes, gathering the courage to ask the question that's been on my mind constantly the last two weeks, but I've been too chicken to actually ask him.

Wringing my hands, I ask, "Did you, uh... Did you ever find him?"

After spending my first few days here asking about Richard and receiving the same answer that he still hadn't surfaced, I stopped asking. I trusted that Kai would tell me when he had something, but more than that, I think deep down, I came to accept that he really was dead. What other outcome could there possibly be after this much time?

Still, as Kai's features shift into the typical expression one wears when they're giving their condolences to the remaining family at a funeral, the little bit of hope I'd been clinging to that Richard was safe and in the hospital, receiving the medical attention he needed, snuffs out. In its place, a much harder-to-tolerate emotion forms—grief and self-loathing.

"I'm sorry, Em." Kai's usually comforting voice barely scratches the surface. "I've been checking regularly with the local hospitals and morgues, but there's been no sign of him."

My brows furrow. "So you haven't found a b-body?"

God, I can't believe I'm even asking that question.

"No, but I wouldn't take that to mean anything," he insists before hope can dig its fingers into me again. "Chances are we will find him when we uncover the identity of your stalker."

"But, what about his friends? Won't they have reported him missing?"

"They haven't yet. My guess is that the stalker is covering their tracks. If they sent an email to Richard's boss, then they probably sent something to his friends as well. It won't work indefinitely, but it would have given them enough time to do whatever they were planning on doing before I intervened."

A shiver wracks through my body. "W-what do you mean *whatever they were planning*?"

Kai's face is serious, shadows dancing in his eyes. "I think the finger on your doorstep was step one in his plan to finally make you his."

My eyes widen in horror, my hands shaking. "And w-what was s-step two?"

"I'm not sure. Perhaps he was hoping to step in and comfort you and take it from there or kidnap you, too. He could even have intercepted your call to the police and pretended to be a policeman just to get close to you." All I can do is stare at Kai in shock, unable to believe that someone would do such a thing. "People like this are unhinged. They don't think like you or me, and they will do absolutely *anything* to get to the object of their obsession."

I swallow roughly, still staring up at him, knowing he can see the fear and questions in my eyes. "You sound like you speak from experience."

I'm not sure if it's just the dim light provided by the television or if his face really does shadow over, but for a second, everything about Kai hardens. An expression like nothing I've ever seen on him flashes across his face. One filled with pain and grief but also deadly. "I do." Those two words are spoken in a gruff, emotion-filled tone. He drops his gaze, looking away from me before getting to his feet, thoroughly ending our conversation as he strides out of the room, and leaving me to stare after him.

I HAVEN'T SEEN Kai since he walked off after our conversation earlier. After he left, I churned his words over in my mind for ages before finally storing the information away and deciding a hot, relaxing bath was what I needed to wash off this shitty day.

When I first arrived, I spotted a gorgeous, deep standalone

tub in the main bathroom on Hawk and Wilder's floor, so I quickly grab a towel from my bedroom and head down to the bathroom.

Filling the tub, I rummage around in the bathroom cabinets for some bubble bath, but of course, this is a guy's house, so there isn't any. Oh well, even hot water will go a long way to easing the tension in my muscles.

When steam rises from the water and it's at risk of flowing over the sides of the tub, I turn the taps off and quickly strip out of my clothes. Twisting my hair up and securing it with a hair tie, I step into the bath with a sigh and sink into the glorious heat. The hot water is on the verge of scalding as it turns my skin red, but it's exactly how I like it, and it doesn't take long to feel the benefits as I rest my head against the rim and encourage my body to relax.

At first, my thoughts center on Richard. I let the tears run freely down my face as I allow myself to mourn him. I may not have been in love with him or wanted the same future for us that he did, but he was one of the closest people in my life. He'd been a good friend, and he didn't deserve what happened to him, didn't deserve an unfeeling bitch for a girlfriend.

Thinking about my relationship with Richard—and honestly, the last four years since I left Pacific Prep—and comparing it to how I've felt over the course of the last two weeks, I can see clearly now just how shut down I was. It's like I'd switched off my ability to feel, to put myself out there and let myself fall in love and get hurt. I was never emotionally invested in my relationship with Richard. I cared about him but was utterly incapable of allowing myself to feel anything more for him.

It wasn't something I was consciously doing. I hadn't even realized I'd closed myself down so completely until I found myself here—with Hawk and Wilder giving me whiplash and ripping open those old wounds I thought I'd long since stitched shut and allowed to heal. But it's like, the second I set eyes on Hawk, this avalanche of feelings came crashing down on top of me. Simply seeing him again had heat strumming through my veins and my vagina perking up with interest.

Even though every encounter I've had with Wilder has been fueled by hate—and pretty much all of my run-ins with Hawk have been the same—I've never felt more alive. Not all of it has been good. I've never felt so rejected, hurt, and stressed out, but all of it has served to remind me that I'm still alive.

I've been going through the motions for the last four years, ticking off the things I thought I had to achieve in order to build myself a life, except while I've been too busy planning for the future, my present has been passing me by. I've been so focused on looking forward that I haven't stopped to realize I'm not happy in the here and now.

Despite the shitstorm that my life has become in the last two weeks, some sick, twisted part of me has actually enjoyed it. I love the thrill I get when Wilder catches me in his space, the adrenaline rush of Hawk watching us. The heat that pools in my lower belly when I set eyes on either of them.

Memories of Kai wearing only a towel flash to the forefront of my mind, and I must admit, I get the same feeling when I look at him too. Like the air around me has suddenly grown hotter, and I can't breathe, even though I don't need to because all I need is their touch—their hands on my body, their lips on my skin.

My body flushes with need, and I glance down my submerged chest and abdomen, half tempted to give myself some self-loving. But, no, that would be weird in someone else's bathroom, with Kai right above me. Instead, I work to empty my mind of any and all thoughts, falling into a half meditative-half sleep state.

Only when the water is cold and I'm a wrinkled prune do I pull the plug and climb out, wrapping the towel around me. I'm wiping the steam from the mirror above the sink when my eyes collide with hard brown ones. I gasp, my body tensing as I spin to face Wilder. With his shoulder leaning against the doorframe, one leg crossed over the other as he casually runs his eyes over me, I curse myself for forgetting to lock the adjoining door leading into his room. *What bathroom has three doors?*

His eyes burn with an intensity I can't decipher as he brushes his thumb along his bottom lip, taking his time drinking me in. With each passing second of silence, my heart hammers harder against my chest, and I begin to sweat. The way he looks at me makes me feel like a mouse trapped in a cage, but some twisted version where the thrill of it is both terrifying and intoxicating. Wilder shouldn't elicit the swirling heat currently coiling in my lower abdomen. Not when he looks at me like that... like he wants to break me until I'm a crying mess at his feet, all so he can lick the tears as they fall from my eyes.

Except, that's precisely how he makes me feel.

The way his eyes glower with a heady mix of antipathy and desire does fucked up things to my insides. Or perhaps it's not the way he looks at me, it's simply him. His close proximity is the catalyst. *He* is my kryptonite. My weakest point. The one person who has the power to build me up or obliterate me.

"Wilder."

His name is the softest whisper, born of a realization. The dawning of understanding. The acceptance of what I always knew yet could never allow myself to accept. That Wilder belongs to me. That I belong to him. That no matter where I would have ran, it wouldn't be far enough. There isn't enough distance in the world to erase what Wilder and I have.

He's the electric shock that brings me back to life every time

I feel myself getting bogged down. The flame that threatens to burn me if I get too close. And I'm the nuke that threatens to tear him apart. Together, we're explosive. Volatile. Cataclysmic.

We'd probably die at the other's hand… but there's *someone* who might just be able to temper the blast.

Someone else who knows when to fan Wilder's flames and when to douse them. Someone who riles me up like no one else and makes my blood heat with a simple glance. Someone who knows me just as intimately as Wilder does and who affects me just as strongly.

Hawk.

Perhaps it *was* always meant to be the three of us, and only Wilder could see what Hawk and I refused to acknowledge.

Except, Hawk isn't here right now, and Wilder is staring at me with a violent sort of lust brimming in his chaotic gaze that promises unending torment.

"Always in my space," Wilder remarks, his voice a dark and hypnotic purr. "It's almost like you *want* to incur my wrath." He pushes off the doorframe and stalks toward me, every bit the predator. "Is that what you want, Angel?" His eyes dart from my eyes to my lips and back again. "You want me to unleash all this pain on you?"

"Yes," I breathe, wanting to free him the same way he frees me. Wanting to rid him of not only the pain I inflicted, but the deep-seated hurt he's been carrying around since before I ever met him. "Please."

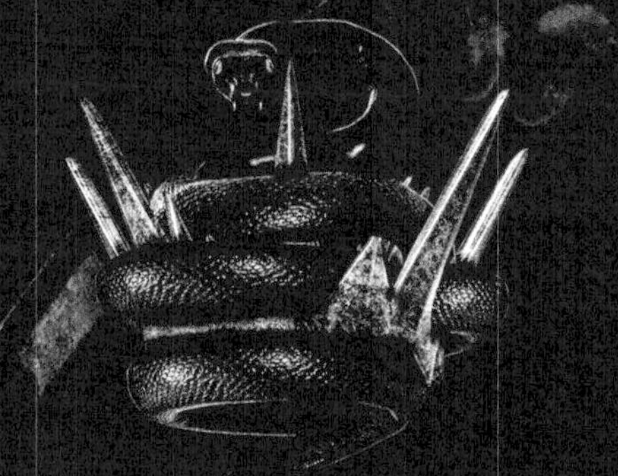

THE RUTHLESS BOYS OF RIDGEWAY

Emilia

CHAPTER 15

"Please."

The plea is barely out of my mouth before I'm spun around. My towel is whipped away, and my hips collide sharply with the edge of the bathroom counter as Wilder uses his tall, lean frame to pin me against it, bending me over.

My hand flies out, stopping my forward momentum right before my head collides with the mirror hanging over the sink, and I raise my eyes, meeting his crazed brown ones. He holds my gaze for a moment before slowly lowering his. Using the mirror, he takes his time analyzing every exposed inch of me—my heaving chest, the sharp peak of my nipples, the flush rising along the skin between my breasts. The countertop prevents his perusal from going any further south, but what he sees is enough, and I can feel the hard outline of his cock straining against his pants, pressed between my butt cheeks.

When he meets my eyes again, I can see just how close Wilder is to losing control. Craziness shines back at me, and a trickle of warning washes over my skin, a small voice at the back of my head telling me I should be running right now, not panting like a dog in heat.

A cruel smirk slashes across Wilder's face as he sees how fucking desperate I am for him. I should be embarrassed; deep down inside, I am, though it's overshadowed by the unbearable need coursing through me. All I can focus on is feeling his skin against mine, the thought of having his hands on me, his cock buried deep between my thighs. I need it—him—more than I need oxygen to breathe.

His fingers trail lightly down my back, causing a shiver to race along my spine. My desire only grows the closer he gets to my ass, and when he finally reaches it, he grabs hold of both cheeks with his hands, spreading them as he grinds his hips. The movement has me bending further over the sink, my feet barely touching the floor as I stand on my tiptoes.

"Let's find out just how wet you are for me." Wilder watches riveted as his hand travels between my spread thighs, and all I can do is watch as his eyes flash with something predatory and undeniably cocky when he discovers just how ready I am for him.

His fingers slide between my drenched folds, gathering my excitement as he teases my entrance until I'm pushing back against him, hungry for more. He chuckles this deep dark rumble that lacks any humor but zings straight to my clit. "For someone who never gave a shit, you sure are fucking gagging for me, aren't you, Angel?"

"Wilder." His name is a panted plea. I want to tell him I always cared. That that was the problem—I cared too much—but I can't seem to formulate the words, and just like last time, he doesn't want to hear them. He cuts off anything else I might have said by pressing his fingers against my clit and beginning to rub until I'm bucking my hips and grinding against his hand as I chase my release. With his body pressed against my back and his fingers working their magic, it takes mere seconds until

I'm cresting the precipice. However, just as I prepare to dive off the cliff, Wilder slows his movements.

I cry out in frustration, and he chuckles, enjoying my pain. "Awh, were you nearly there, Angel? Were you about to come all over my fingers like a filthy whore?"

"Yes," I hiss angrily, my obvious annoyance eliciting another chuckle from him.

"Oops, my bad. Let's try again." Picking up his pace, he pushes me right to the brink once more, and just like before, right when I'm about to implode, he slows back down to a teasing pace that isn't nearly enough to give me what I need and instead just drives me insane.

He does the same thing over and over until my breaths are nothing but shallow, rapid pants, and a dense fog has settled over my brain from the lack of oxygen. Tears burn the back of my eyes, my legs trembling. My entire body is strung tight like a bow. I'm so fucking desperate for a release.

When he slows down for the fifth or sixth time—I'm honestly losing count—I cry out. "Wilder," I beg. "Please."

"Please, what? Use your words, Angel. What do you need?"

In between pants, I manage to push out, "I. Need. To. Come."

My thighs are slick with arousal, and my body temperature is so high that the mirror in front of me has started to steam up, impeding my view of Wilder, although I don't miss the possessive rumble of his chest.

"You wanna come?" There's a sneer in his tone. "And why should I let you?"

"Please, Wilder." Tears clog the back of my throat, my desperate need to come overriding everything else.

A cry rips from my throat when he removes his hand from between my thighs, and my legs buckle as I sag against the sink, but I only get a moment's reprieve before Wilder's hand slides into my hair, fisting it at the base of my neck and pulling hard until my back is arched.

His lips are pressed against my ear, his breathing ragged and uneven, giving away just how affected he is by all of this. I feel his other hand moving between us, followed by the sharp sound of his zipper being lowered before I feel his hard length gliding between my ass cheeks.

"You wanna come all over my cock, Angel?"

"God, yes." His hips undulate as he slides his dick between my wet folds until the tip nudges my swollen clit, making my inner walls clench. He continues with the slow, teasing pace until I'm sure I've soaked his cock and my body feels like it's about to go up in flames. I'm on the verge of losing my goddamn mind, and the tiny fragment that's still somewhat with it wonders if that's exactly what Wilder is trying to do as he holds me hostage at the edge of the cliff. I can practically see the waves crashing far below, and I'm eager to jump off the ledge and feel the cool water washing over my heated skin.

His hand grabs hold of my thigh, lifting it to rest on the countertop, spreading me open and granting him better access. Sliding around my hips until he can dip lower, Wilder's fingers once again start up their torturous rhythm on my clit, matching each thrust as his cock glides between my folds. I push back against him, hungry to feel him inside me, but he pins my body in place with his hips, denying me.

The tears that have been building in my eyes finally overflow, and I wonder if this is what it feels like to be ripped apart at the seams. I feel like my body is being pulled in a hundred and one different directions. My legs are jelly beneath me. Wilder's weight is the only thing holding me upright, and my emotions are all over the place. I can't decide if I want to cry, scream, or break down in hysterical laughter. I'm close to doing all three. So. Fucking. Close.

Wilder uses his firm grip on my hair to tilt my head, licking a line up my cheek and gathering my tears on his tongue. More of them immediately begin to spill over, and he watches, mesmerized. "I can taste how badly you need to come."

The way he says it only makes me cry harder, and I sob against him. He's not going to let me come. All of this torture, and he's not going to give my body what it so desperately needs.

I can feel myself falling apart, and not in a good way. My mind is slowly descending into mad hysteria, and I don't even realize Wilder has shifted behind me until I feel the tip of his cock nudging my entrance. Glancing up at the mirror, I realize he's wiped the steam away and I can once again look into his turbulent brown eyes.

He places his hand on my hip, squeezing tightly to keep me still, and I can feel the tense way he's holding himself as he prevents himself from sliding in any deeper.

"Are you going to be a good girl and cream all over my dick, Angel?"

The purr in his voice tells me that's exactly what he wants. I try to nod in response, but his tight grip on my hair prevents me, and instead, I flick my tongue out to lick my dry lips, my voice coming out in a broken croak. "Yes."

"Say it."

"I'll be a good girl. I'm going to come so hard. I just need you to fuck me, Wilder. Please."

Something flashes across his face too quickly for me to decipher before he buries his face in my neck, murmuring something that I can't hear. With his tip resting just inside my entrance and his hand pinning my hip against the countertop, he lets go of my hair and uses his fingers to work my swollen and oversensitive nub.

This is it. I'm going to come this time. He's going to let me come.

As I climb that hill for the final time, I can feel my inner walls clenching hungrily as they try to suck Wilder deeper, but he holds himself back, even though he groans with pain-tinged pleasure every time I constrict around him. I try to push back against him, but with every attempt, he only grips my hip harder, no doubt leaving fingerprint bruises behind.

He waits until I'm again dangling over the cliff, and I know I'm going to fall apart as soon as he slides inside of me, but that's okay. I'm so worked up, I can probably come several times before he's finished.

His hips begin to thrust shallowly, never letting more than his blunt head make it inside.

"God, I can feel how badly you want me."

"Yes."

"You'd do just about anything I asked of you right now, wouldn't you?"

The significance of his words doesn't even penetrate the thick fog of pheromones clouding my mind. "Anything."

"Too bad you wouldn't have done *anything* to have me four years ago."

It's only when cool air rushes at my back that what he's said penetrates.

"W-what?"

Even though he's put some distance between us, his fingers still move swiftly over my clit, sending me barreling head-first toward an orgasm. His other hand pushes me painfully against the sharp edge of the counter, and when I look up into the mirror, cold, dead eyes look back at me.

"Wilder." This time, I have no idea if his name on my tongue is a plea for him to come back to me or a plea for him to keep going. Using only his fingers, he drives me closer to the edge than he has before. I can feel my release right there, just beyond my fingertips, like flower petals unfurling as the sunlight gets closer with the promise of warmth. At the exact moment when the sunlight touches the outer edges of the petals, someone comes and snatches the sun away, and in its absence, the petals retreat once again.

"No," I sob as the absence of his hands on my body leaves me bereft.

"You see, you aren't a good girl, Emilia," Wilder sneers, his voice icy and menacing. "And bad girls don't deserve to come."

His features are set into a blank, indifferent mask, which he levels my way before turning on his heel and striding out of the bathroom. The second he's gone, I sink to my knees on the floor. Tears are streaming down my face and my entire body is shaking. I can feel my body crashing from the adrenaline, the countless near orgasms, and the cruel, cavalier way Wilder just looked at me. *How can he switch emotions like that?*

I'm not left alone in the bathroom for long before I hear footsteps approaching. Unable to lift my head, I wipe at my nose and sniffle. "Go away, Wilder. I can't cope with you right now."

Instead of doing what I asked, he crosses the room and moves to crouch behind me, his heat enveloping my back.

"Shh, Little Sparrow. I'm here to give you what you need."

"H-hawk?" I glance up at him through tear-stained eyes, watching as he gets himself comfortable on the floor behind me. With his crotch pressed against my ass, he spreads his legs out on either side of me before placing his hands on my hips and maneuvering me into the position he wants. When I'm settled between his legs, my back to his chest, he gently lifts my legs until they are bent at the knee, my feet planted on the outer side of his thighs. The position has me spread wide, my pussy on display for anyone to look at—not that anyone else is here, and I honestly don't think Wilder will be coming back.

The entire time he shushes me softly, trailing his fingers along my arms and rubbing my back in a soothing motion. I'm too out of it to question anything he's doing, and the second his hand dips between my thighs, I come apart with a half scream-half cry.

He presses featherlight kisses to my shoulder as he immediately starts pushing me toward a second orgasm. The only sounds in the room are my heavy breathing and the wet sucking noise as he pumps his fingers into my dripping wet pussy.

I can feel his chest rising and falling in exaggerated breaths, his own desire building as I rub my hands up and down his thighs, occasionally digging my fingernails into his skin when he hits the perfect spot.

I dance along the precipice of another orgasm, but I can feel something is missing. I need more than just a release. After everything that just happened with Wilder, I need something *more*. A connection. I need to know it isn't just me.

Turning my head, I crane my neck until my lips brush Hawk's. He stills, but I push harder, and after a second, he relents, his tongue diving into my mouth. He devours me with his lips, and I can taste the hunger on his tongue. It's that reciprocated desire that sends me catapulting into my orgasm, and he swallows my cries of pleasure, continuing to work me over with his fingers and lips until I squirm against him.

Even then, he doesn't let up. Sliding his fingers out of me, he threads them through my hair, using his grip to angle my head so he can kiss me deeper. He strokes my tongue and sucks on my lips like I'm the most delicious thing he's ever tasted, and I turn over in his arms until my chest slides against his. He hauls me into his lap, our lips never once disconnecting, and I thread my arms around his neck, grinding my pussy against his jean-clad erection.

We drown in one another, both of us content to kiss and grind and simply enjoy the feel of being in one another's arms. It's been far too fucking long since I kissed Hawk Davenport, and as he sucks my tongue into his mouth and runs a hand up my spine, cupping the back of my neck, I make a promise to myself that I won't let so long pass until our next kiss.

"Hawk," I moan when I finally come up for some much-needed air.

I stare into his smoldering gray depths as I grind my pelvis against his, but instead of pulling me closer, his hands on my hips push me backward. I frown in confusion at the regret and indecision in his eyes.

"I'm sorry, Emilia."

Pushing me out of his lap, he climbs to his feet, and I'm again left alone in the bathroom, feeling wrung out and crestfallen. One thing is for sure, though. I'm never, ever having a bath in this house again. It's just not worth it if this is the consequence.

THE RUTHLESS BOYS OF RIDGEWAY

Hawk
CHAPTER 16

"Why aren't we staying at the frat house tonight?" Wilder questions, suspicion coloring his voice as I drive us away from campus and toward the brownstone.

"I told you. I just wasn't in the mood. It's been a busy week and I want the peace and quiet of our house."

Wilder makes a noise that makes it clear he doesn't believe me, and my hands tighten around the steering wheel.

"As for why you followed me to the car?" I glance his way, noticing his lips flatten. "I haven't a clue."

"It's no fun without you there. You're already gone two nights a week, and now you're making it a third? Next, you'll be quitting college and becoming a hermit."

I roll my eyes at his dramatics. I've spent most of the last two days distracted with thoughts of Emilia and her stalker. Until the other night, I admittedly hadn't spent much time with her or given her situation a second thought. The chaotic storm of emotions her mere presence elicits is enough of a reason to keep her at arm's length. I may have understood her reason for leaving four years ago, and while I can begrudgingly admit that some deep-seated part of me missed her, that doesn't mean I want to invite her back into my life. I don't, or at least, I didn't think I did, but Hadley is fucking worming her way into my head and making me second guess myself.

When I walked into the house the other night and saw the meal she was cooking for Kai, I was jealous. Fucking jealous! I wanted her to be going through all that bother for me, which is a reaction that confuses the fuck out of me. I *shouldn't* want her to do that. I *shouldn't* have liked the look of her in *my* kitchen. I *shouldn't* have pictured wrapping my arms around her while she chopped vegetables or stirred a pot, and I sure as fuck *should not* have envisioned bending her over the table and fucking her into it as a thank you. But that's exactly what I did. And when she invited me to stay, well, coyotes couldn't have dragged me away.

The whole night just got weirder as I watched the fear in her eyes and the glimmer of hope that Kai extinguished when he told her about Steven. The way it tugged at some long-forgotten part of me. Only one other person has incited such murderous rage, and that is Hadley—when I learned about the horrific upbringing she'd been forced to endure and the fucking asshole still chasing her.

I'm not entirely sure what it means that Emilia can evoke such strong emotions. I'm not necessarily a *feelings* kinda guy. Honestly, until Hadley came along, I truly didn't give a shit about anyone outside of my best friends. They're the only family I had growing up. It was always just the four of us, and outside of our inner circle, there was no one we could trust, least of all a girl.

Our inner circle has expanded since then, but I've always been content as a lone wolf. I've never had a girlfriend or been in a relationship, and honestly, I'd rather keep it that way. I'm not interested in getting tied down with a girl, and it's not like anyone I've been with has even remotely made me question that. Emilia probably came the closest back when we were at Pac. Even then, we were only eighteen, and I knew she wanted to be tied down in a relationship about as much as I did. It's part of the reason we worked so well—we both wanted the same things.

I'm still not saying I want to settle down and marry the girl, just that whatever the fuck she's doing to me is new and unsettling, and I have no fucking clue what to make of it. After I told Kai to keep me updated on his progress with this stalker, I spent most of the last two days staring at the phone, waiting for it to ring. What's seriously fucked up is that I was torn between wanting to hear that he'd identified the guy and hoping his leads would fall through. How messed up is that?

It's not that I want Emilia to live in fear. I don't get off on that shit the way Wilder does. But so long as this psycho is out there, she'll be hiding under our roof. The second Kai finds the guy and we catch him, she'll be gone again, and I'm beginning to think that's something I don't want. Every time I try to picture the house without her in it, I see her standing in that goddamn kitchen, and I realize I want that—her. In my kitchen. In my house. In my fucking bed.

After I chatted with Kai earlier, when he informed me that the Jack guy was another dead end, I tried to put all thoughts regarding Emilia to the back of my mind and go back to the frat. I lasted about an hour, listening to those idiots blabber on about absolute shit before I'd had enough. Without even bothering to say goodbye, I was out of my seat and heading for the car.

Of course, Wilder was immediately on my ass with a thousand and one questions, not buying a single one of my vague non-answers. Not that I give a shit. I'm just not in the mood to deal with the hissy fit that I know will ensue if he thinks for one second I'm not on team *Let's Make Emilia's Life Hell.*

Honestly, I'm beginning to think he needs to grow the fuck up and get over what happened four years ago. When Emilia first showed up, I felt bad for him. I hadn't realized just how much her presence was going to mess with his head. He's been acting weirder than normal these last two weeks, avoiding the house and barely talking to me, always out doing who knows what. I think it's all so he can keep himself busy. Stop himself from thinking about *her*. I'm just waiting for him to realize that no amount of distractions can fix the problem.

He needs to confront her and unleash all those long-buried feelings so he can unburden himself and finally move forward. For that reason, I think it's a good thing that he followed me out of the frat house. He can't confront Emilia if he's too busy avoiding her.

As for what I need to do when it comes to Emilia? I don't have a fucking clue. Half of me wants to fuck her so good that she forgets all about the reason she's back here with us, and the other half wants to turn tail and run as far as fucking possible from her.

Tension bleeds into the air the closer we get to the house. Anxious anticipation filled with lust, desire, malice, and anger. It's a fucked up mixture emanating from both Wilder and me, but it's potent, and it only serves to spike my adrenaline.

Reaching the house, I park the car by the curb outside and turn off the engine. I move to grab the door handle, but I notice Wilder still has his seatbelt on and is staring out the passenger window with a slight frown. I follow his line of sight, taking in the warmth shining out through the windows from the lamps on inside the front porch and living room. My mind wonders what Emilia and Kai are doing behind the closed curtains, and my limbs itch to join them.

"What are you doing? Come on!"

Despite my insistent tone, Wilder makes no effort to move, instead continuing his perusal of the front of the house.

"How much longer is she going to be here?"

I sigh, not liking the knot in my chest at the thought of her leaving. "I dunno, man. You'd need to ask Kai that one."

Wilder turns to face me. "Isn't he keeping you updated?"

"Yeah, but so far, he's got no leads."

Upon hearing that, his frown deepens before he returns his gaze out the window. I watch him for a moment, trying to figure out if all this pain he feels is really related to Emilia or if she's simply the unlucky one he's chosen to direct it all at. The truth is, despite us having become close friends and living together for the last four years, I don't know much about him—about his past or his family. It's not something he's ever brought up in conversation.

His dad used to do business with my parents back when they were involved in the child mercenary business. Wilder's dad is an arms dealer and was willing to offer up his own son as collateral to secure a business deal, so I can only imagine the sort of upbringing Wilder had. He's never once mentioned his mom, or any other family, or talked about his childhood, but I've seen the shadows that hide behind his broad smile and quirky, unhinged demeanor. They're the same ones I occasionally see on Hadley, and I get the impression that Wilder carries a hell of a lot more pain and hurt than what Emilia inflicted on him. His scars—both physical and emotional—are far more profound than those left by a broken heart. They're the kind born from years of suffering. It's a question of whether that torment was self-inflicted or imposed upon Wilder by others.

"Maybe if the two of you tried talking—"

Wilder's ice-cold glare cuts me off when he whips his head around to face me. "Don't fucking finish that sentence."

Where his glare would have most people folding in on themselves, I simply roll my eyes, more than used to his temper. Hell, it can rival mine. The difference is, I'm frequently in a foul mood, whereas it's rare that Wilder gets this worked up.

Shaking my head, I return his hostile stare with an unfazed one of my own. "Fine. Keep punishing her." Yanking on the door handle, I push open the door and step out, but before I close it, I turn around and duck my head back into the car. "But we both know you're only punishing yourself."

As I slam the door shut, he yells out, "I am not!" However, I ignore him, striding around the car and up the steps to the house. I hear the car door open just before I close the front door, but I don't wait for Wilder to catch up. My mind is already on Emilia as I pop my head into the living room to see if she's there. Finding it empty, I move on to the kitchen, where I find Kai nursing a glass of scotch at the kitchen table.

"Everything okay?"

He lifts his head at my question, and I can immediately see that, no, everything is not okay.

Adrenaline pumps through my veins, multiple possibilities flashing across my mind. "What happened? Where's Emilia?"

"She's fine. She's upstairs."

Hearing that whatever has happened doesn't concern Emilia has me instantly relaxing, and I move to sit opposite him as I hear the front door slam shut, followed by the banging of footsteps as Wilder stomps up the stairs.

We both wait until his bedroom door slams shut before I ask, "What's going on?"

Kai shakes his head, taking a hefty sip from his glass. "Nothing new."

I sit and watch him, noting the dark rings under his eyes and the tightness in his jaw. He's burning himself out with this job, working all hours and never giving himself a break.

Only now, as I take him in, I can tell it's more than just exhaustion and frustration. Kai's first impression is of a sweet, guy-next-door type, but underneath that easy-going, charming persona, he's carrying similar demons to the rest of us.

"This case is hitting too close to home for you."

He shrugs a shoulder, lifting the glass to his lips and downing the last of it. "Don't they all?" It's not really a question, and I narrow my eyes, scrutinizing him closer. I can't imagine how difficult it must be to protect women in similar situations. To *save* those women, especially when he couldn't save the one woman who truly mattered to him.

And yet, this case—Emilia's case—is getting to him more than the others have. Perhaps because she's Hadley's friend or because they're both staying here—a familiar place for Kai, rather than some bland, impersonal safe house. Or maybe it's because the two of them have been spending so much time alone together. Usually, we rotate guards to ensure no unhealthy attachments form and to provide better protection—fresh eyes and all that—but this case isn't like any of the others we've had, leaving Kai to shoulder most of the responsibility on his own.

I momentarily consider getting someone else to take over for him so he can have a much-needed break, but I quickly dismiss it. Not only would it take precious time to get a new guy up to speed, but Hadley was right to ask Kai in the first place. I wouldn't trust anyone else to look after Emilia the way he will.

"Is there anything you need? I can—"

"It's fine." Kai pushes to his feet, setting his glass in the sink. "I just need to catch this guy." Deciding to forgo the glass, he grabs the neck of the scotch bottle, dangling it between his fingers as he strides toward the door.

Before he can disappear, I call out, "I'm here if you ever need to talk." All I get is a nod and a finger wave before he disappears up to his room.

Most of the time, it's easy to forget that Kai has been to hell and back. That, in his twenty-five years, he's experienced more horror than most people witness in a lifetime. I make a note to sit down with him tomorrow and actually discuss Emilia's case, see what leads he's eliminated, and which ones he still needs to track down. I've been so busy avoiding all things Emilia that I haven't had a proper check-in with him, and as his superior, that's not acceptable, even if this is an off-the-books job.

I sit at the kitchen table for a while longer, contemplating everything before deciding to call it a night. Perhaps everything will look brighter in the morning. Climbing the stairs to my bedroom, I hover at the top of them, staring up the stairwell to the floor above and debating going to check on Emilia. Then again, most likely similar to Kai, she'd rather be left alone.

Turning my back on the stairs, I head into my room and close the door behind me, tossing my backpack filled with textbooks on the bed. That's when I hear it. A pained whimper coming from the jack-and-jill bathroom I share with Wilder. On silent feet, I quickly cover the distance and slide open the bathroom door, freezing in my tracks at what I see.

Wilder's bare ass stares back at me as he fucks some broad over the bathroom counter. Horrified and in desperate need of bleaching my eyes out, I turn away, and it's only then that I notice the color of the girl's hair. Black. Turning back around, I mentally block out the way Wilder is thrusting into her as I run my eyes over what I can view of her body. At this angle, I can't see her face. All I can make out is the sweat beading along her skin beneath the harsh bathroom lights. However, the longer I watch, I realize it couldn't possibly be anyone but her. Wilder came home with me, and even though he may be pissed at her, he wouldn't put Emilia's life at risk by inviting some unknown chick back to the house. We very rarely—if ever—bring girls back here. There's no need when we have the frat house.

If I still had any doubt as to who Wilder was currently fucking, his next words obliterate it.

"Are you going to be a good girl and cream all over my dick, Angel?"

So much for his insistence that he wasn't going to fuck her. I roll my eyes at how fucking easily he gave in.

Emilia's whimpered, "Yes," along with the visual the two of them are currently offering, have my cock instantly hard.

"Say it."

"I'll be a good girl. I'm going to come so hard. I just need you to fuck me, Wilder. Please."

His sharp command and her needy response ratchet up my desire. Neither of them seem to have spotted me lurking in the doorway, too engrossed in one another to care even if the house started to crumble around them. So, deciding to stay and watch the show, I unbutton my pants and push them down enough to palm my heavy cock.

I watch them go at it, him driving her insane, as I slide my palm up and down my length in time to his thrusts, pretending I'm the one fucking her instead of him. The entire time, my eyes stay focused on her, but Wilder's larger frame blocks most of my visibility. Shifting to get a better view, I notice Wilder's thrusts are shallow and teasing, and then glancing down to where their bodies connect, I realize he's not actually fucking her. He's fucking *with* her.

"God, I can feel how badly you want me." Beneath his angry snarl, his voice is strained, and I can tell by the tightness in his shoulders and neck that he's struggling to hold himself back. *Huh, guess I was wrong about him lacking self-control.* He's got the restraint of a fucking priest. No sane, red-blooded man could say no when the object of his desire is bent over in front of him, soaking wet and begging to be fucked. "You'd do just about anything I asked of you right now, wouldn't you?"

"Anything." Emilia sounds halfway delirious, and I can tell she's oblivious to the threat hanging in Wilder's words.

"Too bad you wouldn't have done anything to have me four years ago."

As Wilder steps away from her, she turns her head just enough for me to see the side of her face. Her cheeks are flushed a deep red, her eyes glassy as she blinks several times, struggling to process his words. "W-what?"

I can still see his arm flexing as he plays with her clit, his other hand pinning her to the counter. A part of me wonders if I should intervene, and I'm still making up my mind when Emilia begins to tremble with an oncoming orgasm. Before she can reach it, though, Wilder pulls his hand away. Without him there to hold her up, she sags against the counter, her body boneless as she sobs.

Wilder stands and watches her with a cold, despondent look in his eye and a sneer carved into his lips that momentarily makes me fearful for her, and I make a mental note never to leave him here alone with her. Whatever the fuck is going on with him when it comes to her is only escalating.

"You see, you aren't a good girl, Emilia, and bad girls don't deserve to come."

He gives her a dismissive once over as he yanks his jeans up and tucks himself away before heading for the door that leads into his bedroom. The second the door closes behind him, I refocus my attention on the sobbing, trembling, broken-looking girl on my bathroom floor.

It only takes a split second for me to make up my mind before I put my still hard dick away and step into the room, making my presence known as I walk toward her.

"Go away, Wilder. I can't cope with you right now."

Ignoring her scathing words and despondent tone, I crouch down behind her, pressing my knees into the floor on either side of her hips. I gently brush her hair away from the damp skin of her neck and press my lips to her ear. "Shh, Little Sparrow. I'm here to give you what you need."

She startles at my voice, lifting her head to stare up at me through long, wet eyelashes. "H-hawk?"

Shifting, I cushion Emilia between my thighs. The feel of her ass pressed against my crotch makes my cock surge with newfound life, but I mentally berate him. This is for her, not *him.*

Lifting one leg at a time, I plant her feet on the outside of my thighs, her knees bent so her pussy is on display. This is where I seriously regret not putting a floor-to-ceiling mirror in this bathroom. I'd love nothing more than to be able to stare at her pussy right now as I finger fuck it and watch the ecstasy written on her face as she comes for me. *Next time.* That thought catches me off-guard. Next time? There shouldn't even be a *this* time, never mind a next time.

Pushing all of it to the back of my mind and focusing on the shaking beauty between my legs, I trail my fingers along her bare skin, down her soft stomach until I dip between her spread thighs. I can feel her excitement coating her thighs from Wilder's torture session, and her shaking worsens as I slide between her folds. I've barely touched her when she explodes, and I press a soothing kiss to her shoulder, even while I sink easily into her drenched core. It clenches around me, the aftereffects of her orgasm still going strong as I immediately begin pushing her into a second one.

Her heady moans and the way she rocks her hips and digs her fingernails into my thigh have me nearly coming in my pants. I'm two seconds away from pushing her onto her knees and taking her like a wild animal when she tilts her head up.

Her lips meet mine and I go rigid beneath her touch, surprised and hesitant. She pushes harder, and *fucking hell*, the taste of her is too good to deny.

I lick along the seam of her lips, and she parts them, allowing me to delve in and taste her more fully. I can't get enough as I suck and plunder, committing every inch of her mouth to memory. *How the hell did I forget how delectable she tasted?* Like strawberries and cream. Her pussy clamps around my fingers, and she cries her release into my mouth. I drink in every second of it. Even then, her kisses are like a fucking drug, and I can't seem to stop, even after she's come.

Without even realizing I've moved, my hands are in her hair, holding her to me as I devour her lips. Her mouth. Her tongue. When she turns over in my arms, I haul her against me, loving the way her crotch aligns with mine as she drags her pussy over the rock-hard erection pressing against my jeans.

Time loses all meaning as I drown in everything that is Emilia Harrison. It's like we have been transported back to four years ago when, after a single touch, I couldn't keep away from her. She's intoxicating, and just like then, I find myself not wanting to do anything other than bask in her light.

Everything within me demands I do one thing—claim her—and I'm on the verge of giving in to that desire when she moans, "Hawk." My name sounds so fucking good on her lips, swollen from our kiss, and again that overwhelming urge to bend her over and make her mine has my muscles tensing. However, instead of acting on that urge, I pause, staring into her green eyes. They're blown with desire, although I notice something else. An emptiness to them that didn't use to be there.

We both might want this—need it even—but it's only going to create new complications, especially when she's all stressed out over this stalker, and I'm in a war with myself when it comes to what I want from her.

So, rather than doing what every atom in my body demands I do, which is to pull her in against me, rip off my pants, and sink balls deep into her soaking wet cunt, I instead push her away. Hurt and rejection flash in her eyes, making me feel like the biggest asshole ever.

"I'm sorry, Emilia." I don't know what else to say or how to explain that now isn't the time—it isn't *our* time, assuming there will ever be an *our time*. Lost for words and horny as fuck, I do exactly what Wilder just did and leave her on the bathroom floor like she means absolutely fucking nothing to me.

Except that's the problem, isn't it? She's starting to mean *something*. More than something. If I genuinely thought about it, I might actually confess that she's starting to mean *everything*.

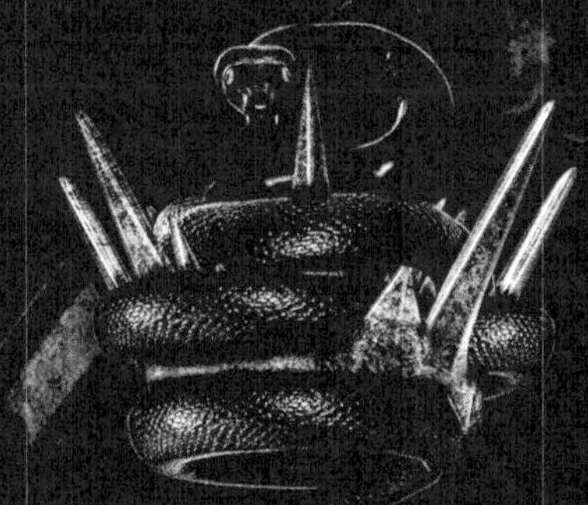

THE RUTHLESS BOYS OF RIDGEWAY

Emilia

CHAPTER 17

After the fiasco in the bathroom, I've holed myself up in my room, only emerging to grab something to eat. Even then, each time I waited until my stomach was threatening to eat itself before I finally caved and went in search of sustenance.

Thankfully, Kai has been giving me my space, probably assuming my antisocial behavior is due to our lack of progress—and don't get me wrong, that is undoubtedly a huge part of it. It's hard to force yourself to get up every day, plaster on a smile, and pretend your life isn't a complete and utter shitshow when that's precisely what it is. I feel like I'm being bombarded from every side, and there's no reprieve or light at the end of the tunnel.

Being cooped up in this house with no sign of being let out any time soon and having to worry about potentially running into Hawk or Wilder every time I leave my bedroom has me constantly on edge, and I can feel myself sinking into that dark hole. I like to think of myself as an optimistic person. I always try to find the bright side of things. When my mom couldn't make it to my high school graduation because she had to work, I focused on the fact that I had my friends. When I got a B in one of my college classes—my first B ever!—I accepted it for the learning opportunity it was and ensured it wouldn't happen again. Life has taught me that shit happens, and if you only focus on the bad stuff, then you'll never see the good things. You won't spot the rose in the thicket of nettles or appreciate the rare moment of sunshine on a wet, miserable winter's day. I've always worked hard to spot the rose, to lift my face to the sunshine, but it's getting harder and harder to do that these days. I don't even remember the last time I bathed in the sun's heat, never mind letting it warm me from the inside out.

After spending the last half hour trying to convince my stomach that it's not hungry, I give up and sneak downstairs. I don't know if Hawk or Wilder are home, nor do I have the energy to face them. So like a thief, I pad silently through the house, crouched and on alert—and definitely looking suspicious as hell.

Reaching the kitchen without any incidents, I peer around the doorframe, checking that the room is empty before daring to venture any further. I let out a breath of relief when I find it unoccupied, and I allow myself to relax a little as I rush over to the fridge and begin piling as much food as I can into my arms.

"About fucking time you showed your face," Kai growls behind me, his loud voice making me jump as I fail to suppress a squeak of surprise. "I was on the verge of dragging you down here myself."

Hoping the cool air of the fridge offsets some of the heat in my cheeks, I peer around the fridge door at a towering Kai. He's standing in the middle of the doorway, blocking my path out of the kitchen as he stares me down with his arms crossed over his chest.

"I just came down to make myself a sandwich."

He nods, watching me pile everything in my arms until I have what I need. Taking the ingredients over to the kitchen island, I set about making the sandwich and pouring myself a glass of water. Once I'm finished and I've put the food away, I grab my plate and glass, hoping he'll let me scoot back up to my room without any questions. Of course, I'm not that lucky. In fact, I'm beginning to think I'm the exact opposite of lucky. Unlucky. Fucking cursed.

"Not so fast," Kai chastises. With a tilt of his head, he gestures toward the kitchen table. "Sit. We need to talk."

Well, fuck. Those four words are *never* followed by anything good.

Reluctantly, I move over to the table and take a seat, feeling his eyes on me the entire time. Nerves diminish my appetite, and I end up anxiously twisting my fingers and staring at the tabletop while I wait for him to sit down.

When he doesn't speak up, I lift my gaze to meet his, finding him watching me with what looks a lot like concern in his eyes. "Eat." He once again tilts his head toward my plate and waits patiently while I nibble on my sandwich. It tastes like sawdust in my mouth, and it's a struggle to swallow every bite, but eventually, I manage to get the whole thing down.

When I'm finished, he nods as though satisfied, and it's only when I push my empty plate away and raise an eyebrow at him in question that he speaks. "I think it's time we talk to Mel."

Well, I definitely wasn't expecting him to say that. It takes a second for me to get over the surprise and hear what he's not saying. "You're out of leads."

He grimaces. "I've looked into literally everyone associated with you. Everyone you work with, those who live in your building, and all the staff at Halston. I've done a basic background check on every student registered when you were, and completed deeper searches into the few you pointed out. Every person who has so much as walked past you since you graduated from Pacific Prep has been searched and eliminated. I—" He hangs his head, looking defeated. "I'm out of ideas, and I'm out of suspects."

"And you think Mel could help?"

"Maybe. She may think of someone you've overlooked or who passed my basic check. Like you said before, she might have picked up on cues you missed."

For the first time in days, a tiny flame of hope builds in my chest. "Yeah, okay. Let's call her. Wait—" I glance around the room in search of a clock. "What day is it? She might be at work."

"It's Friday."

"Oh." My shoulders drop. "She doesn't get home from work until six." It's only midday, which means I need to wait six more hours before we can talk to her. *That's fine. Six hours is nothing,* I tell myself, trying to remain upbeat. I can totally kill six hours with... something.

"It's lunchtime," Kai argues, holding my phone out toward me. "Try her. If she doesn't answer then we can try again later."

Nodding, I take the phone from him and pull up her details. I bring the phone to my ear, worrying my lips as it rings, and rings, and rings.

"Hey!" Mel greets happily, sounding a little breathless.

"Hey. Sorry, am I bothering you at work, I can call back later."

"No, no, you're good," she laughs. "It's a dud day here anyway. I'd literally be on the verge of falling asleep if Cathy didn't keep walking past my desk every five minutes."

For the first time in days, I smile, chuckling while I picture the hard roll of her eyes.

"What's up? Are you coming home yet?"

I flinch at the word *home* because Springview and the life I was building there no longer feels like home. Honestly, it never did. Not in the way being back around Hawk, Wilder, Hadley, and her guys has. Despite all the... issues... I can feel my old self coming back to life. The cold, hard shell I'd encased myself in is showing signs of damage. It's cracking, and with every fissure, I can feel myself reawakening.

"It's not the same here without you," she says, making me realize I haven't answered her.

"Ehh, not yet," I say vaguely, feeling all twisted up inside as I say it. Although, I'm not sure if it's because I'm lying to her, or if it's at the thought of one day going back to that life. Regardless, I push that feeling aside and focus on why I called Mel in the first place.

"I was, uhh, wondering if you remember anyone from Halston hanging around us and maybe seeming a bit weird or anything?"

I cringe as my question is met with silence. I can only imagine she's staring at the phone with a *what the fuck* expression, wondering if I'm on drugs or some shit.

"Why?" she questions.

"I just..." I trail off, not wanting to explain further and drag her into this mess. I still remember Kai's warning from before, about how it could put her in danger. "I'll explain later, but I need to know if you remember anyone."

"Emmm..." she falls silent as she contemplates the answer, before heaving out a long sigh. "No, sorry. Not that I can think of."

"Oh."

She picks up on my disheartened tone, as she tacks on, "But, I'll give it a good hard think, yeah?"

"Please," I plead. "It's important, and I promise I'll tell you everything later."

"Yeah, okay... Is everything alright, Em?"

I sigh, dropping my head to rest in my free hand. "Yeah, it's fine. I'll let you get back to work. Talk to you later."

"Talk later."

Hanging up, I drop the phone on the table, feeling like a burst balloon. I don't even have the energy to lift my head. It's not that I'd expected her to have a name on the tip of her tongue, but... well, yeah, I guess I'd put all my hopes on the fact that she *might*.

Silence stretches out for a long moment, before a warm hand wraps around mine on the table. "I'm worried about you," Kai says softly.

His concern is enough to have me lifting my head to meet his troubled gaze. His eyes roam over my face, and I'm certain he's seeing far deeper than surface level. I feel like he's always watching me, reading me. It's probably just ingrained in him from his Marine Corps days and his time working for Hawk, and yet, I feel like there's more to it than that. Every time I catch him watching me, and our eyes collide, something profound and unidentifiable passes between us.

"Don't be, I'm fine."

He cocks a brow, a small smile playing along his lips. "Really? You're fine? Well, now I'm definitely worried. Anyone who is in your position should be anything but fine, Emilia. Come on, talk to me."

"I—" I'm not even sure what I opened my mouth to say, but whatever it is seems to stick in the back of my throat. Instead, something so much more embarrassing happens. I cry. I fucking *cry*. I don't even know why. The tears just start coming, and I can't work out how to turn them off.

"I'm sorry," I babble, swiping furiously beneath my eyes and sniffing my nose. "I don't even know why I'm crying. I think I'm losing my mind in this house." I wave blindly toward the door. "Around those two assholes." Kai snorts out a laugh, but he lets me continue on with my ramble. "Wilder hates me. Like honest to god *hates* me. And Hawk is giving me whiplash. One minute he's indifferent and couldn't give a shit, and the next, he's staring at me and giving me orgasms on the bathroom floor."

There's a part of me that realizes I'm being highly inappropriate right now, but whatever elastic band was wrapped around my sanity has officially snapped.

"I'm not going to last another day under their roof. I need to get out of here." Blinking away my tears, I focus on Kai until he comes into view. "Please, Kai. I need to get out of this house."

His expression is tight and withdrawn, and I can see the outright denial on his lips before he even speaks. Not giving him a chance to say no, I reach across the table and grab his arm with both of my hands, giving it a desperate squeeze. "Please, Kai. *Please.* I'd do just about anything for some fresh air, to feel the sun on my face, and to know I'm not going to walk into one of them at any second."

His eyes soften, and I can tell he's wavering. He just needs a little push.

"We can go anywhere. Wherever you decide. Hell, we can hang out in an abandoned quarry for all I care. Anywhere but *here*. Please. *Please*, Kai."

I realize I'm laying it on thick, and I don't even mean to. I'm just so, *so* desperate to get out of here for a couple of hours.

His eyes drift shut and his jaw clenches, an inner battle ensuing behind his eyelids. I let him argue with himself while I observe his face for any signs of which side won with my heart lodged in my throat. After what feels like an eternity, he opens his eyes and focuses on me again.

"Fine," he grits out. "But we go somewhere remote, only for

a couple of hours, and you do absolutely *everything* I say. Do you hear me, Emilia?"

I'm already bobbing my head furiously before he finishes speaking. "I hear you. I'll stick to you like glue. Hang upside down from a tree if you tell me to."

He frowns, apparently not a fan of my joking. "Why the hell would I tell you to hang upside down from a tree?"

"I dunno." I shrug a shoulder. "But if you tell me to, I'll do it. Even though I hate being upside down, and I can't even do a handstand because I hate the way all the blood rushes to my head and makes me feel dizzy."

He just continues to stare at me like I'm insane. I'm ninety percent certain that I am. This house—those boys—have *made* me insane. Instead of arguing with him, though, I push to my feet. "We're going now, right? Like, right now?"

His gaze drops down my small frame, and I follow it, realizing I'm wearing an old tank top with no bra underneath, which means my nipples are on display for any perv to see—excellent!—paired with a pair of shorts I found in my bag; my outfit definitely shouldn't be worn outside of the house.

"Oh, uh, let me go change. Five minutes, yeah?"

Not giving him a chance to argue, I race out of the kitchen and up the stairs, changing faster than I've ever changed before. It's not more than three minutes before I'm flying back down the stairs, wearing an old band tee, jeans, and sneakers with my hair pulled back into a ponytail.

"Okay, I'm ready. Let's go!" I bounce impatiently up and down on the balls of my feet while Kai gathers his things at a painstakingly slow pace, mumbling under his breath the entire time. Something about how I'm acting like a dog who has been told they're about to go for walkies.

It's only when he grabs a gun from one of the drawers in the kitchen and tucks it into the back of his jeans that the risk of what we're about to do resonates with me, diminishing some of my joy as I swallow around the sudden lump in my throat.

Catching me watching him, some of the tension bleeds out of Kai's shoulders as he turns to face me. Walking over, he plants his hands on my shoulders and bends down until we are at eye level. "Are you sure about doing this?"

Despite the nerves fluttering around in my stomach, I nod my head. "Yup. I'm sure." I'm not going to back down or change my mind. I'm doing this. *We* are doing this. "Now stop procrastinating and come on."

His lip quirks up in a smile, but it doesn't reach his eyes and I know he can hear the nerves behind my upbeat tone.

An hour later and I couldn't find my way home if I tried—and trust me, I did actually try to remember the route we took here, except after about the eleventh turn, I gave up. But that's okay. I have no interest in returning to that tension-riddled, testosterone-charged house any time soon.

The second Kai turns off the engine and gives me the okay to get out of the car, I practically launch myself out the door, the widest grin on my face as I spread my arms out on either side of me and spin in a full circle. I tilt my head back, allowing the afternoon sun to soak into my Vitamin D-deprived skin, and I just let myself be present in the moment as the light breeze blows into my face.

The horrible cloud that has been hanging over my head for the last few days is chased away by the sunshine, and I feel infinitely lighter and more like myself as I continue to spin in a circle, making myself dizzy.

Right before I lose my balance, I open my eyes and plant my feet, laughing as the world continues to spin around me. After a few seconds, everything comes back into focus, and for the first time since we pulled up, I take in the scenery around me. I can see for miles in every direction, nothing but greenery as far as the eye can see.

"Wow, this is gorgeous."

Kai smiles warmly. "You haven't seen anything yet, Em. Are you up for a short hike?"

Now, I am not an exercise or even an outdoorsy person, so hiking isn't my thing. Still, after being cooped up inside that house for weeks, I'm fast developing a brand new appreciation for the outdoors.

"Hell yes!" I grin, and he grabs a backpack out of the back of his car, then the two of us follow a narrow gravel path as it winds down the side of a hill.

The two of us walk for the next hour, switching between silently drinking in the scenery and chatting easily. Our conversation is light and free-flowing, keeping me distracted from the weariness slowly filling my legs with lead and the fact I'm drenched in sweat and Kai's barely breathing heavily. In fact, despite my obvious lack of fitness, I'm starting to think I should add hiking to my list of favorite things to do—well, hiking with Kai, at least.

"What?!" I exclaim. "How can you even relax if you aren't wearing cozy pajamas?!"

He laughs, this loud, free bark that is completely at odds with anything I've heard come from his lips before. I've loved watching him unfurl the longer we've been out here. It's like he's an entirely different man than the one I've been living with for the last two weeks. More carefree. That's not to say he's not prepared to dive into action at the first sign of a threat. I don't think Kai could ever be relaxed enough for that, but he's definitely the most at ease I've ever seen him.

"Why do I have to be wearing pajamas at all to relax?"

"Because," I argue. "You just do." I groan. "Please tell me you aren't one of those people who doesn't change out of their work clothes as soon as they get through the front door."

"I practically live in jeans and t-shirts. It's not like I wear a suit to work. Why would I need to change?"

All I can do is gawk at him. "You can't relax in jeans. They're restricting and tight, and uncomfortable. Nobody wants to lounge on the sofa all night in a pair of *jeans*."

That earns me another carefree bark of laughter. "Usually I'll exercise in the evenings anyway."

Well, now I'm truly horrified. "Exercise later? Isn't exercise like a mandatory part of your job? Why would you also exercise in your free time?" I scrunch my nose up, horrified at the idea. I mean, exercise like this, I could *maybe* be talked into. It hardly feels like exercise except when we reach a particularly steep part of the path, and suddenly I sound like an eighty-year-old asthmatic trying to climb her stairs.

He shakes his head at my antics. "I enjoy exercising."

"You were undoubtedly dropped on your head one too many times as a baby. Nobody *enjoys* exercising."

He turns to face me, his eyebrow raised as he asks, "Don't try to tell me you aren't having fun right now, because I don't think I've seen you smile so brightly." My grin wavers, a blush creeping into my cheeks as I duck my head. Before I can think of a suitable response, he nudges my shoulder with his muscular arm. "I know you haven't had much to be happy about recently, but you should make an effort to smile more often. It suits you."

Bashfully, I tuck a stray strand of hair behind my ear, muttering, "Yeah, maybe when this is all over."

"I didn't see you smile much *before* your life got tossed in a blender, either."

Brows furrowed, I snap my gaze up to his as I stop in my tracks. "I smiled."

He comes to a stop beside me, clearly disagreeing as he shakes his head. "No, you didn't." Lifting his hand, he traces the edges of my lips with his thumb. My lips tingle where he touches, and I swear I stop breathing, unable to do anything but watch as he stares at where his thumb brushes my skin. "Not like this. I rarely saw a smile that reached your eyes. One that was completely genuine and open. Never a smile like the one you've been wearing today."

It's on the tip of my tongue to argue with him, but he beats me to it with a knowing smirk. "It was my job to pay attention to you. Trust me, I watched you often enough to know. You don't fool me with your fake smiles meant to appease everyone else, Emilia. When this is over, you should smile only for yourself. No one else."

His words leave me utterly speechless as I stare up at him, and after a moment, he drops his hand and continues forward. When I don't immediately follow, he peers back at me over his shoulder. "Come on, it's just up ahead. We're nearly there."

Shaking my head in an attempt to clear it, I turn to stare at where he's walking ahead of me. "Nearly where? What's just up ahead?" I call, breaking into a jog to catch up to him. "I thought we were just out for a hike?"

"Every hike should have a destination in mind," he responds cryptically, not providing me with any more of an answer than that.

We continue on in silence for another twenty minutes or so. So much for our destination being just up ahead, though I don't complain because I am genuinely having a lot of fun. I can't remember the last time I enjoyed myself this much. I'm completely immersed in the here and now instead of thinking about the million and one things I need to do later—or in this case, the reason why I'm even out here with Kai at all.

Maybe, when this is all over, I'll take up hiking as a hobby.

Although, even as I think it, I know I won't. It's not the hiking I'm enjoying. It's the company. I don't remember ever being so at ease with another person. I feel like I could tell Kai anything, and he wouldn't judge me or take offense. Maybe it's the circumstances in which we met or the fact that we've been stuck together under the same roof, but we've developed a solid kinship. It doesn't hurt that he looks like a golden Adonis, especially with how the rays of sunshine make his skin glow, like he was made to spend his days outdoors. He took his shirt off a while ago and tucked it in his back pocket in that hot way guys do, where it's hanging out, and ever since then, I've had a hard time not tripping over my feet. Every golden inch of him is perfection personified, and I'm finding myself parched—and not solely because of the warm weather.

We left the actual path long ago, blind faith my only justification for why I followed Kai into the wilderness. Since then, we've been traipsing through grass and jumping over streams. I'm just about to cave and ask him how much farther we have to go when I hear it—the sound of rushing water. My ears perk up, and Kai laughs at the expression on my face, a knowing grin gracing his very kissable lips.

Wow, where did that thought come from?

It's obvious the heat and exhaustion are getting to me.

"What's that?" I question, looking around for the source.

Grabbing my hand, Kai urges me forward. "Just around this corner."

I have to jog to keep up with his large strides as we skirt around a wall of rocks, and then the area opens up. Giant rock walls reach up to the sky around us, but following the sound of the rushing water, I gasp when I see a waterfall running down one of the cliffs and seemingly disappearing into the ground. Getting closer, I realize the rock we are standing on overhangs a cavern below, where the waterfall ends in a plunge pool and spring. "Wow," I gasp.

"Yeah, it's pretty impressive."

"Very," I murmur, still staring at the water below me.

"I found steps carved into the rock face that take you down to water level."

Snapping my gaze away from the water, I gape at him in excitement. "So you can go swimming in it?"

"Yeah," he grins. "It's nice and warm."

Staring back down, I really regret not knowing in advance so I could bring my swimsuit, but then it was already early afternoon when we left the house. I gaze up at the sky and notice the sun is well to the west, so we probably don't have time to go swimming today.

Turning back to look at Kai, I reach out and grab his hand. "Promise me you'll bring me back here and we can go swimming next time."

His face is earnest as he vows, "I promise, Em."

We only hang around at the waterfall long enough to drink some water and eat the provisions Kai brought, and then we begin the trek back down to the car. With every passing minute, a heaviness seeps into my limbs, and I'm reasonably sure it's more than just exhaustion. Knowing that every step brings me closer to the house and to the very real problems that await me there, threatens to remove all the good that Kai achieved today with this hike.

By the time we reach the car, my smile is forced, my laughter more tense and short than it was earlier as a heaviness bears down on me. Kai can see it too, but thankfully he doesn't comment.

"Uhh, we have a slight problem," I blurt out as he puts his backpack in the back seat. Immediately on alert, he spins to face me, his eyes darting around in search of a threat.

"What?" he asks with a frown when he finds no impending danger.

"I really, *really* need to pee." It's been creeping up on me for the last hour, but now that I no longer have nature to distract me, my bladder is making herself known.

"Oh." Kai instantly relaxes. His eyes take in our surroundings, this time not looking for enemies but for something else.

"No. No! Absolutely not, Kai!" I blurt out when I realize what he's searching for. "I am not peeing in a goddamn bush! There isn't even any toilet paper or hand wash."

"I have some tissues and hand sanitizer," he reasons, but I'm still adamantly shaking my head. I am *not* peeing outside. I've seen horror movies. Even if it is broad daylight, anything could jump out of the bush and attack me. Or there could be poison ivy, or something could sting my butthole. Hell no. It's not happening! My ass is too precious to take that risk.

"Not happening, Kai." I level him with one of my most serious expressions. "We passed a gas station a few miles back. I'm sure they have toilets."

He scrunches up his nose, mumbling something about how he doubted they were any cleaner than peeing outside, but I don't care. It's still a step up from a bush.

"Fine, fine. Get in. I could do with getting some gas, anyway."

We both hop in, and not long after, we're pulling up at the gas station. It's one of those old, rundown places where they're probably lucky to see a handful of customers a week. I imagine it was popular once upon a time, but with the interstate built nearby, very little traffic comes along this road now unless it's locals or someone hiking in the area. I'm assuming that's the only reason Kai is happy enough for us to stop here. Although, as I glance over at him out of the corner of my eye, he doesn't look too pleased about it. His eyes take in the station with eagle-like focus, even though we're the only car here. Only when he's assessed for any potential threats does he give a sharp nod of his head and make a move to get out of the car.

Following his lead, I do the same. As he begins filling the tank with gas, I go in search of a bathroom, finding one for customers at the back of the store. It's about as grim as I expected, yet I still stand by the fact that it's better than a bush hiding god-knows-what.

Finishing quickly, I decide to grab us both some chocolatey snacks to take home, and as I'm perusing the sugary treats aisle I hear my name.

"Emilia?"

I freeze in my tracks, turning in slow motion as my heart hammers painfully against my chest. I can't be hearing that right. It can't be him. He can't be here. Of all the fucking places, there is absolutely no way that he is in the same rundown gas station in butt-fuck nowhere that I am. It's just not possible.

...And yet, as I take in the six-foot-tall, expensive suit-wearing, sleazy asshole in front of me, there's no denying that he's real.

"It is you," he says with a leering smile.

"S-Steven?" I dart my eyes around the small shop, desperately hoping to spot Kai, but I don't see any sign of him before I focus back on the threat standing in front of me.

"What a surprise, running into you, here of all places."

"W-What are you doing here?"

"Just passing through. The band has a gig in Kimeth." He holds up his hand, showing me some sugary drink intended to keep you awake on long drives or when you're cramming for an exam. "And I needed to stretch my legs and get something to wake me up." He chuckles at himself before his eyes drop to my feet, slowly rising as he takes me in with that leery look I remember and still hate. "You look as good as I remember."

All I can do is gape at him, my mind racing in several directions. Is there really a gig not far from here, or did he follow us here? Although creepy, Kai dismissed him as a possible suspect... And yet, is it purely coincidence that I've run into him today? Now? What are the chances?

He raises a brow, staring at me expectantly, and I realize I missed whatever he was saying. "Huh?"

"I asked if you're seeing anyone."

"Oh." That's all I can say. The only sound I can force past my dry lips.

"Babe!" Kai calls out. The tension thrumming through me calms instantly at the sound of his voice. Kai's here. He'll know what to do. My eyes snap to his, widening in a silent plea for him to help. Not that I need to beg. Unlike with Wilder, or even Hawk, there's no animosity or tension between us. Kai's a true-to-life hero. The good guy in the story. In my story.

He smiles warmly at me as he approaches, as if everything's perfectly normal and I'm not freaking the fuck out inside. The easy reassurance in his expression somewhat settles the nerves fluttering in my stomach.

"Did you find the Twinkies?" I stare up at him in confusion as he steps right up to my side and casually drapes his arm around my shoulders, pulling me in against him like it's the most natural thing in the world for him to do. It's not his question or the fact that he never asked me to grab him anything that gives me pause, but the easy way that he's touching me—like we're lovers. And more significantly, the way my body hums beneath his touch.

With his warm smile still in place, he stares down at me for a beat before tearing his eyes away to take in Steven, as though he's only now realizing he's there.

"Oh, sorry. I didn't see you there." Still holding me close to his side, he holds out his other hand. "I'm David, and you are?"

I know for a fact that Kai already knows who this is. All of this is some kind of act; I'm just not entirely sure what the point of it all is. If Steven is my stalker, then Kai could be putting himself directly in the line of fire by behaving the way he is.

At that thought, I jiggle my shoulder, trying to dislodge Kai's arm, only he increases the pressure, squeezing me tighter so my face is practically squished against his chest and his calming sage scent is washing over me.

Steven's gaze darts back and forth between Kai and me, his brows lowered as he tries to suss us out. There's a reluctance to his movements as he reaches out to shake Kai's hand. "Steven."

"How do you know my girl?" Kai asks, his voice coming out as casual as his posture.

My girl? What the heck?

Steven's gaze darts to mine, and I'm careful to keep that fake smile Kai talked about earlier on my face.

"Oh, I know her from a long time ago. Just happened to see her here and thought I'd reacquaint myself." There's an icky undertone to his words that feels as though it sticks to my skin, and I immediately want to shower it off. It takes everything in me not to react as another scrutinizing flicker passes back and forth between Kai and me. "Are you two...?"

"Yup." From my position flattened against Kai's chest, I glance up at him through my eyelashes, catching his beaming smile that shows off his pearly whites. It's hard to believe it's fake, and for a second, I allow myself to believe in the lie he's telling. So, when Steven's gaze once again darts down to mine, I've donned a love-struck expression. I nuzzle deeper into Kai as I secretly observe Steven in my periphery, noting the lines that deepen around his lips as he flattens them.

Kai looks down at me, a twinkle in his eye. Is he enjoying this? "Anyway, we better grab what we need and get going, babe." Glancing back at Steven, he smirks. "Gotta stockpile so we don't have to come out again for the rest of our trip." He winks, his meaning more than clear as my cheeks turn pink, and memories of Kai earlier today without his shirt on mesh with how he looked in just a towel after his shower the other week.

Steven makes a somewhat disgusted noise and forces a tight smile, barely sparing me a glance as he mutters a goodbye, and we watch as he strides out the door.

It's only when I hear a car leave the parking lot that my shoulders sag and I dare to take my first real breath since Steven first approached. As the earthy aroma of Kai's aftershave fills my sinuses, I realize I'm still pressed up against him. Embarrassed, I take a step back. A cool chill runs along the back of my neck as his arm drops away, and I instantly miss his closeness.

It was just a show for Steven's sake. Get it together, I chastise.

When I look up at Kai, the easy expression he was wearing has fallen away, his eyes narrowed on the door and lips pursed as he stares out into the parking lot. "We should go," he says quietly, still staring out the shop's front windows as if expecting Steven to turn around and come back.

"Do you think it's him?"

At my question, he glances down, making an effort to smooth out the lines on his face. "I'm not sure. It's definitely one hell of a coincidence if it's not."

We don't hang around any longer. I put aside the unwanted snacks, my mood officially soured, while Kai pays for the gas and we climb back into the car. The entire time, we are careful not to make our movements appear rushed or panicked in case Steven is lurking nearby, watching.

It's only when we're safely within the confines of the car and Kai is steering us away from the garage that the reality of what just happened hits me and my hands begin to tremble.

"It's him," I croak.

"We don't know that for sure," Kai states, not taking his eyes off the road.

I scoff. "How can it not be? We're in the backass of nowhere, and there is literally no one else around, yet he shows up in the same gas station as us?"

"What did he say to you before I arrived?" Kai asks, his hands flexing around the steering wheel. I repeat what little he told me about the band doing a concert in Kimeth. I'm still in a full-body tremble by the time I finish, and any calm I'd found today is long since gone.

Kai reaches across the center console, grasping both of my hands in his. "I'm going to look into it, but if it is him, then this is a good thing."

"A good thing?" I shriek. "You made him think you were... that we were..." Unable to put a voice to the words, I instead snap, "You made yourself a target!"

"I needed to see his reaction."

"And?"

"It definitely annoyed him, but he didn't give anything away that would confirm he's your stalker."

Sighing, I turn my head to look out the window. "What now?"

"Now, I check to see if the band really does have a gig and that he's supposed to be at it."

I stare absently out the window as we drive back toward Ridgeway, the hedges on the side of the road zooming by in a green blur. Kai's hand is still wrapped around mine, his heat seeping into my skin and grounding me.

Only when we reach the city limits of Ridgeway, do I turn back to face him. His face is still pinched, and his hands clench the steering wheel tightly, deep in thought as he navigates the city streets.

"If he is my stalker, then he killed Richard." I pause,

chewing on my bottom lip as emotion swells within me. "He'll go after you next."

Squeezing my hand, Kai shifts his gaze to give me a quick look, a soft smile lifting his lips. "He can try. You forget I'm a trained Marine. It would take a hell of a lot more than that suit-wearing prick to take me down."

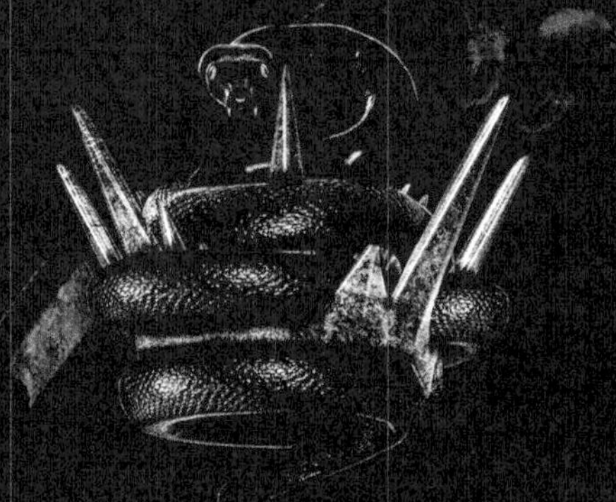

THE RUTHLESS BOYS OF RIDGEWAY

Kai
CHAPTER 18

I manage to keep calm for as long as it takes to get Emilia home, but the second she disappears up the stairs to change, I let loose the storm of emotions bubbling up within me.

"Where the hell have you two been?" Hawk barks out as soon as I stomp into the kitchen. Seeing my expression, his shoulders immediately push back, his anger at me fading away. "What happened?"

"I took Emilia for a hike out near Hollows Park." He begins to protest, but I cut him off with a wave of my hand. "I know it was stupid. I fucking know." I wipe my hand down my face as I collapse into the chair at the kitchen table. God, how did I let a pair of green doe-eyes talk me into taking her out of the house? How could I have been so reckless with her life? "Everything was fine until we stopped at a gas station on the way home. One of those ones by the old highway that never sees any traffic anymore, and fucking *Steven* was there."

My hands ball into tight fists, the urge to go back there and wring his slimy fucking neck overpowering everything else.

"Steven..." Hawk muses aloud, trying to place the name. "The band's manager? That Steven?"

"One and the same."

"What the fuck was he doing all the way out there?"

"Claims the band has a gig up in Kimeth."

"Do they?"

"No idea, I haven't had a chance to look yet. My main concern was getting Em out of there and back home safely. *Now* I can pick apart every aspect of his life and find out what I missed before."

Hawk's gaze shifts so he's staring out the kitchen door into the hallway, and I can hazard a guess on where his thoughts are at. "How is she holding up?"

It's on the tip of my tongue to ask him if he actually cares. The concern etched onto his face implies he does, but other than the night he came for dinner, he's hardly been home since Emilia arrived, not to mention what Emilia told me earlier. Not needing to add the headache from an argument with him to the pressure already forming behind my eyes, I just shrug a shoulder. "As good as can be expected."

Wanting to get answers ASAP, I grab my laptop from where I left it at the other end of the table and begin searching for Death on a Matchstick's schedule. It doesn't take long to confirm that they are performing in Kimeth for the next three nights. *So I guess Steven didn't lie about that.* Still. It feels like too much of a coincidence, and I don't fucking like coincidences.

I frown at the screen, trying to decide my next move. I could just let it go, but it's not in my nature. Not after... I shake my head, dispelling those thoughts.

"What can I do to help?" Hawk asks, his voice startling me. I'd completely forgotten he was here, but as I glance at him over the lip of my laptop, I realize he's been watching me and most likely saw where my mind went.

Clearing my throat, I focus back on the screen in front of me. "You can find out what hotel the band and everyone traveling with them are staying at."

Without another word, Hawk grabs his phone and begins scrolling through it, and for the next hour, he calls around various hotels while I search through everything I can find on social media. For obvious reasons, the band hasn't made the location of their accommodation public, so it takes a while to figure it out. However, after finding a photo one of their roadies posted a couple of hours ago that showed the stucco wall and tail end of a motel sign, I managed to track down one that looks like it matches the photo. A phone call pretending to be someone from the band's management company and I confirm Steven Carmichael has successfully checked into room 217. Apparently only the band is fortunate enough to be put up in a five-star hotel, and the rest of the group is slumming it in a motel down the road.

The second I have a location, I'm on my feet, grabbing my car keys and heading for the door. "What are you going to do?" Hawk asks, having trailed me into the hall.

"I'll figure that out when I get there."

"Do you need backup?"

"No. Stay here and keep an eye on Emilia. I made sure we weren't followed, so I'm confident no one knows she's here, but I don't want her left alone." I turn to face him, waiting until he nods in confirmation. I can see the promise in his eyes. He won't let anything happen to her. Still, I feel the need to say, "Keep her occupied, but stop messing with her fucking head, Hawk. She's one strong push in the wrong direction from losing her mind, and she doesn't deserve to be on the receiving end of whatever the hell is going on with you."

His jaw ticks in irritation. "Those are strong words from someone whose only job is to protect her."

Taking a step toward him, I don't give a single shit that he's my boss as I shove a finger into his chest. "Before we even stepped foot in this house, she asked me if I'd protect her from the two of you." Surprise flashes across his face before he masks it. "At the time, I didn't understand why she would ask such a thing, but this is me living up to that promise. You're my boss and my friend, but you and I are going to start having problems if you don't pull your head out of your ass and stop fucking with her. Same goes for Wilder. Do the pair of you think I'm fucking stupid? That I don't see, feel, and hear everything that goes on in this house? That girl up there has enough shit going on in her life right now, she doesn't deserve to receive backlash from you and Wilder too. Whatever happened in the past is exactly that. In. The. Past. You all have the opportunity to start fresh and make amends, so stop looking backward and decide what sort of relationship you want with her going forward."

Leaving a stunned Hawk behind, I turn on my heel and stride out the door, slamming it shut behind me.

I SPEND the next several hours parked outside Steven's motel with a front-row seat to his boring as fuck evening. When he went out to collect his dinner order from the Chinese restaurant down the road, I snuck into his room and planted a listening device. So not only can I watch him through the window, but I'm privy to everything he says. Not that he's said or done anything interesting or relevant yet. His entire evening has been spent on his phone, making business calls and yelling at people. If I didn't despise him already, I'd hate him for the condescending way he talks to his colleagues on the other end of his phone.

When he eventually strips down to his briefs and pulls the

curtains, blocking my view, I consider calling it a night. The whole evening has been a total bust, but I am now firmly of the opinion that our run-in with him at the gas station was a fucked up twist of fate. This guy is an asshole and a sleazeball, but I don't believe he's Emilia's stalker. After the way I dangled myself in front of him earlier and his close proximity to Emilia, there's no way he'd be so calm and able to concentrate on work. He'd have been researching me as thoroughly as I've been researching him. He'd be doing what I am right now, tracking us down and wanting eyes on Emilia. Not watching shitty cable TV and scrolling through his phone.

Every time I shift in my seat, intending to start the engine and head back to Hawk's, something stops me. However, when the glow of the TV disappears from behind the closed curtains, I decide enough is enough.

Starting the engine, I put the car in gear, and just as I roll out of the parking space, I hear a noise that has me slamming my foot down on the brakes. My eyes flit up to the darkened window of Steven's room, my muscles bunched as my hands fist the steering wheel, and I wait to hear it again.

"Emilia." The groan that follows her name triggers an intense fury inside me. It pumps through my veins and licks up my spine, overwhelming and all-consuming as I throw open the car door and storm toward his room. I can't think straight. Can hardly see through the red mist that has descended over my vision.

I slam my boot into the flimsy wooden door, breaking the lock as it swings open and crashes into the wall, leaving a door handle-shaped hole behind.

"What the—Hey! Get out of my room!" Steven yells, lurching upright at my sudden intrusion. Before he can get another word out, I kick the door shut with my boot and close the distance. He backs up against the headboard, but he doesn't get time to do anything else as I wrap my hand around his throat and slam his head into the wall.

Unbothered by his pathetic attempts to break free, I run my eyes down his chest to where the sheet pools around him. With my other hand, I yank it back and sneer when I find him naked beneath it.

Still pinning him in place, I scour the bed sheets until I find his phone. The screen is still lit up, and I reach over to grab it, snarling when I see the photo he was looking at.

It's a picture of Emilia from the gas station, bent over as she reaches for something on the bottom shelf. Something tells me she wouldn't want this perv jerking off over her, and before I can crush the phone in my fist, I gather enough wit to spit out, "Is this the only one?"

"W-what?"

I slam him back against the wall before repeating my question. "Is this the only copy?"

"Y-y-yes."

Another smack of his head against the wall. "Yes. Yes. It's the only copy."

Focusing back on his phone, I scroll through the rest of his album, making sure he doesn't have any others. There are some seriously disturbing images and far too fucking many dick pics that I will never unsee, but thankfully there are no others of Emilia.

Going back to the one he has of her, I delete it, ensuring I also delete any copies that might be backed up to a virtual drive before slamming the phone into the wall beside his head. The screen fractures and breaks, and satisfied that it's unusable, I drop it on the bed and focus back on the shitstain in front of me.

"Why were you at the gas station today?"

"W-what?"

I'm reaching my fucking breaking point, so instead of

repeating myself, I squeeze his throat until he's gasping for breath and crying like a fucking pussy. When I find the restraint to ease up so he can answer me, he stutters out, "I-I was just after a Gatorade, man. I didn't know she'd be there." I continue to scowl at him until he continues rambling. "I'd been driving all day," he wails. "I just needed a fucking drink."

A tense moment passes as I stare him down, before I hiss out, "You will *never* utter Emilia's name again." Using my hold on his throat, I yank him forward before shoving him back. "You will never *talk to her* again. If you fucking see her, you'll turn around and walk in the opposite direction." I wait until he stutters an agreement before delivering my final threat. "If I find out that you've done *any* of those things, I'll be back, and I'll do a hell of a lot worse than throw you against a wall."

Finishing off my warning with a double punch to his face, leaving him with a black eye he won't soon forget, I storm out of the room and back to my car, high-tailing it out of the parking lot.

My hands flex around the steering wheel the entire drive home, rage still coursing through me far too potently. It's uncharacteristic for me. I'm never this... emotional... with cases. I pride myself on my level-headedness and ability to remain clear-minded in heightened situations, but right now, I feel as though I'm completely unraveling.

Swiping a hand down my face, I shake my head, trying to clear it and gain some perspective. Perspective that isn't the image of Emilia bent over in that shop on that fucking pervert's phone. *God, I should have done worse than give that fucker a black eye.*

Reaching the house, I park outside and relax back into my seat, exhaling a long breath. I need to calm the fuck down before I go in there. The way Emilia looks at me sometimes, like I'm her port in the hurricane, her safety net when everything around her is spinning out of control... I can't let her see me like this, so on edge and frenzied.

I still can't fully explain my actions tonight. The anger behind them or the overwhelming protective urge I felt, but I do realize that something about it felt right, purposeful. It's been a very long time since I felt anything resembling that—that need to protect what's yours.

I'm aware that this job is turning into more than a job, and I'm not sure how I feel about that, but I don't think there's anything I can do to stop it. I'm on this train now. I'm along for the ride, and so long as I keep Emilia safe from her stalker as well as Hawk and Wilder, I guess I'll find out the destination when we get there.

When I once again feel calm, I get out of the car and head into the house. The porch and hall are dimly lit, and through the partially open door of the living room, I can see the flickering lights from the television. Moving toward them, I push open the door and peer in. My eyes immediately land on Emilia. She's lying across the couch, her head in Hawk's lap, sound asleep.

Lifting my gaze, I find Hawk staring at me. His brows are slightly furrowed, and I stiffen beneath his scrutiny. "How is she?"

"Okay, considering. She passed out from one too many glasses of wine about an hour ago. She'll have a hangover in the morning, but hopefully she'll actually get some sleep."

I nod, dropping my gaze to her peaceful form. The lines usually prevalent around her eyes have smoothed out in her sleep, making her appear peaceful. It reminds me of how she looked earlier today, except without her glowing smile.

"How did tonight go?"

Not taking my gaze off her, I answer, "He's not our guy."

Hawk takes a moment to absorb that information. "Tomorrow, we'll sit down and go through everything from the top."

I nod. "I'll carry her up to bed." Crossing the room, I bend so I can slip an arm behind her knees and another under her back. Hawk's hand, slung across the back of the sofa, moves to brush a strand of hair out of her face, his fingers lingering on her jaw before he withdraws.

I lift her up into my arms, and she shifts in my hold until her face is pressed against the front of my shirt. I tighten my arms around her as I duck my head in goodnight to Hawk before striding out of the room.

I take my time ascending the stairs, partly because I don't want to rock her too much or accidentally knock her feet or shoulder against the wall, but also because I'm enjoying the feel of her in my arms. The way she rubs her nose against my top in her sleep and her contented groans.

"Mmm," she hums sleepily, making me chuckle. I glance down to find her wearing an untroubled smile that I feel all the way to the depths of my soul. It's the same one she wore earlier today on our hike, and I find myself promising to do whatever it takes to make her smile like that every day when this is all over.

All too soon, we reach her bedroom door, and I nudge it open with my elbow before stepping inside. Being careful not to jostle her, I lower her down onto her bed. As I go to pull away, she fists my shirt in her hands. "Don't go," she mumbles in her sleep. Her lower lip pushes out in a pout, drawing my attention to her lips, and I swallow back a laugh. "Please." Her tone sounds pleading and desperate, and before I've thought through what I'm doing, I shift her over so I can lay on the bed beside her.

"Shhh," I soothe, stroking her hair and watching in fascination as she relaxes beneath my touch. "I'm not going anywhere."

Rolling onto her side, she wriggles against me until she finds a comfy spot that has her head resting in the middle of my chest. Hesitantly, I wrap my arm around her and relax back against the headboard. Staring down at her, I watch as she sleeps soundlessly, unable to put words to the warm feeling in my chest that slowly radiates outward.

If I had any doubts that this case was different—that *she* was different—they are obliterated with every passing second she's in my arms until my eyes grow heavy and eventually slide shut. Just before I fall asleep, a single thought passes through my mind. A promise. *I won't let the same thing happen to you.*

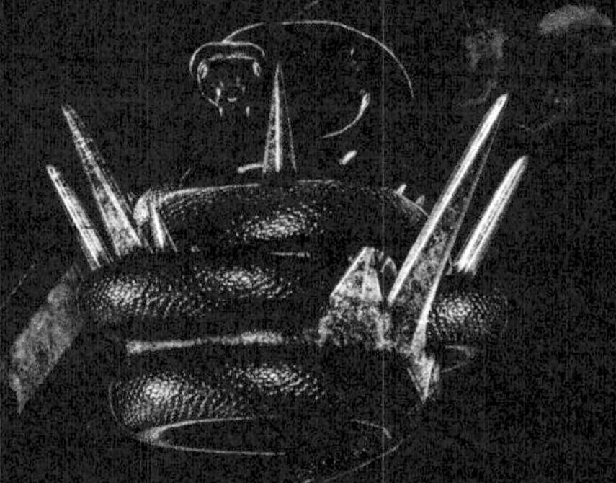

THE RUTHLESS BOYS OF RIDGEWAY

Emilia

CHAPTER 19

I wake with a groan, lifting a hand to press against my pounding temple. *Oh, God. I feel like I'm dying.* Even the simple act of rolling onto my back sends my stomach into an uproar, threatening to revolt as the thudding behind my eyes beats to a faster tune. *What the hell happened last night?*

Refusing to open my eyes because I know it will make my body hate me even more, I walk myself through my hazy memories of yesterday. I remember my hike with Kai, then running into Steven and freaking out on Kai on the car journey home.

When we arrived back here, I rushed up to my room, desperately needing a shower to scrub off the filth left behind by Steven's leer, which is when Hawk came knocking. I'd been putting off going back downstairs. I knew Kai would be in *fix-it* mode, demanding answers and doing whatever it took to either confirm Steven was my stalker or rule him out once and for all.

I smile at the memory of finding Hawk at my bedroom door. I'd assumed it was Kai checking on me, and honestly, I'd been both apprehensive and disappointed to find Hawk. However, when he held out a bowl containing all my favorite sweets, he tempted me downstairs with the promise of chocolate, alcohol, and whatever movie I wanted... Well, who was I to say no? If he was pretending the bathroom incident never happened, then I could do the same.

Of course, one glass of wine turned into two, which turned into two full bottles. Then before I knew it, neither of us was watching the movie, and things had taken a turn for the dangerous.

"Truth or dare."

"Hell no," I shake my head, even though it makes the room spin, and I nearly tilt sideways off the sofa. A drunken giggle escapes as I right myself.

"Okay. Truth for a truth, then."

I chew on my bottom lip before nodding. "Fine, but you first."

He seems to mull over whatever his truth is while I bring my wine glass to my lips. Oh, it's all gone. Oopsies. Distracted, I begin looking around on the floor, trying to remember where I left the bottle. It was definitely around here somewhere. I hope Hawk didn't sneak the end of it when I went to the bathroom. I'll be so pissed!

"I missed you after you left Pac."

My gaze snaps up to Hawk so fast that I see double of him, and I have to blink several times until the two of him merge into one person. "What did you say?"

I feel like I need to hear him repeat himself, this time while I stare at his lips so I can be sure it's definitely him saying those words and not my imagination making shit up.

Instead of indulging me, he smirks and nudges me with his knee. "Your turn."

I chew on my bottom lip while I try to think of something good but not too personal. Should I share something that involves him?

Something light and dumb? Something that actually fucking matters?

"There was never anyone else after you and Wilder."

He cocks a brow. "What about Richard?"

I shake my head. "Richard was the guy I wanted to love. The one I told myself I should *want. Who checked the box for what I naively assumed I needed in a husband in order to complete the perfect little life I had planned for myself."*

"So why didn't you love him?"

"Nu-uh." I shake my head and smirk at him. "Your turn."

A sly grin lifts his lips before he spills another truth. "I'm so ready to be done with college."

My eyebrows lift in surprise. "Really? Huh. I thought you'd be living your best life, going to college parties, embracing fraternity life... working your way through every new class of freshmen."

Throwing his head back, he barks out a laugh. "God, no. Don't get me wrong, I thought I'd be all into it. Hell, after our senior year at Pac, I thought it was exactly what I needed—to let off some steam and actually have some fun."

"So what happened?"

With a shrug of his shoulder, he loses himself in his memories before responding. "It just wasn't what I expected, or maybe it was no longer what I wanted. I dunno, but Wilder ended up dragging me to the parties. He was the one that talked me into joining the frat."

I smirk, knowing exactly how persuasive Wilder can be, and remembering how he and Hawk used to rub each other the wrong way—and no doubt still do at times. I can only imagine the push and pull involved in that conversation.

"None of that shit holds the same appeal it once did."

Nodding my head, I can relate to what he's saying. Senior year changed us all. My time with him and Wilder changed me. It was only when I created some distance between us that I realized just how much I'd changed. How irrevocably *I'd changed.*

I was no longer that freshman who walked through the gates of Pacific Prep at the age of eleven with big dreams and high hopes of one day becoming someone. I wasn't even the same girl who came back for senior year. Meeting Hadley triggered a chain reaction. A butterfly effect that ended with Wilder, Hawk, and me getting all tangled up in one another.

After we crossed that bridge together, there was no going back. None of us realized it at the time, but we came away from that night reborn. The people we once were no longer existed, and along with their demise went every dream, wish, and idea we had for our lives.

Wilder embraced it, Hawk disregarded it, and me? I ran from it.

But maybe it's not too late to make amends, at least with Hawk.

"I get that," I say, giving him a soft smile. "I thought I was doing everything right—school, college, career—" I tick them off one by one—"Then get myself a husband, a house in the suburbs, and settle down with a couple of kids." I flatten my lips as I shake my head. "Except every achievement has felt flat. I'm checking off milestones like they're on a goddamn grocery list—something I have *to do." My shoulders drop as I confess aloud, "It's like, I work my ass off to achieve something, and when I finally do, I don't feel any of the joy or accomplishment I should. I just feel... empty. As though I'm sitting on the sidelines of my own life, watching from a distance, but unable to embrace it fully."*

A moment of silence falls between us until I laugh awkwardly. "I'm drunk. I don't even know what I'm saying." I reach over to grab the remote in need of a distraction, but Hawk's fingers curl around my wrist, stopping me. When I dare look up into the swirling depths of his hurricane eyes, I'm surprised to find nothing but compassion and understanding.

"Nobody should be a passenger in their own life, Em. If that's how you feel, then do something about it."

His words feel like a challenge, one he's begging me to accept. Unintentionally—or maybe my subconscious is trying to tell me something—I lean toward him until his breath fans my face. His eyes drop to my lips, and he slowly lowers his face to mine.

My heart slams painfully against my chest, but right before our lips can touch, images of me on the bathroom floor and him walking away assault my mind, and at the last second, I tilt my head to the side, breaking off our would-be kiss.

His lips end up skimming my cheek, and knowing they're bright red and scorching hot with embarrassment, I cough and mumble, "Umm, how about another movie, yeah? I think a movie sounds good." Grabbing the remote, I make a point of not looking in Hawk's direction as I flick through the channels until I find the first half-decent movie I can find. Ensuring there's plenty of distance between us on the couch, I sit steel-spined and fixated on the television, and that's the last thing I remember.

My cheeks heat with embarrassment simply at the memory of last night. How close we came to kissing—again. I can't believe how badly I wanted to feel his lips on mine one more time, but I'm so damn glad drunk me had the foresight to realize that could only end one way—badly.

Hawk keeps portraying himself as my ally, only to give me whiplash with how quickly he turns on me. Fool me once, shame on you. Fool me twice, shame on me, but fool me three times, and shame on both of us. I can't keep hoping Hawk will be anyone other than who he is. He's not a savior. At least he's not mine. He may not hate me the way Wilder does, but he's not on my side, either. I have to toughen up and learn to stand on my own against these two devils in disguise, and that starts by not fucking kissing them.

Finally wrenching my eyes open, I groan against the bright light streaming around the edges of my curtains. I slowly push up onto my elbows, and when my stomach doesn't climb its way up my throat, I swing my legs over the side of the bed while giving my head a second to stop spinning before standing up.

I take my time going through my morning routine before I venture downstairs, reminding myself that I did nothing all that embarrassing last night so I don't need to hide from Hawk. At least this time he didn't leave me legless on the bathroom floor after delivering the world's most mind-rendering orgasm.

Stepping into the kitchen, my shoulders drop in relief when I find it empty, and I go about making a cup of coffee before taking a seat at the island. Even though I'm enjoying the peace and quiet, I can't help wondering where everyone is. I hadn't seen Kai again after we got home last night—at least, not that I can recall—and seeing as it's a Saturday, Hawk should be around here somewhere, unless he's already run off back to the frat house with Wilder.

I sigh, wishing there was some way to magically fix things with the two of them so that we can get over this awkwardness. With Wilder, it's pure hatred, and no matter what I say, he doesn't want to hear it. However, with Hawk, it's so much more complicated. I don't even know what is going on between us. All I know is that I enjoy the feel of his hands on me and the taste of his kisses on my lips. And I think we kinda get along. We had fun last night. I'm just not sure what any of it means. I'm trying not to look at any of it too closely. I have a tendency to psychoanalyze these things, and for once, I just want to see what happens rather than planning out every second. Besides, with some psycho out there threatening and killing every guy I date or sleep with, now probably isn't the time to be thinking about how good Hawk tastes.

The sound of the front door banging shut startles me out of my thoughts, and butterflies take flight in my stomach when I hear Wilder's voice.

"Yo! Did anybody order something?" he yells loud enough

for everyone in the house to hear him. "I found this on our doorstep."

His voice gets louder as he approaches the kitchen until he steps across the threshold, his eyes connecting with mine. His expression becomes carefully blank when he discovers me sitting there, and his eyes run briefly down my body before he glances away. "I see you're still here."

"Looks like it." Faking nonchalance, I lift my coffee mug to my lips and take a sip, all the while watching him over the rim.

After what happened in the bathroom, I'm fucking done being nice to Wilder and feeling bad for invading his personal space. I didn't ask for this, and despite how badly he may want me gone, I can't fucking leave. I'm not even sure I *want* to leave. I hardly miss my old life. Yeah, I miss having a purpose and getting out of the house to go to work every day, but that's about it. I don't miss the girls from work I'd sometimes grab a drink with or curling up on my sofa in the evenings with a book and a glass of wine. Hell, I've barely even given Mel a passing thought, and other than Hadley, she's my closest friend.

It makes me realize just how removed I was from my own life. It's like I was playing a part in a play—going through the motions but never really engaging. I hadn't realized just how numb I'd become until everything went sideways and I ended up here. It makes me angry that I let myself get that way—like my mother. Oblivious to the problems in my life and pretending that everything was fine by burying my head in work. I never let myself slow down long enough to actually assess the life I was creating for myself, but with very little to do these last few weeks, it has given me plenty of time to honestly think about it. To understand that the life I was living, while on paper it had everything I wanted, was missing the crucial aspects that make life enjoyable.

The only problem is that those crucial aspects that *my* life requires come in the form of two insufferable assholes—one who hates me and the other who enjoys messing with my head.

And let's not get started on Kai, because without his constant presence these last couple of weeks, I'd be a curled-up mess in the corner, rocking back and forth and begging for all this to be a horrible nightmare. He's the reason I haven't completely fallen apart. The reason I even feel safe in this house—both with regards to my stalker and the two cavemen that live inside these walls.

"Shame. I was hoping your stalker might have found you by now."

Ouch. His words hit their target, and based on the smirk that tilts his lips, he knows it.

I quickly wipe any trace of emotion from my face, and ensuring my tone is carefully neutral, say, "Why, so you could stop hiding out at the frat house?"

I watch as his hands tighten around the box he's carrying and his jaw ticks in irritation, but he doesn't immediately hit me with a comeback. Instead, he casually crosses over to the kitchen table and sets the box down on top of it before whirling to face me. Rage burns in his eyes, his nostrils flaring as he descends on me.

"Why the hell would I be hiding? From you?" His coinciding laugh is cold. "You must think pretty highly of yourself." Leaning down, he presses his palms into the edge of the island on either side of me, bringing our faces within inches of one another. "Not everything is about you, Emilia. I've got plenty of girls on campus to keep me occupied. This is my senior year, after all. Gotta make the most of that easy pussy before graduation."

It takes everything in me not to let him see the angry snarl threatening to lift my lips or the tightening of the muscle at the back of my jaw at the picture he's painting. "So that's why you nearly fucked me in the bathroom—because all that *easy pussy* just isn't cutting it for you anymore?"

"I did *not* nearly fuck you. I was *toying* with you, 'cause that's all you fucking are to me—a toy." His lips are so close to mine that spittle hits the corner of my mouth as he snarls.

Removing one hand from the island behind me, he lifts it up to my hair and begins winding it around his finger, stroking the soft strands with his thumb. The anger slowly falls from his face as his gaze shifts to where he's playing with my hair, before a wicked smirk that makes my heart skip a step replaces it. "How many times have you tried to get yourself off, picturing my dick sliding into that sopping wet cunt of yours? *Please, Wilder,*" he mimics in a high-pitched voice before laughing cruelly. "So fucking desperate for me, aren't you, Angel? You don't even care that I hate you, you still want what you'll never get."

My thighs clench on reflex, and Wilder catches the subtle action, glancing down to my apex as though he's got x-ray vision that can penetrate through the layers of clothing. "You're wet right now, aren't you? Despite how I left you—turned on and begging for me—you still fucking want me." Another cruel laugh, but I see through his act. He can't hide the dilatation of his pupils, and when I squirm in my chair, his nostrils flare with primal hunger. "Tell me," he growls, his voice dipping an octave. "How many times did you make yourself come after I left you on that bathroom floor?"

Although my nipples are chafing against the fabric of my top, and I know he can tell how turned on I am, I'm proud of the way I lift my chin to meet his eyes head-on. "None."

"Tut tut, Angel," he tsks. "Don't lie to me."

My own smirk plays out, and I take great satisfaction in my next words. "I'm not. Hawk did the job for you."

As soon as his name passes my lips, Wilder's hand clenches into a fist, yanking on my strands of hair still wrapped around his finger, but I bite back my cry of pain, keeping my eyes on him as I watch the vast range of emotions flicker across his face. Eventually, he hisses, "You're lying."

"Am I?" I know I'm only adding fuel to the fire that is Wilder Clearwater and, no doubt, putting a wedge between him and Hawk, but I can't care about that right now. I need to start leveling the playing field between Wilder and me, and this right here is strike number one of my attack. "Why don't you ask him?"

I could almost laugh as I witness his face change. A red, angry flush fills his cheeks, and his nostrils flare, his jaw repeatedly clenching and unclenching as his brows pull down. His eyes bounce all over my face, attempting to find the lie behind my words, and I let him look his fill, having nothing to hide.

Eventually, he scoffs and looks away. "Yeah, well, don't go thinking Hawk is your hero. He's only looking to get his dick wet." When I open my lips to protest, he continues. "Do you know why he calls you Little Sparrow?" He glances back and forth between my eyes before answering his own question. "Because Hawks eat little Sparrows like you for breakfast. He's going to chew you up and spit you out."

I swallow around the lump in my throat, mentally replaying every interaction with Hawk and wondering if there was an ulterior motive behind it all. Is he just playing me the same way Wilder is?

I'm scanning his face, looking for any tell that he's lying, when I hear approaching footsteps before Kai and Hawk enter the room.

"Uhh, what's going on?" Hawk asks, moving toward us, while Kai walks over to peer at the box on the kitchen table. Still not looking away from Wilder, I notice out of the corner of my eye that they are both wearing loose basketball shorts and tanks, having apparently come from the gym downstairs.

Finally releasing me from his incensed gaze, Wilder lets his hand drop away as he spins to face Hawk with his indignation. "You tell me, brother," he snarls.

My eyes dart back and forth between the two. Animosity is palpable in the air, practically crackling between them as Hawk steps up on my other side, so they're both boxing me in. I barely get to appreciate the musky scent wafting from him or the sheen of sweat still coating his skin as though he stopped mid-workout to come up here, before Wilder's angry snark interrupts my thoughts.

"Is this why you've been spending all your nights here instead of at the frat?"

Hawk rolls his eyes. "Don't be so dramatic. It's only been a couple of nights."

Wilder scoffs in response. "Try every night for the last week."

That information piques my interest. I obviously knew Hawk was around more these last few days than he had been since I'd gotten here. But I hadn't realized he'd been here every night.

Hawk opens his mouth to respond, but Kai's snapped, "Hey!" cuts across whatever he was going to say, as all three of us turn to face him. "Where did this come from?" He tilts his head to indicate the small, plain cardboard box on the table.

"I dunno." Wilder shrugs. "It was sitting by the door when I got here."

"There's no address label on it or any indication of who it's for."

"So?" Wilder gives another unbothered shrug, clearly finding Kai's questioning pointless, but as I stare at the bland, brown box on the table, goosebumps form along my skin and I shiver as though a sixth sense is warning me away from it. "Which one of you ordered something?"

"I didn't," Hawk immediately pipes up.

Both of them focus on Kai, who shakes his head. "Not me. I haven't ordered anything to the house, just in case."

All three of them turn to look at me; by now, my hands are trembling uncontrollably. "Why are you all looking at me?" I squeak.

"Em, did you order anything?" Kai asks, but I can see he already knows the answer. He's no longer looking at me, instead bending to carefully inspect the box.

"N-no. I don't even have access to the internet to buy anything, and Kai's already told me not to use my cards in case they can be tracked."

Before the words are even out of my mouth, Hawk has moved over to stand next to Kai, the two of them frowning at the box as though that's enough for it to spill its secrets.

A tense moment of silence fills the room, and I'm certain the only sound is my erratic heartbeat, but Wilder scoffs. "Jeez, the three of you. It's probably something meant for one of the neighbors."

"Then why is there no address label? No postage stamp? Nothing."

"I don't fucking know, but what else could it be?"

My hand whips up to cover my mouth, even though my shocked gasp still breaks free. "Please don't let it be any more body parts."

Hawk immediately takes a significant step back, as if he thinks it's about to explode and cover him in blood and bits of flesh.

The three of us continue to stare at the box while Kai walks in a circle around it, inspecting it from every angle.

"We should check the security cameras," Hawk states. Kai nods and grabs his laptop, moving to stand beside me. Hawk and Wilder crowd around us as he pulls up the relevant program, and the screen fills with numerous small boxes, each one showing an image of a different room in the house.

"Wait, do you have cameras in every single room?" I question, not quite able to believe my eyes as I gape at the screen.

"What the fuck, dude?" Wilder growls, outraged. He points at an image on the bottom left of the screen. "That's my bedroom!"

My face heats as all the dirty things he and Hawk have done to me in various rooms of this house bubble to the forefront of my mind. *Oh my god, did Kai see any of that? Kill me now! Please, God, just open up the ground and swallow me whole before I die of embarrassment.*

"That's an invasion of my privacy!" Wilder argues.

Uncaring, Kai just stares at him. "So? Maybe if you were here, we could have talked about it. But since you were MIA, I had to make executive decisions for Emilia's safety."

Wilder bares his teeth like a rabid dog.

"Pull up today's footage of the front door," Hawk says, getting us back on track before Wilder can completely derail us with his tantrum.

Obeying, Kai pulls up the video feed for the front door, and zips back over the day. I watch cars and the occasional person walk past, until the entire screen goes fuzzy.

"What the hell?" Kai mumbles under his breath.

"What just happened?" I question, staring at the white noise as he taps on the keyboard.

"The camera went out."

"What do you mean it went out?" I frown.

"Someone must have interfered with the signal. It stopped recording."

"So we don't have anything that can identify this guy?" Wilder asks, sounding furious, although I'm willing to bet he's still pissed over his invasion of privacy, rather than the fact we still have no idea who my stalker is.

Kai shakes his head. "No. They must have had a signal jammer."

"But how did they know we even had cameras?" Hawk argues. "You wouldn't see them unless you knew to look for them."

Kai's only response is a shrug of his shoulders. "Either they knew to look, or they brought a jammer just in case."

With a sigh, he closes the laptop, and as if lured in by its ominous presence, my gaze zeros in on the box sitting on the kitchen table. I'm not the only one. All of us stare at it for a long moment, no one daring to move closer as if sensing the life-altering secrets hiding inside.

Eventually, Kai approaches and eases off the lid. I don't even realize I've moved, but the next thing I know, I've slid off the bar stool and stepped toward the table for a closer look.

Hawk's arm flies out to hold me back, and I stop, leaning forward as far as I can in his grip to get a better look at what's inside.

Kai pauses with the lid in his hand as he stares at the item on top before slowly resuming lowering the lid onto the table and carefully reaching into the box.

"W-what's in it?" I ask, not wanting to know but *needing* to know. I don't see any blood or body parts, not that that necessarily means anything good.

Kai shakes his head, not once lifting his attention from the box. When he doesn't explain any further, I push against Hawk's arm and march closer. The movement draws Kai's attention, and he immediately yells out, "No! Hawk, stop her!"

Hawk jumps into action, wrapping his thick muscular arms that may as well be steel bands around my waist and hauling me back against his chest.

"What?!" I cry out, fighting against his hold while yelling at Kai. "What is it? Is it about me? Is it from the stalker?"

"You don't wanna see this, Em, trust me." Kai's cryptic words only make me more curious, and I fight harder against Hawk.

"NO! You can't keep this from me, Kai! This is my life! My livelihood! My fucking sanity that this asshole is messing with. If it's from him, I deserve to know what is in it."

Kai finally lifts his usually emerald, green eyes to mine. Today they are clouded over, appearing more jaded than normal. Something about them gives me pause, but before I can rethink my decision, he gives a slow nod for Hawk to let me go.

Slowly, as though reluctant to do so, Hawk loosens his hold, and I slide out of his arms and move toward Kai. Not that Hawk lets me go far. He remains on my right side, and surprisingly, I notice Wilder move to my left, the three of us approaching the table as one united front. Their silent support bolsters me and gives me the courage to face whatever is in that box—so long as it doesn't contain body parts belonging to someone else I care about.

My mouth is bone dry, and something hard and unyielding sits in the back of my throat as I approach, yet I refuse to cower. Refuse to let this psycho take one more thing from me.

As I reach the table, Kai pushes the box toward me, and I swallow nervously as I meet his gaze one final time, reading his silent plea for me not to look and ignore it before lowering my eyes to the contents of the box.

The first thing I see makes the breath stall in my chest. My eyes bounce all over the picture staring up at me, seeing it but unable to truly process its significance. It was a ghostly pale face, smeared with streaks of red and offset by dark brown eyes that would usually look at me with such warmth and a type of kindness I just wanted to fall into. Except, in the image, those eyes are listless. Vacant. Dead. They're dead because *he* is dead.

"Richard." His name is no louder than a whisper as I continue to stare at the picture. I should be screaming or crying or *something*. I know I should, but I'm not. I can't. I'm entirely fucking numb.

Kai clears his throat, but still, I don't look away. "There's, uh, more." He says it as kindly as one can, and I simply nod, unable to respond in any other way. "I'm sorry, Em."

Another paralyzed nod. I can't stop looking at his face and wondering what his last moments were like. Was he in pain? Did he die quickly? God, I hope so. I can't bear the thought of him being held captive for the last two weeks only to be brutally murdered. A single tear slips down my cheek, the only emotion I'm capable of, but I make a promise to Richard—and to myself—that when this is all over, I will have a proper burial for him. He was a good man and a great friend. He deserved far, far more from this life than he was given, and for that, I am truly sorry.

"I thought you hadn't found a body?" I ask absently, still incapable of ungluing my eyes from Richard's lifeless form. It wouldn't matter even if I did, I'd still see his body crystal clear in my mind's eye.

"I haven't."

God, somehow that makes all of this even worse.

When Kai speaks again, his voice is still soft and soothing, even though his words are anything but. "There's more than just him."

It's enough for me to tear my gaze from Richard and gape at him. "W-what do you mean?" My stomach rolls just thinking about there being pictures of other dead people in the box, and my brain goes into overdrive trying to figure out who else this psycho could have killed. Surely he wouldn't have gone back to those few guys from college whom I slept with? He'd already scared them off, and other than Richard, there was no one else. So who the hell else could be dead?!

Tactfully reaching into the box, Kai lifts out the bundle of photographs. He's careful not to let me see them as he flicks through the first however many before lifting them off the top of the pile and setting them upside down to one side. I can only guess that they are more of Richard, and before I can punish myself any more than I already have by demanding to see them, I instead focus back on Kai as he spreads the remaining photos out on the tabletop.

My hand flies to my mouth, and I gasp as my eyes bounce from one photo to the next. Images of Hawk and Wilder coming and going from the house, of Kai in the front door or peering out a window, even one of me sitting in this very kitchen late one night making a hot chocolate. Upon seeing it, I snatch it up and walk shakily over to the kitchen window above the sink. There's a small outside terrace with steps leading down to the garden below, which is also accessible via the double doors at the back of the large gym in the basement, and it only takes me a second to realize the photo has been taken by someone standing near the steps.

"H-he's been watching us." I spin back to face them. "*All* of us."

"Yeah, and he doesn't seem to be too happy about the fact that you're living with three guys." Wilder plays it off as a joke, but I can see the worry in his eyes as he turns the photo in his hand around for me to see. It's one of him walking on campus—demonstrating that this psycho hasn't just been watching the house—but what is even more disturbing is the fact that his eyes have been crossed out. I stare in horror at the image before anxiously crossing back over to the table and glancing over all the others.

They're all the same. Every image of Kai, Wilder, and Hawk

has their eyes or faces scored out. Some have been done so vigorously that the person has torn right through the photo.

I'm still staring slack-jawed at the photos when Hawk speaks up, his tone all business as he, presumably, directs his question to Kai. "What do we do? How do we deal with this?"

My thoughts race as I try to think through the fog of panic clawing at my insides.

This has to be Steven.

I hadn't even realized I'd spoken that thought aloud until Kai responds.

"It's not Steven, Em."

Lifting my head to look at him, I insist, "It *has* to be him. He must have followed us home yesterday. H-how else would this person know where I'm staying?"

"Em." The steel in Kai's tone stops my rambling. "It's not him."

My lips part to argue further, but Kai lifts his hand, and I spot something I hadn't noticed before. The knuckles on his right hand are red and swollen. *They didn't look like that yesterday*. And he and Hawk would have worn gloves if they were sparring this morning. It's on the tip of my tongue to ask him what happened, but he speaks first.

"Just trust me, Em. It's not him."

I meet his eyes that are such a similar color to mine, only lighter and filled with so much more warmth and conviction, and I find myself believing him. "Okay."

But if it's not him, then who is it?

Frowning, I go back to scanning the photos on the table while Kai and Hawk talk back and forth, spitballing ideas. I'm not paying them—or Wilder—any attention as I reach for the box, spotting a piece of paper wedged at the bottom of it. Ensuring I only touch the edges, I extract it from the box and unfold it. My breaths are unsteady and rough, and the world around me feels as though it disappears as a whooshing sound rushes through my ears.

None of them can give you what I can. When will you open your eyes and realize it should be you and me? How much longer will you make me wait, Em? Am I going to have to dispose of every man in your life before you see what's right in front of you?

"I have to leave." I'm still staring at the note, my words too quietly spoken to be heard over the argument that seems to have broken out between Hawk and Kai. But the more I think about it, the more I realize I'm right. Lifting my head, I repeat myself in a tone that slices through whatever they're bickering over. "I have to leave."

Both of them turn to stare at me, blinking before my words register, and their eyebrows dip in mirrored aggravation.

"Hell no!"

"You're not leaving!"

They both speak at the same time, their words brokering no argument.

Tough. I refuse to let anyone else suffer because of me. I will *not* let them end up like Richard.

"I have to! You're all in danger if I stay here." Kai opens his mouth to argue, but I already know what he's going to say, and I cut him off before he can get so much as a word out. "I won't *let* you put yourselves at risk for me."

"That's not your call," Kai growls, glaring at me.

"It's exactly my call. This is *my* life. *My* stalker. I appreciate that Hadley was trying to help by getting you involved and bringing me here, but she's only put all of you at risk. Our best chance is if I sneak out without being seen tonight. In a couple of days, he'll discover I'm no longer here, and hopefully when he realizes none of you know where I am, he will leave you alone."

"And what about you?" I can tell Kai is only indulging me. He has no intention of letting me simply disappear into the night.

"I have some spare cash," I say, shrugging a shoulder and totally making this up on the fly. "And I'm sure you know how to get a fake ID? I could travel under an alias."

"And what happens when this psycho catches up to you, and you have no one around to protect you?"

Scowling, I snap, "The point is that he *won't* catch me. I just have to stay low, keep my head down." Even as I say it, I know it's far-fetched, and honestly, the thought of going out there on my own and facing this stalker by myself should he find me is absolutely terrifying. It's not what I want to do, but I know I can't continue to stay here and endanger any of them.

A scoff behind me has me whirling around to glare at Wilder. Of course, he has something to say now. He's been far too quiet. "I doubt you'll get very far."

"Well, thank goodness I don't give a crap what you think."

Rolling his eyes at my attitude, he holds up a photograph for me to look at. It's a different one than the last one he showed me. In this one, Wilder is at a party on campus. I grit my teeth as I glare daggers at the girl curled up against his chest, his arm slung over her shoulder as he dangles a beer between his fingers.

"You at a party. Wow. What a surprise." My voice drips with sarcasm, earning me a hard stare from him.

"This party was two weeks ago." He waits until his words sink in. "Only a couple of nights after you arrived here."

"Are you sure?" Kai barks, moving to snatch the photo from Wilder's outstretched hand.

"Yup." He pops the "p," displaying as much attitude as I did a second ago. Leveling me with a deliberately blank expression, he says, "I remember because I intentionally went out with the aim of forgetting all about you."

Kai whirls on him. "Yeah, and in the process, you could have talked about Emilia to anyone, and you'd have been too drunk to even remember."

It only lasts a second, but I catch it when Wilder's carefully placed mask slips, and the reality of what he may have done hits him. By the time Hawk speaks in his defense, he's already concealed the little blip of emotion he let spill.

"He didn't. I'm not in that photo, but I was there that night, keeping an eye on him."

"And what about all the other nights when you were here, and he was alone on campus?" Kai continues to berate. "Did you go to any parties alone where you got drunk? Or talk to any of your frat buddies?"

"No," Wilder growls, glaring furiously at Kai. "I wouldn't have done that."

Stepping up to him until the two of them are chest to chest, Kai delivers his final blow, "But you can't be certain. You don't know for sure that you never mentioned her, and therein lies the problem."

Wilder shoves Kai in the chest, pushing him back a step. "What problem? What the hell does it matter how he found her? He knows she's here, so what the fuck are we going to do about it?"

"*You* aren't going to do anything. Why don't you go back to pretending she doesn't exist and let me and Hawk handle the situation." Kai shakes his head in disappointment. "The less you know, the better."

"Fuck that shit!" Wilder yells, but before he can continue,

Kai once again steps up to him. They're both the same height, but Kai straightens his spine, giving him an extra half an inch.

"What? You suddenly give a shit? Or are you just trying to protect your own ass?"

Wilder snarls, but before things can escalate, I place a hand on both of their arms. "Stop." Neither one of them looks at me or acknowledges my presence. "*Please*, stop. There's enough to deal with without you two at each other's throats."

"Emilia's right," Hawk states, backing me up. "Wilder, you're either in or out, but if you're in, there are no more parties or getting drunk or hiding out at the frat house."

"Like hell, I'm going to let myself get wasted when there's some vindictive psycho on the loose who wants to scratch my eyes out." Wilder tries to make light of the situation, but when both Hawk and Kai continue to stare at him, waiting for a serious response, he sighs and rolls his eyes, his shoulders dropping as he lets go of some of the tension. "Fine, I'm in."

Stepping back, Kai nods in acknowledgment before pinning me with a grave stare. "And you're not fucking going anywhere either."

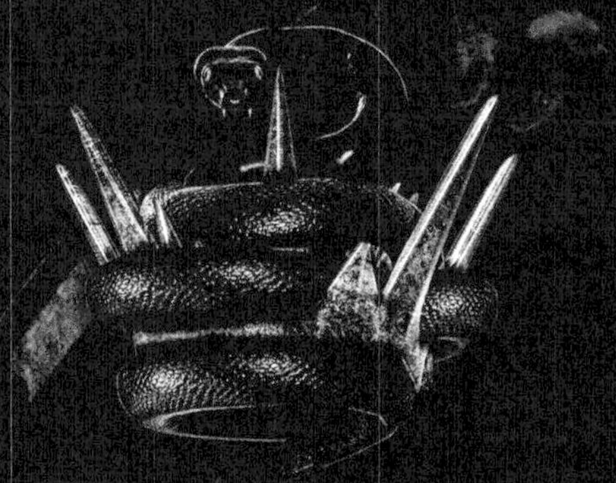

THE RUTHLESS BOYS OF RIDGEWAY

Emilia

CHAPTER 20

The rest of the day is spent in heated arguments. The only thing everyone seems to be able to agree on is that things need to change, but with every idea suggested, someone points out a fatal flaw that sends us back to the drawing board.

I'm still of the opinion that I should run as fast and as far from here as I can, and every time a new plan falls through, I get closer and closer to thinking that's exactly what I need to do.

The ringing of a phone draws me back to the current argument—whether I should stay here or go to a safe house.

"I don't want to go to a safe house," I argue as Hawk pushes back from the table and steps away to answer his phone. "Clearly, whoever this is knows I'm associated with you, so even if I go to a safe house, they'll probably just track me down again." Besides, I'm sick of hiding and letting other people stand between me and this asshole. I realize running isn't much better, but at least it would just be me—no one else taking the fall for my shit and getting hurt in the process. And at least I'd feel like I was actively doing something, instead of just sitting here, hiding out like a wimp.

Kai spears me with a narrowed gaze as though he can read my inner thoughts, and not wanting him to read anything on my face, I quickly distract him by asking, "Did Mel ever get back to us?"

His shoulder's instantly drop. "No, Em. I'm sorry."

I just shrug a shoulder. "It was a long shot, anyway," I mumble dejectedly.

An awkward silence falls between us, until Hawk calls out, "Emilia."

I practically jump out of my chair, happy to momentarily forget about the fact every turn we take seems to be a dead end.

"Hadley wants to talk to you," Hawk explains, handing me the phone.

Hawk had called her earlier, but she'd been in class, so he'd just left a voicemail telling her to call him back when she got home. I'm guessing she's home now, and Hawk has just gotten her up to speed on the drama happening over here.

"Hey." Despite the tiredness in my voice, my smile is genuine as I answer the phone.

"God, how are you holding up?" Hadley asks, never one to beat around the bush.

"Oh, you know, I'm great."

Hadley scoffs. "The truth, Em."

My shoulders drop as I dispel a long exhale. "I've been better," I confess.

"I'm so sorry, Em. I didn't think he'd be able to track you here. Kai got you out of your place so quickly, and there was no passenger log for you on the plane. I don't... I don't understand how they even tracked you here."

"Same." I sigh. "I haven't even left the goddamn house, except for yesterday, and whoever this is already knew I was here." I chew on my lip before saying, "Kai thinks Wilder maybe got drunk and blabbed at a party."

"No way," Hadley quickly interjects. "There's not a chance in hell Wilder would have done that. He might have his issues, but he'd never want to see you hurt. Not like that."

Refusing to think too deeply about what Hadley is saying, I shrug. "It's not like it matters much now anyway." With another sigh, I say in a quieter voice, "I don't know what to do. I can't continue to stay here and put them at risk, and whoever this is knows I'm associated with you now. I—I..."

"So help me God, Em, you better not be thinking what I think you are!"

"I won't let him hurt them."

Hadley snorts on the other end of the phone. "Please. Kai can more than look after himself, and Hawk has an entire company to back him up. One word, and there can be dozens of security surrounding all of you." There's a moment of silence before she speaks again, her voice more insistent this time. "Emilia, they know what they're doing, trust me. Trust *them.* Don't do anything foolish."

The two of us talk for a while longer, and she fills me in on what's been happening with her. It feels good to lose myself in something mundane and forget about my own personal crisis for a while.

By the time I step back into the kitchen, Hawk, Wilder, and Kai are huddled around the table, talking in low voices. They look up when I enter, and Kai smiles encouragingly. "We think we've got a plan."

My eyes shift to Hawk and Wilder, their expressions not quite as reassuring as Kai's. "Okayyyy..." Walking over, I take the empty seat beside Kai. "What is it?"

"We lure this fucker out." My head swivels to gape at Kai.

"What?!"

He just stares at me like it's the most obvious plan ever. "Hiding isn't working, and if anything, we're even further from figuring out who this person is than we were when you first arrived. The only two options we're left with are running—which we've already established you aren't doing—and luring him out."

"Uh, okay, but how do we lure him out?"

"We bait him."

At hearing Hawk's voice, I turn my head to look at him, frowning. "Bait him? With what? Me?"

Hawk makes a *sort of* gesture with his head before flicking his gaze to Kai. Following, I glance back and forth between them until the penny drops.

"You." The word snaps off the end of my tongue as I continue to bounce my gaze between them. "You mean *you'll* be the bait."

Hearing the refusal in my tone, Kai gives me a placating look. "Emilia, this makes the most sense."

"Putting yourselves at risk makes the most sense?" I seethe, glaring at all three of them. "No. I'm saying no." Fixing Wilder in my sights, I demand, "How are you on board with this?"

Holding up his hands in a conciliatory gesture, Wilder says, "I agree with the logic of the plan, but I'm not the one putting myself at risk for you."

My eyes narrow before I dismiss him, focusing back on Hawk and Kai.

"*I'm* going to pretend to be your boyfriend," Kai states, like it's the most natural thing to say.

"Boyfriend?" I croak.

"No, *I'm* going to be her boyfriend," Hawk growls, smacking his hand on the table.

The two bicker back and forth for a minute before Wilder speaks up, a condescending smirk on his lips. "You must be so proud of yourself, Angel. You've got these two fighting over you."

"I don't want anyone fighting over me," I snap irritably, a headache forming at the base of my skull. Pushing to my feet, I plant my palms on the table and stare at all three of them. "I don't want any of this. I don't want *any of you* to put yourselves in harm's way. This is *my* problem to solve. If Hadley hadn't involved Kai, none of you would even know about this.

"Yeah, and you'd probably be locked in some whacko's basement while he tells you to put the lotion on," Wilder drawls. I'm left momentarily speechless as images of exactly that flicker across my mind.

Hawk jabs his elbow into Wilder's side, making him grunt, while Kai tells him to shut the fuck up. It's enough of a distraction to pull my thoughts back to the present, and despite the new chill in my bones, I force my features into a scowl.

"I'm vetoing this plan. Either come up with a different one that doesn't involve any of you possibly dying, or I'll—" I hesitate, not entirely sure what to say. "Or I'll think of something myself."

That was a bit of a lame-ass ending to my speech, but regardless, I stomp away from the table before any of them can argue. Heading up to my room, I close the door shut behind me and collapse onto my back on the bed. In the silence of the room, my headache begins to dissipate, yet my thoughts only grow louder as everything they just bombarded me with and Hadley's plea for me not to do something stupid play on repeat in my head.

I can't let them put themselves in harm's way for me. I can't let anyone else die *for me.*

Yeah, but you aren't asking them to do this. They're volunteering. They want *to help.*

And what? I'm just supposed to stand back and let them put themselves at risk?

It's not like they don't know what they're signing up for. They've all seen what happened to Richard, yet they're still willing to help. Besides, didn't Hadley say they could more than handle themselves? Between them, they have experience and resources on their side. Richard didn't have any of that, plus he didn't even know he needed to be on the lookout for a crazy-ass stalker. If anyone's going to have a chance of catching this guy before he catches you, it's them.

I groan aloud at my inner thoughts, rubbing at my eyes in an effort to dispel them.

At a knock on my door, I lean up on my elbows, arching a brow when Wilder steps into the room. He closes the door behind him and leans against it, his eyes focused on me as he crosses one jean-clad leg over the other.

I scan his face before lowering my gaze, running my eyes along his body. This is the first time he hasn't been staring at me with hostile aggression, and I take my time noting the changes in him since we were at school. He's bulked out some —probably having been dragged downstairs to the gym with Hawk—but he's still lean in all the right places.

I have to fight a smirk, noticing he still has his quirky sense of style, with his black and purple vans, dark jeans, and a black t-shirt that says *story of my life: I knew better but I did it anyway.* I wonder if that's meant to be some sort of reference to us, but I don't dare ask.

"Do you remember that whole thing with Deke back at Pac?" I frown, not sure where he's going with this. "You were so pissed at me because I got him to stop harassing you."

"He was my problem to solve." Pushing myself upright, I cross my legs on top of the bedsheets.

He nods as though he understands, but his tone says otherwise. "That's the thing about you, Emilia. You always have to do everything yourself. You never ask for help, even when a situation is beyond your control. I used to admire your independence, but that pride of yours will get you killed one day."

Frowning, I feel a tad defensive as I explain, "My whole life, I've been taught to be self-sufficient. To rely only on myself. To fight my own battles. My mom..." I duck my head, pulling at a loose thread on my sheet. "My dad hurt her—badly—and she never really recovered. I—I never wanted to end up like her."

"Fair enough, but those two guys downstairs aren't asking for you to rely on them. They aren't waiting around for you to find the balls to ask them for help. They're already committed. You let your hubris get in the way once. Are you really going to let it kill you this time?"

Finding the courage, I lift my head to meet his eyes. "Wouldn't you prefer if I just left? Why are you trying to talk me into letting Hawk and Kai help?" When he just shrugs, I push harder. "I'm honestly surprised you haven't shoved me out the front door and left me to fend for myself."

He smirks. "Maybe I'm not done torturing you myself."

"Oh great," I grumble, rolling my eyes. In the split second where I take my eyes off him, he pushes off the door and closes the distance between us until he's towering over the bed. Leaning down, his close proximity forces me backward until I'm resting on my elbows once again, his hands planted in the mattress on either side of my hips and his face looming above mine.

"You complain, and yet you keep putting yourself directly in my line of sight."

"Not on purpose, asshole."

When Wilder chuckles, his warm breath fans over my lips. "Keep telling yourself that, Angel."

His words only add fuel to the flames catching fire inside me, stoking them until it's a raging inferno. "If anything, you're the one that keeps seeking *me* out."

He doesn't like that if the snarl that lifts his lips is any indication.

"If that's the case, then it's only because I feel the need to punish you."

"Because the punishment I dealt myself just wasn't enough."

"No!" he snarls furiously. "It wasn't. *You're* the one that did this to us. You took something that could have been amazing and twisted it into this hateful thing that eats away at everything around it until there's nothing left but this gaping black hole of nothingness."

Tears slip out and run down my cheeks until they drip off the edge of my jaw. "I know." The words are barely more than a broken whisper, yet Wilder is too incensed to hear any of it as he continues on his rampage.

"The only time I feel anything other than empty is when you're crying and screaming and begging beneath my hands. It's not fair, Emilia. It's not fucking FAIR!" The last word comes out in a furious roar, his brown eyes nearly black with anger and his nostrils flaring.

The tears are streaming continuously down my face now. Blinking them away, I reach up a hand to soothe the tic in his jaw. "You're right. You deserve to feel something other than nothingness." My fingers move to trail along his lower lip, my eyes following the movement. It's the first time since I've been here that he's let me openly touch him, and *god*, I've missed the feel of his heated skin beneath mine, the coarse hair of day-old stubble. Lifting my eyes to meet his chaotic, wild chestnut brown ones, I murmur for only him to hear, "So punish me."

His gaze bores into mine, giving nothing away, and then all of a sudden, his hands are on my hips and I'm being flipped over onto all fours. "What the—"

A hard slap to my ass makes me cry out in surprise. "Shut up, Emilia. You asked for this, remember?"

My mouth slams shut, and I don't say another word as he

rips my leggings down my legs, taking my panties with them until I'm bare from the waist down. Grabbing an ass cheek in each of his hands, he uses his thumbs to spread them apart, giving himself an unobstructed view. "Always so fucking wet for me, aren't you, Angel?"

I twist to look over my shoulder, wanting to see him, but the movement catches his attention, snapping his gaze up from between my thighs. "Nu-uh. Hands on the bed, face forward." He waits until I obey before he spreads my ass wider, and in the next second, I feel his nose running along my slit. "I can smell how turned on you are."

God, he has no idea. Even though I know exactly how this will end, I never want him to stop touching me. I know exactly what he meant earlier. One of the only times I feel alive is when I'm breaking apart beneath his touch, or when I'm arguing with Hawk, or hiking with Kai. Everything else just pales in comparison. It's like every tingle or skip of my heart that I've gotten around another guy has been a watered-down version. I simply hadn't realized it until I met Wilder and Hawk. The effect they had on me was the other extreme. It was undeniable and all-consuming. Overpowering and terrifying all at once, yet it exhilarated me and made me forget about everything other than being with them.

Back then, it sent me running far from the two of them, but as Wilder dives in to feast on me, licking, sucking, and biting until I'm squirming and muttering incomprehensible pleas, I let myself sink into that heady, potent feeling. It crashes over me like a wave, tugging me down into its depths until I'm surrounded by everything Wilder. Nothing exists except the two of us.

Time loses all meaning until I'm trembling, barely managing to hold myself upright as I begin to fall apart.

"No," I cry when he slows his pace, pulling back until his

tongue only skims my sensitive skin. He chuckles against my folds, the vibration sending a new jolt of pleasure through me, but it's nothing more than a tease.

He shifts behind me until he can grab my hair, wrenching my neck backward and forcing me to arch my spine. Bringing his face to mine, he licks along the seam of my mouth. It is by no means a kiss. I'm not even sure what I'd call it, but it's far less intimate and more primal than a kiss. "Do you taste yourself? Taste how much you want this?" Flicking my tongue out, I lick along my upper lip before sucking my lower one into my mouth. I can taste myself, but I also taste him, and the combination, together with his possessiveness, makes me moan.

Releasing his hold, he moves back between my thighs. This time his fingers join the party as he coats them in the mess he made before dragging them upward until the tip of one is pressed against my asshole.

He groans at the tight ring of muscle that pushes against his finger as he slides the tip in. "I still remember how fucking tight you were. I thought you were going to hold my dick hostage and never let it go."

With another push, he slides his finger all the way in, and we both groan this time. He begins to finger me slowly, igniting new nerves and stoking the flames. "Has anyone else ever been here, Angel?"

I shake my head. "No. No one. Only you." I push back against him, needing more than his slow teasing, but he doesn't oblige me as he continues his maddening pace, not acknowledging my answer to his question.

A few more pumps, and he adds another finger, upping his pace until I'm panting and pleading with him for more. "What do you need, Angel? Use your words?"

"Your." Pant. "Fingers." Pant. "On my." Pant. "Clit."

I'm so shocked when he actually does what I want, that I cry out and throw my head back, riding both of his hands as I race toward the light.

"God, you look so fucking sexy when you drop your inhibitions," Wilder murmurs, and I'm pretty sure he doesn't even realize he's saying that aloud. "You should see how hot you are taking what you want—what you need."

"Yes," I moan. "Oh, God, yes!" I'm right on the precipice.

"Too bad I can't let you have it." Wilder's tone is cutting, lacking any of the awe I heard a second ago.

"No!" I sob when his hands suddenly leave me, and my legs give out, sending me crashing into the mattress.

He tsks behind me. "Don't tell me you're done already, Angel? We've only gone one round so far."

He slaps me across the ass, and I whimper before searching deep for the energy to push myself back onto my knees. The second I'm in position, he starts all over again, edging me just as badly as he did in the bathroom the other day until I can't physically lift myself off the bed anymore.

Seeming to realize I'm out of energy, he rolls me over, using his knees to shove my legs apart and settling between them.

His eyes slowly roam over my messy hair, tear-stained face, and flushed skin until they linger on my apex, where he can see the sticky mess coating my thighs from multiple near-orgasms.

The further south he gets, the more the look in his eyes turns from lust and desire to anger and irritation. No longer able to look him in the face, I drop my gaze, noticing the way he runs the palm of his hand over his jean-clad erection. Is that what has him so annoyed? The fact that he's turned on by what he sees? Well, if it annoys him, it has the opposite effect on me. Seeing how much I still affect him is the only true pleasure I get from these sessions. He may be fighting it, but he can't deny the physical reaction he has to seeing me spread out in front of him, horny and ready for the taking.

"Please, Wilder," I plead, lifting my eyes to his once again and hoping if he's looking me right in the face, I can push him to cross that bridge he's so vehemently avoiding. "I need you."

He smirks, still palming his dick. I'm pretty sure he's punishing both of us at this point, but if this is what he needs to feel something, then I'll happily oblige. I'd do anything to offset some of the pain *I* caused. And maybe the only way out—the only way for us to move forward—is through. Perhaps we both have to go through this in order to come out the other side, reborn as something new, something that has a future—whatever that may be.

"Is that so? And what exactly is it you need?" My eyes flick down to his dick, my answer more than evident. "Your words, Angel."

"Your cock inside me."

"Is that so?" He moves his hands to slowly undo the button of his jeans, lowering the zipper before lifting out his heavy dick and fisting it in his hand until precum leaks from the end. "Is this what you want?"

"Yes," I pant, my chest heaving.

"And where do you want it?"

"I-In my pussy."

He arches a brow. "Are you sure? You don't want it in your ass? Or your mouth?"

"No," I groan, growing impatient.

He shifts forward, and I tilt my hips, bringing my knees up to grant him more space and enable him to slide in deeper, but of course, I should have known Wilder wouldn't cave that easily.

I catch the harsh glint in his eye a split second before he moves, but it's too late. My top is yanked up before I can react, pulling my arms together above my head, and he pins them to the bedsheet with a firm hand on my wrist.

His other hand fists his weeping cock, tugging on it until the purple vein running along the underside begins to pulsate. "Open your mouth," he bites out, and seeing that he's about to come, I obey without question, parting my lips as warm cum spurts from his tip and hits my tongue, lips, and chin.

Panting heavily, his hand still pins my arms above my head, his face looming over mine. "Swallow." Holding his unreadable gaze, I do just that, swallowing the slightly salty substance. "Open your mouth."

When I do, he uses a finger to gather the cum on my lips and cheek, pushing his finger into my mouth. My tongue instantly wraps around it, sucking the cum off before swallowing.

Everything about him hardens in the blink of an eye, and I stiffen beneath him. "Don't bat your eyes and demand that I fuck you ever again," he snarls in an icy-cold voice. "You lost that privilege a long time ago. Now, we're playing on my terms." Swinging a leg over me, he climbs off the bed, tucking himself away, but I'm too boneless to move, instead following him with my eyes. "And don't go crying to Hawk this time to finish you off."

Finally, I snap, my temper flaring. "Don't worry, I can finish the job just fine by myself."

In a flash of movement, Wilder once again hovers over me, his eyes wild with fury. "Don't even fucking think about it!"

Before I can so much as gather a retort, he's gone, the door slamming shut behind him, and I collapse back onto the bed, wondering how my run-ins with Wilder always leave me feeling so alive and wrung out all at once.

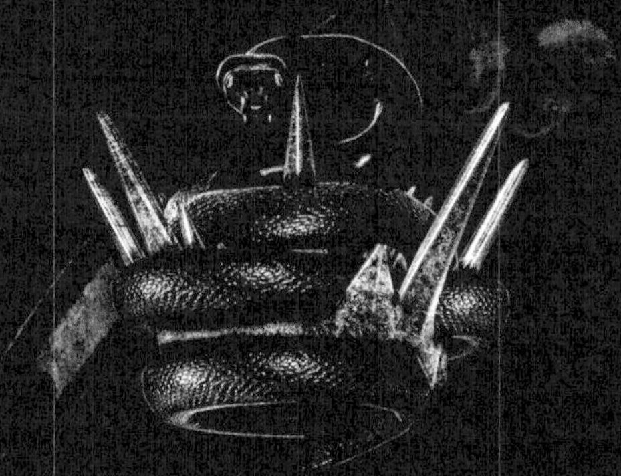

THE RUTHLESS BOYS OF RIDGEWAY

Kai

CHAPTER 21

"Given our history, it makes the most sense if I pretend to be her boyfriend."

I snort out a laugh, shaking my head. "Pretend? Funny, I didn't hear that word earlier when we were telling Emilia the plan."

Hawk glowers at me, and while his ire might terrify some people, it has literally no effect on me. I have seen far scarier things than Hawk Davenport when someone calls him on his shit.

"Look," I try to reason. "I know you want to stay close to her, but you don't have the same training I do. I know it, and you know it."

The muscle at the back of his jaw tightens, yet the fact that he doesn't immediately snap back at me implies that he knows I have a point.

"Fine, I'll agree with you on that, but how are the two of you going to make a fake relationship look believable to this psycho?"

"All I have to do is put my arm around her in public, smile at her, maybe even give the odd brief kiss. I can do what needs to be done." I've had to do far worse than smile and pay attention to a beautiful woman to complete jobs. This should be no hardship, especially since I've grown rather fond of Emilia. *Too fond*, a voice in the back of my head pipes up, but I squash it down.

Hawk scoffs, clearly not believing me. "Didn't you say this stalker only intervened with Richard when he was about to propose?"

I cock a brow. "Yes."

"So, until then, he didn't think Richard was a true threat. Since Richard was clearly all in when it came to Emilia, that means whoever it was *knew* Emilia didn't feel the same. That means it's not only *your* acting skills that will be tested, but hers as well. The two of you will have to look pretty damn believable if you're going to pull it off, and you *have* to pull it off, because we won't get a second shot at this."

"I can do it." Upon hearing her voice, we both spin toward the kitchen doorway. She's changed into a pair of shorts and an oversized tee, her dark hair scraped back into a ponytail, but it's her flushed cheeks and bright eyes that draw my attention.

Is that where Wilder disappeared to? To get his latest fix of tormenting Emilia? Can that idiot not see that now is hardly the time for him to be riling her up and denying her, although I must confess, the afterglow is doing inappropriate things to me.

Flicking my gaze to Hawk, I notice the way he's scrutinizing her, too, his eyes zeroed in on the aftereffects Emilia hasn't been able to hide.

When she steps into the room, my focus switches back to her, noting the determined set of her jaw. "I can do it," she repeats. She looks nervous as she licks her lips, her eyes jumping between Hawk and me. "If this is the plan, then I'm in."

Settling her attention on me, she pauses as though expecting me to have a sudden change of heart. Still, if I'd had any reservations before—which I didn't—at seeing the scared look in her eyes and the way she's holding herself like a wounded animal, then I'm all in now.

"Okay, take a seat. I'll grab us a bottle of scotch—and wine for you—and we'll get you up to speed."

"I'll, uh, take a scotch, too." My eyebrows lift in surprise, remembering one of our first conversations here when she told me she was more of a wine girl, and she explains, "I'm guessing I'm going to need it for this plan of yours."

A WEEK LATER, I stroll across Ridgeway's campus with my hands in my pockets, like I don't have a care in the world. It's incredible how much can change in a week. We've now got a state-of-the-art security system installed at the house—something we probably should have had before, except there had never been a need for Hawk and Wilder to have one before Emilia arrived. Sure, I'd installed small, undetectable cameras around the outside of the house and in each of the rooms, but there was no alarm system. If we'd installed one back then, it would have looked suspicious. Not that it would have mattered, now that we know her stalker has known her location the entire time she's been here, but still.

Thanks to one of the junior English teachers getting pregnant over the summer break, the English department was in need of a substitute for the rest of the year. We were able to pull a few strings, fudge a few documents, and get Emilia into the position. It's not the high-flying career she pictured for herself before she was abruptly uprooted from her old life, though I can tell she enjoys it—or, at the very least, she's enjoying *not* being stuck inside the house all day.

Every day, I drop her off and pick her up, and she eats lunch with Hawk, Wilder, and Hadley and her guys. Since her stalker knows she's here, there's no point in her hiding any longer. She may as well live her life as best she can, and that includes being seen in public with other people. The more she can do to aggravate this psycho, the better. If he sees her enjoying herself, spending time with others—aka people who aren't him—laughing and having fun, then it can only serve to piss him off further. However, Emilia is watched at all times. She is never truly alone, even when it appears as though she is. We even have plants in her classes—men and women from Nocturnal Enterprises, who are undercover as college students there to protect Emilia and look out for anything suspicious.

Reaching her classroom, I peer through the windowpane, watching as she talks away to a long blonde-haired woman—one of the ones we've planted. They've all been instructed to stay behind, pretending to ask a question or whatever, if they are in her last class of the day until I arrive. Some days I come before the class is out to throw off any suspicion, but on a couple of days, I've deliberately shown up a few minutes late.

I rap my knuckles gently against the door before pushing down on the handle and opening the door.

"Thank you so much, Ms. Harrison. That's really cleared things up."

"You're welcome, Fiona," Emilia says, practicing our rehearsed speech. "I'll see you on Monday."

With a nod in my direction, Fiona steps past me and out the door.

"Hey, babe," I greet. "How were your classes?"

Emilia smiles, and it's warm and genuine. I'm constantly surprised at how easily she's adapted to her role. She makes it look so effortless, not that fake dating her is difficult, by any means. "Good. The students are so engaging. They actually want to be here and learn."

I laugh, and as is the way around her, I never have to fake it. Our relationship may be fake, but our interactions aren't. "Isn't that how college works? They are paying a fortune to be here, after all."

"You'd think so, but I know at Halston and the same at Pac, the ones from the rich families never really gave a shit. It was the scholarship students who were hungry for knowledge. Everyone else was too focused on parties or getting laid or the latest handbag that had just been announced." She chews on her lip for a second. "I guess I'm just surprised to be on the other end of it and rather enjoying it."

I take the stack of books from her arms, tucking them under one of mine, and when she's no longer laden down, she pushes onto her toes to press a kiss to the corner of my lips. The two of us share an easy moment, staring at one another as though we genuinely are in love, before I wrap my arm around her shoulder. "Come on, let's get out of here. We have a date night to get ready for."

Emilia talks my ear off as we make our way back across campus to where I parked the car. Every now and again, I throw a, *huh* or *you don't say?* into the conversation, so it doesn't seem so one-sided if anyone is paying us any extra attention, but Emilia knows the drill by now. It's not that I'm deliberately ignoring her or that I don't give a shit about what she has to say; I'm just busy subtly scanning our surroundings for anyone who stands out or who may represent a threat.

When we reach the car, I open her door for her and wait until she slides in before closing it and rounding the front of the vehicle. Dropping the books in the backseat, I climb in beside her and start the engine, reversing out of the parking space.

Emilia waits until we're on the road, heading away from campus, before asking the same question she asks every day. "Did anyone stand out?"

"No." I hate that that's my answer every single time. I hate it even more when her shoulders drop with disappointment. Reaching across the center console, I wrap my hand around hers. The lines between us are becoming blurred, though I'm not sure that I care. "We knew this would take some time. Whoever this is is smart. They're going to wait and suss us out first." I glance her way. "Tonight should help."

It's not long before we're back at the house, and Emilia tells me that she has to go get ready for tonight before disappearing up the stairs. I'm sitting at the kitchen table with my laptop open in front of me, scouring today's security footage, when Hawk walks in.

"Hey." He nods toward the laptop. "Anything from today?"

It's the same routine every day. With Emilia on campus during the day and Hawk and Wilder with her, I've been back in the office. I won't be taking any cases while I'm still working on Emilia's, but I can consult, not to mention the pile of paperwork calling my name I'd been putting off before Hadley approached me, asking for my help.

"Nothing yet."

Grabbing a drink, he joins me at the table. "How are you feeling about tonight?"

I shrug my shoulder, not taking my attention away from the screen as I watch the mailman deliver a letter in the mailbox. He's been Hawk and Wilder's mailman since they first moved in here, so I don't think there's anything I need to look into there. "It's just a night out. We'll have dinner, talk, hold hands and come home."

I notice Hawk shaking his head out of the corner of my eye, nonetheless I don't engage him. Not that he needs my attention in order to continue. "Man, you're wasting a perfectly good Friday night. Em's going to be all dressed up, probably in a nice dress with easy access—"

"Jesus, Hawk, I'm not looking to fuck her," I bite out, glaring at him over my laptop and ignoring the traitorous voice in my head calling me a liar.

The asshole cocks a knowing brow. "Isn't that exactly what you're *supposed* to be trying to do? I can guarantee you trying to get in her pants is exactly how *any* guy on a date with her will behave." When I lift my lips in a disgusted snarl, he raises his hands placatingly. "I'm not saying to throw her up against the first hard surface and fuck her brains out. But every nice gesture any halfway decent guy on a date would do, like pulling out her chair, opening her car door, will be with the intention of getting his dick wet at the end of the night."

I continue to stare at him, not understanding what the fuck he's trying to say.

"Dude, when was the last time you went on a date?! I'm saying you need to act like a gentleman and think like a horn dog. That way, your actions will come across as believable to anyone watching."

Lifting a hand, I wipe it down my face, feeling so far out of my depth. "Oh god," I groan. "What the hell was I thinking when I said I could do this? I haven't been on a date since Laura. I have no fucking clue what I'm doing. I don't know how to even be on a real date, never mind a fake one."

"And this is why *I* should have fake-dated her." I level Hawk with a deadly glare, and the corner of his lips lifts in a smirk, telling me he was joking. I knew he was, anyway, his attempt at lightening the mood.

"What's going on with you two anyway? Do you actually want to date her, or do you just like the transience of fake dating her?"

"I dunno," Hawk says with a frown. "I take it she filled you in on our past?"

"Yeah. The tension coming off the three of you when she

first arrived was palpable. Since no one seemed all that eager to fill me in, I tempted her with a bottle of wine until she caved." He laughs. "Seems like Wilder was pretty hung up on her, but what about you?"

He shrugs, but it lacks any of its usual casualness. "I've been asking myself that same question recently."

"Okay, well, forget about back then. What about now?"

"*Fuck*," he hisses, a mysterious smirk on his lips as his thoughts clearly drift away from the table. "There's been a couple of unexpected moments when she's slipped past my defenses. She's been worming her way into my head, like cancer infiltrating my cells and gnawing on my bones, and now it feels like she's so ingrained in the very fabric of my DNA that I dunno if I'll ever get rid of her."

Shaking his head, he leans back in his chair, still staring at a point on the table as he continues. "I find myself wanting to be here more than at the frat house. Jesus, I'm even fucking jealous over your stupid fake date tonight. When I thought that Steven guy was the one stalking her, I wanted to be the one punching his fucking face in, and then when I saw how scared she was after those photos arrived, I just wanted to pull her into my arms and comfort her."

"So why didn't you?"

"I don't fucking know, man. Everything is so much more complicated when it comes to Emilia. If we cross that line, there's no coming back from it. It wouldn't be like before. There's far too much on the line this time."

Getting to my feet, I close the laptop and clap him on the shoulder. "Sounds like you need to figure your shit out, and soon. Meanwhile, I've got a date to get ready for."

Half an hour later, I'm back downstairs, wearing a black shirt, dark jeans, and brown shoes.

"Just calm down, man," Hawk reminds me for the millionth

time, yet no matter how many times I tell myself this isn't real, my heart won't calm the fuck down.

"That's not fucking helping," I snap at him.

He chuckles as I spin to glower at him. However, something behind me has his attention lifting toward the ceiling. I quickly turn back, falling still as Emilia descends the stairs wearing a deep red, sleeveless dress that flares out at her waist, swishing around her thighs until it falls to her knees. *Holy shit.* It looks like a sexier version of that dress Marilyn Monroe wore over that subway grate.

It's only when she reaches the bottom of the stairs that Emilia lifts her eyes to mine. I can see the nerves fluttering on her face. Her cheeks are even stained red beneath her makeup. "It's not too much, is it? I can change."

My mouth opens and closes as I struggle to find the words, but Hawk beats me to it, obviously having more grace than I do.

"You look beautiful, Em."

Her eyes dart to his, her cheeks deepening in color as she smiles nervously.

I clear my throat. "He's right, you look amazing. Are you, uh, ready to go?"

"Yeah." She offers me a tentative smile while I hold out my arm for her to slide hers through. Somehow this feels more *real* than anything else we've done this week.

"Have fun, kids," Hawk calls as we head out the door. The only acknowledgment he gets is a two-finger salute as we descend the steps to the car.

The entire way to the restaurant, Emilia twists her hands in her dress before smoothing it out, only to repeat the action all over again a few minutes later. Her nerves only serve to set me more on edge, and I have to keep loosening my hands around the wheel.

We don't really talk, both of us absorbed in our own

thoughts as I drive us across town. A valet greets us as we pull up at the restaurant, opening her door before I can round the car. Slapping my keys in his hand, he passes me a ticket before driving off with the car, and with a palm at the base of her spine, I escort Emilia up the steps and into the restaurant.

"This looks fancy," she mutters, low enough for only me to hear.

"From what I gather, that's the whole point of a date." The volume of my voice matches hers, but unlike the nerves threaded through hers, mine is lined with humor, trying to ease some of her tension.

"But..."

"Relax. We're putting on a show, remember?"

Except it's not all for show. I *want* to impress her. I spent hours searching for the perfect restaurant, and it wasn't just because I knew it mattered for whatever creep was watching her.

Her shoulders marginally relax, and I keep my hand on her lower back as the concierge shows us to our table. She continues to fidget while I peruse the wine menu, identifying her favorite type and ordering it when a waiter comes over.

"Two wine glasses, sir?"

"Just the one."

"No, two," Emilia interjects as I hand over the menu. The waiter glances from her to me, and I nod in agreement before dismissing him. "It's a date. It will look weird if you order a bottle and only I drink."

"Fair enough, but I think you need it more than I do. And will you stop fidgeting, you're stressing me out."

She chuckles under her breath, making a physical effort to stop as she places her palms on the table. "I guess I'm nervous, although I don't really know why. It's not like we haven't shared a meal together."

"Exactly. The only difference is we have to hold hands and give each other googly eyes while we do it." One side of my lips lifts in a smile, and it turns into a full-blown one when she tips her head back and laughs too. "Come here, give me your hand."

She slides her hand across the table until I can wrap my fingers around hers. "I know none of this is easy on you, but I have a feeling it's working."

"How do you know that?"

"How could it not? If I thought you were my girl and I saw some guy pawing all over you, I'd be furious. I wouldn't be able to stay away for long."

One side of her lips lifts in a smirk. "Pawing all over me? Is that what you've been doing?"

We both chuckle, and it breaks the tension. The wine helps when it arrives, and before I know it, we're halfway through dinner, and the conversation has flowed smoothly.

"How are you enjoying teaching at the college?"

Emilia swallows the sip of wine in her mouth before answering. "More than I thought I would. I didn't think teaching was really my thing, but I genuinely enjoy watching the looks on the students' faces when something clicks with them." She smiles, remembering something. "It's like a light-bulb moment. You can see it in their eyes. The way they widen ever so slightly and a smile brightens their faces. It's that moment when everything I've been saying for the last hour that sounded like total gibberish finally makes sense."

I lose myself for a moment in how her face lights up as she talks about her students and classes. It reminds me of the way she looked that day we went on our hike. That similar essence of joy and freedom that she's doing something she truly loves.

I realize I was so caught up in staring at her that I completely missed what she was saying when she glances around the busy restaurant before leaning in toward me. "This dinner was delicious, but I'm not sure it's enough."

"What do you mean?"

"Do you know of any bars or nightclubs around here?"

"Ehh, yeah, wh—?"

"Okay, let's go." She's pushing to her feet and setting her napkin on the table before I can wrap my head around what's happening. Not sure of what else to do, I follow, thankful I've already paid the bill as I scurry out of the restaurant after her.

"I don't understand," I say as we climb into the car.

"We need to do something that will really get this asshole's blood boiling. The couply stuff we've been doing all week, and tonight, is great, but it's not enough. I was thinking about what you said earlier, that if you were him, you'd be pissed seeing me with another guy. And while watching me hold hands and getting walked around campus by some guy is probably irritating, I think I can do one better."

As she smirks, I find that I quite enjoy this playful side to her, even if I still don't get what she's saying. She glances over at me, a mischievous smile on her face. "How good are your dancing skills?"

"Ehhh." She bursts out laughing at what is no doubt a look of panic on my face. I navigate the streets until we reach Club Envy, one of the more popular nightclubs on this side of town.

Once we've queued up and paid the cover charge, we step through the doors and are instantly greeted by the deafening beat of hip-hop music. Placing my hand in the middle of Emilia's back, we push our way through the crowd to the bar.

Leaning in so I can talk into her ear, I ask, "What do you want?" when we finally make it up to the counter.

"Gin and tonic."

Nodding, I wave down the bartender when he passes, ordering a gin for her and a tonic water with a lime wedge for me. Half a bottle of wine is more than enough when I'm also keeping an eye out for this stalker of hers. The absolute last thing I want is for him to sneak up on us when I'm too busy focusing on Emilia instead of everyone else around us.

Our drinks arrive, and we move over to a small table for two at the side of the dance floor.

"Now what?" I shout over the music, after we've spent a while watching the crowd bump and grind around us. The couple at the next table are practically fucking each other against it, and it didn't take me long to remember why clubbing was never my scene.

Setting her now empty drink on a table, she threads her fingers through mine and pulls me toward the dancefloor. "Now we dance." She's grinning as she says it, looking like she's having the time of her life.

She drags me into the middle of the dance floor, the dense crowd barely moving aside to give the two of us enough room. She's still smiling as she begins to sway her hips to the beat, lifting her arms above her head. "Dance," she urges when I make no effort to move. With a roll of her eyes, she grabs my hands and places them on her hips before sliding her palms up my arms and winding them around my neck.

I can feel every point at which her body is pressed against mine. I react to it like her touch is a visceral thing I can feel all the way to my core, my fingers pressing into her skin and pulling her closer as my body instinctively curls around her.

She tilts her head up, scanning my face as if checking that I'm comfortable with our close proximity while we both sway to the music. "If it were me, this is what would annoy me the most." I can feel her breath on my face as she talks, so close that she doesn't even need to yell to be heard over the music. "If I were the stalker, seeing this would send me over the edge. The intimacy. The sensuality." Her eyes dip to my lips, and holy shit, if it doesn't go straight to my dick.

I cough to clear my throat, mentally picturing Hawk dressed up as a giant baby in order to calm the rush of blood that has started traveling due south. Yet, my hands slide further around her waist until my fingers trail over the curve of her ass.

Lowering my head until my lips are at her ear, I murmur, "You are truly an evil genius," before trailing kisses down the column of her neck. For the next couple of hours, we touch and dance and grind on one another, and the entire time I keep one eye on the crowd around us and the other on the beautiful woman in my arms. I can't remember the last time I permitted myself to let loose, and yet twice in the last week, I've done exactly that. There were even moments cooped up in the house, when it was just Em and me, where she chased away the demons usually clinging to my back. I've never felt peace like this, like I do when I'm with her.

We never once leave the dancefloor, and by the time we finally call it a night, Emilia's hair is plastered to her face, and both of us are slick with sweat and panting heavily but still sporting mirrored grins. I realize, to anyone looking at us, they'd see a real couple out having a great time, who are now most likely going home to fuck. That simple thought is enough to have my dick surging with newfound life—not that he'd really died down all night.

As we stumble into the night, laughing and carrying on like two love-drunk—and very real drunk—idiots, Emilia fists the front of my shirt, pulling me toward her. "Kiss me."

My eyes flick down to her plump pink lips. Lips I've been thinking about and denying myself all night. It's the one thing we haven't done—properly kissed. There have been chaste brushes of lips but nothing more. However, something in her tone has me closing the distance between us, powerless to do anything other than obey her. My lips move against hers, electricity crackling in the air between us, and I quickly pull back just enough to search her eyes for any change of mind.

Her grip instantly tightens on my shirt, preventing me from moving away, and my lips hover over hers. "Kiss me like tonight was real. Like we were on a real date." Her hand that's fisted in my shirt flattens over my heart. "Like you actually like me, and we had a great time tonight."

At her whispered words and the pain she fails miserably at hiding behind them, my hand lifts up to cup the side of her face, my thumb running along the angle of her jaw. I stare deep into her bottomless green eyes, slightly dilated from alcohol and adrenaline but filled with more life than I've ever seen before. "It *was* real. *All* of it felt real to me. Every blissful moment." I slam my lips down on hers, and she moans into my mouth, her hands digging into my shoulders as I wrap my arms around her waist and pull her closer, not giving a shit that we're standing in the middle of a sidewalk outside a busy nightclub and drunken nobodies are wolf whistling at us right now.

All that matters is ensuring this magnificent woman in my arms knows tonight wasn't just a job to me. That *she* isn't just a job. Somewhere between the talking over wine and silent sessions studying yearbooks, the hiking, and fake dating, she became more to me; to mean more than anyone has in a very long time.

Breaking off our kiss, I thread my fingers through hers and hurry us back to the car. I'd parked in what had been a busy enough parking lot when I'd arrived, but now that it's the middle of the night, only a few other cars besides mine remain.

When we reach her side of the car, I push her back against it, my lips colliding with hers once again and already hungry for another taste. It's like her lips are the forbidden apple, and one taste has sent me descending into madness as my hands swipe over her ribs and down her sides, until I hitch one leg over my hip.

"Oh god," she gasps, tilting her head to the side in an invitation for me to lavish her neck with attention. Our hips collide in a matching, frenzied rhythm as our hands roam over one another, never settling in one place for long. "Kai."

I return my lips to hers, losing myself in her taste until we both grunt and groan our releases, panting heavily as we cling to one another.

"I can't believe we just did that," she eventually says in a breathless tone, making no effort to untangle herself from me. "If that doesn't get his attention, I don't know what will." There's a joking smile on her lips, but concern is hidden in the depths of her eyes.

Catching her chin between my fingers, I wait until she lifts her eyes to stare at me through her thick eyelashes. "I hope it does, but that wasn't just for him."

Her responding smile is soft and warm, and sincere, and I plant a final kiss on her lips before lowering her leg and waiting until she's fixed her skirt around her waist before stepping away and allowing her to open the door.

As I walk around to the driver's side, a rare genuine smile on my face, I'm still riding the high from the twist tonight took, but one thing is for sure, I won't let this asshole ruin this one for me.

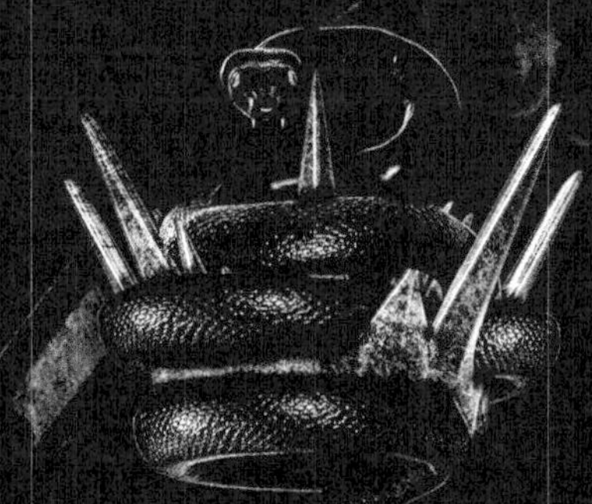

THE RUTHLESS BOYS OF RIDGEWAY

Emilia

CHAPTER 22

I'm still grinning like a lunatic when I step through the front door of the house.

"Ah, the lovebirds have returned," Wilder jests from the kitchen doorway, startling me. What the hell is he doing just hovering there like a creep? Was he waiting for us to come home? "Did you catch yourselves a stalker?"

"Not yet, but hopefully soon," Kai states confidently.

Wilder cocks a brow, his sharp gaze jumping back and forth between us, and I have to resist the urge to reach up and flatten my hair or fix my makeup, wondering if there's anything that might give away what we just did. "So you think you pulled it off?"

My gaze darts to Kai, and I find him smirking at me. "Oh, definitely."

I snort out a laugh, making Wilder's other brow jump skyward as he scrutinizes us before seeming to force his expression into something blank. "Whatever, it's not like I care. As long as you're not planning on having some sort of post-fake-date fuck. I don't need to hear that shit."

Kai snorts. "Like the rest of us don't hear when you're getting your rocks off."

My cheeks must turn bright red as my eyes widen in shock, and my gaze drops to the floor, remaining glued to a knot in the floorboard. However, Wilder clearly isn't as embarrassed as I am, as he simply chuckles. "You think you'd be grateful. I'm giving you something to jack off to." At his crude words, I glance up at him through my lashes, noticing when Wilder's gaze flicks to mine, heating with liquid lust. "Doesn't she sound way better than the fake moans on those porn sites?"

"I wouldn't know. I'm not sure I've actually heard the poor girl come... at your hands."

Fucking hell, this is turning into some sort of pissing contest, and I'm not sure I really want to be here for it.

One of Wilder's cheeks twitches, the muscles in his jaw repeatedly bunching and unbunching as he struggles to keep his composure, before giving up and storming up the stairs. He makes sure to slam each foot solidly against every step, alerting the entire house to his tantrum. *God, he acts like a five-year-old who was told he had to share his toys.*

"I'm sorry," Kai says, looking chagrined when Wilder's bedroom door finally slams shut. "I shouldn't have said that. It was childish."

I chew on my bottom lip before venturing, "So why did you?"

He sighs, his shoulders dropping as he shakes his head. "I don't know. The way he treats you pisses me off." Holding up his hands in a placating gesture, he adds, "Not that it's any of my business what the two of you have going on. I know it's complicated."

"It is," I agree, although not harshly. "I can't begin to explain it any better than you can. I just... I think it's what he needs right now. Anyway," my lips quirk up into a soft smile. "I had fun tonight. Thank you."

Kai's returning smile is full of boy-next-door charm, the same as it has been all night, and I swear every time he dazzles me with it, it makes my knees go weak. "So did I. Sweet dreams, Em."

Giving him a lame wave goodnight, I head up the stairs, feeling lighter than I have in a long time. My lips still tingle from Kai's kiss, and I'm not entirely sure how tonight changes things between us. I just know that it has.

He's been my safe port in the storm these last few weeks, and perhaps it's some twisted form of Stockholm syndrome, but with his easygoing personality and reassuring aura, it's hard not to feel safe and protected around him. Don't even get me started on how right it felt to be in his arms tonight, with my back pushed against the car. I've wondered once or twice—okay, maybe a few more times than that—what it would be like to be in his arms. To be the person Kai focuses *all* of his attention on. I've no doubt he'd give a hundred percent to any relationship. He's perfect boyfriend material—a touch of darkness encapsulating a wholesome interior. I'm not fooled, I know something happened in his past that he doesn't like to discuss, and it's left him jaded, but it hasn't eaten him alive like Wilder's past has.

I'm still replaying my evening with Kai when I step into my room and flick the switch, coming up short when I find Hawk lounging on my bed in just his boxers.

"What the hell are you doing in here?" His hands are clasped behind his head, his feet crossed at the ankles, making it obvious he's been waiting for me, but why? Unbidden, my eyes trail over his exposed, toned chest and muscular thighs. Hawk has definitely not lost his enthusiasm for the gym since he left high school, not only maintaining the bulk he had back then, but adding to it with brand new muscles that I don't even know the name of.

"How was your date?"

"Fine," I answer carefully, unsure whether his presence in my room is a good thing or not.

He cocks a brow. "Just fine?"

"What do you want, Hawk?"

He slides to the edge of the bed, the movement effectively placing him opposite me. My room isn't large, and if I wanted, all I'd have to do is take two steps forward and my dress would brush against his knees. "To know how your date went."

"Why? Why do you care?"

He gives a casual shrug of his shoulder that only aggravates me further. "Call me curious."

Frowning at him, I push off the door and move around the bed to the dresser, barely sparing him a glance in the mirror before I begin removing my earrings and necklace. "I'm not discussing that with you."

"Why not?" A creak of the bed frame has me flicking my eyes up to the mirror, finding him prowling toward me. "Did he get you off?" he purrs in my ear, making heat rise in my cheeks as I refuse to meet his eyes, knowing he'll read the answers in them.

A surprised laugh escapes him. "He did, didn't he? Damn, I've never known Kai to cross professional lines like that." He mutters the last part to himself, though I hear him anyway, his condescending tone pissing me off as I whirl to face him.

"Don't cheapen it," I snap, spitting fire at him with my eyes.

He takes a step back at my hostile defense, seeming surprised at my outburst. "I'm sorry, that's not what I meant. I'm just surprised, that's all." He hesitates, seeming to deliberate over something before his gaze drops to take in my dress, and he tacks on, "And a little jealous."

"Jealous?" I question, confused. What the hell does Hawk Davenport have to be jealous over? He's got a body made for sinning, he's richer than God, *and* he can do or have anything and anyone he desires. There is absolutely nothing Hawk could want that he can't get with a simple click of his fingers.

He gives another infuriating shrug of his shoulder as he closes the distance between us. "I was hoping to be the one tearing that dress off of you tonight."

My mouth opens and closes several times before I find any words, and even when I do, only one manages to make it into the atmosphere. "Oh."

"Is that so surprising?" Another step forward has his fingers sliding through the fabric of my dress. "You're beautiful, Emilia. Even when your hair is pulled back, and you're wearing ridiculous guinea pig pajamas, there's still something captivating about you."

"Bunny rabbit," I correct, remembering the pajamas I wore in our senior year of high school.

Hawk doesn't appear to be listening, though, as he takes another step forward, eliminating the sliver of space between us until his thighs press against mine, his hand landing firmly on my hip and rubbing circles through the fabric of my dress. His gaze rakes over my outfit, heating with each passing second. "But like this, all dressed up for some lucky man to show off and call you his, you're completely breathtaking."

"Is that what you want?" I question, unsure whether he's just after sex or something more. "To call me yours?"

With one hand still on my waist, holding me against the dresser, he lifts his other to my face, brushing his thumb along my lower lip. "That's something I've been struggling with recently. Trying to figure out what this is between us. The sex was great, and we had fun in high school..." He drifts off, losing himself to a memory while I wait with bated breath, wondering if there's more to come or if that's it.

"I missed you when you left." Recollections of him saying something similar the night I got drunk and we played a truth for a truth bubble to the forefront of my mind. Even though he's told me this before, the genuineness in his voice takes me by surprise, nearly knocking me off my feet. We both knew the deal back in high school, but I was surprised to find myself missing him too. I just never expected him to have felt the same way. Isn't it usually girls who get emotionally attached, and the men move forward with their lives like you meant absolutely nothing? And yet, although brief, my tryst—for lack of a better word—with both Hawk and Wilder left a permanent mark on all of us.

"Having you back here has opened old wounds and gotten me thinking shit I never thought before." He frowns as though thinking through something. "I thought I was happy. Hadley would nag me to go on dates, and occasionally I would to keep her happy, but I told myself I was never truly interested because I didn't want to settle down with anyone. That a relationship just wasn't for me."

He seems to get lost in his thoughts, and when he doesn't continue after a moment, I hedge, "And now?"

At my question, he lifts his head, his eyes staring into mine, and I can see the turmoil within them. "That's the fucking thing, isn't it? I don't want to go out on dates or be in a relationship or do any of that shit." My heart sinks, and I have to work to keep the disappointment off my face. "Unless it's with you. I don't know what the hell it is about you, but I can't stay away. I've been trying—*God,* have I been trying, but I'm fucking done." My eyes bounce back and forth between his, not truly understanding.

"I don't... What are you saying?"

"I'm saying, yes, I want you to be *mine*. Mine to date. Mine to fuck. Mine to protect and hold and comfort. I'm saying I'm done holding back and pushing you away. I want to be able to wrap my arms around you when you're upset. I want to drink wine and talk shit with you until you pass out." He tugs at the skirt of my dress. "I want to see you get dressed up for me, all so I can throw the outfit on the bedroom floor before I eat you out and make you scream my name to the heavens."

I hesitate with one foot over the ledge, ready to plummet headfirst into the unknown but absolutely freaking terrified of doing so. "Are you sure about this?" I chew on my bottom lip, trying not to let excitement consume me. "This wouldn't be like before. We won't easily come back from this."

"I don't want it to be like before. It isn't just sex this time around, Emilia, but you're right. There won't be any coming back from this for us. We either jump off that ledge together, or we walk away and never take that leap. It's up to you."

It doesn't take me long to think through the decision. It's not really a decision at all. I think my subconscious already knew before I did, and my body has been sending me signals since the moment I first saw him again. I pounce, wrapping my arms and legs around him and knowing he'll catch me before I fall as I slam my lips down on his. "I'm in. I'm all the way in when it comes to you, Hawk Davenport."

One arm bands around my waist, the other sliding up my spine until he cups the back of my neck, using his weight to push me against the dresser as he devours my mouth.

We kiss until we are both starved of oxygen, our chests heaving and our eyes glassy, before he spins us and sets me down on the bed. He hovers over me, leaning in for another breathtaking kiss as his fingers slide beneath the fabric of my dress, slowly pushing it higher up my thighs.

Pushing my legs further apart, he gets to his knees in front of me. With my dress bunched around my waist, his hands holding it out of the way, he has a perfect view of my core. Desire flashes across his eyes when he sees the damp spot on my panties, and he groans as his fingers stroke back and forth along my skin.

"Some days I wake up, and I swear I can still taste you on my tongue." He runs his nose along my inner thigh until he reaches the lining of my panties, where he licks along the wet patch before groaning. "I'm a starving man, Emilia, and all I want to eat is you."

It takes me a second to find my voice, his touch and words making me feel lightheaded, dizzy, and hungry for more. Only when I do, my voice comes out raw and husky. "So eat me."

His eyes flick up to mine, his lips hovering over my center, and I take a mental snapshot of this moment, wanting to remember it. The moment Hawk Davenport got on his knees for me, ready to worship at my altar. Seeing how badly he wants me, and knowing it matches my own hunger for him, makes me feel beautiful, powerful, and sexy in a way I've never felt before.

"Kiss me, taste me, fuck me. Do whatever you want with me because I'm all yours. I always have been."

Those words are Hawk's undoing, and he loses control over his restraint as he rips my panties off and dives in to sate his hunger, feasting on me like the starved man he claimed to be.

"Oh, god."

"Fucking hell, you taste even better than I remember," he growls in a low voice, dripping with need and desire, before diving back in for another taste.

I fist his hair in my hands, arching my back and throwing my head back as I ride his face, mewling like a kitten as he sends me headfirst into an all-consuming orgasm.

I'm still trembling through the after-shocks as I drag his face up to mine, hungrily kissing him. I groan obscenely at the taste of me on his tongue, the combination of me and him toxic and possessive but also light and fruity.

"Fuck, I need to be inside you. Now." The urgency behind his tone is followed by the quick, sharp movements of his hands as he pushes his boxers down and fists himself a few times.

"C-condom," I gasp as he lines himself up.

His head lifts to meet mine, impatience written all over his face. "Are you on the pill?"

"Yes, but—"

"Then we're fine." He focuses back on the task at hand as his tip nudges against my entrance, but my hand pushing against his chest stops him, and he sighs irritably. I know it's not aimed at me; he's just as impatient as I am. "I haven't slept with anyone since you came back, Em. Plus, you are the only person I've ever fucked without a condom, so I'm clean."

My lips part in a silent gasp, remembering the time he bent me over a desk in an empty classroom and fucked me 'til I couldn't walk straight. It—and once with Wilder when he practically busted down my door and pinned me to the bed—were the only two times I've ever had sex without a condom. The only times when it has slipped my mind. After that first time, I immediately ran out and got a Plan B, and I didn't stop panicking until my period arrived two weeks later.

"Besides, we both know you haven't slept with anyone since you've been here."

"How the hell do you know that?" I snap, narrowing my eyes at him.

He lifts an eyebrow, a knowing look in his eye as he smirks. "Are you telling me you have?" He presses a kiss to the hollow at the base of my neck. "Because I know Wilder is punishing you by denying you both what you ultimately crave." Another kiss over the pulse point in my neck. "And you and Kai have been ignoring your feelings for one another, until tonight." His lips brush the sensitive skin behind my ear before he moves to trail kisses along my jaw until he reaches my lips.

Our eyes collide, and it feels like he can see into the very depths of my soul, the connection between us roaring to life and solidifying itself as he slowly eases himself inside of me. I'd forgotten just how fucking big Hawk is, the stretch bordering on painful as I bite down on my bottom lip, stifling a cry.

Hawk's hand strokes my hair and the side of my face, muttering reassurances as he slowly splits me in half with his dick. "That's it, baby. Nearly there. You're doing so good. You were fucking made to take all of me."

When he's all the way in, he allows me a moment to adjust before sitting up, staring in awe at the point where we're both connected. "Fucking hell, Em." He gives a testing thrust forward, and I groan at the bite of pleasure and roll my hips for more. "You should see how fucking good you look swallowing all of me. *Fuck.*" He can't seem to look away as he continues to rock into me, watching himself slide in and out.

With his hands on my knees, he pushes them further apart, stretching me wide as he increases the power of his thrusts. With every brush of his cock against my bundle of nerves, stars explode behind my eyes and pleasure races through my veins.

"Hawk," I whimper, lifting my hips to meet his.

Raising his eyes from where we are joined together, I see awe and desire shining back at me. Today, his gray eyes remind me of a summer storm. The charge you can feel in the air that makes your skin prickle and the hair rise along your arms right before that first lightning strike hits, followed by the relief of a rainfall after days of sweltering heat.

My nails dig into Hawk's arm as I arch my back. "Oh, God, Hawk." I lick my dry lips, barely able to suck in a breath. "Hawk, I—I..."

"I know, Little Sparrow. I feel it too. I'm right there with you." His words are spoken between breathless pants and hard thrusts, and I can tell he's on the verge of coming too.

He presses down on my clit with his thumb, giving it a hard rub, and it's enough of a catalyst to spark a fire that rushes through my body, sending it up in flames and incinerating me from the inside out as I scream out his name and tighten around him, initiating his own release.

Spent, he collapses on top of me, not pulling out as he shifts us so we're both lying on our sides, his softening cock still snug inside me.

My heavy eyelids start to drift closed, exhaustion weighing me down. "I hope you're not planning on going to sleep just yet," Hawk says, his voice low and laced with humor.

"Nope. Just a five-minute power nap."

He chuckles. "Good, 'cause I haven't even gotten you undressed yet. There will be no rest until I have you naked and have tasted every inch of your skin."

I crack open an eyelid at his heated tone, finding his incensed gaze on me as my lips lift in a playful smile. "You think you've got another round in you?"

Hawk scoffs, looking highly offended as he lifts my leg to rest over his hip and uses the angle to thrust inside me. I can already feel his dick waking up for round two. "When it comes to you, I could go all night."

My grin is wide and sated, as I lean in to give him a tender kiss. One he happily deepens as he cups the back of my head, preventing me from escaping as he rolls onto his back, taking me with him.

"This has to go," he orders, tapping a finger on my dress. "I want you completely naked while you ride my cock." Laughing, I do as he says, and we spend the next few hours intimately committing each other's bodies to memory, until we're both too tired to move.

Later that night, I'm curled up in his arms, sated and happier than I ever remember being. "Why do you call me Little Sparrow?" I question, chewing on my bottom lip.

"Mmm?" he mumbles, clearly half asleep. I don't repeat the question, instead waiting him out, and deciding if he doesn't answer the question then maybe I'm better off not knowing. At least for tonight.

Eventually he asks in a husky voice, "Do you know what sparrows symbolize?"

"No?"

"They represent pleasure and happiness. They are all about finding joy in the little things in life."

I frown, unsure how that relates to me. "And I'm your sparrow?"

He kisses the top of my head, pulling me tighter against him as he murmurs. "You're my sparrow."

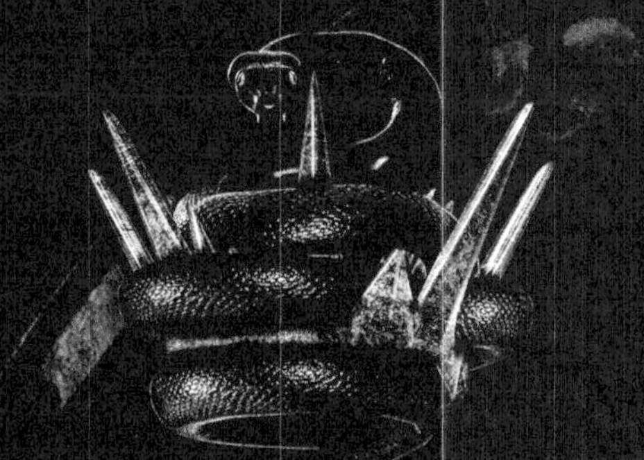

THE RUTHLESS BOYS OF RIDGEWAY

Emilia

CHAPTER 23

I wake with a smile on my face, my eyes still shut as I stretch out in bed. I think that was the best night's sleep I've ever had.

"Well, don't you look far too comfy."

My eyes snap open, my hands flying to tuck the sheet around my naked body as my bewildered gaze lands on Wilder. He's leaning against the bedroom door, his arms folded and his posture appearing far too casual considering the wicked gleam in his eyes and the cruel curve of his lip.

He's working hard to *appear* casual, but inside, he's furious.

Oh, fuck.

"What are you doing in here?" I seethe irritably, darting my gaze to the other side of the bed and finding it empty. *Where the hell is Hawk?*

"Thought someone was being murdered in here last night. Thought I should do my due diligence and see if that was actually the case."

"Well, as you can see, everything is fine, so feel free to show yourself out."

His smirk only deepens. "Nah, I think I'll stay."

"Get out, Wilder," I snap, my good mood officially ruined.

He scoffs with derision. "You can't tell me what to do. This is *my* house."

"Yeah, and this is *my* bedroom, which *Hawk* offered to me. So I'll say again, *get out.*"

"So crabby this morning." Wilder fake pouts. "I guess last night wasn't all you'd hoped it would be." He pointedly glances at the empty spot beside me on the bed before wincing. "Can't have been that good for him either if he snuck out before you woke up."

"That's not..."

The protest dies on my lips, doubt taking root.

Is that what he did? Last night was... *everything* I hoped it would be, but perhaps that wasn't the case for Hawk.

Wilder snorts. "Sure it's not. Classic Hawk M.O. Let me guess, he saw you all dressed up last night and spouted some pretty words to lower your guard and make you fall into bed with him."

I can only frown as I try not to let what he's saying germinate and ruin last night.

"What I'm less sure about, is *your* game." He cocks a brow.

"My game?" I question with a frown, not understanding what he's trying to say. "I'm not playing any games." My temper boils. "The only one playing games around here is *you.*"

His face shadows over, his features turning menacing as my heart skips a beat before speeding up. Now I'm definitely scared to be alone with him.

"If you think I've been playing, *Angel,* then you haven't been paying attention. And if you think sleeping with Hawk will endear him to your side, then I have some news for you: Your pussy isn't that good. As for Kai? He'd never go for a heartless bitch like you. Plus, he's a professional. Your *date* last night was just that—a job. No matter what he said or how he acted, you are just a *job* to him, and once he's caught your stalker, he'll be done with you too."

Each hateful word drives like a dagger into my chest, ripping me apart and leaving me cold. Knowing his barbs have landed, he tacks on a smug smirk, finally leaving me alone.

My hands shake with anger as tears gather in my eyes, but it's my thoughts that are the hardest to deal with as I go back over every interaction last night with Kai and Hawk. Was everything Kai said and did just for the job? He said it wasn't, but perhaps he got caught up in the moment like I did and is currently somewhere in this house, regretting it.

And what about Hawk? He didn't have to say all those things last night to get me into bed... unless he's been playing me like Wilder has, only his games involve stealth and mental manipulation.

"Ughhh," I groan, rubbing my hands over my face. I don't want to believe Wilder, but there's no arguing that he's planted doubts. Doubts that scare me because I don't want my date with Kai to be only a job. I had more fun last night than I've had in a long time, and I've *never* enjoyed myself so much on a date. Usually, I'm a nervous wreck or self-conscious, never sure what to say, or my thoughts have drifted elsewhere. I've never just been in the moment like I am when I'm around Kai. When I'm with him, all my concerns and worries fall away. I stop thinking about everything I need to do or wondering if I left the stove on or if I remembered to pay the electric bill.

But perhaps it's not like that for him. After all, I *am* a job to him. And I've no doubt Kai would go to the extremes to protect his charges. Is that what he's doing?

Sick to my stomach, I climb out of bed and hurriedly get dressed, needing to be anything other than naked in case Hawk decides to come back from wherever the hell he disappeared off to.

Cracking the door, I peer into the hall, making sure no one else is around before sneaking out and sprinting up the stairs. I only breathe again when I slam the bathroom door closed behind me.

Showered and dressed, I pull up my big girl panties and march downstairs, not entirely sure what my game plan is. All I know is that I can't hide in my room until the end of time. Although, admittedly, that thought is appealing.

I make it to the kitchen before my steps falter. Kai is sitting at the island with his back to me, working away on something.

Mustering confidence I don't feel, I push back my shoulders and keep my head high as I step into the kitchen. "Morning."

"Hey," he greets, glancing up from his computer and giving me an easy, boy-next-door smile. "How did you sleep?"

My cheeks immediately heat, and a new, terrifying thought strikes me. If I'm *not* simply a job to Kai, and what transpired between us last night was real, then I came home from our date and jumped into bed with Hawk. Hawk, who is his boss and friend.

What the hell was I thinking?

"Fine," I squeeze out through a tight throat, immediately turning away from him as I move to grab myself a cup.

Keeping my back to him, I clear my throat as I pour myself some coffee from the pot. "What are you up to this morning?" I ask, changing the topic.

There's a moment of silence, and I swear I can feel his gaze digging into my back, probing and prodding with a silent demand to turn around.

When I don't turn to face him, he thankfully answers me, "I reached out to the owner of Club Envy, asking if I could see their security footage from last night, and they just sent it over."

"Oh?" Curiosity piqued, I turn, thankful to find his eyes back on his laptop screen as I walk around the island to stand beside him. "Anything interesting?"

He chuckles. "Plenty of interesting stuff, but nothing with your stalker."

My gaze flicks to the screen, watching people dance and grind on a packed dance floor. The screen flicks to a different angle, and I spot Kai and me in the upper left corner of the screen. My arms are around his neck, and I'm staring up at him with a painfully obvious *fuck me* expression.

Oh my god. Did I really look like that last night? Crap, if this is only a job to him, then that is incredibly embarrassing, and I feel awful for putting him in such an awkward position.

"About last night," I begin, needing to clear the air before it suffocates me. "I—"

His laptop pings with a notification that flashes up at the corner of his screen, alerting Kai to a new email, but the subject line catches my attention.

Police Report - Girvan.

"Girvan?" I question, my voice sounding shaky. "That's Richard's surname."

Kai immediately opens the email, hesitating with his mouse over the attached file.

"You might not want to see this," he hedges, turning his head to look at me.

"I already know he's dead. How much worse can it get?"

His lips pinch, his expression telling me that it can always get worse, but instead of arguing, he simply gives a curt nod and clicks on the file.

Some sort of handwritten investigative report opens, filled with so much information that I don't even know where to look as my eyes bounce all over the screen. I note his full name, address, and date of birth have been filled in. *Definitely my Richard*, I think, even as my stomach roils. I already knew he was dead, but somehow this feels even more real than the photographs.

Kai scrolls down, more new information filling the screen and flooding my brain. I skim over most of it, but words like *stabbed with a sharp object, advanced decomposition, exposed to the elements,* all jump out at me until I have to sit down.

Tearing my gaze away from the screen, I take several concentrated breaths, willing my stomach to calm down. "Maybe you should just tell me what it says," I say in a strained voice, deliberately keeping my eyes averted.

"They estimate that he died about four weeks ago," Kai states, his voice soft and calming, helping to soothe the pain left behind by his cutting words.

"Around the time I—"

"Yeah," Kai confirms when I stop mid-sentence, unable to say the words aloud.

At least he wasn't held captive all this time, right? It's the only silver lining I can find, although it does nothing to reassure me.

I frown, words that I don't understand catching my attention. "Why do they think it's a possible drug deal gone wrong? Richard didn't do drugs."

Kai skims his eyes over that part of the report. "Looks like they found drugs near his body, and given the part of town he was found in. It's known gang territory and his missing finger fits the M.O. of Devil's Dynasty, a well-known gang that operates in that part of town."

My face screws up in disgust, having no words.

"Looks like he was stabbed multiple times," Kai continues, reading aloud. "They think that's what killed him."

"They aren't sure?" I question with a frown.

"He, uhhh..." Kai winces, and I brace myself for what he has to say next. "He was found in an alleyway in a rundown suburb of Springview."

"Okay?" I frown, not understanding.

"He was there for a while, Em. Probably since he was... killed."

My entire body stiffens as the other words I read on the report assault my mind like a battering ram. *Exposed to the elements. Advanced decomposition.*

I close my eyes against the onslaught, yet all I see is Richard's kind face as his skin turns gray, his eyes lifeless before his skin begins to rot and slew off.

"I think I'm going to be sick," I groan, placing my forehead against tabletop. I wrap my hands around my waist, breathing deeply until the wave of nausea calms to a low boil. At the sound of Kai's chair scraping against the floor, I turn my head, placing my cheek against the cool granite.

"Here, drink this," he says, placing a glass of water down beside me.

Making no effort to move, I instead watch as the occasional bubble of air forms against the glass. "How do they even know it's him?" I ask in a weak voice.

"Dental records. Looks like one of his friends eventually reported him missing."

A suffocating silence falls, or perhaps Kai is talking and I just can't hear him over my chaotic thoughts. My mind churns with all of this new information, but one thought, in particular, keeps circling back around.

"This is all my fault," I murmur, my voice low. I'm not capable of speaking any louder. Not capable of moving. I could easily curl up and die right here.

"Don't say that." Although Kai's voice still has that same soothing quality, his words are spat out in a bite.

I grimace, still unable to gather the energy to lift my head, as I stare blankly at the kitchen wall. "Why not? It's true. I strung him along. If I hadn't made him think there was the possibility of a future there, then he wouldn't have bought that ring." A tear escapes the corner of my eye, running down the side of my face until it pools against the cold granite beneath me. "Richard was a good man. One of the best guys I've ever known. He didn't deserve this." Another tear overflows. "Wilder's right. I am a heartless bitch."

"Richard loved you." Kai's voice comes from somewhere nearby, but I just continue to stare pointedly at the wall. "Maybe you weren't able to give him your whole heart, but he was obviously happy with what you were willing to give. Otherwise, he wouldn't have considered spending the rest of his life with you." He releases a long sigh when I don't respond. "The responsibility for his death lies squarely with this psycho. *Not* you. Besides, since when did you start listening to Wilder?"

I can tell he's trying to lighten the mood and pull me out of my funk, but this, on top of the doubts Wilder instilled this morning, are pulling me down deep beneath the surface.

"I shouldn't be doing any of this," I mumble to myself. "We shouldn't be fake dating. We definitely shouldn't be making out like we did last night, and I absolutely should not be sleeping with Hawk." My tone lacks emotion, the numbness chilling my bones and distancing me from the horror of my situation. "He's going to get you too. Both of you. Then it'll just be Wilder left, and he'll spend the rest of his life reminding me that your deaths are all my fault."

I'm yanked upward so quickly that the kitchen spins. I blink, getting my bearings, and I find myself settled in Kai's lap, encased in his arms with his pissed-off expression inches from my face. "I won't sit here and listen to you talk like that," he growls angrily.

His anger surprises me so much that I'm completely taken

aback for a second. Kai is always calm and placid. I've never seen him so worked up. Didn't even know he was capable of it.

"I am sorry about Richard, but nothing can be done to change the past now. Stop beating yourself up. If Richard was unhappy with your relationship, he would have said something or he would have left. He definitely would not have bought an engagement ring."

Kai's eyes simmer with pent-up rage, turning his irises a dark green.

"You say your heart wasn't in it. Don't let that be the case next time. So Richard wasn't the one. That sucks, but don't make the same mistake again. Next time you start something with someone, make sure you can give them every part of you. Give everything you have to that relationship and have no regrets."

He pins me with his intense gaze. "As for you and I..." His hand moves so his thumb rests along my collarbone, his fingers curled around my shoulder. "I'm not doing anything I don't want to. I know the risks. I know what's at stake. I *want* to protect you. I *want* to catch this guy. And I definitely want to kiss you again."

His hand slides up my neck until his thumb brushes the underside of my jaw. His eyelids fall to half-mast as he leans in to close the distance between us.

"But Wilder said—"

"Again, why are you listening to anything Wilder says?" Kai questions in a husky tone, his breath skimming my lips before he seals them with a kiss. It's tender and cautious, testing the waters. There's none of the heat or desperate hunger from last night, however, his kiss is no less passionate and far more deadly. It's the kind of kiss you could fall into. The kind that will stay with you long after it's over. The kind that speaks of complete and utter self-destruction.

THE RUTHLESS BOYS OF RIDGEWAY

Wilder

CHAPTER 24

The second I hear Hawk's heavy footfalls as he descends the stairs, I crack open my bedroom door. I watch as he disappears out of view in his workout gear, off for his typical early morning gym session, before I sneak out of my room and up the stairs to Emilia's. Silently, I turn the door handle and push it open wide enough to slip into her room.

My nose wrinkles, even as my cock hardens, at the pungent smell of sex. *There will be no fucking,* I remind my dick as he strains against the cotton fabric of my sweatpants, dying to get to the only woman he has any interest in anymore. The one woman I've been denying him and will continue to deny him.

My eyes slowly rake over her sleeping frame, lingering on the top of the sheet where it is draped low across her chest. A slight tug and it would slip low enough to expose her nipple. A harder tug and she'd be naked and entirely at my mercy. My hand fists at my side as I hold myself back from doing exactly that.

The problem is, I'm too angry. I don't trust myself not to fuck her into the mattress in an attempt to remove all traces of

Hawk's touch. To fuck her so damn hard that she forgets exactly what it felt like to have *him* inside her.

Why the fuck am I even here? I ask myself, my body vibrating with the effort it's taking to remain by the door. I heard the noises last night; I didn't need to fucking see this. To subject myself to this. To see Hawk's betrayal. His stupidity.

Emilia shifts in her sleep, rolling so I can see her face. My breath hitches and I'm suddenly reminded of why I started calling her Angel all those years ago. She's the epitome of everything I never knew I needed. The balm that soothes my jagged edges. The calm to the storm raging inside me.

At least, she was.

Until she chose some boy band over the thing brewing between us.

Didn't she feel what I did? Didn't she understand how special that was? How rare it is to find something as pure as what we had?

Obviously not. That, or she didn't care, because she tossed it away like it meant nothing. Like *I* meant nothing.

There was once a time when I would have taken on the world for her, but now all I want is to destroy *her world.* I need her to feel what I feel. This raw pain that, no matter what you do, continues to feast on your insides until there's nothing but an aching emptiness. A giant gaping hole where your heart used to be.

I hadn't even known I had a heart until Emilia pried it open. But every second I spent around her, I felt it more keenly. I felt it beating... for her.

Until the second she ripped it out and stomped all over it, crushing it like petals beneath her feet as she strode off into the sun with her fuckboy musicians.

Why the hell didn't she turn to them for help if they were so close?

I bet she was treated like their number one groupie all summer, and the second their tour was over, she was kicked off their bus and sent on her way without so much as a goodbye.

It would be the least that she deserved. I hope, in that moment, she understood what she'd thrown away. That she realized the huge mistake that she'd made.

Bitterness coats my tongue as Emilia begins to stir. A satisfied smile spreads across her face, causing my scowl to deepen with every second it grows wider.

"Well, don't you look far too comfy," I snipe when she's mid-stretch. I smirk at how her entire body tenses a split second before her eyes snap open, and she jumps into motion, trying to cover herself up. I've already seen every inch of her, committed it to memory, so I can fantasize about it in a moment of weakness that threatens to consume me late at night, when I'm alone and regret how things worked out.

"What are you doing here?" she snaps, panic flaring in her eyes as she realizes she's alone in the room with me. No Hawk to protect her. If she thinks fucking him over to her side will actually protect her from me, then she's only fooling herself. Nothing and no one can save her from me. Not even her stalker.

She and Kai are fake dating in the hopes of luring out this weirdo, but I'm not ready for him to take her yet. I'm not done punishing her. She's scared and on edge. However she's not yet broken, and until she is, I'm not finished with her.

Even when she is broken, do you really think you'll just be able to walk away? a snide voice pipes up.

Blatantly ignoring it, I quip, "Thought someone was being murdered in here last night. Thought I should do my due diligence and see if that was actually the case."

"Well, as you can see, everything is fine, so feel free to show yourself out," Emilia snipes, making me smirk.

"Nah, I think I'll stay."

I relish in watching the metaphorical steam pour out of her ears as her face turns sour. "Get out, Wilder!"

My lip curls up in a sneer. "You can't tell me what to do. This is *my* house."

"Yeah, and this is *my* bedroom, which *Hawk* offered to me. So I'll say again, *get out.*"

"So crabby this morning." I push my lower lip out. "I guess last night wasn't all you'd hoped it would be." Making a point of glancing toward the empty spot beside her on the bed, I add, "Can't have been that good for him either if he snuck out before you woke up."

"That's not..."

Her protest trails off into nothing, glee rattling my bones at knowing the satisfied, happy feelings from when she woke have been replaced with self-doubt and questions.

"Sure it's not. Classic Hawk M.O. Let me guess, he saw you all dressed up last night and spouted some pretty words to lower your guard and make you fall into bed with him," I say, driving the knife deeper, until a deep frown is carved into her face and I can see the wheels churning behind her eyes.

"What I'm less sure about, is *your* game." Narrowing my eyes, I cock a brow in question.

"My game?" I'm so not buying her faux-innocent expression. "I'm not playing any games. The only one playing games around here is *you.*"

She thinks what I'm playing are games?! Oh, if that's the case, then she hasn't seen anything yet. I'll happily show her just how serious I fucking am.

"If you think I've been playing, *Angel*"—I spit out my old nickname for her, knowing how she always winces when she hears it—"then you haven't been paying attention. And if you think sleeping with Hawk will endear him to your side, then I have some news for you: Your pussy isn't that good. As for Kai?

He'd never go for a heartless bitch like you. Plus, he's a professional. Your *date* last night was just that—a job. No matter what he said or how he acted, you are just a *job* to him, and once he's caught your stalker, he'll be done with you too."

The cold, detached anger that had washed over me after hearing the two of them fucking in here last night has given way to a boiling temper, spewing like magma as it burns everything it touches. Before I can do something I'll regret, like rip that flimsy sheet away and shut her up by shoving my aching cock down her throat, I stalk out of the room, slamming her bedroom door behind me.

Fuming, I stomp down the stairs to the basement. Betrayal and hurt gnaw on my insides. *And there I've been, feeling fucking guilty for betraying his trust. What I did is nothing compared to this! He may as well have stabbed me in the back with a fucking butter knife. Well, I hope the sex was worth it because it's absolutely going to come back to bite him in the ass, and I hope it takes a sizeable fucking chunk when it does. Maybe rip off his dick while it's at it.*

Ouch. Fuck. Maybe that's too far.

Fuck it, no, that's not too far! I haven't been able to have sex since that fucking hussy showed up here. My *dick is going to fall off soon, so Hawk can damn well lose his too.*

I blast through the door into the gym with all the finesse of a hurricane.

"What the hell is eating your ass?" Hawk asks, far too fucking casually.

Instead of answering, I stride up to him and, pulling back my arm, I drive my fist into his face.

His head whips to the side as his hand comes up to touch his eye.

"What the fuck?" he snarls, glowering at me with murder on his face.

"You fucked her!" I yell in his face, ignoring his anger. It has nothing on the shitstorm raging inside me.

His face softens with some emotion I don't care to identify.

"Are you going to do it again?"

"I plan to do a lot more than just that," he says so seriously that I'm momentarily taken aback.

However, a new wave of anger surges. "How could you be so fucking stupid?" I demand. "You think she won't do the same thing to you? You think she isn't going to go running back to her nice little life as soon as this psycho is caught? She's going to do to you what she did to me."

"Haven't you been listening to a word she says?" Hawk argues with a scowl and fuming eyes. "Things won't be like last time. She's not the same person she was at eighteen, and neither am I. Neither are you, for that matter."

"No, I'm not," I agree, "*because* of her."

Hawk rolls his eyes, pissing me off with his nonchalance. "You need to stop blaming her for all your problems."

I gape at him for a full minute. "Are you fucking serious right now?"

"She didn't hurt you on purpose. It's not like she *made* you fall for her. None of us could have known how messy things were going to get. I really think if you'd just talk to her, that it would clear the air."

"I can't believe what I'm fucking hearing. Her pussy must have manifested magical abilities because it's obviously scrambled your brain."

"Hey!" Hawk growls in warning. "Watch it. I get that the way things played out, you got burned, but she was always going to leave, man. Didn't matter if it was the start of summer or the end. She was always leaving, you just didn't want to accept that."

"I would have gone with her!" I yell into his face. "I just needed more time to be sure, but I would have gone with her."

Hawk's eyes widen, his shoulders dropping some of their tension. "Did she know that?"

My body tenses before I drop his gaze. "No, she didn't. But that doesn—"

"It *could* have changed *everything*," he argues.

"Whatever," I snap, refusing to give his words any bearing. "I'm not ready to forgive her yet."

"Fine, but hopefully, with all that punishing you're doing, you'll realize your problems run deeper than just Emilia's hurt. You showed up at Pac with shadows on your tail. All she did was send them scurrying into the corner, and when she left, they re-emerged with a vengeance." My eyes narrow as he purses his lips. "But Wilder, it's not her job to banish whatever it is you refuse to deal with."

With gritted teeth, all I can do is scowl at him before storming back out of the gym. Stomping up the stairs, I head straight for the front door, not even stopping to grab my coat to fend off the autumn weather.

What-the-fuck-ever.

Hawk has no idea what he's talking about. He didn't even know me back then. My fingers subconsciously touch my side before I rip them away with a snarl. I've accepted that part of my past. Accepted that it was my fault. Accepted that I was reborn in those ashes into this uncaring, selfish bastard. Emilia made me forget for a little while, but ever since she left, I've been seeing clearly again.

This is who I am. Who I was always meant to be.

And it's time Emilia realized that.

My feet hit the pavement, and I turn left down the street with no destination in mind. Just anywhere away from this house. *From her.* At least when Hawk was on my side, I could vent to him. I doubt he will be quite so understanding now that he's getting his dick wet.

Pathetic asshole. I should have known he would cave sooner rather than later. I'm still not convinced it's anything other than sex. It's not like Hawk has ever wanted anything more from a girl. Even with Emilia, it was simply her pussy he was after. Whatever the fuck that woman is hiding in her vagina, it's like catnip to our dicks.

And now she's got her hooks in Kai, too. Poor man. She's dangling a fucking plastic fish in front of his face and hoping he'll take the bait. And because he's a red-blooded male—not to mention a huge fan of the big, tough bodyguard trope—he'll fall for it, hook, line, and sinker.

I'm still stewing in the heat of my anger when the squeal of car brakes has my head snapping up to where a blacked-out car has slammed to a stop at the curb beside me.

Three men wearing all black with balaclavas hiding their faces spill out, their eyes set on me.

I quickly back up. "What the—"

One launches at me, and I throw my arm out, clocking him in the jaw, but the move has me losing sight of the others. One of the sneaky fucks attacks me from behind, grabbing my arms and attempting to restrain me.

I fight against him, but three-on-one is not a fair fight, and I'm quickly overwhelmed. Zip ties snake around my wrists, securing them behind me, and I'm unceremoniously shoved into the back of the car. A hood is thrown over my head, and the world goes black. The driver presses down hard on the accelerator, and I'm pushed further into the seat as we speed away from the house.

No one has any idea where I went, and given the way I stormed out of there, it will be a while before they even know to come looking for me.

Fan-fucking-tastic. Just one more thing I can blame Emilia for.

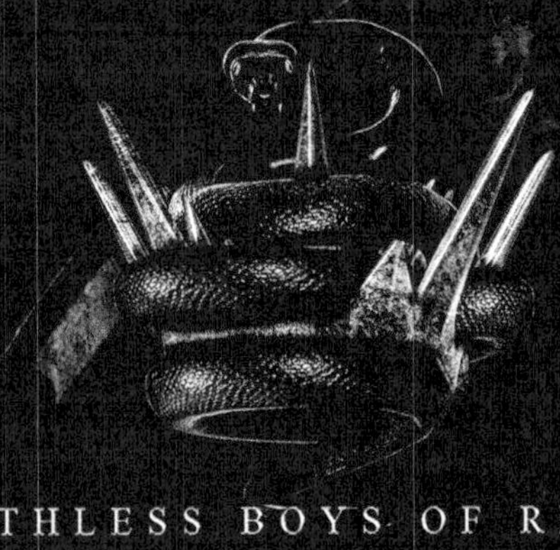

THE RUTHLESS BOYS OF RIDGEWAY

Emilia

CHAPTER 25

Rain pelts against the classroom window on Monday afternoon, and I have to raise my voice until I'm practically shouting in order to be heard over the loud patter.

"I think we'll stop there for the day. All of you should get back to your dorms before this storm gets any worse!" I'd heard on the news that we were supposed to be getting the tail end of a hurricane passing further north. I expected some strong winds and rain, but about half an hour ago, the sky darkened out of nowhere and the wind picked up until it was howling. The new addition of the rumbling thunder and flashes of forked lightning is what finally made up my mind. I can't teach in this, and half of the students aren't even listening—too busy staring out the window, waiting for the next flash to light up the sky.

The class filters out, and as usual, one of Hawk's men stays behind, pretending to ask a question so I'm not left alone. We're mid-conversation regarding the Chaucer essay assignment I handed out last week when my phone rings, Kai's name flashing across the screen.

"Oh, sorry, Nigel, this is my boyfriend. Just give me one sec."

With a smile in his direction, I answer Kai's call. "Hey, are you nearby?"

"I'm about ten minutes away. Damn storm. All the roads are flooded. It's a nightmare out here." I can hear the aggravation in his tone and the sound of a horn blaring in the background. "I've told Hawk to get you and left a message with Wilder—if he bothers to check his phone. One of them should be with you in a few minutes."

I chew on my bottom lip, worried about Wilder. Hawk hasn't heard from him since he left the house on Saturday. Hawk assured me he was probably at the frat house blowing off steam and to give him some space, although he promised to check in on him today. I don't even know why I'm worried. I shouldn't be, especially after the way he planted doubts in my head.

I felt better after talking to Kai, but I haven't said anything to Hawk. I don't want to drive a wedge between him and Wilder, and honestly, Hawk hasn't given me any reasons to doubt what he told me.

"Just drive safely," I plead with Kai, putting all thoughts of Wilder to the back of my mind for now. "I'll be fine."

"Is one of the security team with you?"

"Yup, as usual."

"Good. Stay with them until one of us get there."

I roll my eyes and laugh. *As if I don't know the drill by now.* "I know, I know. I'll be here when you arrive."

We hang up, and I return my attention to Nigel. "Sorry, he's caught in the hurricane and running late."

"I'm sure it's crazy out there."

I nod in agreement before circling back to the conversation we were having. "Anyway, uhh, we were talking about—"

The lights flicker, drawing both of our attention, before they seem to settle again. "Ugh, I hate thunderstorms," I grumble aloud, rubbing my palm over my chest to try and soothe my racing heart. It's not even that I hate storms. I've never really minded them, but with everything else going on, this one has me on edge.

Before either of us can speak again, we're plunged into darkness, my adrenaline immediately spiking as I strain to see through the dark. "It's okay," I say aloud, more for my benefit than anything else. "The college's generator should kick in any second."

Unfortunately, my words aren't followed by an explosion of light, and as the seconds tick by, my concern ratchets higher until panic turns my mouth dry and nearly has me spiraling into a frenzy.

"What the—" I hear Nigel's shocked voice and spin to face the direction it came from at the same time something heavy hits the ground.

"N-nigel? Are you alright?" I stretch my arms out in front of me, squinting through the semi-darkness toward where Nigel had just been standing. My eyes have adjusted to the lack of light, but with the dark clouds outside the window, there's not much to help me see. However, I can no longer see the outline of his body. Placing one hand on the edge of the desk, I guide myself around it. "Nigel?!"

I can hardly hear over the hammering of my own heart, and when my foot collides with something solid, I freeze. The only sound is my heavy breathing as I work to calm myself, forcing my body into action as I bend my knees, my arm outstretched.

I feel warm skin beneath my hand, using my fingers to feel out a shoulder. "Nigel!" I call, my voice laced with panic. "Nigel!" What the hell happened? I don't understand. One second he's standing and talking, and the next, he's unconscious on the floor. Did he trip and hit his head?

Remembering I set my phone on the desk before the lights

went out, I stretch up to find it, but as I do, I feel something sharp slide through the skin on my neck, sinking into the muscles.

A strangled gasp escapes as something cold plunges into my system, and my hand flies up to my neck, its task of finding my phone abandoned. What little I can see of the world is already starting to tilt until I'm no longer sure if I'm the one falling or if the world is spinning out of control. The last thing I remember is landing on a cushioned yet hard surface, before my eyes roll back, and I'm lost to eternal darkness.

My stomach roils, and my head pounds as I'm dragged reluctantly back into consciousness. *What the hell happened?* I take short breaths in through my nose and mouth, fighting the overwhelming urge to vomit until I find the energy to crack open one eye.

The dim light burns my retinas, and it takes another few moments before I'm able to see past the blinding light. The first thing I see is the concrete floor beneath my shoes and the zip-ties tying my wrists to the wooden arms of a chair. As my brain slowly processes what my eyes are seeing, my adrenaline spikes, pushing back the fog clouding my brain and allowing memories of my office to come flooding to the surface.

I pull against the restraints, noting that both my arms and legs are tied to the chair. Goosebumps race along my skin, and there's a chill in my bones that wasn't there before. My wet clothes are suctioned to my skin, so I must have been carried outside of some point. That knowledge terrifies me. Knowing that I'm not in the same building where I was meant to meet Kai. Where all three of them were heading toward.

If I'm not there, how will they find me?

My breathing picks up again, a fresh wave of terror rocking me to my core, and I whip my head up to take in the rest of my prison, needing something to focus on. Something to help me determine where I am.

Brick walls stare back at me from every direction, and I notice the absence of any natural light. Only the single bulb hanging from the roof offers any illumination, and as I force my heart to slow down and my brain to *think* instead of panic, I notice the wall in front of me is covered in photos.

Leaning forward, I rake my eyes over them, each one more terrifying than the last. Images of me on campus, more of Wilder and Hawk at the frat, and of Kai coming and going from the house and his work. But what really freaks the shit out of me are the photos of me on all fours on my bed, Wilder crouched between my legs. Me sound asleep on Hawk's lap in the living room. The three of us the night Wilder told me to suck his cock. Kai and I out on our dinner date, dancing in the club, practically fucking against the side of his car. Every intimate moment I've shared with them, all of it is on the wall for me to see. Privy to the eyes of this psycho. Fear and fury twist around one another in my gut, forming a two-headed, pissed-off serpent, ready to strike when this asshole shows his face.

While I wait, I catalog each photo to memory. Every private moment, stolen. Any sense of safety and security, ripped away. Every solitary moment where I felt weak, powerless, or lost was on display for him to gawk at and revel over.

How. Fucking. Dare. He.

This is *my* life. These are *my* moments. *My* memories. He has no right to them. No right to invade them, to take them as his own, to tarnish them. These photos make me look weak, cheap, easy, yet what they don't capture is the very real connection I'm forming with Kai, the battle Hawk is slowly losing with himself, the war waging inside Wilder that only ever lessens when he's doing what he thinks he has to do —punish me.

It doesn't show how we're all stripping back our defenses and slowly forming one cohesive bond. Self-reliant, yet we're learning to lean on one another. Right now, it's fragile and easily broken, but I know that, given a bit of time, a little love, and some attention, we could form something durable and special. Something most people search a lifetime for and never find. The one thing I never thought to plan for but can't live without. I made the mistake once of turning my back on this feeling, and I lived to regret it. I won't make the same mistake twice. This time, I'm fighting. I'll fight my own fears, Wilder's demons, this psycho, because I'm sick of feeling empty. Sick of being numb. Sick of being scared and living life the way society dictates.

The disengaging of a lock, followed by the sound of a heavy door being opened from somewhere behind me threatens to shatter my resolve, but I hold firm. I'm doing this for Kai, for Hawk, for Wilder, but most importantly, I'm doing this for me. I don't know how much time has passed, but all of them were on their way to me. I trust Kai to figure it out. I trust Hawk to do whatever is necessary, and I trust Wilder to bring his usual brand of crazy to the table and do what needs to be done.

Footsteps echo out behind me. The sound of someone descending wooden stairs makes me think I must be in some sort of a basement or underground room, which would explain the lack of windows and the fact I can no longer hear the raging storm outside.

With each step the person takes toward me, I have to work to push back my fear, refusing to let them see me scared.

There's movement in the corner of my eye as they walk past, and I take in their worn boots, jeans, and slim build before they turn to face me.

"Hey, Em."

My brain goes on the fritz as my eyes bounce all over the person in front of me and I struggle to put the pieces together and figure out what I missed—because I sure as fuck missed something.

I have to lick my dry lips, only managing to force out a single sentence. "*You're* my stalker?"

THE RUTHLESS BOYS OF RIDGEWAY

Wilder

EPILOGUE

"See you at the inauguration, initiate," the hooded asshole calls after tossing me out of the car.

All I can do is snarl at him, as I climb out of the muddy fucking puddle he shoved me into. I jump to my feet in time to watch the back wheels of the souped-up Honda Civic spin as one of the asshole's friends applies too much gas. I give the car both of my middle fingers as it speeds away through the campus car parking lot, the crude gesture doing nothing to abate my anger.

Only when the high wail of the modified engine has petered off into the distance, do I turn with a scowl on my face and slowly trudge through the downpour, across campus back to the frat house. I've been wearing the same clothing for the past two days and desperately need a shower—ideally a warm one, rather than the freezing cold shower I'm currently subjected to.

I don't know what the fucking point was of that last task, but I'm guessing by the asshole's remark that I passed. They had me sequestered in some sort of interrogation room the entire time, demanding to know which initiate blabbed about the King's Elite to an outsider. *How the fuck should I know?*

All I could tell them was that it wasn't me, but that didn't stop some dude I'd never met before from screaming in my face, denying me fucking food and piss breaks, insisting that I knew who it was and demanding that I give him a name.

Took until about half an hour ago for him to finally fucking realize I didn't know jack shit. *Fucking douche canoe.*

I pull out my phone, intent on cursing Robbie out for not giving me a heads-up. I'd at least have made sure I ate and pissed before I was so rudely kidnapped, taken hostage, and denied my basic human rights!

However, I pull up short when I find more than a dozen missed calls and texts from Hawk and Kai. *What the hell could have happened in the space of forty-eight hours?* Pretty much all of them are from this morning, so I doubt it was because they were worried about me after I stormed out of the house. Something must have happened, and my body tenses as my sluggish, sleep-deprived brain connects the dots. Emilia.

The phone vibrates in my hand, Hawk's caller ID flashing on the screen. I immediately answer, bringing the device to my ear.

"Where the fuck have you been?" Hawk roars down the line. He doesn't wait for me to answer before firing out his next question. "Where are you? Get to Emilia's classroom. *Now.* She's missing."

Something in my chest lurches at those two words, but it's his next ones that push me into action.

"Her stalker has her."

Hanging up, I take off in a sprint across campus.

Emilia is *mine* to break and torment. I won't let this psycho of hers do the job for me.

ACKNOWLEDGMENTS

I have so many people to thanks for this series. Firstly, to everyone who read and loved Pacific Prep. If not for you guys, Emilia, Hawk, and Wilder would probably not be getting their own series. And what a shame that would have been, right?

I have to thank the amazing team I have around me—Nikki, my PA, my alpha readers, and betas for all their hard work perfecting this book. Angie for being such an amazing editor and friend. Stephanie for making such a kickass cover. Everyone on my street team, along with Peachy Keen for all their help promoting this book.

And I can't forget my husband for always being a solid source of support and for putting up with me all these years.

And finally, to all of you who have picked up this book and made it this far. My readers are so important to me, and I hope you are enjoying reading about Emilia's journey as much as I'm enjoying writing it.

Love, Rachel xXx

ALSO BY R.A. SMYTH

Crescentwood Series

A dark, high school bully reverse harem with a stalker and gang element.

Pacific Prep Series

A dark, academy bully reverse harem with a taboo relationship.

Black Creek Series

A rival gang-mafia reverse harem with a vigilante FMC. Contains MM.

The Ruthless Boys of Ridgeway

A college, friends-enemies-lovers, second chance reverse harem with a stalker and secret society elements.

ABOUT THE AUTHOR

R.A. Smyth is best known for writing contemporary dark romance filled with unexpected twists, mystery, and plenty of steam. Rachel lives in the UK with her husband and two golden retrievers, and when she's not busy thinking up crazy cliffhangers to drive her readers insane, she enjoys inflicting the same torture on herself by reading incomplete series.

She has always been an avid reader, starting from the Harry Potter books as a kid. It's an interest that has grown into an obsession over the years and becoming an author has been a secret lifelong dream of hers.

Printed in Great Britain
by Amazon

45240141R00202